DIVA

JOSEPH KINNEBREW

072723-1

Copyright © 2023 by Joseph Kinnebrew

ISBN: 978-1-77883-116-4 (Paperback)
       978-1-77883-118-8 (Ebook)

All rights reserved. No part of this publication may be reproduced, distributed, or transmitted in any form or by any means, including photocopying, recording, or other electronic or mechanical methods, without the prior written permission of the publisher, except in the case brief quotations embodied in critical reviews and other noncommercial uses permitted by copyright law.

The views expressed in this book are solely those of the author and do not necessarily reflect the views of the publisher, and the publisher hereby disclaims any responsibility for them.

For orders or information please contact:

Kinnebrew Studios LLC
siristruble@gmail.com

4294 Birch Bay Lynden Rd
Blaine Washington, USA
98230

(269) 967-3241

Bookside Press, Toronto Canada

BookSide Press
877-741-8091
www.booksidepress.com

CONTENTS

BOOK 1 1

BOOK 2 33

BOOK 3 121

BOOK 4 147

BOOK 5 157

BOOK 6 183

BOOK 7 199

BOOK 8 237

THE DENOUEMENT 261

"I have many questions, Doctor. Some I did not have before and now realize, most likely there will be no answers to them. That has been unnerving for me. Diva is the thief who stole answers that proved perishable, changing with the weather, circumstance, and our gestalt.

I feel like a man standing in winter with no shoes. Perhaps answers would never have been of value anyway. Odd that maybe her theft was a gift, don't you find that ironic, Doctor?"

Writing a "real" story, better to write it as fiction, then an author can elaborate at will.

Truth is stranger than fiction but often, by necessity, shared as fiction.

Could someone make this story up? Consider the following:

I have a friend who, for years was a deep cover operative with a three-letter governmental agency. Imprisoned in various foreign countries and on more than one occasion having done Tom Clancy book worthy things, he is also an author who repeatedly says, "Truth is more often found in fiction."

Names and places in this book are fictional and any resemblance to real persons, living or dead, is purely coincidental.

When protecting the author and others who deserve protection, the author has taken license chosen to change names, places and for various reasons embellish events. The reader may choose to decide for themselves where, when and for what reasons. Some aspects may possibly be "factual" or summarizations while others may not. The Diva exemplar referred to herein may well apply to no one, many, or one in particular. Such disclaimers are, in our times, necessary for legal reasons.

Writing can be risky business.

VANAPRASTHA

(SANSKRIT, GOING INTO THE FOREST)

TO BEGIN

For patient and physician, the question is simple.

"Why did you stay?"

There are many kinds of abuse, mental and physical, but as we know well, these include degrees of blatancy and subtly. Abuse is not just domestic nor only physical; however, in this book both apply. A basic question for the abused is, if they have a choice, *why do they stay*? The victims, who in their innocence are unwittingly connected to perpetrators who hated their jobs, their bodies, their families, their lives…their impotence. Frequently two people looking at each other, interacting with each other in sadistic satisfaction of one brutalizing the other. Why do victims stay? Ask them and listen carefully for in their explanations you find parts of yourself. La Rochefoucauld said, "Hypocrisy is the tribute that vice pays to virtue."

A diva is defined several ways, in this book it refers to a *prima donna grotesque*. The dictionary says a prima donna is, "*A vain or undisciplined person who finds it difficult to work under direction or as part of a team.*" Clinically reduced to ASPD or Antisocial Personality Disorder, this term is central to our subject Diva.

Sociopathy or Psychopathy, The DSM IV, Diagnostic, and Statistical Manual of Mental Disorders, fourth edition, lists symptoms that must be present in an individual in order to be diagnosed as suffering from ASPD. Elaborating, according to the DSM IV, this disorder falls in the Cluster B list of personality disorders. This is also defined as Sociopathy or Psychopathy. Every single checked box describes "the diva" who is the primary subject of this story

And now to proceed…

The doctor was experienced. Matters of the human mind. Professionally educated in the northeast and having served her residency at a prestigious hospital she repeatedly heard abuse victims' answers and their justifications to questions of why. She came to believe she would never know the precise answer. Most commonly the explanations were simply because they were human and if they endured and survived, they persevered for many reasons. The first reason, and easy part was humans do inexplicable things. Sometimes horrible things. The second was not always irrational as it may have seemed to others. The third part remains the greatest puzzle: why?

Ergo, first you must imagine if you cannot imagine and then how could you wonder?

or perhaps:

Can you imagine what it would be like to not wonder?

Wonder the noun: a feeling of surprise mingled with admiration, caused by something beautiful, unexpected, unfamiliar, or inexplicable.

Wonder the verb: desire or be curious to know something

Who?
This is the story of Diva, a person whose story in the telling may help others better understand themselves and people in society who, by degree, pose a threat to them. It is a cautionary tale. *Diva* herein does not wonder. She lives on the surface, wandering in the moment, just like many of her friends whom you soon will meet in these pages. She, Diva, is a wannabe diva among wannabe divas. Not enough of them to swarm but enough to harm if you get too close, and yes, there are male versions, perhaps referred to as "divors." Collectively their reality is most likely not like yours, not like most normal people. Among people, *sociopaths* are, by degree, malevolent parasites sucking life blood from us all. Clinically defined, this diva is a sociopath!

Wonder is for everyone, even angels if you believe in them along with poets, firefighters, mothers, children, generals, all people except ones like Diva. A sociopath's wonder and creativity are mostly limited only to expressions related to their personal physical and social benefit, not to be confused with "well-being."

La gratification personelle. For a sociopath, experiences that do not promote or enhance feelings of self-gratification are discarded. Trashed with disagreeable and sometimes fatal consequences. With a distorted sense of entitlement, capital "D" diva is amoral, exclusively in pursuit of personal pleasures.

A very interesting aspect of "our" Diva is what she is not. This is sometimes referred to as the *reversed mirror image*. You might wonder how the image got there and does it have integrity in the reverse? A mirror image, is it really what appears to stand before it? After all, one image is three-dimensional and the other only two. Each a metaphor of, and for the other reversed left to right but not top to bottom. Diva's image is more like that of a vampire who has no reflected image at all.

Of the two, and poetically in the case of Diva, probably the two-dimensional image is more correct. Diva is no poet, does not wonder about such things and therefore accepts the one in the mirror for that is how she chooses to see herself. For a stranger, the absence of an image in the mirror speaks volumes. For her, life is more fun with redactions of the complex. When you cannot imagine, "things" are nothing more than the reductionist's empty two-dimensional reflection.

BOOK 1

1.

The pungent odor of hormones hung heavily in moist night air. Musky body fluids and perfume mixing together, in here the lust of rutting season lasted all year, 365/24/7. It was hot in the room, not warm because while her partner sweated Diva always complained she was cold. She liked it this way and often described it as "Sweating like a Turk." The same cutesy anonymous woman who coined the ah.... endearing term "muffin top" also said, "Women do not sweat, they glow." Nevertheless, in this darkened room, with soft light coming from a partially opened bathroom door two bodies were writhing, slobbering, slipping, sweating, wet thrusting moaning groaning shapes. Sharing. Glowing was an illusion; a cacophony of audio and piquancy of the olfactory overpowered with belly jiggled flopping jowls of a bulldog.

On other occasions, in the bright light of day with every detail visible, every texture, curve and lump exposed, fleshy sex was mighty meaty. All of it blatantly literal in cruel intense light. Not completely ravaged but revealed quite clearly in age, Diva preferred the light. For a simple-minded slut, it was unvarnished. She could watch "Lover's" every move, obey "Lover's" every request and instructional demand, sometimes sharp and sometimes alluring. With no imagination to fill in the blanks this literalness was important, with it Diva could better understand the demands of her *partenaire de l'amour* and, in fact, she usually needed them, demands that is.

They took turns changing positions but that was always Lover's idea, Lover's instruction/suggestion. With no imagination Diva could only do as she was bidden by another or those recently seen in pictures she collected and secreted away. When she was alone, *ex parte*, they were re-viewed and promoted *extra sessions*. Diva's memory was poor so knowing where the collection was and using them like flash cards for a dysfunctional child, Lover often showed Diva pictures. For her part Diva bought "adult" toys because she was good at buying and they were her special contribution. It made her feel aroused and important. When she and Lover were not together, buying was a project she could handle herself, reminders of their recent interlude(s), as well as those soon to *cum*. Selections were easy, she simply bought all the new toys. Sometimes three. A pair and a spare of the same in case someday there were three for(e) play and even greater pleasure. Mega battery packs of AAA's and AA's. Replacing batteries "midstream" was a minor interruption accompanied by giggles and sometimes in real darkness, fumbling awkward silence.

Only one of Diva's lovers understood love but that lover was infrequent and eventually deemed then finally nonexistent. Keeping others distracted he had been a show-dog lover, really only for public scrutiny, general admission easily accepted for swallowed impressions. Using him the show couple projected a picture of normalcy, missionary position passivity. In these matters she wasn't stupid. This woman's duplicity was something a diva's mind could understand and what she and Lover skillfully intended everyone else to accept. If the "normal" others were still having sex with their original or legal partner at all, that was most likely "missionary" predictable. Perhaps the only one who didn't suspect was the naïve show-dog himself. He might actually know while usually graciously avoiding the advances that saved other's the embarrassments from their rejected overtures. Handling it with diplomacy and politeness, foolishly her for-show-man believed "they" even cared about flirtatious rejections. He was "slow" about such things. A few of her friends even thought it refreshing and charming.

Diva moved in the company of people who thought themselves intellectually accomplished, complex, and sophisticated and, in fact on rare circumstances some were. Never with literally observable dirty hands, the clean hands of swells were metaphorical in name only. At least this is what they hoped others thought. No one knew the witty lawyer regularly visited an expensive dominatrix who baby diapered him, Pampered and spanked him until he wet and messed himself. None of them knew about the chain-smoking vodka marinated woman whose "trainer," with more than coke in a can, regularly visited her lush apartment when she was in town and husband not. His specialty: training her using "special exercises," for every puckered orifice of her unnaturally enhanced and increasingly pickled body. Their secret pleasures, if or when known, were presumed unique among the more prosaic tastes of commoners.

Diva's Lover, the secret one with capital "L," was the real thing. "L," that nobody figured out until too late. Nor in real life was it meticulously dealt with anywhere outside the pages of a secreted diary kept well back in a bedside drawer. The circles of wannabe divas would never dare imagine a drama such as Diva's on this particular night. The real thing Lover with Diva, vibrating, licking and eventually to sum it all up, thrust plunging with pussy pegging. Each chapter and verse awarded the full ten points. This was no occasional tryst, it had gone on for years and if she'd been a belt notch girl cutting gunslinger, she'd have gone through many belts by now. Diva had banged and been banging the gang for years but nothing like this. In plain sight only one observer finally confirmed for sure what this was actually about. That witness is for later, much later, closer to the end and believe it right now, that wasn't bean bag!

It took years but eventually the suspicions of others were inevitable. With "the troubles" confirmed the near impossible lewdness of it all, back in the day bona fide details were sketchy. There were exceptions in coven circles of "society," ones with access never granted to those who threatened and thus for a long time Diva was protected. Fear of her retribution prevented anyone from uttering anything other than a rare whisper, Diva, at times clumsily Machiavellian, at others definitely not subtle; frequently using a pipe wrench when tweezers would have been just fine.

If you are a diva, you worked diligently to hide flaws. Aging didn't help, it was the enemy, the great race in life the finish line... death. Common among older women of inherited but more often married or with divorce settlements, this can mean old-aged cheesecake =s mold and tastes like it. It had been some time since, in public "our" aging diva had worn a swimming suit. Even the slightest suggestion of doughy puckered flesh was literally and figuratively just too much scrumptious fluff of the bygone years. While aging men unabashedly were exhibiting their own new-found breasts older women like Diva were concerned about underarm waddle flap, flap. Fewer oldies appeared at the beach anymore. Once upon a younger time the beauties had paraded in the briefest and most revealing attire but these days our Diva's most common and somewhat effective resistance exercise was pulling and stuffing her copiousness into Power-Lycra pantyhose. This exercise augmented, of course with power walking from store to store.

In today's afternoon light, she was instructed to roll over, draw her knees up beneath her, spread her legs apart and lean forward with elbows on the satin pillow. With plenty of lube Act Two for the doggie was about to begin.

2.

A spring day, bright, sunny, winter past, daffodils blooming, expectant tulips on the rise. With anticipation trees were starting to bud, life was returning after a seemingly endless dreary winter. Opening the door, nodding her head slightly and gesturing with her hand, in a pleasant voice the doctor said, "Hello, please come in." Attractive and ever professional, the woman gave every appearance of congeniality and that he quickly decided matched the day just perfectly.

As she usually did she smiled, particularly when seeing "a patient" for the first time. They introduced each other formally and exercising caution did not to touch him physically. Drawing him in pointing across the room quite pleasantly said, "Sit over there if you'd like. That chair is far more comfortable for conversation than the couch. I actually keep it just for appearances sake, and really, the occasional nap." Her voice was even and casual, the introductory comment not new but it usually did the job.

"Thank you." The man dipped his head briefly and she replied in a somewhat no-nonsense demeaner. With an expressionless face he first walked to the far end of the sparse but competently furnished office then turned back. Sitting down in a shallow tuxedo arm lounge chair it occurred to him the short depth probably made it easier for anxious female patients to sit up straighter and modestly keep their legs together. In a similarly designed chair the doctor took her seat opposite, knees together. Although he had never been to this kind of doctor before, the gentleman assumed this was all quite pro forma. Separated by a rectangular beveled glass topped coffee table with magazines, an ashtray, a bottle of water was placed at either end. Inexperienced as he was in these matters, he took note of the absent copy of Psychology Today.

Adjusting her dress, she smiled again and looking down at the clipboard in her lap, the doctor took a moment to review her margin notes, then got right to it. "So, let's see, and what brings you here to see me today? You really didn't write or tell my assistant much." Looking up her smile was again pleasant, inviting and kind.

"I want to talk to someone, that's the bottom-line Doctor." There was a pause, "I have questions." It was abrupt and direct. He looked, no, instead one might say drilled into her eyes like he wanted to get right to work. The intensity of it especially so soon made even this experienced psychiatrist slightly uncomfortable. She glanced to her left, unconsciously confirming the panic button nearby if situations got out of hand. Once again, straightening and smoothing her dress she looked directly back at him, establishing her own direct eye contact and maybe, if needed, even the playing field.

Clean-shaven, well dressed, the man appeared to be in his late sixty's and in his own style rather professional looking. Casually dressed in an open collared subtly striped shirt that appeared custom made there was no neck chain, wrist ornamentation, or rings. She especially noted the absence of the power watch common to many accomplished self-confident men. Obviously, an expensive English cut tweed sports jacket, pleated tan gabardine trousers and with no tassels, instead expensive loafers,. He wasn't wearing socks. She wondered if this was a fashion statement or protest, certainly not an oversight.

And for her, the plain black wool jumper over a gray cashmere turtleneck sweater, opaque black hose and two-inch black heels. Auburn hair cut relatively short; no jewelry other than a modest wedding ring he knew was to keep the bears away. He'd done his research and knew she wasn't married. On the wall requisite diplomas from recognizable schools, MD, PhD. State license to practice and hospital certifications. All quite professional. Frankly just as expected and after his Internet research rather normal.

Not to be too obvious he inquisitively looked around the room, taking mental snapshots of the environment. If one knew him better, they understood that was just what he was doing. He was a professional observer sizing up things very quickly, taking in a great deal of information. Lately, his information gathering had been more for defensive purposes; later, in his mind, he would review and contemplate the images for further decisions and actions. Perhaps the observations would prompt questions or determine his future interactions with this woman.

"Well, ummmm," furrowing her brow and tilting her head slightly, "do you have friends to talk with or are there things for us to talk about more privately?"

He hesitated, then using his deeper voice began slowly. It had changed somewhat, was more personal sounding, sad and remorseful. He spoke, as if beforehand having carefully considering his words with organizing purpose, accuracy, and impact. A burdened memory or awareness of something regrettable, she could tell that, but then this was her job. As he was a trained observer, she was a trained listener and skilled reader of body language. She sensed pain in his voice and heard it change quite quickly, it was now different in the way he carried or presented himself. Heavy, no *lightness of being* here. In the Caribbean, the West Indians called it "carrying a stone."

"None who will listen long enough, and none who really want to hear the whole story." He was talking a little faster. "Actually, none who would believe this story anyway. People don't want to think about unpleasant things, and I can assure you they don't want to hear this one. They are cowards really, especially those who know the woman I will speak about, those who only want sweetness and endless bliss. Not people you would count on for things that matter, nor if you knew them would you trust enough to confide in."

His voice grew stronger and slightly louder, there was more energy now. "The biggest problem Doctor, and the reason I am here and not there with them, is others simply would think this is about revenge or worse, made up. Deniers who believe what is convenient for them. In their self-deception they ultimately betray us all, and Doctor, there are many of them out there." He eased back in the chair already sounding weary and disheartened. Oddly, even with this brief beginning his sad story she felt he had been here before, talking for a long time. Long ago she learned to trust her instincts about such things.

She again looked down at the clipboard her assistant had handed her moments before his arrival. "I see here Mr. ah," the pause was palpable, "there's no first name on the form. Is there a reason for that, is this really your last name or first? It seems a bit peculia... ahhhh, shall I say unusual?" She paused to read it again, "Chevrolet... really? It's quite unusual, French I suppose. Am I correct?"

He relaxed a little but now sitting up straighter just a bit more comfortably, "You don't need this information Doctor, at least not yet. Rest assured I can, and I will pay you in cash at the beginning or end of this talk." Reaching into his inside jacket pocket he withdrew a long thin tan wallet. Seeming to take some offense the doctor ignored the gesture.

"Oh? And is there a reason for that? Your name I mean."

He answered quickly, a bit testily, "Just not necessary yet. Do you have a problem with this, Doctor? If so, I can leave, there are others with whom I can talk." Opening his wallet, he took out what looked like five new one hundred-dollar bills and carefully laid them on the table in front of him. He did not count them nor from her distance did she.

She paused. When he did not respond further, she continued "Well then, let's just let this be for the moment. For the time being, I don't need your first name, but it would make this a bit less formal. What are we to talk about today?"

Leaning to one side he resettled, again resting his arms on the high arms of the chair, and this time crossed his legs. The pose of a monarch, the doctor interpreting this an expression of presumed superiority and control. He paused then spoke, this time just above a measured whisper and she once again made note of his ability to move quickly with his emotions.

"Doctor, how often have you thought about morality, the truth, how people wonder, or if they even can? Isn't that what you do, don't you wonder about them and these *kinds* of things?" Continuing, "You ostensibly want to make people better if they are broken then make them whole again, isn't that right? But in some ways aren't we all broken?" He paused and added, "I think so, don't you?"

This time, sitting back in her own chair and crossing her legs at the ankles she replied. "Ah, well, … yes, that's why I'm here. This is generally what I do." Quickly not wanting to abdicate control to this man, "And you sir," tapping the clip board with her pen, "do you think about such things? Do you think you are broken?"

In his near whisper and drawing out his first word, "Ye…es! I think about them a great deal… all the time actually."

Again, tilting her head slightly this time, in a questioning tone of voice she responded. "Have you been damaged by others, someone who has no regard for such things, or the ideas you think about? Can I assume this is what you want us to talk about? If so, maybe I can help."

"Yes, and yes, I see myself on a journey. You and this…" with his raised hand he gestured around the room, "are a part of it. You might say getting from H to M at this point but having started from "A" not yet getting to Z. I've already come a long way and am quite sure there are more episodes to come. This is, what shall I say, …a validation, a check-up. Yes, that is what it is, just checking and confirming I'm still on the right track, why I'm here."

She didn't challenge him. Instead, she intended to remain comforting and sincere. "Well, I have the balance of the hour sir. Perhaps then we can discuss whether you would like to make another appointment. Does that work for you?"

"Perhaps," he said. "I'll tell you at the end of the hour. How about that." And this time he smiled.

More control she thought. "Have you sought help from any other doctor such as myself?"

"No."

"May I, just for a moment ask how you decided on me?"

Responding. "Because I know about you Doctor. I do my research."

And that was it, with this implication clear, and some unease she pressed on. "How would you like to begin?"

"There is no real beginning Doctor. It was all so gradual I guess, but it starts I suppose a long time ago just as most things do." Now he was pausing again, stop start, stop start recalling. He looked up to the ceiling, caught for a moment in a memory then wrinkled his forehead, closing his eyes and pressed his lips as if expecting pain.

"Then why don't you just begin wherever you wish? We have time."

3.

"I spend long hours alone with my work. I am certainly not co-dependent but like most people I want and need some limited companionship. My privacy is important for many reasons but still I don't really wish to live entirely alone. I enjoy intellectual conversation, abhor gossip and can be quite nonverbal when the conversation turns to things I know little about, or have limited interest. I have no time or passion for sports and generally nearly every day I work. Like others dedicated and committed to their work I have few recreational interests. Those few I do have tend to be mindful and solitary. You could say I am more of an observer who records what I think about, see, and hear."

"I can, under some circumstances, and with those I'm interested and comfortable with be quite sociable. I'm innately curious and like listening to others talk. These need not be subjects directly connected to my work but sometimes might eventually be part of it. And I am passionate about music."

"This is a lot about myself, but I thought you ought to know. After all, it is "self" who brought me here and your business is, I think, or assume ultimately all about 'self.' I should add I have disdain for those who are factually incorrect by choice and those who lack compassion for others less fortunate. In spite of suspicions, I am not exclusively liberal and as often suspected I am not religious, at least not the way others usually define it. A few have said I'm spiritual and do not suffer fools gladly. I agree with these characterizations but feel some other aspects of my make up are, shall I say… undesirable and would benefit from self-improvement."

"I am a fool. With all my years of carefully honed powers of observation I have blind spots. No big surprise here but when I believe there is no reason to suspect others I am often easily deceived. When I say I am a fool I mean I am embarrassed and should have known better. Presumably, you are well read enough to know there are two definitions of a "fool." Most know little of the second."

"For several years I associated with a woman who eventually, and regrettably I discovered led a double life. Until recently, I'd no idea this dichotomy existed. Discovering what I now know were her malicious actions to rid herself of me, and I can assure you they were devastating, I had few options. In short. I was torn down, reduced to the most basic necessities and my ability to exist. I won't dwell on these details but please believe me, my getting here has been, by any measure, a great struggle."

"She lies, cheats, steals, and makes no distinction between fact and fiction. She is a duplicitous gossip, genuinely hates people of her unapproved ethnic origins and those of her unapproved religious faiths. She has no faith of her own other than money and social standing. You see I was such a fool not to have reacted at the beginning, and knowing this you could well I agree, just shake your head, doubting this all, either in disbelief or out of pity for a qualified idiot, but believe me... it is not that simple.... What I did not understand until it was too late, was the depth or reach of these traits and the affect they did and have had on me along with others who were eventually her victims. In short this is why I am here, Doctor. Do you want more because I do my homework? This woman I call the diva is a sociopath."

"This woman has a child of questionable parentage. One whose disposition is reminiscent of unpleasant stage and movie characters. Behind the scenes manipulators easily come to mind, back-stabbing Brutus characters, pernicious greedy people. In real life at his age, he has yet to see or experience anything resembling legitimate success, and like his mother, blames everyone else for his misfortunes. Clearly his mother's son, but from what I was told, most probably not his father's."

"In a moment of weakness and too much wine, the mother clearly suggested he *thinks* his real father is not the one he's been led to believe. She told me she strongly believes the son knows the real truth and secretly resents this, blaming not his father but her, the mother which I think is about right. Beyond that, most failures this mother and son believe, result from unnamed imagined conspiracies intended to relentlessly persecute them both. A QAnon thing and believe me, both of them are conspiracists themselves. He, with an added disagreeable druggie's paranoiac attitude, basically waiting for his trust fund to disgorge its contents so he can resume blurry-eyed, coke whacked golf lessons. I am not alone in my opinion of him, these traits are well known discussed assessments of the man child most know as corrupt. In short, he is a wasted human life. Detritus if you know what I mean, but my primary issues are with the mother."

"Six years ago, this woman contacted me and would never disclose how she found me. Whatever the source, she used it and other services often. Later, and much too late, I would find out she was a Black Widow who ensnared unsuspecting men. More than once she told me how she used different names and sometimes, for her own amusement posed as a man seeking women. These kinds of female predators are not and do not always search for men. With her remodeled and unique web of deception, she and I became entangled in a destructive drama. Hateful might be more correct."

"Her first lie was age, the second her "dating" experience and the third her intentions and motivations for being connected with another person. The fourth on the list of her lies were endless stories about her former husband and then her own "adventures." Most concerned itinerate affairs with previous lovers, all of which were proven disasters. In the opening scenes I did not know any of this, then it was mostly cake and ice cream."

"After her affairs, before and after the eventual divorce, her social position, she told me, deteriorated rapidly. Her need for trophies grew. She didn't use this word, but she wanted showstopper consorts. Not a man from the world of business, finance, or law, they were too common. Too much like men her friends were married to or themselves collected for various reasons. Instead, she wanted someone from academia or culture related. For what I see now were obvious reasons, her friends had little firsthand experience with such people so I, for show, would be unique. The desirability of people more like myself was not about wealth but presumed sophistication, academic or intellectual achievement, culinary taste. Resumes well documented, legitimate, by her standards, esoteric accomplishments with unique but poorly understood abilities. This, even though I suspect she didn't even know the meaning of "esoteric.""

"Unknown to me, I would be another front man. A distraction from her "other" life that took me a few years to discover. She and her very secret co-conspirator I'm sure agreed, I would be ideal for their purpose. A necessary show prop at her side for parties and society page photographs.

You can still see them in media that never forgets. But I must point out here, men with more, shall we say esoteric qualities, were not easy for her to find. Most, if not nearly all wound up being like those running to the type she normally associated with socially. I was a good choice mostly because of the way I work, intensely focused and just occasionally come out to play. It was perfect for her purposes."

"As I said, when we met, her position in society was in free fall. To her credit, she was somewhat forthright in saying she wasn't being invited to parties that mattered to her. New in this city I knew little about such things and had little frame of reference nor had I previously cared about such matters. So, much to my detriment, I let them pass unnoticed, grievously misunderstanding the consequences."

"She made quite a point of telling me her friends did not like single women in a "co-ed" room, especially at the dinner table. There is, I have since learned, a musk like odor about these women predators known as cougars. I was eventually told, by jealous women alleged to be confidants, Diva surreptitiously lured their spouses into her nest's nest. A close friend of hers told me Diva's former husband had for years tried desperately to get her fixed. Her mental illness issues worsened over time and they both had affairs. He for a marriage that was wrong, she for the sheer gratification of pernicious conquests. While he tried to repair the damage with money and counseling doomed to failure from the start, she constantly resisted therapy. She was a hard case, not taking prescribed medicines proved frustrating and expensively ineffectual. Like others who have ASPD (Antisocial Personality Disorder), she would not, could not be cured. As with the alcoholic, we know to heal the seeming incurable you first must admit you are a drunk. If you're a sociopath admitting you are destructive, if not evil is particularly difficult, and some, even professionals, say impossible."

"Diva was a cougar through and through. Predatory sexual compulsion exacerbated the situation for everyone. Her obsession increased needs to ignore or cover other aspects of her life, she needed more than a diversion and impressive dance partner for all occasions. Foolishly I was in no position to see or understand that at the outset. I was just a damned fool and have paid a terrible price for it."

"I think enough said for today."

4.

As daffodils waned with gusto the second act of tulips unfolded in full bloom. The patient was learning to trust the doctor and she realized they were making slow but necessary progress. There were still many questions and that was always part of the process. Talking now for the third time this was how it was supposed to work but lack of trust is always the first obstacle. A delicate balance between trust, compassion, and professional empathy. In this case the primary issue was betrayal and ambush. Negotiating these hurdles successfully was an art only somewhat related to the science of medicine.

A gift when well-practiced.

At this appointment, her patient looked drawn, appearing not to have slept well. She thought he'd lost weight asking if that were so. He had lost several pounds he told her and late at night walked long distances thinking and smoking alone. He was lost, not yet finding his way and indeed wondered if he ever would or could.

"Tell me again, how did you meet? We are to call her Diva, is that still correct?"

The man grimaced and shook his head, first yes and then from side to side. "I was attending a tennis match where a friend was playing; this was the first time I met her briefly but then forgot. I was by myself. She had been sitting across the way and unbeknownst to me, when it was over, made her way over to my side and then yes, it was an old line and I fell for it.

"Do I know you from somewhere, you look familiar. Oh dear, tell me where? You seem very involved, do you play?"

"I have an interest in attractive women but had grown tired of traipsing around for a date, driving, flying, wasted dinners with no continuing reason to repeat. I talked to my dog and told him, with nobody else of interest we might just go on to the end together. That was fine with both of us. I was increasingly wrapped up in my work and now my dog has died a few years ago."

"But the truth, Doctor, is I wanted somebody else in my life just didn't realize it. When this woman reached out, I responded, I thought, one last time. That was the beginning, I made an exception just one last time. The trajectory was to be up, up, and away and then, pardon me but eventually shit happened, a long out of control dive to the deck. Eventually she would try to, metaphorically cut off my hands, end my career, stop all my work and then content, I believe force me to suicide.... I have no doubt about that! She was an unrepentant thief, took everything I had and left me literally penniless. With intention and no remorse, she nearly succeeded ending my life."

"Humm, I see," she said. "I am so sorry and can only try to imagine what this did to you. But sir, please tell me more about how it actually began. Did you at once go to see her, what was the scenario? Was it fast, were you both equally drawn to each other, what was the chemistry?"

"She was with her auntie whom she had taken to Europe in the early Spring. With her there and me here we occasionally emailed back and forth for a month or two. When she returned, we arranged to meet again, since the first time was rather perfunctory."

The doctor took a small notepad from the table beside her and began to write. She had not been taking notes during their previous sessions. For a few moments there was silence as she wrote then looked up and asked, "And when you met up the second time, what were your thoughts about that meeting?"

"Frankly, I had none or maybe just few. I was in neutral. I had no particular expectations other than being open to possibilities. At that point I really knew nothing about her personal life or social status. There seemed little likelihood of it going further because of my work-related issues and our geographical separation. It was easy since I was quite comfortable living with my dog and working which is, as I said, my passion."

The doctor looked away, up for a moment and then back, "So you really were not intent on being, shall we say... intimate with her, or seeking a long-term relationship... nothing like that?"

"That's right Doctor... I just cruised in easily and I should add I dated her because I thought we just both enjoyed each other's conversational company. Had that not been the case, I doubt we would have ever continued."

"Surely sir, there was more to it than that."

"Because I lived some distance away, I infrequently travelled to her city, combining our visits with other business I had there. No, with her I looked to politely take care of business matters, then afterward have a nice lunch or maybe dinner with a pretty woman. She was an attractive woman with no obvious commitments or demands and soon, after we met, I told her that. That didn't seem to be an issue or a problem for her."

He sounded irritated. "Surely, Doctor, you must have heard what I just said. For all the reasons having to do with the outcome, my being here now is not an act of self-deception, it is one of painful self-discovery and regret. I had no agenda with or for her then. That really does happen you know. I was reasonably well off, happy in my work and truly loved where I lived and worked. That is what I am telling you and was made clear to her."

Again, she believed he was playing for control so quickly changed direction. "Okay, I get this. What about before? You had previous lovers? How long did they last? Tell me a little about them and then I am going to ask you how they compared to ah... Diva as you call her. That is how you refer to her right? You still call her Diva, or I thought you said The Diva?"

He thought for a few minutes, nodded yes, and said, "Really only two affairs of any consequence duration. They were dramatically different. No permanent or shared living was ever on the table, just mutual companionship and as some would say, "sometimes with benefits." One ended badly, the woman fell in love and that was something we had both agreed in the beginning was not going to happen, in so far as it led to marriage. We were to be just companions. You see I was a widower and not looking to replace the wife I had lost. The other was quite different. I still occasionally hear from her, and we share genuine feelings of affection, but both know we can never go back."

The doctor interrupted, "But tell me, were they at all, or sorry, both like what I assume were the sexual experiences you eventually had with Diva? You said before, in the last session, sex became an important issue. Have I recalled that correctly?"

"Yes and no." He was thinking again, an effort to be candid but respectful to past women's privacy but not Diva's and certainly in the end not deserved. "They were exciting and playful but also included genuine affection. This was never the case with Diva. You would have to know how she approached this. Diva was never what one would call a good or even satisfactory lover. Sex for her was more like filling a physical need, but then that wasn't something I sensed at the outset because we did other things together that were actually just fun."

"As I may have said she was an actor and in the beginning, I would later discover her emotions were easily and successfully contrived. This isn't something we typically look for in the beginning of a relationship, or at least I don't. Not the way we analyze a relationship, at the outset it's sort of exciting, so I for one did not see her obsessions or understand motivations that would only appear gradually over a longer period of time. There were other distractions and questions that took precedence. After all Doctor, I am not exactly a youngster in heat anymore. I also must say I was quite willing to let things evolve on their own. Urgent or immediate sexual satisfaction was neither expected nor the primary criterion."

"In retrospect I see intimacy with her was more an urge of the moment she needed to have satisfied. Almost like a purchase. It could be there with exigency and at others before anything could be done often it was gone. It was as if once she mentally masturbated there was no longer any interest. Does that make sense to you? I'll tell you more about the origins of this but now, after what happened, I am unsure whether anything she said to describe it to me was actually true."

"Diva is a compulsive shopper. That was something immediately apparent. Everybody knows about her buying things. Even when I first met some of her friends it was mentioned. It was far beyond normal. An uncontrolled obsession with her and yes, many people knew this, but I was new to it. I'd never seen or experienced this kind of thing before. More or less, I just accepted it, again not paying much attention because most of it was done when she was far away from me. She hid her hoard or dumped it all over the guest room, in the city house, and behind closed doors in rooms I was asked and told not to go into. In her city house, the first year I knew her I was instructed to never open closed and locked doors into the dining room, guest room or several closets. Once quite by accident I did get a look I was shocked to see the total chaos. Shoes, purses, scarves, and clothes everywhere. You'd have to have seen it to believe it. In her homes, she had two, there were locked rooms and closets with serious keys and serious locks. To tell you the truth I still can't understand why I did not react to these things and especially the locked dining room. I'm a reasonably neat person however, I respect other people's privacy and I'm not a snoop. That has been a long-standing issue with me."

"I think, for the moment," the doctor replied, "it seems a reflection or more an extension of how she acquired things. Is this right? It seems she liked material things, she horded but I am guessing, might have never used them again after she was satisfied. Is that also correct, fair to say? To your knowledge was she somewhat aware this was dysfunctional and didn't want others to see what she was doing? Do you see it that way, did anybody else? And another thing, when did it occur to you that she treated people like she did her clothes or other purchases? You said she treated people like objects."

He slowly nodded in agreement. "Yes, well... I think that's right. I did eventually see it when I started to put a bigger picture together but that wasn't until quite a bit later. You see there were weeks and sometimes months we were not together. I was busy, usually occupied far away from her. She talked endlessly about things she wanted, but never really followed through with most of them. Diva was a lot about just talk, but again, I wasn't paying attention, seeing the signals, or sensing danger. With the distance and time, I simply was not following up on all the things she talked about. Back in those days, when I saw her where she lived, not mine, it was often because of some big party, sort of event related. Extravagance was part of her life… essential really."

"Little by little the bigger picture became clear. I was not the first for all this, and really Doctor, that didn't bother me either, at least not at this age, people have their idiosyncrasies. What I was a bit surprised at was the diversity of partners she'd had and told me about but even that didn't seem particularly important. We get used to this these days when we've had more experiences but back then I was not close enough to really see the effect on other people or how they themselves operated. And with more time the picture also became somewhat byzantine. The details still really didn't interest me until I started to see some of the actual theatrics, then it became quite a different picture."

Power corrupts but so does extravagance.

5.

Diva was in her dressing room. Once very large but now very small. Costumes and itinerant pieces of clothing draped, dropped, thrown, pushed, stuffed, and hung around the space leaving only a narrow path down the center. Clothing on the floor outside, thrown over doors and hanging from open drawers. Everywhere, under furniture, stacked in corners that were no more and had not been cleaned in years. It looked like a ransacked murder movie set; certainly no real or sane person could live this way.

"With time marching on what I saw was a not very cute or beguiling "re-formatted dumpling woman" in her late sixty's. Barmaid pinafores, shorty crinolines, fairy costumes with wings, high heels saturated with rhinestones and sheer peek-a-boo lingerie covered with ribbons and bows; she often liked to remind me she was an actor. She spent days trying on, taking off, trying them on, the off-on-off-on occupied entire days. More than a pastime, constantly adding new things to see herself again in mirrors of confirmation. Twirling, bending over in reflection to theatrically show her ruffled panties, primping to fluff a miniskirt with tiny multicolored crinolines and crotchless garter panties. Head tilting one-way then another, performing her favorite little Judy Garland dance routine waving arms, open palms and spread fingers, oscillating back and forth with bumps and grinds. Lacy gloved fingers in the mirror beckoning back to herself. Mind-fucking Diva seducing herself."

"A made-up scene you say, well maybe you had to see it to believe it. And yes, I caught the repeating scenes, sometimes by accident and others witnessed at her insistent requests. Diva loved the stage when she was the only performer, this was a 60 then 70-year-old woman performing just barely beyond the sight of others who would never have believed it."

> "And yes, ladies and gentlemen (I use the term loosely), you see before you, all the way from the West Coast, unadorned and unashamed, the one, the only Miss Diva."

"Diva sincerely wanted to be a stripper and often brought the subject up. Here and there, amidst the clutter, wig stands she'd pull from the top shelf of her closet. So many to choose from. Different colors, styles, and lengths, as many in a wig store. Over and over, trying them with newly acquired sparkled barrettes, bows, tiaras, and combs. Diva was not good at this exercise but always persistent and the results could be simply bizarre. Rhinestone tiaras were her favorites; after all, she, with pasted glitter on her eyelids and nipple ends was a glitter princess. The rhinestone panties and bras with holes in front for the nipples were favorites."

"Later, she again asked for my witness to little dramas she'd rehearsed for days in front of the worn-out mirror. Reminding me often, she was an actor, but... teasing stripper. Never to be touched, only she, worn-out aging stage stripper would do the touching. The men before were not to have her by touching the showstopper. This was a real strange thing to get used to. Only Diva reflected in the mirrors could have herself, playing herself with herself in dramas of erotica. Imitating her special versions of the Tease Please Strip Tease always insisting I, he, we or a new she watched her performances, she loved the role of stripper. On one occasion, twirling atop the dining room table she broke the table leaf support. Demonstrating how she self-pleasured, Diva time and again spoke about how she wanted to be a porn actress and would be a great one. Her squeaky little voice, imitations of what she'd seen in the many (and I mean many) porn tapes she bought and both day and night rewatched alone. Perhaps an alluring idea to some watchers years ago, but no longer for most older adult audiences. She would pout for days after I told her I wasn't interested claiming they were boring."

"These movies were addicted foreplay performances but because we saw each other rarely in the beginning, that was not at all understood. Diva had her own, *by-my-self-only* devices for before and afterward self-pleasure. I was, for a very long time completely unaware of this. When she felt like it, I was advised, she encouraged others of her choice to watch them too. Repeatedly reminding others she was an actor and loved an audience. She was once a walk on in a laundry commercial and thus a self-qualified "actor."

"I learned prepubescent Diva learned to masturbate while her sister slept nearby, sometimes in the same bed. Inducing pleasure for herself she claimed was the result from years of experience and taunted her captured men with demonstrations, showing them how much better at it she was than they ever could be. A taunt illustrating successes far better than he, she or it could ever manage themselves. Only one other could make Diva scream with pleasure, and it wasn't these lovers. Of course, they were never to know that and only in one of her very few drunken episodes, I was told this and was rather flabbergasted."

6.

More general background: The next lies, or perhaps more charitably elaborations with multiple realities were self-described descriptions of her diva status. She loved to tell the story about how she and another man, well known in the city and supposedly seen on national television, had been voted the nicest people in their fair city. She never said by whom, what, where or when. Claims by her with no displayed recognition for verification or further evidence other than just her say so, were not uncommon. If true, nothing was said about what this "nice person award" may have cost her, i.e., with what or how she was willing to pay. When asked, others did not seem to remember this *alleged* city-wide recognition accolade, listeners suspected another fiction. It is, of course not uncommon for people to lie about their resumes.

Being a diva is hard work unless you come by it legitimately and most do not. Of course, this diva did not, she was not a natural, she was a fraud talent. This never occurred to her, or if it did, she pressed on with a plunger in one hand and bucks in the other. Like a politician, she had to first work the neighborhoods, move to the precinct level and on to the district always looking to the horizon of bigger times with the swells. Like politicians, every step of the way she needed to be careful, and like them, at some point she'd get tripped up, just a question of time. What goes around comes around. As things progressed, and because she was substantially a fake from one day to the next, she was far more careful. Also, like too many politicians, her relationships were routinely bought and sold. Glitter prized far more than palmed pay offs. The person nobody could buy was the one she held closest in her chest of pleasure treasure. Only she knew 'precious pernicious' would never be for sale, that was certain and sometimes it made her wet just thinking about it.

Necessary attributes for divas are good looks, being an actor/actress, little to no regard for facts, ethics, morality, or truth. You had to be willing to fuck anything, anywhere and by anything. Particularly important traits if you came from humble second-generation beginnings and one who scrupulously hid banal blue-collar histories.

Humble beginnings were regarded as distastefully unclean unless you told a great story of overcoming the coming over. No Mayflower bible here, no matter how much bleach she used, Diva could never turn a soiled blue collar into white, so she just lied about it… what the hell!

Physical beauty counts, inner beauty is wasted inefficient distraction. If you can't see it, you can't show it. If you can't show it, it's worthless.

Historical note: In her youth Diva had been a great beauty.

One could be a regular housewife diva but those were delusions of unfulfilled desire, the heart, products of too much over the ironing board daytime television. Diva did plenty of daytime television viewing, but her show selections were different, flat on her back, lying in bed eating foods most tell us not to eat and lots of sex. Here presented, we focus on divas with big money, anointed star quality, social standing along with persistent and regular pedicures of the spirit.

Diva was asked what was the most important thing in life. The quick, unrepentant answer was… "money." When her for show man asked if she wanted to get married, the response was… "You couldn't buy me a big enough ring." With this statement Diva, who repeatedly claims to be a thespian, reminds again it is all about her. When asked if she dreamed, she said no and if she had a favorite book, she could not remember having read one. A favorite painting, she couldn't recall, a favorite piece of classical music she admitted quite candidly she hated them all. To be sure, Diva had many unread books on her library shelves. These were necessary trappings for impressive others' viewing; same folks who also played games of décor. Asked where the books came from, she said used bookstores and the Goodwill, you never pay full price. When observed and some said many of them look new and unread, she answered they were probably donated by her friends or actually when she heard of a new book others were reading, she'd make an exception and immediately go out and get one for her own shelves then later report she'd already read it. It's only money and chump change after all.

Asked if she had a favorite food, she said no. Favorite wine, no, they all tasted the same, but she'd never tell anyone else that. A favorite anything, she said it was again, again and again money, oh well, yes, and jewelry.

Some of the wealthy tell of self-made fortunes and they are sometimes admired. Usually, but not always, they are men, their strength of will and intellect well regarded. Generally these folks try to avoid too much scrutiny, and few will be remembered after their inevitable demise. All very man-up stuff.

If you came into the circle of society as a trust funder you might be admired if your name and lifelong association with wealth was historical… or perhaps even hysterical. A life of privilege, "nipple poky" Ralph Loren shirts (male and female), tennis, crew, lacrosse, and a school where you may well have been "legacied in."

In fairness, a few rare admitted 'trusties' are actually capable genuine collectibles. They are better that what used car dealers call sparkle, different than anyone else and associated with legitimate cultural elitism. All this said such people are never involved with the lower-case aspiring divas. Diva liked to tell others, a few blowjobs and you can ride that puppy home for dinner, dancing and on into a comfy bed.

Even when running to type there are, as with all things, exceptions. A few legitimate were genuinely liked and admired, none however, in Diva's collection of the infernal *inferno*. There is nothing particularly admirable about most of them, they are gratuitous cowards, no guts other than poisoned usury. Diva loves to tell people she graduated from Vassar, she has no idea a few checked her out and found nobody home. Typically, they just smiled, nodded and as is their way, let it pass hoping others will not investigate their claims as closely…PHEW! Diva barely made it out of high school but in some things, she is not stupid.

Being a social climber is Everest level work. Roping up with lies can be precarious. Like doing Everest without oxygen.

7.

In the wild, watching divas can be interesting. Gay men are tolerated in diva circles but lesbians rarely or at least not openly. Many gay men love divas, and nearly all wish they were Shirley Temple. The serious gay men hang back and roll their eyes when watching straight men trying to, at least in their dreams, cop a feel without their wives catching them. Straight husbands or *companions* stand by looking at diva's posture, back straight, breasts out, glancing side to side, toe, heel, toe-heel walk gyrating hips up, down and around.

When 'at prey' divas are flirtatiously tilting heads slightly this way and that, out of the corner of their eyes checking to see who-what's on the field in competition. All the while, perhaps unnoticed a worthy opponent is likewise feigning for attention. Looking subjects in the eye only briefly, they hook the unsuspecting with tease then turn away, passing from one to another for other evaluation situations, it's all catch and release. Keen eyed as a cheetah hunting for dinner before bedtime, and far more sophisticated than the now passe hair flipping stage of their cute-n-perky breasted youth.

An experienced diva sizes up a room in seconds. It has nothing to do with intellect, everything to do with the smell of raw meat. All very carnal, all very primitive and expensive. No one ever said a jackal was smart, they said they were crafty, efficient, and effective scavengers. If jackals were smart, they'd be hushed puppy dogs and live a lot more luxuriously. The uncommon but obvious problem is if you ever smelled one, you'd never go back.

When conversing with a man, in diminutive fashion these female predators look to momentarily catch subjects whose eyes are, predictably and in anticipation, looking down the front of their dress. This is all, of course, by design and intent. Generally, these "crevasses" of cleavage are no accident, they are instead a sculpted achievement of constructed pressure, hooked and eye(d), strapped ensemble. Pressed flesh suggestion of a high up vagina. You might say complimentary marketing enhancement, market slogan "Viva Vagina" in plain text. On these occasions our diva smiles appreciatively, faking interest in uninteresting topics of talk, not flesh. To further enhance the listening, side pressing arms tighter against breasts deepens come hither décolletage. With just a little more squeeze, another inch, C to D elevation projection atop murderous high heeled legs imperceptibly moving with thong a'rubbin. Next stop Venus's lower divide.

Misogyny? I think not, rather observations of closeup and tempting personal encounters. It is well known men and certainly the "show man" adore women, particularly one's of exceptional beauty. A well-practiced and placed coquette act is amusing; when seeing Diva operate it's like watching a cobra disguised as a harmless rubber snake from the circus. Mice are everywhere and so are the rats.

These lovelies know their physical assets well. Like the virtuoso playing a violin, wannabe soloists concertize for targeted elites using rhapsodic music of the flesh. But alas in Diva's case the music is off key, dissident, blinding to the eyes, ear splitting, but what the hell, these are times of tempestuous circumstance so who really cares about harmony and musical genius. Many associate these self-loving women as ever-present operatic personages of the Bunny Rancheras. Gold foil wrapped, socially centered delectables. Godiva may be a chocolate to many, but the other "go-divas" were there first. These creatures are plenty smart about the whole-body potential, also, most of them have too much time on their hands and don't cook. Our diva's full-time job is shopping, watching television and along with Brazilian management, she, and others like her amuse themselves by perpetually updating the wardrobe, eating out and sucking lollypops.

Diva says she never wears tricot, she only wears silk, but let me tell you, she has plenty of tricot and no cotton underpants.

Expanding on the above and no matter the season, Diva nurtures her garden of chaos with more chaos. As if there's a rash between her lower cheeks, in heels she walks bow legged. One man commented, "looks like she's got a corn cob up her ass."

8.

Spent, exhausted still breathing hard they collapsed into each other then fall away. One nipple already purple from first a clamp then vicious sucking with pain that had her screaming with pleasure. Copious dripping lubricant without an oil pan she was still sore 'down there.' Insides feeling raw she loved this, Diva loved the inside and out pain that brought waves of pleasure. "Fuck me, fuck me harder you bitch." Lover answered with a pounding war cry, these two were a terrific match. Perfect really. Later, when *he* arrived, and after dinner, she would tell her cardboard companion no sex tonight, headache or something. A yeast infection perhaps, always a good excuse and no one wants to go near that. What most men only know, or think they do, and wonder or care about yeast infections is they gotta be catching.

For now, and long before dinner, their breathing slowed, overtaken by blurred drowsiness then a short sleep. It had been a brief time window for their escape to go unnoticed. In these circumstances Lover must never be seen or even suspected by others, but for now they were safe, resting until it was time for her to leave and Diva prepare for dinner with 'him.'

After "L" left a few more minutes. Reaching down she smiled and took up "Blackie." A true nymphomaniac, she always wanted more and could handle this baby herself. Using Blackie's tip, ever so lightly she touched the secreted button of sensitive flesh. Starting with the lowest setting Blackie went to work and soon desire again was reaching the heights followed by another cascade of endorphin loaded hedonism. Time to hit turbo and shift Blackie to high fly. She lost count of her orgasms this day, which was odd since she usually liked to count and record them with little bows added on her garter belt.

Endless energy from the wall plug at one end and at the other Blackie could reverb for hours, days actually, but even Diva had never tried that.

9.

The doctor looked perplexed. "Could I revisit something that has been bothering me, sir? Would you mind if we start there today?"

"Ah…hem, you say you are not a misogynist. Why is that? You seem bitter about this woman in particular and quite cynical about others like her. Just how many women are you referring to? Really, who are they, not their names of course but the others since they seem to be quite different than the one you address quite directly as Diva. I think it would be helpful for us to explore this a bit."

"An interesting question Doctor, and no, Diva is nothing like the ones I told you about before, the other two really. The women I speak of now are ones Diva consorts with regularly. I put it this way for a reason. These women of diva, ones I met more recently have their own idiosyncrasies and believe they are her friends, they are fools. She is as loyal to them as a mother hamster, who is known to devourer her offspring. You see there are groups and subgroups in Diva's world. Circles within circles and then some beyond reach and affecting others outside their little groups. It's like an alien universe. When I first met her, the people I saw at the beginning were outside, or I thought they were. Later I understood many were of the notorious inner circles. That's circles plural, cleverly overlapped and circumstantially gathered. With all due respect, a spymaster could probably not have done better. Discovery and understanding of how this all works takes some skill and plenty of experience."

"Those people who Diva knew, and all thought they were friends, knew how to hide from each other inside or outside their circles, but I assure you it took me some time to understand this. The nasty truth is they know each other and yet, just out of earshot, speak the unspeakable about one another. A few of them would sometimes take me aside with intriguing whispered conversations. At the time, in the beginning, I couldn't understand why but gradually it became clear, this is how they function. Conspiracies and spreading rumors are a way of life for them. They do it in their alleged polite society, in business, various transactions as well as their own beds, beneath the sheets with others, plural. You would never, and I mean now knowing better, never consider them loyal or scrupulous people. They are corrupt, amoral human waste. Taking you aside they'll speak in confidence, and this is how I know some of these things. Talking in hushed tones, giving me inside scoops so I can be a better player, especially with them. To draw you in they don't sell you the drugs of conspiracy they just assume we eventually share."

"In the world of not even great wealth, drugs and money are not as related as one might think. There are other bonds movies don't touch because in the movies those people are not the same outside as in, movies are pretend. These people I call the Divatonians don't realize they have descended into their own netherworld of depravity, sometimes, or too many times accompanied by hate. But here, in Diva's world of B maybe C class society rating I would nod and say thanks and habitually play the Columbo card pretending, dah... I didn't know what they were talking about just nodding saying thanks. These disclosures were intended deeper explanations so the next time I would be ready and not so ignorant, just one of them. Pretending gratitude for them being my new "inside" friend. Believe me madam, I could tell you things about some of these people that might shock even you. You see, a few of Diva's friends wanted me to be an attacker like they were. It was a set up and I was to eventually be the sacrifice."

"Faking an orgasm is just the beginning. As an actor/actress, being one includes trickery, motive, and goal setting. At this level of play we are in with pros and sex is a tool for construction as well as demolition. Do you read history Doctor? Have you read about the courts of Europe, like the life of Catherine the Great? Those intrigues included people fucking themselves sometimes literally to death. It's not a shared expression of passionate emotion or satisfaction, and certainly not lasting commitment."

"Do you understand this, Doctor, are you getting what I am trying to tell you? I hope so but most people who are not like this do not. I call these people I'm telling you about social animal people, Diva's friends, Divatonians. For them it starts early but further along, marrying for money and position you grab the genitals and move out from there. Oh my God, the seductions, the blatant invitations offered, at times it was an effort to keep a straight face wondering who wrote their stuff. The lines could have been written by a sixteen-year-old horny teeny bopper rather than a sixty somebody in heat. Those women, and the men too, who say they get out lots, needed to get out further, somewhere else or hire a better writer. Finally, it was embarrassing when hearing it from one who just told you yet again they were Diva's best friend. Listening to them you came to hear Diva had many best friends when in reality she had none."

"And then there's this matter of the other side of the coin but I rarely heard or saw the men work this way. In truth I wasn't there often enough to be part of their club. Their actions I suspect were more along textbook criminal lines and because of my quite different kind of work I was usually excluded from those conversations. However, make no mistake, most were no better than the women … just different with their means and methods. The women had more discretionary free time, but for keeps they always played dirty."

"The diva I am talking about was different than others, and they only suspected how or that she had another authentic, well-hidden source for real sexual satisfaction. Everything else is about strategy, show and tell. It's a game they play; usually there's no opening gambit they just jump right into it and let the chips fall wherever they may. Real satisfaction lies outside the definitions of reasonably acceptable gaming rules. Every relationship is about impressions; when relationships wear out, they are garbage and treated that way. We are talking disposable people here."

"One of Diva's favorite dramatic rants was yelling, "sterilize them all" and believe me she was serious. This applied particularly to those south of the border. She just hated Hispanics and I never knew why. One thing I can tell you, Hispanic, blacks and Asians are never, and I mean never part of the Divatonians inner circle. Never invited to anything unless they have money or position, and you want a piece of it…never. Oh, I take that back, there's one black couple. He was quite charming, but I don't know about her."

"All this said, participants can play with different cards, they aren't only sex cards. They compete by holding business or charity board positions, buying clothes, jewelry, buying homes, cars, boats, trafficking in friendships, and for a few there are airplanes. Those with the planes usually don't know how to use them to advantage so they don't last long, boats seem better. All used to position for greater recognition and power. You listen to them in disbelief, while they plant disinformation as well as any national security group, political party, or media rag. Using all manner of deceptions they fight dirty, create fake news, plunder with stolen wealth from family trusts and estates. Lots of whispered suggestions about bisexuality and incest, sometimes all of it in the same breath. Talk of drugs, alcoholism, fat farms, institutional padded rooms, believe me I've heard it all at one time or another and I was enrolled in the short course. Survivors talk of those who used others and ruined them in the process, but soon return to the front lines of abusers. Bellringers are the occasional suicides and sounds of those range from spoons beating cotton to shrieks from the hubs of hell."

"In this crowd if you ever made the mistake of thinking you had a friend who would someday never turn on you, you're a fool. It is literally and figuratively said there are those who have been screwed and those have yet to be screwed, literally and figuratively. Their life is speeding while constantly watching for a cop's flashing lights in the rear-view mirror. You never close both eyes, especially if you're in the "ladies' room" doing a line."

"So this, Doctor, to set the stage is the opener. This is what I dealt with, the people Diva introduced me to, her friends and enemies. A few might have once been kind reasonable people, but in the end, in my case, after Diva unleashed her war of attrition, only one person stepped forward with courage and personal decency."

"She could not have known for sure, but I think Diva sensed I knew too much. I didn't realize that was a serious liability for her or for me. The rest of those I got to know were simply spineless. Toothless cowards who wouldn't recognize shame if the Pope's inquisitors held their feet to the fire, and for this reason I regard them as no better than Diva herself. Those who turned their backs and with no comment walked away conspirators and quislings. Human detritus dead or alive to eventually be eaten by dogs."

"But I still know where bodies are buried and maybe someday should let the authorities know."

BOOK 2

1.

Let's set the record straight. I am respectful of women. However, when Divatonians are in the picture these are not women we imagine. These diva friends are abusive predators who bring shame upon all descent civilized women. They corrode and destroy the worthiness of all people and only exist because of money and their burned-out tortured souls. Without their money they would be commoners, dirt under our feet, wind-blown foul-smelling dust across a landfill.

What my experience did not prepare me for, what I'd never experienced before, was a woman of Gollum offspring who was willfully, or to be more precise, viciously and maliciously deceitful. Other than in books, movies, or theatrical tragedies I had never met a person like this and was unfamiliar with the term *sociopath*. Initially I thought maybe, since she does not or cannot read books, she learned this behavior from movies or television trash she watches with such animated dedication. Not knowing anything about this mental torment, I certainly didn't know it most probably came in her original package. I thought perhaps it was recognition or choice that premeditation worked to draw the unsuspecting into what can only be described as a classic honey trap.

Gluttonous consumption, snaring for a spider's courtship known to involve females eating their males after coitus. It is inherent in their warped personalities, the illegitimate ones like cannibal spiders who have trouble controlling their innate desires. One eventually concludes such creatures are not made; they are born this way. But this, unfortunately is not the end of the prognosis, it is progressive, getting worse with age.

I'm no prude I can assure you, but even I, who am reasonably well bred, read, and modestly suggest experienced, was ill prepared for such egregious sexual adventurism, ethical impropriety, blatant racism and prejudice. This was a curious example of how high society, the stuff of how Town and Country like media works. Naïve at my age, I should perhaps have known better, but this is easy to say after the fact and probably unrealistic when later learning a great deal about sociopaths. I must add, parameters of sexual expression appear limitless in this tale but for good reason there are limits to nearly everything and reasons herein, are primarily for personal safety.

I do not look for deception. By nature, I believe others are generally good while cautiously accepting many are not. Certainly, I had not previously met a two-legged Iberian Cannibal Spider this close.

The nuanced differences of avarice are synonymous with greed and the way it played out with Diva. When perpetrators, using years of practice, are done and successful at practiced obfuscation, witnessing and reporting their behavior takes time and done at considerable personal risk. When life is pleasurable why turn over rocks? What for, to what end? Unless you intend to poke the bottom to see what the inside creamy flavor tastes like why disturb the chocolates. That all comes later with consummation (aka consumption).

I am no outsider to communities of accomplishment, wealth, and privilege. I've had the good fortune to know those who were passionate about genuine and legitimate qualities of life. In my work I was selectively and professionally sheltered from most of the frauds. There are those who present, wear, and use privileged positions well but unfortunately others, cons by degree and in my longer experience, most cons were exceptions. Real friendship, real loyalty, and knowing those who one can actually depend upon when things go wrong simply do not exist in Diva's world. Using friends for cannon fodder or when cannibalizing families are eating their young, Diva's world is much more than merely dysfunctional, it is poison.

A sociopath is a successful fake of the worst order. They can be deadly even to those who think themselves experienced, safe, and immune. Understanding and accepting the cost benefit, I think it fair to have such people tattooed with a skull and cross bones on their forehead. Marking them to warn and save others from harm. Divas should be red inked onto her ass as well, since that's a view she often likes to share.

Oh, this all sounds like such a tirade, it wears me out. Perhaps this is just a long cautionary tale.

2.

The diva and I were going to talk over dinner. This is unusual, she had agreed to cook. After her very exclusive and expensive cooking school, her single culinary accomplishment is beef stroganoff, and we are enjoying it. There is wine and thankfully no fair and unbalanced. Usually we are competing with locomotive sounds of derivative television rants along with Diva's extravagant heated responses. Shouted invectives of hate and agreements for her supported conspiratorial plans of exclusion and executions of the great unwashed. Last week, at breakfast time she threw a full glass pitcher of orange juice at the wall for her cleaning lady to pick up and clean walls in the kitchen.

Not even four bites into the stroganoff she unloads.

> *"You know I fought hard for my social standing. I served on boards. I went to luncheons, decorated for parties and grand balls (uh-huh). I met fashion designers, bought, and wore their gowns but it's the jewelry I love."*

Mentally I ask myself why did we get on this subject? Jewelry is a qualifying competition engagement item usually reserved for girl talk. Neck, wrist, finger and elsewhere piercings. For a qualifying female contestant, jewelry shows what and who you are.

"You can't begin to buy me what I want; that's why I buy for myself." I'm asking myself, is this explanation, apology or editorial? Why are we talking about this?

"Do you really think you could please me this way? You don't know what it takes." Phew, gratefully I sit back, relieved to be out of this game but still wonder why the attack mode. However, what I don't realize is that this dinner is a time for instruction.

> "How many times must I tell you, the most important thing is money and then comes social recognition? The rest are trinkets to keep those people away from our homes, out of our lives. That's why we do charities. Those others are pigs." If she had a more expansive vocabulary, she might even add something about satiating the masses.

Diva rolls on, my mind drifts going somewhere else, it really doesn't matter where, nodding occasionally to affirm I have not gone to sleep and am eating quite well actually! With no vocal utterances necessary, confirming I am here I pretend to listen. How many times have I ignored these kinds of conversations? In my mind I am instead thinking about pleasures of my work and maybe a beach in Fiji. Some SCUBA perhaps.

With feigned interest I'm trying to tune this out for the sake of sanity, healthy digestion, and a decent attitude. I've heard this so often; her invectives like fingernails down a blackboard… she actually believes this crap. The subject abruptly changes from the bounty of booty to social politics, and eventually to revulsion for her apartment neighbors in the city. The mousey mild-mannered man and his Little Orphan Annie wife with electrically charged kinky hair.

Oh, and yes, I often wonder about why I am even here. I wondered, back in those days why and in domestic violence cases, why do couples stay together. I often debated this idea remembering there are/were good times, usually when Diva is calm, funny, happy, and actually, despite our age, quite attractive. It's a spiral thing that defies common sense and so, as many do, we continue. I should also add, thoughts of difficulty associated with a breakup at these various times were often just too much to contemplate.

This talk of jewels is enough to make you believe some women are descended from crows; they love things that sparkle and shine. They also like things that go hump and bump in the night. Twinkle is far too restrained a term for this subject. Diva, like a crow, is a feathered scavenger searching for carrion, finally picking at raw dead meat. Swallowing without even tasting.

For her tinsel, for him roar of the engine. Así es la vida.

"Jewelry, we all watch for it." She is continuing, as if I need more, teaching me a lesson on how it all works.

"I know exactly what *she* was wearing last week." She stabs her finger in the air, "I know when she will wear it again because she has to with the little she has, and I'll tell you, it isn't much. The stupid bitch asked me if she could borrow my diamond necklace, can you imagine that? Actually, borrow it. I really don't know why we even put up with her. What a bitch!"

I know what she says is all true. You can watch the competition from across the room; cataloguing what hangs from ears, around necks, wrists and God knows where else.

Speaking of which... "And let me tell you sweetie, there is jewelry in other places too. Want to see mine again?" She winks, I wince thinking about the piercing pain down there. For a guy, this kind of makes you slam your knees together.

There are all kinds of ways to accomplish and promote the perception of wealth. It ain't always Tiffany's or Cartier; eBay is one. She buys dozens of precious and semi-precious stones on eBay. When coming from foreign countries of origin they are amazingly inexpensive, especially when labeled "Kitchen Utensils".

Hours spent, days and nights in front of her laptop. The trick is to get them cheap, have them then refined by a cheap foreign source to finally present them with pedigree. An estate purchase perhaps, goodies acquired by a well-known auction house or jeweler who knows your preferences and gives you insider info. Who will argue except behind your back, and they do argue behind her back.

In the drawers (furniture ones), inside and behind the reinforced locked doors of her home, are boxes of cut-polished inexpensive semi-precious gemstones. Unless you were a Euro queen, more stones than one would most likely ever have made into legitimate jewelry. One thinks of Cinderella's evil stepmother questioning the mirror with a wink and a smirk.

All you do is send stones and a picture. Diva always goes shopping with her phone, cell cameras were a godsend for Divatonian collectors of baubles. While the man at Sax Fifth Avenue brings out their latest estate treasures on black velvet covered trays and returns to the back room to get more loot, she surreptitiously changes into a practicing spy photographer. Soon a packet of stones along with her cell photographs will go off to Thailand, China, or India where copying is endemic and cheap. Just like her ersatz Rolex she thinks nobody has yet figured out. The watch however, significantly better than the street vendor or souvenir store's copy....... And yes, the girls did notice.

A catty conversation. Diva has gone to pee and given the nature of undergear struggles and stuffing, this will take a while.

Naughty, Naughty... friends do talk behind Diva's back,

> *"It's from Thailand Sweetheart. You can get them there for a song. She seems to think we don't know this anymore than we don't know she married a Jew. Now she's after that new one over there, he's bi you know, just like so many of them. I love it when they later tell you about "her" hidden treasures and open-door policy. A few are my "special" friends. Such gossips they are, just delicious. Georgie told me he wanted to actually survey and then measure her labia."*

Back to our dinner story. By the time we finish the stroganoff Diva has had two glasses of wine. Not a big drinker she is too drunk for more talk and thankfully for sex. I'm relieved by the reprieve and while this has not yet become a deal breaker it increasingly is less inviting. I'll help her up the stairs where she will fall into bed sleeping farting and snorting in her clothes. Three or four hours later, under the covers and still in her clothes she will wake, reach for her laptop and resume eBay searching for more loot. I hope by then to be down the hall in the guestroom, blissfully sound asleep.

But not yet. Replaying the evening's drama in my head I roll over and resume trying to get to sleep between snorts and 'breaking wind' from Diva's bedroom active somnolence. It is not easy but still not all was lost. The night ended with humor unnoticed or appreciated by Diva. Just before collapsing she continued her rant that turned to criticism of a soon to be widow. Using words and suggesting actions to be taken, she believes display her sophistication and superior intellect, the old girl likes to show her worldliness at the oddest times.

> *"...and that last time, she's wearing that old fashion emerald green taffeta dress. Did you see it, notice her brassiere, how it kept riding up over that pathetic low neckline? You'd think he would have said something to her, but she was just too lazy to do all the hooks and eyes around back. That's the real problem."*

Diva is referring to last Saturday's "event" and the woman she is working on. Over the past few weeks, Diva has made several references to her friend's husband's recently serious diagnosed form of cancer. It appears he has only months to live. This is sort of a last hoorah. They have a home in Diva's fair city and another far away. Many of her friends have visited their far-off estate but she has never been invited. This makes Diva furious.

It seems a cycle. After we see this couple every time Diva goes into histrionics about how she has never been invited to the 'other' grand estate. This eats at her because she can't figure out why. She's showered them, *a' la zee* bribe with expensive gifts. Her's far better than others who've been invited guests. She's had the dying man and his lady to dinner at her downtown club several times, but nada. In return they occasionally invited her to parties they have given in town but never at the distant estate *La Grande*. This makes Diva nut case crazy and one night, really worked up, for punctuation she literally peed in her pants.

With the announcement of cancer Diva is frantic about her bucket list. She has repeatedly told me she hopes "the old fart" doesn't die before she can get to their far away other home. She needs, no, has to be, on the list of those who have visited. It's a prerequisite, an important bauble for continued recognition. With more routine outbursts the man's pending demise has renewed her obsession on the subject. The latest was, "You'd think that if he's going to die, the least they could do is invite me before he does."

Much later she declined to attend the funeral but sent her trademark orchid for show.

3.

It is morning, breakfast time, I enter the kitchen to, as usual, make my breakfast. Diva has been up early loaded for bear. "Fair and Balanced" news blaring from the television in the corner. Agitated, the reason isn't clear, but I easily recognize the potential of this bubbling soon to be torrential state of mindless stupidity. Leaning over the sink she manically scours a pan that most probably is already quite clean and probably worn thin. She hears me enter, stops and snaps around to face me.

"I want something, and you can help me get it."

I try to speak calmly knowing a storm front is moving in and we will be swept away yet again. The day will begin in chaos and there will be no "Nice Job Brownie'," President Bush's infamous old FEMA comment to save me.

"And what is that?"

"It doesn't matter what, only that you help me and do what I want."

Someday I'm going to smack down her imperious manner, and hard but not today. Diva usually asks for nothing from me other than I show up shaved, appropriately dressed and on time when she never is (on time I mean). I await the surprise request.

"How would I do that?"

"I have your money, or the pittance compared to mine but it's not enough. Now that there is so little left, and until you get more, I want you to go on public assistance. I watched a program this morning (fair and balanced) and they told how it's done. You just call up and get food stamps. It's free and all the Mexicans do it and I'm sure the Orientals."

I'm shocked. What does one say? Several moments of silence before... "But you and your friends hate those who are on public assistance and especially if they are Hispanics. We hear their party line every week at the club. What if your friends found out?"

"They won't because you won't tell them, and neither will I."

I squint my eyes thinking and say, "What's this all worth to you? How much money are we talking about?"

"Oh" she says... "maybe about $1200 a year."

"And with your money (several million) you want me to go on public assistance for $1200 a year?"

Now she softens her tone, realizing she's overstepped she smiles sweetly. "Yes sweetheart, it's really my money, my tax dollars and I want some of it before those filthy Mexicans and Chinese get it. I want it now. You can call them this afternoon. I know you can find the number."

I ask her, "And what are you buying again?"

"Not your business, just help me. In a little while I have to leave, I'll be going to the city for a few days, you call me when it's done. Just tell me how much we will be getting every month so I can figure it into the payments if I decide to do it that way."

"Diva ... this is crazy!"

She has already left the kitchen, Fair and Balanced blares on, I can't find the remote under her pile of mail etc. so just yank the plug. I've lost my appetite and leave without breakfast, thinking about all those conversations over dinner tables with her friends. Their constant vilification of people less fortunate, the great unwashed, filthy (while picking their crops for country club dinners and mowing the greens) because, as she always says, "They know nothing different, they're just animals" or, as a soon to be elected president will say, "shitholes."

4.

When one reads about television ratings, I wonder about those who really watch and listen. I wondered who listens to the programs she listens to everywhere including her car. I always thought among the listeners were Farm Program Subsidy beneficiaries, cruising endlessly back and forth in their enclosed government financed farm program tractor cabs with onboard refrigerators, microwaves, and televisions to keep them company. In their monotony they listen to voices reinforcing beliefs they had a right to expect government subsidizes for their business and nobody else's. In years of drought low prices and government guaranteed purchases, which after all cover the risks of being in their business, if others want to eat, they believe all citizens should bear these business risks on their behalf.

Speaking of public assistance, alas we know the government subsidizes many businesses including people who do not need it. Diva's country house is on a river in the middle of farmlands, where "the party" subsidy business has a firm grip on every farmer's neck. Most of the non-home-boy-transient-country-swells are big time city grifters but they love to yammer at the club while writing checks to "the gotcha covered party." Hating the immigrants who all around them work in the fields, not just a sport of anti, the rants over immigration and 'white is right' is a religious commitment in these parts. Mantra madness.

As a genuine independent that has voted on both sides, I admit to having known more liberals than conservatives, but I too have a conservative streak. In my past what I have not known are those whose vehemence burns the soul, tears at the heart and whose loathing of others disembowels their hate filled brains. Listening to politics from her and friends, it was no wonder they were so morally corrupt, filled with hypocrisy, anger and always ready to take from the government while denying its benefits to others. Diva was much more than conservative; she and nighttime Internet friends were closet radicals waving flags of sedition or treason.

I once asked Diva if she would deny birth help to a Mexican woman in the emergency room of a local rural hospital. Her response, "They are pigs who deserve to die. They don't belong here." Diva loves the word "pigs" it is synonymous with Mexican. Jews, she repeatedly says, are kinky haired dogs, another of her favorite targets along with several other ethnic "despicables."

Our diva exemplar was born into plain and humble circumstances, second generation Germans. Mother a failed wannabe beautician and father a bartender in a big city westside neighborhood Cheers tavern. The father seemed to have been a standup guy, but I never met him personally. Hearing Diva tell it, the mother provided an early example of out of balance self-interest, a clue to Diva's future performances.

Perhaps some shared genetic explanation for Diva's eventual conduct. When I knew the mother, she was old and appeared to be quite sweet, but "Mom", I'm told stole the college piggy bank funds so she could go to hairdresser school. Sometimes the story changed, and the college fund was a sometimes family vacation fund. The "Mom" story continued, she separated from the husband and took up with another man of questionable lineage and no employment.

To Diva, her parents were mongrels, sometimes she called them Mongols and privately called them mutts and Mongol/mongrels. All terms Diva loved to call those of unverifiable pedigree and of course, with no discussion, this meant she remained unsure of her own verifiable linage. Her city neighbors, she said in a whisper, were mutts.

According to Diva's account, when she was a kid Mother and "other man" lived in Diva's small childhood row house where she first heard sounds of humping with expletives. Mother eventually got tired of this other man, returned to former husband while "other man" continued living in their basement. With husband upstairs, on occasion in the downstairs the humping sounds resumed. This again all according to Diva, who after her mother's death sanctified Mommy with stories of love and unconvincing soapy affections of grief. Oh, and at the same time, behind her back telling wild stories about her sister, whom Diva alleges after Mom's death "stole" all the good stuff from mutt mom's house. Oddly, sister seemed to be quite normal, generous, and quite unlike Diva. Parental models can be powerful, sometimes unpredictable influences, especially for those who are impressionable, sociopathic, and greedy.

Diva learned from her schoolmates one doesn't question anything or their body unless they have power (aka money). Young girl Diva had no power or money, but she did have the body. She vowed early not to let powerless and penniless happen later in life. She wouldn't put person of the basement, presumably on call, when finished she'd throw him in the garbage, since there was always an ample supply of rooster replacements. This was a plan she employed on more than one occasion, but that took some time to find out and not in time to save me from my own dumpster discard. Means and method details of our final episode she carefully concealed from her supposed well-bred friends. Listening to Diva describe her parents to friends could, at best, only be called a fantasy.

Money is power. Power is money. It is just that simple for the diva and like-minded associates. If you can buy anything you want, this includes allegiance and detritus from the web, Peachtree Street, Paris, Goodwill, Rodeo Drive and T J Maxx. She had eclectic tastes and just like Midas, she always said you are most of all careful about your money. You know how much, where it is and carefully spin stories of disinformation about it. Secrets are taken and allocated on a scale easily as truffle drools dry cleaned out of fur. If you ingratiate yourself to above ground friends while others pay full price, you can attend pricy functions in Europe and elsewhere for free. How naive they are, it's just scammed of the damned.

The diva's ignorance is breathtaking, but she is very smart about her money. While she keeps spending, she thinks she outfoxes her financial advisors when they tell her to cut back. But they're not stupid and someday the IRS will come-a-callin'. Even I came to know where some of the loot was stashed and why. Thanks to her former husband, the well of wealth was, for a short time, still rising with just barely enough to keep up appearances. Frustrated advisors are paid to be cautious, but she is not. Having attended a few of these "annual wealth reviews," oddly at her request, I watched the dance for profit continue, while advisors right on their annual schedule, quietly before tendering fees withdrew advice and admonitions. Resuming their next twelve-month pillage via fees, the Robin Hood bandits were simply robbing the robbers. They all deserve each other, but Robin Hoods benefiting the poor they ain't!

Her primary and favorite source of so-called hard news is a web site viewed late at night. One frequented by far-right extremists who believe bat-shit crazy conspiracies and when not benefiting them directly, cry foul over the intrusion of government for any reason. All essentially Timothy McVeigh Ted Kaczynski thinking. Online they actively share comments and conclusions with utterly witless naïve readers, who still think the tooth fairy is out there for them, and Santa can only be a white man for white children of Euro descent. Everything Diva doesn't like is an outside conspiracy but in polite conversation you're not to know this. Not even the FBI, who rarely, if ever, looks at swells probably since they would be the last to want the capitalist system brought to its knees.

In the presence of others, she wisely and rarely ventures an opinion. Some are reasonably well read and up to date on the news, so best not to lift your skirts there. Inside her city and country houses it's a very different story. In those decorous halls there are bombastic screaming tirades and on occasion airborne objects. Who's to know? No New York Times here, just "fair and balanced" cable news in the kitchen, bedroom, bathroom, and all around the house. On the Internet, more extreme right QAnon in the bedroom deep into the night, until there was an agreement. No more television news, I say, "unless you are by yourself or with ear buds." I'm thinking, but do not say it, please jerk off your brain with the television room door closed.

Verbally masturbating for the pleasure and reinforcement of hate is a well-developed habit of this woman and a few other similarly diseased creatures she knows. Nothing is about something; I didn't want to hear it or see any more. This warped often blatantly fake information is only part of Diva's carnal carmel pleasures.

And The Housewives of Whatever. These fans are true mind-warped devotees. They love fights, the accusations, the hurters and the hurtees. It is their ritual nightly television dogfighting experience. Blood sport, bare fisted boxing for women or as Diva calls them "The Cunts." In addition, if she misses primetime airing, she watches reruns after midnight, sometimes several repeats over and over into wee hours of the morning. We know what we call women who love women and men who love men, and men who hate women, but what's the word for women who hate women? Female misogynists!

5.

We are in Paris instead of the annual London. I am hungry. When we are here together this story repeats often. Since I drink little and rarely before 5 P.M. the canapés and champagne at the last afternoon invitation visitation de jour is not enough. In our five-star Parisian hotel, between the last event and dinner I suggest we go to a nearby street café. The food will be inexpensive and dinner that evening fashionably late, just about the time most people like to go to bed. This Paris trip is not one I would have chosen for any reason, but the diva needs and insisted on an escort.

Since it was her idea and she is paying to be with friends, she has not opted for the hotel's inclusion of breakfast. Diva says, "You're hungry, go to the McDonalds. It's cheaper." It is only three blocks away and I do this several times. She figured it was cheaper than nearby street cafés by about $1.25 US and she never eats breakfast. At McD's in downtown Paree you stand since there's no space for tables or stools. I discover it is interesting to watch the French eating McDonald's American food in France. I wondered if the sausage or hamburger is horse or dog meat?

For appearances we will this night, as usual, appear the perfect couple. She dressed to the nines and in fairness looks great as long as you don't peek or climb around underneath. Her preparations began eight to ten weeks before our departure from "the states." For big time travel she selects and reselects wardrobe ensembles months in advance. She has grown out not up unless flat on her back since the last annual trip to England. Moving from "muffin top" on to "dumpling" bound, I believe headed toward "loaf." Each new voyage requires pre-trip purchasing at familiar home city stores, more new white pants and the etc. I once counted a pile of white pants, discarded on the floor in the *guest-less room,* many still with tags. There were seven. She always says she will return some but rarely does. They will be added to the country house collection a'la garage. Wandering through favorite stores she adds items, most of which will never be worn and generally not returned. One repeated trip mission is the white pants purchase. Necessary because she likes them skintight and has inevitably embellished zee-bellee and dairy-air.

Diva does nothing in moderation. Her favorite slogan is "More is More." Repeatedly I tell her this may sound offensive to some, like

Jack Benny's snarky old smirk at Rochester her wordless response is condescending. In a dream state of denial, she usually buys clothes too small. With the white pants I am introduced to a term I had not previously known. Camel toes. Tight white pants on old and young women create, I am informed, unmistakable camel toes. This is not amusing to me, kind of like Steve Martin's references to dress right for men but in this case for women "*right* down or up the middle."

Most amusing it's the shoes. Exceptions to the rule of small she buys sizes large, too large then stuffs the toes with toilet paper adding some clear jelly like plastic slices in the inside sole. They are flattened clear Gummy Bears sticking to the bottom of one's shoe and foot for added security. If you look closely, and I often look carefully at how women are dressed, there is a gap between the inside heel of the shoe and her foot's heel. The effect is to stay in the shoes when leaning forward she shuffles the sticky Gummy Bears when she walks, shuffling along lest she come out of them. Hence, on occasion, unstuck she's fallen out, having to explain to an officer or passer bye she was not drunk. The upper diva arrived first then the shoes. There is a similar or related treatment inside the bra she likes to call a brassiere because some upscale lingerie salesperson told her that's the right term for "a lady" to use. Prior to this I always thought "a brazier" was something you cooked raw meat on.

More than once she fell out of her shoes, but this can't be said of the bra . This shuffling and leaning forward walk has the effect of her walking like a primate, but boobs on the street or table is another matter entirely. To help beyond an inevitable denial, I once photographed her to show how the shoe shuffle walk looks. She was enraged, screamed, making more than casual death threats if I didn't delete. I tell her I was deleting anyway but just wanted to help. To this day she continues to walk like an early homa-drooping erect-ass.

Buying shoes too big and clothes too small. Pouring her into a dress or skirt and managing to zip her in there is a dangerous exercise. Kinda like trying to stuff a mattress one handed. No street variety foundation garment can withstand such material or structural challenges. Diva requires industrial strength. I had never heard of or seen a woman wearing a girdle + some added extremely tight Lycra garment over that. A twofer. Apparently, she can't be half safe since, like a house, if the foundation fails, engineers call it rotation, the framing and siding (costume d' jour) go with it. Splitting open, fur will fly. As if launched from a slingshot, fur has flown. I once heard and saw a rouge breakaway garter crack a window in her bedroom. Could have been my eye. I considered protective clothing, starting with a helmet and eye protecting goggles. She didn't think my suggestion was funny. In retrospect I think this may, to some degree, have later accounted for her despicable actions toward me. Dangerous job site conditions, where was OSHA?

Bras too small… Once again, a subject I can never figure this one out either. Breasts spilling over the top gotta feel uncomfortable. She's particularly conscious of her breasts. A failed cosmetic surgery from her younger days, right misplaced nipple that looks over her shoulder. If you're a man into breasts this is not a pretty sight. Not exactly attractive, sexy, or alluring. Somewhat like looking to see the dot not over the "i" but missed and over the h. It first seemed like a joke in poor taste. The poor soul, a years ago bad surgeon. Vanity de la grotesque and that "pig Jew doctor," You will recall Diva loves the word pig and hates Jews.

Most of Diva's clothes are rarely worn again. Closets and racks jammed with clothing, many still with original tags. I say sell or give them away but Diva never willingly parts with anything. Some people know about the reputed off-site storage areas where she accumulates and rat holes away older clothing. These rental storage locations are never discussed, and she continues to believe nobody knows about them. She says she's not been to some of them for years. As for racks and piles in the houses, this is the cause and effect of locked doors to inside rooms and others off hallways. Some contain her video porn collections and other more personal off-limits items.

6.

"You seem to be quite observant. Why is that?" The doctor is writing furiously, trying to keep up with my dissertations that are getting longer. Today I am on a roll, spilling memories like boiling oil dumped through crenellations.

"It is a professional discipline. I am a careful and professional observer. I look for things people often miss. Others in my field do the same thing. I examine people's faces carefully but forget names easily."

"Does this bring you pleasure, or do you do it to judge others?"

"Sometimes it brings pleasure. I enjoy seeing all, but especially attractive and interesting people, which does not necessarily mean beautiful as most people would define it. I like complimenting them, that brings me particular pleasure but regardless of their circumstance it is people of character that interests me most. I know it isn't allowed but if it were, I would have told you before how attractive and nice you look." He smiled and added, "Well done, madam. We all judge, even when we say otherwise, but I have tried hard not to. Sometimes I succeed and too often I don't. I don't like this quality in myself. I'm sorry I often judge people by their actions and attractions. My greatest disappointment is not having found genuine loyalty in friendships, so I, in my vulnerability, sometimes succumb to my own lesser qualities."

"What kind of actions do you look for Mr. ummm... Chevrolet? Do you really still want me to call you that?"

The man ignores her question, as she thought he might.

"It's picky but bothers me when people have poor table manners. I was raised in a home with a mother who was an aspiring diva herself but definitely no sociopath. I used to say her biggest problem was she wasn't Jewish, and she wasn't a princess... just an ordinary American WASP. Manners, we were told, spoke volumes. You'd be amazed, attending special events and sitting at a table with the swells, how many talk with their mouths full and use their eating utensils improperly. Turn their knives out instead of in, a used fork laid down end on the tablecloth hooked over the edge of a plate. The diva often talks with her mouth open and full, holding her hand up and slightly away to cover it thinking we don't see the garbage disposal at work. The odd thing is many others who really should know better do this too. Odd. I guess perhaps they really don't know better, a reminder money can't buy everything. Maybe finishing school would have been a good choice, or at least a better investment for several of them. On numerous occasions I watched Europeans observe American etiquette with obvious distaste. Just no class."

"What else annoys you?"

"Those who talk about their success, not to inform but boast. I was taught this too was poor manners. Socrates said, 'Strong minds discuss ideas, average minds discuss events, weak minds talk about people.' Gossip is a quality shared by those with feeble minds and malicious intent. Most of my life I have enjoyed the company of those who talked about ideas, it's part of my job. Diva's smallminded world is only about people. Their talking about others, I assure you isn't about ideas. Despite having been well educated many of these people are not well read. For sure not the diva, she fakes it. She talks about her college days but actually never went to college, and I doubt she could have been accepted into one of any quality. Yes, I am an educational snob, but Diva is an unmitigated uneducated liar."

"So, you're a snob?"

"Yes, but certainly not a swell."

"What's the difference?"

"Snobs I think are those who think their interests and positions are superior. I work professionally in a world of rare exclusivity and believe I understand this well."

"And a swell?"

"People who, like Diva, see themselves through a filter of accumulated material possessions. They like to think they are snobs. They have many of the trappings and accumulate material objects but few of lasting value, rarely ones of spiritual or philosophical significance; it's ignorance and poverty of the soul. Most have no historical pedigree of authentic entitlement but still fabricate to claim it. Having "stuff" isn't bad when it reflects need, appreciation, and achievement, but it isn't necessarily privilege or prerogative. Enlightenment is a path. Most of these people think once on a path they are leading a charge to the bank. For starters, their sense of being first in line makes my headache."

"I think perhaps you are a snob sir."

"I already agreed with you."

"Okay, a point we can agree on. Let's move on."

7.

One end plugged into the wall, the other into the plugged. Both are receptacles.

Once in a while, she is even happy when Lover leaves since she's taken or received enough from her and will shortly continue business on her own. Diva's bedroom is off limits to everyone except a select few necessary and up to the task. After I complained in the master bedroom there was no longer an open pathway to my bed side, I moved out to sleep in one of the guest rooms, I got tired of crawling over her side. Actually. I preferred the guest bedroom, it smelled better, was lighter and uncluttered. Interestingly, from that decision forward, Diva always kept her bedroom door locked. I assumed it was because of the mess she didn't even want the sometimes housekeeper or certainly not the rare overnight guests to see. Truth is I wondered and doubted she ever changed the sheets.

Diva sleeps but only really catnaps. When she sleeps, she sounds like a pig, she snorts. It can wake the dead and is often accompanied by the unsavory odor of sulfur. This might lead one to believe the devil herself has made a nighttime house call.

It is evening and for her the day began with drawn-out pleasure. It started shortly before lunch when Lover (aka L) arrived at the *cuntrey* house. The floor strewn with sex toys and clothing, Diva was messy; in her bedroom lubricant stained the bedding and carpet. Spots all over, but she blames them all on the dog that pees or defecates anywhere and anytime it chooses. But finally, who cares since nobody else goes in there, including myself, I suppose she is used to the smell. The pooch doesn't like the grass especially after rain or snow. There is hard dried fecal matter in corners and dark crevasses of her closets. These canine additions, in part, contribute to the offensive odor of the bedroom but there are other sources as well. Good thing the door is closed. Tomorrow she will again buy a mat to soak up the slippery joy juice before she slips and breaks a hip.

Later, in the mirror walled bathroom Diva showers. With her razor she grooms and tidies up the down-there mustache. Patting herself dry and looking over her shoulder at the reflected image she pirouettes (quite badly). Hollywood style poses of the elderly. There are drawers full of makeup, but she wears little and routinely has her nails and hooves done elsewhere. The diva looks at her sagging self with cognitive bias, ignoring the deepening overlapped folds. Soon, if she is to find her navel, she'll need bookmarks. Cognitive bias can be such a deceptive but sometimes merciful thing. In the mirror imagining, Diva sees only the younger woman of 30 years ago, and to be fair-minded, back then she was quite something.

Always ready plug in "Blackie" never needs recharging, she's and sometimes he or it, plugged into the wall socket always ready for action. Dependable and mobile when required, high buzz, low buzz in between needing no instructions, but with guidance Blackie knows his/her/its job, how to get there and do it just right. With gyrating hips and convinced now she hasn't aged a minute; feet apart, Diva moves to masturbate on her small dance floor. In the mirror, perfectly timed and admiring the trimmed Brazilian, finally head thrown back... a scream. Pleasure heard round the block. Diva is addicted and when they were there, close neighbors knew it too.

Even those in the sex business take a day off but for Diva it is a fulltime 365-24-7 job.

8.

People lie, cheat and or steal for many reasons. Some by necessity others for no particular reason other than reasons pathological. Still delusional, others do it for personal gain. Diva is well beyond adolescent shoplifting; she steals because she can afford to and gets away with it. In later life her records of theft will become serious crimes, requiring serious money to escape the consequences. We all have deficiencies that we try to hide, keep under control, maintaining some balance. Most people are good or wish to be, but Diva borders on or completely fell into the intensely malevolent. She's out there, way out of balance with acid on her tongue, oil and water in her veins. At best, she, along with her dysfunctional son, is litter, garbage really. He's been raised in her self-imagined image, a grinning Diva-man in Lauren Polo pants but no balls.

There are those, in high society and out, whose generosity is subtle and gracious. Surely, Diva has met some but failed to take note of what worthy people are like and why. At times, when with her I recall having met some and now wonder what became hard to reconcile: why, after so many years, didn't they see who Diva really was? Were those few people of quality that blinded, or just insight stupid? It was difficult to understand why they even acknowledged her. Her facial expressions rehearsed, everything about her Botoxed, mind and body, even her mannerisms were predictable. Her smile demure, banal as Marzipan. Surely, they must have seen something in conflict. At other places and in other times, people I have known would not even bother with the gossip, would have cast her out ignoring her completely. But this was Diva's world of make-believe incarnate, a confection of rat poison that, quite foolishly, all nearby her nibbled on. And the final question of course, what about me, why or how did I miss it all?

Not the best but almost high society all for show. In spite of what men want to think, studies show women actually dress to impress other women, not men. Females watch attempting to mimic those they consider worthwhile, better than themselves. It is well known girls, then women, have self-esteem issues. The gross reality of this is Diva's worthiness can only be equated with T.J. Maxmoney and the like. The assumptions others make are, by association, beliefs that Diva is a big giver and one to saddle up to for charities of choice. If you look at her financial records, as I have and still retain copies of, you see she actually is a smalltime donor. Just barely enough, to get a listing in the right places. I hear her telling others, "Perhaps next year darling, because as you may have seen, anonymously, just this past week there was a significant donation," ...to some undisclosed charity. I try not to roll my eyes and spoil the dodge. I mean really... she is riding on the back of someone else's anonymous donation creating the illusion it was hers. This is, to my mind, like people who sell counterfeit airplane parts that cost real lives. Diva's name will never appear over the entry door.

Returning for a moment to the issues of self-esteem, women, and sociopathy. Matters of self-worth are, of course, not limited to only women but in Diva's case they are woven into the actions, affects and side effects of malaise and her disease. Diva wanted to erase her youth, her origins because she could or would not accept who she was. Instead, she created a myth, a story she would tell herself and require others to believe. Just more to know about the interwoven complex mysteries of sociopathy.

Donors. Statistically and proportionally, middle- and lower-income people, give more generously than the upper class. This seems odd to many since the name on the hospital, library, or museum is more often than not one associated with great wealth, privilege, and position. Yes, yes, there are exceptions but when disaster strikes the little guys pony up. The name on the lion house at the zoo is different from those many on small tiles in the pavement and on the walls outside. Individual names in small print, the folks with their names on the tiles who every night see to its dinner and makes sure the cage is clean. The hot shots went to Africa to shoot one, stuff it and show it off in their "exotic wooded library."

Privilege comes with responsibility, it is for sale she says, and carries no particular responsibility. The woman, not a lady, has no special skills, little to offer to most and selects antiseptic environments so as not to be tainted by the unwashed heathens (her terms). She can't cook or decorate her own table but claims she can do a hell of a job for someone else's if you give her enough to spend… and… it will be seen by those she believes are important. She knows the deserving attendees would never RSVP to a party of her own. Doing this, and to be seen, she scurries around in a dust powder scented cloud of pomposity, making sure the "others" give her credit. She is quite crafty after listening to their ideas and later claiming them as her own, all, of course, to be invited to attend and asked back for more empty-headed wisdom and stolen ideas.

The price for privilege is steep and packed with perfidy. In Diva's universe of ill intent there are lacy edged minefields of murder and mayhem. Sometimes victims were driven close, then pushed over the edge. One thinks of driven over the cliff Indian buffalo hunts in the old west. What seemed like an innocent error, accidental or fate often ending with the victim's demise was, in fact, a product of the willful and devious manipulation of others. Diva has murdered many creatures, once she has them down, she delights in backing up and running over them again. Panty pulling talk amongst panty pulling B-C grade aging socialites is delectably malicious… and so, after the party the now pathetic, formerly melodious Melanie blew her brains out one early Sunday morning. The obit failed to reveal the true cause of death, but Devatonians knew it well and in detail.

The rest of the story: Melanie, a now *former* friend of the "friends," fell from grace. Unable to accept the truth and consequence of unredeemable circumstance. All because the family was, and these days still is, pathetically poor with only remaining cans of beans in their dark, dirty, now roach-infested kitchen cabinets. Overnight a family scandalized by legal miscalculations of the patriarch. No doubt enhanced by unseemly efforts to profit in a system that eventually caught the problem hence, the precipitous drop from pseudo-polite society was long hard and apparently to Melanie's mind irretrievable. Disgrace profundo. Accusations abounded, banishment complete, self-death the only solution. Ironically, there are others in "the group" whose crimes are every bit as egregious.

There but for the grace of…

It really wasn't the infraction itself; nobody really cares if you bought the drug bank that laundered money or screwed people. You were sued, authorities and others won, but you have hidden the money they won to cover losses you caused. Careful now.... just enough apparently to still reside in the walled off family compound up in Swell Town. Money really is not the issue; the deal is you're now poor or say you are until everybody forgets and you swim offshore to where, on a secret island, you buried the goodies. Your children continue in the good life of sorts by hustling, using the slim charity of others and time to time a few bucks under the table. It's all a mess ending in deadly tragedy. This drama has absorbed hours of delicious dinner table conversation with aftereffects of desserted flim-flam flan.

When the mob gathers this story just keeps getting legs. Each time luscious updates from someone who had a recent peek.

Yea, into the shadowed valley of darkness, now death behind the wall. They neither saw nor feared evil.

Reported refutation was only the loss of visible trappings associated with money and while not evil it was still a thrills killer.

Other lepers of Swell Town, their pathetic lives led in shut off portions of once great houses, with second and third houses now property of "the bank." In a swanky suburb of the rich, behind different walls now hiding overgrown once expansive lawns, they eat spaghetti out of a can, Dinty More Beef Stew and past date fruit off formerly elegant porcelain plates, these days unwashed, now chipped and fruit flies abound. Only a few habitable spaces heated with space heaters running on subsidized electricity. For insulation we are told, walls hung with blankets then draped to hide closed tight heavy maroon damask curtains. Cobwebs everywhere, contemporary Havisham's.

Like those who attend feathered cock fights, in Diva's circles players are mean and motivated. Costumed in designer attire, unfeathered cock fight attendees view regular affairs with zippers down and she-she martinis served. All reminders that down really can mean out. Losers finally, just unpaid misery entertainment.

I write a letter of recommendation to help a child into an eastern school of some reputation. The kid's smart and worthwhile. Diva signs it but could never write anything articulate so asked me to ghost write it. The parents knew this, never said thanks, never said boo. They are worshipers of Diva still, slobbering dogs in anticipation of a biscuit. The fools think Diva loves them and will one day be there at the moment of their redemption. Perhaps they deserve each other after all.

The list goes on, there are still more alone, fallen swells, but thus far Diva is not among them. The fallen create opportunities, vacancies to fill by those waiting outside in the rain. She and some of her friends know how to fight without showing dirt under their manicured nails. The trick is you just paint over it. Not so much as a smudge or trace of remaining canine shit on their Gucci shoes. When or if it happens you just throw them out and buy new. To stay relevant in tough times, one progressively waters down the perfume until it is truly toilet water. For the moment there is still England first then France and Morocco, Germany, or Naples in Italy and perhaps Florida. Naples Florida where old elephants roll over belly up and die.

And tails of tales go on stretching further. For yet another scandalous fallen family, borrowed money is collateralized with a full-length black sable coat, about $8000 never to see its original two-legged owner again. Once upon a time friends don't leave casseroles on the doorstep anymore. Can't happen since the givers don't cook and certainly don't eat casseroles. You'd think they might at least leave supermarket frozen lasagna. Certainly not a serving of Oysters Rockefeller.

Faithlessness abounds, re-acceptance occurs for some, but re-upping fees can be substantial. Some act of notice is required, one party in, the other out, cycles of deception with tacit unapologetic excuses. It was terrible the other party wandered they say, but there had to have been a hidden cause. Diaspora even among the goyim, swells and swelling. Whisperers repeat the mantra, "Somehow it was deserved, their retreat into a dark corner of the great house, literally and figuratively." The places now filled with garbage piled on The Pearl Carpet Of Baroda because they can't get rid of it, the now the cracked empty swimming pool and patio, where once, to swelling proportions, The "Grand's" gathered on warm summer days to sip and suck.

Talk of sex is again juicy. Always a conversation hit, speculation morphs to fact. Watching Housewives of the Decadent continues to be good fun and even better when it's real life. With little else to do, *between the parties* this is luxury life and how you fill your days. The "Housewife's" show is really best when there's an emotional breakdown, live on camera the complete destruction of someone deserving. Who said boxing was the roughest… generally at least in boxing the loser survives? The combat of mortal gossip, denial or death, all better than talking ideas for sure, humiliation is so much more fun. The television orange haired fop yells out, "You're fired." Innuendo is far too sophisticated a term for them, quickie slop mind-fucking is easier and more accurate. Come to think of it fucking anything is easier.

Diva's friend's son died. A drug overdose among the faithful referred to as, "What a terrible accident. Hit and run you know." It's witty, ha ha. Sitting at the dining room table she is surrounded by wads of paper on the floor, for show a token dictionary amidst boxes of expensive scented stationary. Profanity erupts. Lots of blame on the "fucking worthless kid who deserved it." Ha Ha Ha.

> *"God damn it, come in here and write this note for me… how do you spell condolence, this shitty dictionary doesn't even have that word in it."*

Many believe visitors to the race car track go to see the accident, chaos, confusion, destruction, and pain. Ambulances are great but a hearse is a twofer. In the stands, holding drink and a hot dog everything witnessed from the safe distance, Diva has more than once said how much she looks forward to the complete public sinking of one of her yacht club women friends. Driving home in the car, after a particularly ghastly winter Friday dry fish fry dinner, she comments on the evening's most recent melt down. She chuckles to herself, relating to me how deserving the melt-down-ee that evening will soon perish, gone forever. Never to show her face again in the dining room at the club, her boating days over. "That bitch will never poke her head up and out of their shit filled bilge again. Oh, and along with her fat little husband who is so smug, the notorious ever smiling mooch with a fancy car. You know he begged the city banker for it."

"Did you hear the latest about ah-ha? She's taken up with the tile man who was doing her and her kitchen floor at (or on) the same time. Even one of her offspring (name undisclosed) authored a book about it, "<u>When Lucy was Juicy</u>," I mean can you really believe that? Poor thing, seems by writing the goria of Gloria, she may have lost her trust fun(d) or was it a truss." Such unusual wit from the diva, I'm surprised and laugh some myself.

At the downtown luncheon, laughter over stories of the countess and tile man is bitter. "I mean really girls, who wouldn't want a young stud after, or maybe for lunch. She told me "dessert" is best when it doesn't cum circumcised. ... then she told me last week, ah...," the woman speaking squeaks, pauses with private giggles and unseen dabbled dribbles, "she's being treated for some social disease. Just think girls; at our age we can still get one... they're cheap. He, I mean the tile guy, even *did it* to her, she says, during his break still holding on to his thermos coffee cup. I mean this guy's a sportsman, a real jock." The laughter was loud in the private room of the lady's club where allegedly they Kegel exercise together every so often. How do I know this because Diva loves to repeat it to me later... My recollection is at least twice.

Sex isn't usually discussed in crude terms, so they have euphemisms, fuck is not a word generally used, "the in and out" is preferred. Outside the house, but inside is another story. In fact, many sexual acronyms are used inside and often vindictively. The old in and out, not to be confused with fine hamburger joints of the same name around San Francisco.

One wonders why so much sex. Don't these people play golf, tennis or paddle a canoe? It is sort of thrilling sport for the diva, titillating, naughty and dangerous. The real estate tycoon's wife was dying to tell everyone about her vagina re-do in LA. "Really dears, everybody's doing it. You can get a new one just like the trannies do."

Naughty is fun. Hers began long ago with oral sex when Diva was thirteen. She on her knees in the janitor's closet at school with a "Jew boy" standing in front of her with pants and panties around his ankles. Wanting to tell me all about how to do it the way she said "the stinking Jew" did it. Telling me this as if it was an instruction with expectation to be followed. A drama she wanted repeated in her advanced age, she really wanted to act it out all again inside any closet upstairs or down, it really didn't matter. The "Jew boy" reference or suggestion was not well received. Something about racism and sloppy seconds.

Her comment: "So what do you think? Which closet shall we use for your BJ tonight?"

Instructions about sex with Diva is delivered in many forms. Soon after we met there were copies of Cosmo Magazine left on the pillow. Usually opened to an article about "How to Please a Woman," "What Women Really Want" and more. All instructions for men who most probably didn't buy the magazine or struggle with ED.

"How to Find the Elusive G Spot," map included or if necessary, use your iPhone GPS. Books on oral sex, as if at our age we didn't know. She wanted to be sure her new servicing escort could deliver well-crafted pleasurable experiences with other a la carte menu items on demand. The odd thing was she was a stroker who rarely wanted to be touched. That, she did herself, sometimes asking for an audience. She was an actor performer after all. That was what the satin covered chaise was for. After seeing something like it in an article with photographs about sex clubs she bought one for her own performances. On dress up (or down) nights this was one of her favorite bedroom stage props.

Sorry to be so specific but more books and little packs of condoms with vibrating penal rings, scented and flavored lubricants, colored fluffer dusters. It was clear, unless a fellow wanted to dust himself up or ride one, the vast majority of sex toys were for women, so they were available in profusion, handily waiting for skilled practitioners who want or needed more practice. "Just visit the toy box sweetheart and select one for me. Remember now sweetheart, practice makes perfect."

Jumbo Costco packs, fresh batteries with use by date on the package ignored, they'd be gone long before that. Diva could open a secondhand sex shop. Certainly, she had the inventory, got into this early, vintage model of devices that must, by now, be collector's items. I am sure many were from limited edition runs that ended years ago, perhaps even museum pieces. How about a pawn shop for antique sex toys only?

Question here: Do people pawn sex toys?

We visited a sex shop where the young nattily dressed male clerk knew her by name, she was a regular frequent flyer. Always nice when the maître d' knows your name. "Let me show you our newest vibrator, Diva." Emphasis on the French pronounced *vib-er-a-rat-eeur*.

An afterthought, "And for the gentleman?" ...God damn, I never thought they could be so formal and polite here.

9.

I had suggested lunch, but she requested our first meeting be at her apartment and maybe, depending, later dinner. On a spring afternoon, when the door opened, she was beautiful. Modestly dressed in a light colored, slightly above the knee silk skirt and semi opaque ecru blouse and hint of lace beneath. White patent leather three-inch heels, gold earrings and a tasteful necklace. The bracelets and rings on her fingers were conspicuous. Light pink shade of nail polish that matched her lipstick, all just perfect. Lordy it looked like a great start, but one learns (or should) to be cautious, particularly of older women and especially if they were divorced and had a small dog, and she did.

In I went, not overly wary but I thought reasonably cautious and certainly polite. The apartment was large, I was immediately given the five-minute tour, a fast look, and I wondered why the hurry. A few things poking out here and there. Was there stuff under the bed she didn't want me to see? In his divorced days, my then single father once opined that when living alone single women could be very messy. Back in the living room I was quickly invited to sit on the short sofa that wasn't quite a love seat. We talked for a few minutes, and she moved closer. I was conscious of this but chose to ignore it thinking she was just being cordial. Moments later, and as we continued to talk she moved closer again. Tilting her head slightly she put her hand on my thigh and looking directly into my eyes said, "You may touch my breasts." I wasn't counting but I think I had been there less than 15 minutes. No wonder the hurried house tour!

To say I was unprepared would be an understatement. Guys may dream about such things, but at my age and in this setting, it was unnerving if not just plain stupefying. It was still early but dinner had indeed begun with early dessert. I literally didn't know what to say so responded as I hoped James Bond would have. "All in good time my dear." Dumb, but it was all I could come up with at the time. Privately amused at my own joke I have subsequently grown fond of the phrase and now use it often for different purposes.

Some might say this was the moment to run, others might say it the moment to pounce. Given the elements of time, age, and just plain good sense I might say it was certainly perhaps one of the most inappropriate thing I had heard from a mature woman in a very long time, but men are forever dreamers, and we have all seen the movies with hooker approaches at the bar. Make no mistake I adore seductive women, but this was far too much like a quickie at the Bunny Ranch and while I have no objection to them, prostitutes had never been an appealing choice for me.

Thinking the roaming Presbyterian Police might break down the door on us yelling "Gottcha," putting my hands in my pockets I stood up. Later, since the Presby-Cops didn't show, I figured she just paid them off.

Despite the distance, I visited a few times over the next few months. What I concluded was I had a wild and wooly sex partner on my hands, whose experience, and shall we say "style," had, on occasion, exceeded what I'd previously known and at times by a wide measure. Thinking this my youth revisited I had no complaints. Occasionally at dinner I assumed, in consideration of my age, a little blue pill was placed right there by my fork... standard fare, compliments of the establishment. Very busy, I'd been on my own for a few years and perhaps during that time societal norms had changed, perhaps even progressed. We were off to a rip snortin' start. Actually, the snorting came later when she catnapped through what was left of our first night together.

Divas know how to use sex but as time passed, I would discover, as far as I was concerned, things seemed more private theater of the increasingly absurd, but that was much later. For a while, admittedly I was curious and game for it; but eventually a nearly seventy something woman prancing around in a raunched up tooth fairy costume seemed ridiculous. Despite this, I figured we were still courting, it was early in the game and in time would play out into more normal territory. Not so, like not quite knowing what some of the words meant; her pillow talk was more like a child trying to talk dirty. She sounded mechanical and at times seemed in poorly accented French working from a script; however, as most males know, when on the rise, and acceding to a bigger picture, we can easily be undeterred by the small stuff.

There would be plenty of theater and costumes along with toys she bought in abundance, accompanied by other curious and inventive accessories. Some still remain a mystery to me. Lube everywhere, I figured enough to get a diesel truck back on the road. Once I was embarrassed, fearing she had no shame when her city neighbor mentioned she had found a bulk pack of six personal lubrication tubes on the kitchen counter. Thank God there wasn't a chalk gun to go with. I wanted to tell her we were fixing squeaky hinges around the place. Perhaps more truth was never spoken. I turned bright red at the ditzy neighbor's question but fortunately I thought the extraordinarily ordinary neighbor was too dense to fantasize. She looked like a cartoon. On a close to elderly woman with the Grand Ole Opry in decline, kinky big hair looked much too Little Orphan Annie for me.

Diva determined the base line of sex was it's a man's job to initiate, but that's not at all how it worked out. There would be lots of talk about variations on the woman's schedule, her terms, and ways to comply ASAP. I had not ever experienced such direct specific conversation like this before. New house rules were, it was a woman's call to call for action, whenever the spirit or whatever moved her. In the interest of experimentation I watched with interest and in early cases sometimes complied.

I'm not entirely naïve but looking back rather sheepishly, I must now say I missed early signs that in a more rationally sensible time might have been a tip off. I was only beginning to suspect the conflicting signs and much too slowly, that as an aspiring dominatrix, she was becoming less attractive. Experimenting can be enjoyable, fun and sometimes refreshing, I have no problem at all with that, but her approach was just less appealing to me. As she talked and quite explicitly, intimacy became a duty, not shared pleasure, or an expression of affection. To that point it was clearly not about love, fortunately we never got that far and when the opportunity may have presented itself, looking for longer intermissions it didn't take much for me to go AWOL. I tended to work a lot. "All in good time my dear," sex would play a role in the undoing of it all, but the influence of her demented son was beyond anything I could have predicted.

These are the kinds of sensitive details generally nobody wants to talk about. By this age presumably we are all experienced enough to know what they are in one form or another. Now I digress to add there certainly were moments of humor, if you could see it that way, and I sometimes did. Nuff said for now.

10.

"I am unclear about this." Shaking her head slowly the doctor squinted, furled her brows, and asked "Aren't you complicit in all this?"

"Of course. However, it was mixed with other things. That's the trouble in discussing it this way, words and events taken from context as if there was nothing else in the picture, before or after, nothing in between. And I'm guilty of this, but where does one start and where do you end? How do I complete the picture, right now, it seems all about sex, but I assure you there was plenty more. The problem was in one way or another Diva made sex part of everything and it took a very long time to understand why. It was hard to get a clear view of the other secretive things through this clouded lens that eventually turned very dark. Much later I would see why, but in the beginning, there was no obvious single rational explanation for it. Remember we were not together all the time, sometimes there were long intervals. Certainly, you can see there were concurrent paths, they crossed... it's just not that easy when they crossed back and over again. I sometimes thought Diva subconsciously knew this, and it protected her. Sort of the old, 'dazzle them with details and baffle 'em with bull shit.'"

Doctor; "Like what? What kinds of paths?"

"Grand houses, a lifestyle of excess which, I must admit I was initially taken with. Even my children and close friends thought I had finally lucked out after years of hard focused work. When I met Diva, and we began our relationship I was moderately well off. I bought a second house in the mountains, there was no need to use her funds. Then my business was blindsided with a major fraud. I was no longer as financially secure or comfortable as before. I wanted to fight the legal battle, but Diva wanted to play, insisting we just put it behind us and have a good life together. I resisted but in time became convinced it could work, as long as I managed to continue my work albeit at a different smaller scale."

Doctor, "Be more specific, I'm not getting the picture here."

"Divas don't cook they go to restaurants. I prefer to cook, but in the city, it was much easier to eat out every night, that is what she was accustomed to. When we were at the other house, in the country she ate like a rat, very little so I quite happily fended for myself, I cooked and did it well. In the city I learned to decline joining her in shopping sprees and even sometimes dinner out with her friends. I chose instead to continue working, which with the distance from my home base, I could easily do for shorter periods of time. When seeing her I would always take my laptop and work through the days so we could play at night. There were times when attendance at social events was compulsory, and I didn't have a problem with that. Typically, I enjoy peace and quiet but socializing to a limited degree is okay and Diva was an exceptionally social creature. That was her real life.

Diva's preoccupation, you might say her occupation is acquisitions and manipulation. She had a nice car but preferred her luxury van because she could pack it full of purchases. She had plenty of money, so I really didn't pay much attention, or frankly care one way or another. When the van was full it was time to return to home base, unload, and sometimes she'd go back for more that same day. For the next upcoming holiday season, Diva was ravenous, in heat waiting for after Christmas sales. If I happened to be there, in the city, when she needed help with purchases it could take several trips taking the "stuff" up to her apartment holding areas. Here, I have a few pictures on my phone would you like to see them?"

The doctor got up and walked over to stand beside and look down at photos as they slid by on his cell phone.

"My god, you say she did this often?"

"Yes."

"Are you a collector as well?"

"Well, yes I suppose but not in her league for several reasons, but yes, I accumulate things. But not clothes, I can certainly tell you that and nothing remotely on this scale for sure."

Returning to her seat, "So let me ask you, did you ever love her?"

He thought a moment, deciding how best to phrase it. "Maybe in the beginning I thought I eventually might. I was in no hurry, and we were having fun then so conversations about that never happened, we were just close friends. But no, at some point it turned into more of a custodial obligation. I honestly really didn't think about love, but I did feel genuinely sorry when she had a serious illness. I took care of her, taking time away from my work I went to her city home to take daily care of her. I did that long before we decided to, off and on, you might say, live together. In fact, when the health situation arose, I was the first one who insisted she go to the hospital."

"During the time of her illness I could see she was frightened. Out of control, but again you had to be very close on the inside to see the profound unusual dysfunction of this. I stayed with her for weeks. Genuinely sorry for her during those long days. I believed the stories she told me about her divorce and what her husband had allegedly done to her. Supposedly, and according to her he beat her often, had affairs, was stingy with money, mentally and physically brutalized her in countless ways, well outside the sight of others. She would frequently refer back and talk of the terrible feelings of hurt and betrayal she endured. He was a beast she said. Now with lots of regret, I misread this as genuine, and her pain hurt me. I didn't know then it was all an act, but you see this is how her web was spun, rarely do people blame the woman. Later I found out her husband was a very nice, caring person and I'm sincerely regretful of the feelings I once had about him. It would be nice to apologize."

The doctor quickly followed up, "So what did you do about it? I mean you're an adult, surely, you're not that naive."

"I mostly had conversations with myself about all this buying, her habits and the absolute bedlam, which normally is difficult for me. I considered her pain, my age, and what I could do to help and shelter her. Frankly, I just made a pact with myself. I looked at my situation and for a time felt she really needed me so what was I to do? That might change but I needed time and I felt I couldn't just walk away from her back then. I decided to stay until some logical end which frankly I had yet to define. I'd protect her until she could regain her footing and continue on her own. That would be my contribution and since she took no interest in my work I too could move on. I felt that I had been honorable with my intentions and helpful to her as a friend when she was in trouble."

"Her story of the hurtful divorce was very convincing, believe me, she is really an actor. On one particular occasion I went to one of her friends, telling him how much he and others had hurt her. They had continued to be friends with her former husband. Later the supposed intent of Diva's friends proved wrong, she made it all up and I apologized to her friend I'd spoken to. Diva had not told me the complete story. Believe me I felt like a fool."

"So," the doctor paused, "while you were exceptionally close friends and with benefits at the beginning, it didn't last long; you decided to serve a sentence and take care of her, is that what you're telling me?"

"Yes, and quite frankly I have described it just that way to myself. The way you just did, so we're on the same page here."

"What did you get out of this?"

"She and others will say some nice travel and my place to work, but I have travelled plenty in my life doctor, so really that wasn't a big deal to me; it had been our original agreement I would sort of be her consort for respectability. For some years, I had been seriously trying to cut back on my travel, I'd had enough. Furthermore, travel with her was not to places I would have chosen, where I would have gone. I often suggested she go on to these places of her choosing and leave me back. I really preferred to work."

"So why didn't she?"

"I told you Doctor, she didn't want to sit with widows and divorcees, they were competition, and she was stigmatized. She repeatedly told me when she was alone and single, she didn't get invited to parties and other social events. Believe me, cougars smell cougars, put a bunch of them together and smelling like a rutting herd, they reek of Shalimar. As my grandfather used to say, "They shit where they eat."

"Sir, if you don't mind my saying so, I think you both have problems. Very different, but problems just the same. This pact with yourself was a Faustian bargain."

The man raised his outstretched arm, pointed at her and smiling said, "Gotcha."

11.

Sitting on the washing machine she is naked beneath the sheer filmy pink peignoir, the one with spots and torn lace along the hem. Sitting on her negligee so as not feel the cold glossy finish on her bare bottom, with feet on the chair in front she is waiting for the spin cycle to begin. Vibration of the machine starts slowly, and all lubed up she wiggles around. Wiping her hands to clean off excess lubricant she gets a firmer grip on her favorite battery joy-toy. Spinning with greater vibration to intensify the experience the "handheld" is slipped between her thighs then further north. She starts slow, accelerating circling motions as the machine beneath speeds up. When the crescendo arrives, she is pushing the vibrator further inside and beginning to howl. Sometimes the actor requested an audience, but I only heard it a few times from downstairs and there was no mistaking what was going on.

The washer reaches it top speed, the spin cycle peaking just when Diva does. Orgasm races through her, they spin together, washer and woman are one. If she hadn't had her feet on the chair, she'd have fallen off, it's a quickie just before leaving for luncheon. She'll go with a smile on her face. You have to see this to believe it and now remembering once I did very briefly and at the actor's insistent request. Such a waste of water and energy I thought. There weren't even any clothes in the washer. I recalled it takes 850 gallons of water to make a Big Mac, but I don't know how much for a load of wash.

Tomorrow Diva will return from city to country but today, after lunch she'll drive to the sex shop in search of a new toy. It's always important to have a surprise for Lover. The real one and much better than flowers.

Diva reaches for her bra. She's not a hook in front and slide around girl. Much better from the back, hooked then leaning over to drop them puppies into position, with one in each hand she flips each breast into its lace pocket, but really this is senseless because the bra is too small, she needs to hand stuff 'em. Like all her others, by choice, not design, this bra is too small, she likes them this way and particularly loves this ritual. Smaller means pushing breasts up so "cups runneth over." Just too biblical for a girl that only believes in full passed collection plates delivered to herself. Sometimes, even after reassessment of the situation, padded augmentation is required.

Years before there was breast reduction surgery but now she wishes she had a little back, more to show for, or of, herself. Once set up and in position one more adjustment. Her fingers reach inside to adjust the nipples so one is not seen quite so much in its wrongful place. Her right nipple is misplaced place because she had more than once explained to me, "That bastard doctor botched the job." She hates this personal failure, breasts are a pain, too much maintenance for the ROI. No matter how often the subject comes up she gets angry all over again. The Doctor of Creatively Placed Nipples was a Jew and this of course, adds to her fury. Diva's secret hatred for Jews is not new; I am one of the few to know this.

At lunch, the "girls," as they like to call their aging selves "girl" talk is about those not present. They are not because in this particular circle of "friends" they were not invited. Every circle has its own admission policies and practices. There is the occasional guest who joins them, mistakenly thinking herself a qualified candidate and future permanent member. Today's *Lambie to the slaughter* is the wife of a prominent banker. She is younger, certainly more fit, and better looking than any of the aging circle girls. Strike one against her she's also smarter but has a shrill voice, strike two. Finally, strike three, an insane ear-splitting laugh that turns heads across the dining room. She sounds a little out of control, off her meds and after three glasses of afternoon Chardonnay, she is. With strike three she's out but *the girls* knew that when they invited her. This was to be a game of cats playing with a dying mouse, their guest that day an amusement. Their "special" guest will never come back and wonder why, because she wanted in so badly, never understanding how lucky she was.

Amused by the lunchtime game Diva leaves the club and waves down a taxi. On the road again she is dropped off where the sex shop is next door to a men's clothing store. There is an order of march here. She shops for men's things first, sex shop next and finally bargain binges at a discount clothing store across the street.

In the men's shop some black and red nylon briefs, briefs for balls. She knows Lover will love them for her strapon appendages. And new ties for the silk shirts… no, why not three of the shirts today and separate ties to go with. She needs them very small for times when Lover dresses like a little man. Lover is petite and is particularly fond of this role.

She asks the clerk if they sell garters for men. The young girl has never heard of such things but says she will ask. Walking away she turns back and says, "Oh, you mean those things they use to keep men's shirt sleeves up?" "No dear, the ones for men's hose." Moments later a stooped cadaverous looking man, wearing suspenders and with his own shirt sleeve garters, emerges from the back room. He asks Diva if that is what she really wants? She says yes if they have them. He says he thinks so, but he will have to take some time searching downstairs. She waits and picks through various men's clothing offerings.

Finally appearing again from the back room and blowing dust off the top of an old box, he opens it and hands one package to her. "Six pair, very well made, still in the original cellophane wrappers. $4.65 in those days." He says he hasn't sold these in 30 years. Diva takes them all, grabs six pairs of sheer men's d'Orsay hose to go with, pays, and is on her way to Toys For You and Me next door.

12.

Very selectively the diva shared past experiences. I was told my predecessor, second one back, was a dress salesman and undercover marijuana farmer with daughters. Diva claimed she was sincerely fond of the daughters and corresponded with them still. I never saw any evidence of this nor, so as not to embarrass her, did I ask questions about this or anyone else who might have led the way. Sometime later I was told by a friend of hers "*he*" was a "drunken brute."

While I didn't ask, she wanted to tell. They met on the Nordstrom designer dress floor where after her little bump and grind to lower the price he suggestively asked if she wanted to see his private showroom that had things more fun and interesting than just dresses. That night was the first of many trips to what they giggled and called the "show room." As frequently happened, I would hear about this secret from others, and told this episode in her life never actually happened. It was all fabrication but not without benefit and introduction to another real one much later. Diva didn't imagine this idea because she couldn't. One of her friends told me it came from a short story in Cosmo, the 'truth be told magazine,' monthly reference for young honeys. At the time I still couldn't figure out why Diva fabricated this unless she was going to claim she inspired the writer of 50 Shades.

My most immediate predecessor (as told by the diva) was, according to her, a former CIA man who preferred rough sex. His "showroom" had many 'true-life' makes and models, and Diva wanted to know if I could find a place to buy them for us. She knew what and where they were because she had, of course, looked. They were not available on eBay so the task was delegated to me, I must add, with virtually no memorable success. I did some hunting, looking, wondering, and saying nah a lot, but per her descriptions I would like to have seen some of the gadgets for real.

Convert and create a room at the country house on the river, she wanted her own and had decided just where and how it should happen. To get started, fur handcuffs and a pair of nipple clamps, no further equipment immediately necessary, the rest would easily follow "all in good time my dear."

CIA man had apparently given her many gifts and she introduced me to her laptop collected sites of Internet equipment stores. Before she went to California they corresponded regularly, prepping for their first *meat* and greet. There would be later trips and it sounded to me like they must have scorched portions of the Internet. I was "privileged" to read a few exchanges and can personally attest to the fact that they were steamy and very explicit. His were quite spicy but by comparison Diva's responses predictively dull, obvious, and unimaginative. At best, I thought she copied somebody else's homework. After reading them I could not imagine I was very good competition.

Apparently on her last visit and after the first few days of non-stop sex in non-stop California, it seemed she became frightened. I deduced CIA man was feeling emboldened and had made several changes to "the room" as well as onerous additions to his *toy-box*. In those days it was apparently more than even she had bargained for. I was told heavy bondage episodes were regular menu items, but they were not described in detail, I think only because her mental limitations wouldn't let her recollections go that far. She might have thought water boarding while tied up naked was next.

Now for a woman who in her first email asks if you like seeing women in lingerie and writes her first stop after landing in France and arrival in Paris is at a well-known risqué lingerie shop (web link provided), in the French manner, what would you think? Bondage man, aka CIA guy, may well have received similar messages and assumed he had found a, lick your lips, marinated, wild and pre-moistened riding partner.

She did say the bruises were hard to hide. She fled California and the man never to return. Or, so she says, not because she didn't like it, but because she was afraid others would see polka-dot hickey marks etc. in odd places. Diva, the presumed expert, said hickeys could last for up to a year. She couldn't swim at the athletic club that was for sure. I knew she belonged to this club but during my tenure never once went there to exercise or swim. More talk.

The only swimming costume I ever saw was in the summer, at the country house, her prancing around the yard wearing a bandeau style swimming suit. The no strap top edge inevitably slid down and needed to be routinely adjusted but rarely made it far enough to satisfactorily cover unmistakable dropping breasts and on rare occasions the peeking over the shoulder right nipple.

From more Diva tales from the crypt, another immediately but relevant former lover tale, this time a female-partnered encounter. She claimed it was truly spectacular. She said with enthusiasm, "Better than you, better than anybody, *almost* the best of my life." I wondered at the time if this was more a passive aggressive suggestion than recollection. While no one supposedly knew who exactly the object of this affection was, or specifics of her reported pleasure I eventually deduced the friend was in "a circle" where Diva was crazy afraid others would find out.

Accordingly, the break-up was unpleasant as lesbian and gay affairs can sometimes be. Such a discovery, of course, would be the "kiss" of death in her world of circles, and most certainly a tempting luncheon morsel for "the girls" to chew on, even those who would undoubtedly be envious and privately had more than a few similar licks in themselves. The hypocrisy of this charade was astounding since there were plenty of bi-sexual relationships in other buffet bedroom-sharing groups. I knew this partnership was not unique, and if necessary, believed I could prove it to the dismay and disbelief of diva group players and wider audiences alike. An afternoon nap in an English country inn with paper-thin walls provided easy enough and lasting confirmation of a permissively continental, real-life, memorably audio-erotic experience. All it took that time was a wall pressed water glass and the recorder app on my iPhone. At the time I thought it was wise insurance.

On a few occasions I did meet Diva's woman partner and the encounters were amusing. She was embarrassingly forward and flirty with me. I apparently was the "i" of the "Bi" and fanaticize, as many men are wont to do about lesbians, but assuredly this was not a pretty picture. In my opinion, the "other" woman appeared skeletally gaunt and unhealthy. One evening, after having observed conversation between the zombie and myself Diva took me to task, ordering me to cease and desist any further conversation with this woman, she was off limits. I responded, with some irritation, saying she had her tit-a-tit, mine was just a tete-a-tete. This went over her head, so confused she walked away.

I thought the comment rather witty.

13.

"I suggest we need to clarify what your intentions are. Why, sir, are you seeing me each week?"

"That's fine Doctor. What exactly would you like to know? When you're in the service business is it customary to ask the customer why they are a customer? Is this customer satisfaction week?"

Yes, the man could be testy on occasion.

"Well let's start with separating fact from fiction. Can you do that for me?"

As he sometimes did, the man briefly sat forward, hunched with hands on his knees. "You, Doctor, first tell me what and why you wish to know and then what you propose to do with the information I provide? For the money I pay, am I not worth if just for entertainment or at least professional fodder without names. If nothing else, I think I'm a good storyteller, you do have to give me that." Smiling, "I don't think you should even care if this is all true or not, unless your concern is whether I am delusional and a threat to myself or society."

"Just telling it out loud is a great help for me. Actually, I must tell you, I have been recording our conversations for the book I'm writing." He reached into his inside jacket pocket and withdrew a slim tape recorder with its small green LED light on.

By now he saw she too had affectations. The doctor liked to look up at the ceiling when she was thinking or frustrated, the man knew this. Looking up this time she said, "Oh god, what have I gotten myself into here... and you say you are recording all this?" She looked down and back at her patient.

Speaking slowly, not in anger but deliberation, "It is... my job. I am the professional here. I want to know if I am to help you in some way or are you just amusing yourself, and, I might add, at your own expense. Yes, you bet, it is important to know how much of this is true. All of it, some of it, none of it."

"I know you're angry, that's obvious. I have told you that is easy to see, but I want to know how this anger affects you outside my office. Just telling 'the' or even 'a' story can be therapeutic, but at some point, I would hope we could discuss some form," she paused then resumed, "...some expression of positive constructive action. A way for you to go forward constructively. You need to confront your abuser sir, in a meaningful way. You see Mr. ah...ah...Chevrolet. This is what we do with victims of abuse. Why don't we reset. So again, tell me, is this all true?"

Putting his index finger to his lips he looked away, as if thinking but then turned back and quickly picked up the question. "Doctor, do you treat people or children who have been abused?"

"Yes"

Nearly snapping and raising his chin to her he said, "And what do you do for them?"

"I help them identify and confront the abuse, and then help them create a path forward to acceptance so they can move on. It is essential that they move on. Do you *want* to move on?" She emphasized the word *want*.

"Not so fast Doctor." Now he spoke slower, nodding his head and leaning toward her, "Let's.... talk about abuse. What, in your professional and personal experience do you know about abuse of the heart, of the spirit, the mind... and the soul? Is that what you see and treat in the children? Those who were innocent and had done no harm to others."

Responding, "This is a question I need to ask you sir. What do you know of such things? Perhaps this is what we should be talking about here."

Shaking his head and smiling, "Ah, ah, ah, Doctor, I'll show you mine if you'll show me yours. You first tell me what you got. I asked you, what do you know about such things?"

"But that's not the way it works Mr. Chevrolet, you see this isn't about me it's about you. You must find the truth, a path forward. You can't hide or perhaps best shouldn't, in my experience you're the patient, I'm the doctor. This is not a debate Mr. Chevrolet, we're trying to solve real problems here, your problems, and don't tell me you don't know this. I well suspect you know a great deal about the process we are going through, even though you told me some time ago you had never been to a psychiatrist before. Would you like me to refer you to another doctor?"

Nodding his head slowly up and down the man was silent for what seemed a very long couple of minutes. With somewhere a second hand ticking the room seemed frozen, about to crack wide open. She waited.

The clock ticked making only the faintest sound. He squinted and pursed his lips in thought. She thought she had lost him but from earlier experience, knew he was thinking, debating what to do, what to say. She waited while he rubbed his hands repeatedly and then finally spoke.

As if he had not heard, ignoring her offer to refer him "Yes, I agree, but we will discuss truth later. First, we need to know about the abuse. Yes, what it looks like, what it smells like, how it defines my days. What happens with the rest of my life is something we may discuss and perhaps even find some answers for, but now I want to define the abuse, put the betrayal in quotes, isolating it. I'm trying to tell my story and paying you to listen. Isn't that right, isn't this enough for now?"

"I have been raped Doctor. My life has been threatened by the actions of a demented person. My deepest thoughts and values have been violated by a sick woman who cannot, will not tell the difference between right and wrong, she is a sociopath, Doctor, we both know what that means don't we. As Elizabeth Browning wrote, "Let us count the ways."

14.

"Doctor, you know I am not a doctor, but I do my homework. Sociopaths are hard to define because outside your field of medicine we usually don't want to. Like many forms of mental illness, you know it comes in different shapes and sizes and from limited, but in some cases known sources. Sociopaths can be deeply hidden using cunning strategies of their own design, you and I know this. A dysfunction overlooked by people who want to see what they want to see and hear what they want to hear. Those people, her friends and acquaintances seeking an easy path to justify their own indifference to the suffering of others. But there is an animal dead behind, in the wall, its foul odor spreading through the house. As long it cannot touch them directly, they stay outside, those viewers have no interest in isolating or punishing people who are creating havoc. These viewers are the ones who watch a crime unfold from the opposite street corner and do nothing to aid the victim. There are many of them and while they would never admit it, they too are betrayers, no better than the perpetrators."

"Sociopaths are," and here he reaches inside his coat pocket to remove a folded paper then holds it up for her to see, "I borrow from a well read and reliable source you know doctor:

Glib and conning. Never recognizing the rights of others. They see their self-serving behaviors as permissible.

They appear to be charming. Yet, they are covertly hostile and domineering, seeing their victim as merely an instrument to be used for their own purposes and pleasure.

They have a grandiose image and sense of themselves. Their entitlement to certain things they view as their individual and personal right.

They are pathological liars. Forms of pleasure-purging to justify more rage. Have no problem lying coldly, easily. It is impossible for them to be truthful and honest on a consistent basis.

Speaking ill of others to different groups with the intention of setting them against each other.

Malicious gossip disguised as legitimate useful information is a favorite choice.

No shame, remorse, or guilt.

They do not relate to emotions as others do.

Deep-seated rage and abuse. Physically destructive.

Does not see others as people but only as opportunities.

The end always justifies the means. Only their own law applies and prevails.

Shallow emotions. Warmth, joy, love, and compassion are feigned experiences with ulterior motives.

Easily outraged by insignificant events or matters.

They are not genuine nor are their promises.

They can easily be provoked to violence and conspiracy.

Incapacity for love. Cannot show genuine affection.

Need for constant stimulation.

Verbal outbursts and a history of promiscuity.

Callousness or lack of empathy.

Unable to empathize with the pain of others, having only contempt for their feelings or distress.

Poor behavioral controls, impulsive nature.

Alternating small expressions of love believing they are entitled to their every wish.

No sense of personal boundaries.

Early behavioral difficulties.

Academic difficulties.

Uncontrolled and improper actions, and associations with others.

Irresponsible and unreliable. Paying little attention to schedules, appearing early, late, or not at all. Blames others, even for acts they obviously committed.

Poor work ethics, bad uses of time.

Addictive behavior.

Habitual buying and spending.

Hording, secretiveness, hiding their addictions behind locked doors, secret rooms, fear of discovery.

Failure to plan ahead.

Spending days alone on the Internet, addictive television and solitary endeavors then hidden or lied about to others.

Paranoid persecution complex. Believing others will destroy their reputation or money.

Believing others are taking advantage of them.

Incapable of real human attachment.

Values skewed.

Favor material objects and money over spiritual qualities.

Purchase of loyalty.

They use their children as pawns and convince them to act as surrogates to clean up their problems.

Scapegoating. Always someone else's fault. Not taking responsibility for their own actions.

Surrounded by conspirators.

"You are, of course, familiar with this list, right, Doctor? Because if you are not, we have little to discuss. What I have told you about this woman fits nearly every single descriptive symptom on this list, created and certified by your peers. She is certifiable and so is her son. I have looked deep into the open jaws of this carnivore."

15.

Why am I seeing this doctor? Indeed, I asked myself this question many times before. I am the one who decided and made the appointment. Self-diagnosis is dangerous but I concluded I was being eaten alive with hatred for this sociopathic woman. I needed to do something about it and so the self-diagnosed person became a formal patient with bona fides. I thought I at least knew when and how to reach out for help.

What those who study terrorism and violence have long known is violent despicable acts often begin with inadequacy and hatred, particularly of oneself. The poison spreads out from there taking many forms. Hatred is a key that opens a door for others to come inside and join. Down deep, in her core Diva is a hater. It took some time but eventually I saw it in how she spoke and treated others. Some of it was obvious, mostly subversive, hence, covering her tracks to give the impression of normalcy. Those in the circles of her duplicity came through that door of her hatred and didn't feel a thing. I was not sharing her designated targets for hate; I was catching the disease itself or rather beginning to hate the source… Diva herself.

What I did not clearly see, what I could not see because of my own outlook on life is the very thing that brought me to this place of suffering. I must take responsibility for it and am saddened by the words I say to myself. Striking deep into my heart they are harsh. They tell me I have been a fool and yes, certainly naïve, perhaps even opportunistic. My own words and actions hold me responsible, suggesting temptations of opportunism. Things I don't like to hear, don't want to admit. And yes, of course, I am not alone, Diva-like associates surround us all.

None of us are perfect, but clearly some better than others. Many if not all of the diva's friends are takers, albeit well disguised with unrecognized serious flaws themselves. But as exemplar Diva stands alone. Her schmoozing friends ride along using the often true and false largess of others. Not all dim witted, just oblivious to the nature of themselves and others, a few token blacks whose reflective white teeth among the many whites are capped Chiclet teeth still separating them like commas. Hispanics and Asians, anxious to agree, all the time knowing they are despised and rejected by those different in appearance than themselves. Even the handicapped rejected suffering, considered damaged and useless. Then finally those less fortunate than the divas and divors who see them as mistakes, flawed, unworthy even of birth and human existence.

Diva has yet another set of friends whose financial situation deteriorated. They could no longer afford to live in the city and did everything possible to cover it up. Knowing she would be gone for several months they presented themselves on Diva's doorstep asking to borrow her city and country houses while their more affordable house in the country was being refitted for full time occupancy. They pleaded for secrecy since if known to their mafia collected friends, a fall from financial grace would be their social death sentence, no recourse. Appearances meant a great deal to both husband and wife. Wife, queen of cattiness and husband longtime serial moocher. Their friends, already gossiping for years, explained their history of mooching went back a long way. I just listened but watched and confirmed my own suspicions while "the friends" tore them apart to again smile and welcome the Moochies to dinner table at "the club."

It had been planned; Diva was going to spend an extended time where I lived. While she was away her Paddycake gardener, AKA spy, was instructed to keep tabs on the... *ah hem*... Moochie house guests in her country house. Diva's financially distressed house-borrowing refuge-seeking city folk friends. Paddycake, known to most as Diva's weed pulling gardener who, for those who will listen and not laugh, likes to refer to herself as a professional "landscaper." When the house borrowers shifted to city, kinky haired neighbor and milk-toast hubby were assigned as watchers of the downtown digs and *ummm*... guests.

The spies emailed reports almost daily and stirred up Diva's regular tirades. In the country and city, moocher guests left lights on, left heat and air conditioning running when they returned to the river house renovation projects, doors unlocked, broke and misplaced stuff. Their garbage was dutifully hand sorted, Paddycake's suggestion, and prying eyes hunting for broken things supposedly hidden to disappear unnoticed. Passing the time, Lady Moocher reorganized things inside the diva dwellings, filing items never to be found again. It was suspected and more strongly believed she took the missing items to her "being renovated" house down by the river away from the city.

Each day, along with her increasingly foul language, the diva's mood grew darker. Coloring in redder, her face changed with thin veins more apparent. I started to worry she might have some sort of breakdown, stroke or a heart attack. She slept less than normal, alternately depressed then manic with rage. Any suggestion the Moochies be asked to leave was ignored. Confirming, as far as I was concerned, their torment of her, another deity's punishment visited on hapless Diva. It was she who would be biblical Job.

The city neighbor watchers were calm, but Paddycake fed routine fires with excitedly malicious purpose, both real and I believed, much of it made up. Consistent with her mental illness Diva, in fact, looked forward to these calls and emails reporting the misdeeds and Moochie treachery. In weird ways, each of the spies benefitted from the reported abuses and codependence of Diva on her so-called friends.

Finally returning back home, Diva did not confront the Moochies of no gracias. It didn't work that way, there were other ways and other times when and where pestilential stories would be told and mooches would sweat. From sewers of duplicity wells were poisoned, I was to have been the only first-hand witness to vivid Moochie descriptions, then sworn to secrecy since, after all, Diva was so generous, and we were all just one big happy family. But alas not so, not to be, gossip is like a leaky diaper, there was more to come. In return for the Diva accomodations, especially amusing was the Moochies move of household goods from city to renovated country house. After staying in her house for nearly three months, they requested Diva buy some of their furniture at an inflated price and the topper...they asked her to pay delivery charges from the city to river bend corn field country.

Others are themselves not without sin. Everything has a price since, it is, once again and after all, about money. Benefactors, like the pseudo wannabe French Grand Mom-ah-ha who does the annual Britain brouhaha would easily sell you for a cheap martini after taking your check, the London Lavish.

I think about those who take the many forms of gifts from Diva. They use similar methods on their own, branded following surrogates. Patriots and believers, flag lapel-pinned profiteers who pay others to take their place in times of war. Friends with benefits, benefits with conditions, pasteboard patriot beneficiaries with acknowledgments hanging on their walls, no medals other than those from Rotary and Kiwanis pancake days etc., framed proclamations of meaningless promotion.

What else is it we do not see in life? I am rethinking all this seems a bit late, maybe I should have been doing it quite differently all along. How much did I take and requite? Not every day is sunny, sudden squalls appear, storms roll through, seasons change, we grow older closing in on death. We think we look and see but signs for the pathway are missed. We are imperfect, ah yes... but Socrates said the unexamined life is...

The allure of comfort is attractive to most of us. I have worked hard over the course of my life, demonstrating, I hope at least on some occasions, a sincere sense of obligation to others. I have uncommon abilities I did not ask for, including characteristics and artifacts to match. I didn't ask for them either, but carry them, sometimes light other times very heavy. Each of us with a different vision and version of comfort and accomplishment. For me chief among them would be unending sources of opportunities to benefit others, materials with which to work along with time and circumstances to do all that. I eat little, have never used or abused drugs, drink moderately and dream of creating as many new ideas as I can. Perhaps it is the Calvinist background, maybe something else I do not understand. I should not blame the Presbyterians for my youthful upbringing but then again maybe I will.

With Diva I wasted precious time in my life. Every minute I'm racing against time and there seems no way to catch up, every day, every month counts. My relationship with her was squandered time, I compromised when I should not have. Lure of the honey trap, the web, the spider that takes pleasure offering up only death as thanks for pleasure and self-continuance.

Yes, in my own defense, there was a time when I wanted to be a part of making her happy, but then was foolishly blinded by the trimmings of wealth and social position she bought for herself and paid for at others' expense. Previously, nearly all of it meant little to me so it is odd I should have succumbed to this. In retrospect, retrospect itself can be useful, far more instructive than nostalgia. Even in my own family there are those who lost their way ethically, morally, and even common courtesy. We are not genetically immune, there are no guarantees. Depending on your immediate point of view, to survive the selfish gene knows to be selfish, but the charitable gene is also part of the mix.

Sociopaths are good salespersons. If you have no regard for truthfulness, no compunction about fabricating stories and if you present them well or as acceptable fact and truth, you can succeed with those who are blind, dumb and deaf, or in my case, not paying attention. Ask the proverbial car salesman. Ask her dress salesman… he got her into the "show room" of his and her sexual fantasies.

Like those born with talents they did not ask for, perhaps Diva should be considered more compassionately. She may not have asked for this flaw of heart, body, and mind. Like thalidomide babies of 50 years ago she's a victim, albeit a dysfunctional product of nature-nurture and yes, breeding. But she also made choices and unlike others, the choices and this malady makes her a predator, a villain, a criminal to damage us all. Are we prepared to apply the lists to describe the serial killer? Knowing they can pass it on to their progeny what are we do with out-of-control predators? Back then, had parents known, would Hitler have been aborted? The victims suffer when unknowingly kept as pets, repeatedly used and abused. The sociopath is a villainous reptile, hypnotically swaying back and forth, taunting, titillating us with mesmerizing swaying… like the cobra.

In the zoo, with no warning, the deadly cobra spitting venom strikes the glass separating us. She can see it clearly but not feel it physically… only fear it. Where and what are the right questions about actions taken to protect ourselves from such deadly creatures? For the safety of others, instead of the Hispanics, Jews and others she hates, it may be divas who should be sterilized and kept behind enclosed safety glass.

Divas, a case for eugenics……?

At the insistence of another, friends knew Diva was in therapy for years. She claimed it wasn't true but as far as I know she was the one on the calm-down meds. Rarely did she take them as prescribed. Counseling and therapy didn't work, most likely because in her case they never could.

When confronted and because the explanations can be long and tedious, we often miss the deeper, more revealing stories. Carefully orchestrated sights and sounds of pitiful individuals torn asunder. Stories seducing friends and judges to pity the undeserving. How are we to know, can we ever? Yes, in the beginning I felt sorry for her, pitiful helpless waif who'd, according to her, been abused and tormented by men and especially her husband. Oh, the stories she could tell. Beatings, the destruction, reported yelling coming from terrible men who sexually and emotionally abused her, poor thing. Eventually, in her case all or mostly lies of course, but those explanations and revelations didn't come out until a long time later. By then abusers were long gone with circumstances never fully or truthfully explained. Who's to ever know now what really happened, why the arrangement between us didn't work. It didn't largely because you can't talk rationally to a sociopath or their off-spring who inherited their me-first gene. You don't fix or heal a cunning sociopath. There is no known cure for psychopathy. Psychopaths and sociopaths share similar causes and effects. Some experts believe they are one in the same.

We had problems with rational discussion, even greater problems with subjective ones involving emotions. No matter how many scripted "I love youszz" with no real heart, how could there ever have been genuine feelings? Conversations easily became convoluted facts with no value when fictitious sources and fantasy circumstances were thrown in under the Diva guise of truth. It is distracting when trying to help her understand that no, Mexicans are not the first immigrants to flood into the country. No, large numbers of North Koreans are not streaming in from Canada to take over the good old Uuu Ess of Ayaa!

What does one say? The diva belongs to a cult of nightly website visitors, who in cyberspace gather to spew and consume their special version of news and information that by any reasonable measure are extremist, conspiracy driven illusions aka crap. News designed to enflame those who don't put two and two together, never graduated or progressed from anything other than comic books, real guns and Cracker Jack trinkets. People just like her who have no concept of empathy, only contempt. People with short memories, no understanding of history and spell love H.A.T.E. The web creates gathering places for devotional like-minded comic book people, devotees functionally dysfunctional. So yes, it is a concern there are many QAnon people out there like her. You can go there and find out how to make a DIY bomb and she loves to tell me just where she would put them. My repeated question is and was, who actually writes this stuff since there are no specific facts to substantiate such nonsense and it is very dangerous?

How do you maintain a line of thought when conversation jumps from one's favorite online deity or candidate to restricting births, banning books and euthanizing "undesirables"? I thought we decided eugenics was a bad idea but apparently not. Diva believes if you don't have a job, you absolutely should be sterilized or eliminated. Please note she, like her son has never had a real job for any length of time. The diva thinks if you are Mexican, black, or Asian you should be sterilized. This is no joke; she visits her Ayn Rand mania often. Her son, Ne'er-do-well, worships Rand. They hate government but expect it to solve all manner of problems using death penalties, bulldozing portions of cities they live in deemed breeding grounds for disease resulting in plague.

From her mouth I repeatedly heard how vermin-infested ethnic groups carry diseases designed to destroy white Americans in particular. The bible doesn't say this, but her favorite website says it does. Diva wanted food stamp money for her expensive new car. The biggest problem is people will not believe these things I am relating, they think them fantasies, the product of my own present loathing for Diva. And I wonder how much of this applies to them because yes, I have witnessed and heard this hatred for others often from many of them.

Forecasting Armageddon is easy. The signs will be clear says Diva. When blacks become Jews, it is over and if Mexican Catholics turn Jewish the world will be hell. She's just getting warmed up, next are the Muslims who will cut off your head and blow up your kids. First, these kinds of people will take her money then come for her jewels, and this is why she has so many jars of peaches in the cellar. Not only does she like them but also, they will save her because, for extended periods of time, people under threat can live in their big house's basement shelter eating canned peaches from Del Monte, or so she says. I can't make this up; I heard it regularly and watched her buy more peaches every time she shopped at Costco. Do you really think this is rational? You want verification, look in the cellar and help yourself. There's plenty for all before we peach ourselves to death by choice or force. Better death that way than at the hands of "the great unwashed" flooding in from the desert slums south of town.

When I think of stupidity, I scorn it but when I think of ignorance, I forgive it. We have all been guilty of both, but most overcome it, albeit temporarily, and don't willfully feed either one when better more reasonable options have been offered and understood.

Sociopaths think they have it all figured out. When one reads the psychological assessment items most commonly used to rank psychopathy and then relates it to our very own specimen, sociopathic Diva, the correlations are confirming and compelling. I did not say damning, but you might. I am certainly not qualified to draw such conclusions, but now I can't resist. I am reminded, "If the shoe (aka glove) fits…" it is probably just peachy.

16.

There are people who from an early age are constantly at war with those they meet. If or when needed there are official labels for them, sometimes referring to them as type 1 or type 2 psychopaths. The former have superficial charm, are pathological liars, callous and manipulative. They sell past-dated food, medicines, flawed counterfeit airplane parts and conspiracy mumbo jumbo ideas to the unsuspecting. At various times they are us in one way or another and this is how they succeed.

> *FYI: Clarification is difficult and often confusing. Some believe psychopaths are born, but sociopaths are made. Both share similar traits and behaviors. Both can be considered extremely dangerous and difficult to recognize.*

Ted Bundy was a psychopath; Hannibal Lecter was a sociopath.

No matter you think you're above such things, you're probably not completely, hence matters of degree and sincerity. Bernie Madoff, considered a sociopath, fooled a lot of intelligent people, showing no remorse. He tore into and destroyed lives creating horror and mayhem and should have, or perhaps, been tried for the murder his own son by suicide. Bernie sat at tables, in clubs and rode in limousines with luxury minded friends, some were friends of Diva but later certainly would never say so. Nobody saw it; nobody imagined anything other than more money and greater success. Diva is no different than Madoff was, just smaller potatoes.

She has a friend duped by Madoff; he invested his client's money with the flimflam man. Afterward Diva sat by as others called her friend the filthy little faggot Jew. I only heard this repeated but know who said it and am ashamed to have known such people. The accused friend knows who said it, and so does his wife. In spite of this they too love the diva et al. His loyalty was proven to be for sale and despite it all, the wife remains one of Diva's best chums. Still, I liked him and for a time his wife as well, but she soon proved little better than Diva herself. Interesting side story here. Diva secretly loathes this reviled man's wife because I, on occasion, mentioned how attractive and interesting she was. It was quite a scene, first feigned hurt, then outrage and accusations. The issue, she claimed, was she never heard me compliment her as often and with as much enthusiasm. Retrospectively, and in some cases, it is a pity, I guess they all deserve each other, just more souls of and for the sewer.

Always at war with something or someone, Diva needed a target and too often I was it. She was habitually reviving her war on everyone and accusing me… I talked too much or not enough, I was remote, poorly, or inappropriately dressed or forgot to cut the hairs in my nose and ears. Hoping to defuse persistent criticism, anger and confrontation, I occasionally tried turning to humor.

"Diva, I have decided to grow a beard in my nostrils and say I'm Jewish, I've also taken an oath before Yahweh to never pull the hairs out of my ears again. Older men need hair in their ears to keep eardrums from freezing. Diva let's not argue about this, it's silly, we don't need to deal with it, I'll get some scissors. Diva, no, I am sure the man who pumps the shit holding tank at the country house is not a communist or a closet serial killer, he's just fat, smells like what he pumps and has no teeth. Oh, and by the way, FYI Yahweh is God of the Jews if you didn't know (and probably didn't)."

I am no patsy and there are limits, sometimes we would hit them. Among the issues were her complete and utter disdain for those infirmed, damaged, or less fortunate. That was a hot button for me. She has a friend with a mentally handicapped child. After they leave, every time we see them, she starts in again on how these "types" of people should be institutionalized and sterilized or put down at birth. It goes downhill from there.

New tale of diva horror: "Let me tell you what has happened to her." Diva is telling me why I should not feel sorry for Judy or her family and why I must know all this.

Judy has cancer of the plumbing, aka something cervical. "I can tell you this has been coming for a long time. Judy is not like us, and I don't understand how "the girls" tolerate her. We all know she's a slut, the whore's been shacking up with that trainer of hers for years. Richard (the husband) is dumber than a post for not having seen it, and he's fucking their, not old enough, babysitter." I'm being filled in on the scoop, not for the first time. Diva continues with gusto. "Because of that trainer guy Judy's had two abortions, and at her age, let me tell you, this is the result. She got this cancer from him, herself." Followed by a few more, "Judy's just a fuck slut." In my mind only, I follow, recalling something about calling kettles black.

Now the implication is clear and unavoidable, I get it. Judy does have cancer. As for the slut part I don't know, and I don't care other than actually Judy is pretty good looking. That's as far as my interest went. As for Richard the husband, my guess is he's paying the trainer on the side. Probably telling him to do this because I know Judy can rag at him on and on, along with others; I was often a witness. I thought he hated her but loved her father's money and would screw her father if she asked Richard to... as it is, I just thought the father asked Richard to fuck his daughter and keep her the hell away from him. Such is life in the *valley of the dollies*.

Diva continues and figures, for as long as we are at it, she might as well educate me on another dolly "friend" of hers. "The pathetic woman doesn't know how to dress, how to act like the rest of us." This from the same woman who overflows her clothes and for good measure and a rash, adds another rash *between* her lower cheeks when slop-walking in heels. The same woman who really thought a muffin top was something endearing and cute along with quoting that former dress salesman gentleman, "Let's do the Tootsie Roll in my candy shop." Give me a break. Love poems of John Keats this ain't. *Titsie* rolls in a box of turds it is.

Ed note: Judy has since died; Richard has not remarried her father, but instead her sister whose husband died of AIDS. Good luck with that Richard, at least you're still in line. Hope you didn't mess around with the sister's husband.

Repeating, repeating: Diva lives in a constant state of bedlam, huffing and puffing out of habit, as if pressures of the world are too much for her to *bare!* She is usually late, confuses dates, we arrive for a party one day early, but they still invite us in and feed us. We arrive to another party an hour early, they ask us to go for coffee and come back at the right time. For still another soirée we don't arrive at all, and for that one I couldn't have cared less. We miss planes, wait for another but in Mexico have to stay overnight at the airport because she can't get the itinerary straight. After trying (unsuccessfully) to blame this on the agent, the ticket man calls for airport security and there is a scene. I follow her and the Aeropuerto cop to a glassed enclosed room. Standing outside I watch as she gestures wildly, repeatedly telling the airport police she wants, right there, at the Aeroporto Internacional de la Ciudad de México, to immediately see an attorney from the American Embassy.

They finally call it a draw and she walked out, as the cop opened a drawer and through the glass window, I watched him reaching for his bottle of Tequila.

She insists on being in charge of itineraries, claiming she is an expert in such matters. Since she can't keep them straight and hiding travel plans like they were a list of goodies in her "joy-toy" box, she reschedules and pays the additional fees often. Twice, one hour apart for a 6-hour flight we had two booked flights to the same place. Once I ate four salads in one day, I try to eat healthy on flights and in airports usually do salads while Diva eats candy, crackers with cheese and peanut butter and always, because she thinks it's free, she drinks too much. On a long flight in first class, she usually gets smashed to the point where they cut her off and "phew," they, not me, help her from the plane, "phew again." She tells the cabin crew it is because she was so excited to see her nonexistent grandchildren and had little sleep (bull shit). When I could, I told cabin attendants I had no idea who she was and while I sat next to her, worried the entire time she would throw up on me.

Preparing for a trip or simply going out for an evening is a trial. Total confusion. You'd think this was a Marco Polo journey. I finally figured it out, Hannibal took elephants over the Alps to carry his wife's luggage. This is the way Diva travels. My back aches just thinking about the lugging part.

We are headed to the airport; the taxi waits while she goes back upstairs to put on different colored heels. She comes back down only to remember to go back up and get an extra pair of panties for her purse. I don't quite understand this packing panties habit but remain quiet about it. It makes me somewhat apprehensive thinking about bad things happening that I want no part of. Twice we needed two taxis because we were late and the first one couldn't get all the luggage in his so he called another Pakistani brother whom we also could not understand. We missed the flight, got another while apparently the luggage went on another, never to return to the destination of its choosing. Other than on airplanes she is usually not a heavy drinker. One whiff and she's out, this is a bartender's daughter who should have been a pro.

It's Christmas Eve. "Thank you so much for a lovely evening. You really are a dear. Happy Holidays, and I brought a coat."

Ah… well yeah, there is a blizzard raging outside.

The host helps her with a floor length black sable I refer to as "the animal skins."

In an astonishingly coherent voice, again and again she tells our hosts, "Oh thank you sweethearts." Finally, establishing who's in charge here, dropping an octave to use her best commanding voice she turns to me, "We must go now." At the dinner table she has put on a good front and is mostly quiet, but I know she is smashed. At least in public she is generally a quiet drunk.

The private elevator descends. As soon as we're out the door and beyond sight of the doorman she collapses in a snowbank, too much wine. Very windy with saucer size snowflakes falling, she is flat out on her sable furry back, giggling hysterically, swinging her furry arms making angel wing patterns in the snow. I prop her up, get her to her feet, take her arm and we struggle down the snow-covered walk, there will definitely be no cabs tonight. Through the December blizzard night, we are on the four-block journey home to city digs. It's colder than a dead bitch in Iceland. Back there, buried in the snowdrift, I missed the boots she was carrying in a zippered bag, but I have her small purse in my overcoat pocket. Freezing, windy and plenty of driving snow. No cabs in sight. We're on a tree lined street of expensive brownstones but I'm imagining how arctic explorers died out in the frozen open.

On the slippery snow disappearing sidewalk, she repeatedly falls; it's getting deeper by the minute. I repeatedly lift her to her feet although intervals between up and down are getting shorter. She is laughing hysterically at all this… even in the now roaring wind it starts to sound manic. A drunken crazy person in the night, on this very upmarket street, I pray to a god I have long been certain doesn't exist.

"Dear God please have all the people asleep. No one call the cops, PLEASE." Finally, I cannot lift her again, I have a very bad back so must do what my backpacking time in the mountains taught me. We have one more street to cross and three quarters of a block to go. I only have two reasonable options, first, leave her out there to freeze to death.

Tempting. Second, sled drag the KY queen across to the closest shelter, dump her and leave.

This time Diva is sideways on the ground, animal skin wide open and dress up to her crotch. I'm an Eagle Scout and know what to do. I rearrange her clothing so as not to offend or frighten passersby. Looking around for witnesses I roll her over further on her back, grab the animal skin by the collar and pull.

She bumps down over the curb into the snow packed street. If it had been dry pavement, to wear fur off, I'd have done the same thing. Near the other side but not quite over the snow-covered curb I see a shoe is lost... I need to go back across and grab the shoe... Looking away from her and over my shoulder I see huge bright lights two blocks away. Christmas Eve, a snowplow coming, ... got to hurry. Oh Christ. Seeing me and shattering the peace of silent night the snowplow horn blasts.

Everyone has to be awake now. Surely lights will start popping on everywhere. Do I leave her for the plow and save the shoe? Grinding sounds, I hear the snowplow downshifting, oh sweet Jesus, he blasts his horn again this time twice and long, a waker upper. As fast as I can, sliding her bumping up over the curb we are barely on the other sidewalk. She's grunting now, not laughing or crying, just grunting like some unpleasant animal. The snowplow is close, bearing down on us, more slowly now. The shoe's a goner.

The plow passes, we are in a dense cloud of blowing "after" snow.

One more maybe half block to go for home but I'm worried someone has peered out their window to probably see a homeless mugger dragging an old lady in an animal skin around in the snow. Probably headed for a dumpster to first relieve himself, then her of her jewels and soon maybe go to work on her body. I can assure you, at this stage and age the jewels are only the ones around her neck, wrist, and fingers. Rape is always a repugnant idea but tonight especially, who the hell knows or cares?

Her purse has fallen out of my pocket, and I realize, or hope it must be somewhere on the other side of the street. Diva always carries lots of cash. Forget the shoe, save the purse but no shovel to dig with. The snowplow gone, passed, gawd he's a witness, did the driver see my face in the headlights? Slipping and falling myself, I dash back across to at least look for the purse. There is a long gold chain on it. Miraculously I find it, partially sticking out of the snow. Hanging it around my neck but falling again I can't see the shoe. You get the picture?

Sensing a heart attack coming on I can see we are now about fifty feet or so from home base, the doors and the apartment's doorman. Clutching my chest, I leave her laying in the fur sled and stagger away for help. I stumble up the few stairs to the locked glass doors and pound on them silently mouthing to the doorman behind the desk, "I need help."

As if from a cuckoo clock, out pops the doorman. Late at night an old guy, whistle in his mouth to get me a cab. I'm gasping for air, grabbing his arm I point down the sidewalk where Diva is piled up in a dark shadowy heap of trouble. She has become ill and I'm standing there with a jeweled purse around my neck. Even from this distance we hear loud moans and puking sounds. "Please," I say between breaths, "Help me get her inside."

Doorman panics, has his cell out dialing 911. I grab it from him before he can speak and say, "Just get her inside and in the elevator, I'll take over from there." I hand him back his phone. As instructed, he lumbers off to get her, thank God the old girl's dress was pulled down closer to her knees, otherwise the sight might have caused the old guy to stroke out. I arrive at the scene a few seconds later to see the snow stained with chunks of mixed grill dinner and red wine vomit. Part of the animal skin has been dragged over the mess as the doorman tries to lift her up. He is willing but too old for this and has no strength to lift her by himself.

What we don't need here is another fellow's heart attack. Wind roaring, I yell to him we should just each take a sleeve and we both start to drag her up the now snow-covered invisible sidewalk. But he has grabbed a side of the coat's collar, not the sleeve, it tears off so we each grab a lapel. I have rescued the long fur collar, it's around my neck now with the purse. If someone finds it, God only knows what sort of investigation will follow in the morning. Two old men dragging a skirted body down the street in a vomit covered animal skin. Looking out a window, what would you think?

"We got'er," he says as we fold her in half and stuff her in the elevator, and I punch the button to the eighth floor. Adios and good night.

Dragging her out, with her no longer puking, praying she stays quiet in the eighth-floor lobby, I fumble for keys and remember they are in her purse. Thank God I got the purse! Just inside the apartment hallway she is laying on the floor giggling again about some private joke I obviously don't get. With one shoe sticking out of my pocket and pulling her feet inside and shutting the door, I leave her there. Go get a pillow for her head, wipe off her face and coat then disgustedly throw the puked-on coat over her and go to bed. Next morning is hell on earth. I should have let her freeze. And now by the way, Merry Christmas!

I have not yet seen the Sunday paper but envisage headlines, "Man mugs, kills, rapes (you must be kidding) and in snowy blizzard drags elderly woman across town in full-length animal skin. Body still missing but hunt continues." I think, boy, are old men dumb. In some ways I wished we had called 911 then the cops could have dragged her up the last block into an ambulance or maybe hearse and be done with it. I might have spent the night in jail but that would have been better than this morning after. I'd never have the chance again; I know I should have left her out there to freeze.

No fresh muffins for that Christmas Sunday brunch. Airborne cup whizzed by my ear, hit the wall breaking into a thousand splintering pieces, almost killed the bird inside her cage. She's seen this before; I saw the bird duck. You really think birds are dumb and I made all this up? I say again, you can't make this stuff up. I should have let her freeze out there.

The web tells me there are two kinds of sociopaths. Type 1 and Type 2. Roaming the streets like a moose in Manhattan, she's the worst kind, a two.

17.

"So, you just ignored all this? If I may say so, the woman sounds like a real cunt. But I also have to say some of this is sorta funny."

"Well, I'm not sure that is the word I would use, cunt I mean, but yes, I tried to, let's just say overlook it, or get beyond it. I took shelter in my work."

"And how would you do that?"

"I just say "enough," leave and go to work. The place I did that was some distance away. Since I was spending so much time near her, I arranged for office space. One of those co-op places with a shared receptionist etc. Diva knew all about this and the loft apartment that went with it where she couldn't fling a plate or cup. The explanations were I often worked very late at night and sometimes weekends. I didn't want to drive all the way to her places. Fortunately, she never went there saying it is too "*ordinaire*.""

"I still don't know for sure what you do but I am finally getting some sense of it. Can you tell me what you do?"

"Soon, perhaps I will tell you but for the moment it isn't relevant. It's a distraction that will complicate your ability to understand why or how I could endure or tolerate the madness. What I came to learn was and still is a menace. Believe me, without even touching you, this woman is a socially transmitted disease."

"This sounds a bit like control sir. Do you like to be in control?"

"I suppose, but let's put it differently; since that sounds like psychobabble to me, I don't like things that are out of control. I live in a world where details are important, and organization is critical. In the physical world I prefer order. I don't like loud noises, screaming, or unpleasantness. I pursue things that commonly don't fit, but jelly filled belly rolls are not among them."

"Seems to me that, with her, you must have had a high threshold for pain."

"Yes, maybe I do or did, but I do have a high threshold for ambiguity. Initially I saw her as an adventure, you might say a diversion in my life. Sometimes I thought I was too organized and needed some lightening up."

"Do you read sir?"

"Yes, a great deal."

"Why is that?"

"I like to learn things. I enjoy research. The Internet is a godsend to me and a place where I apply what I learn and know."

"What do you read?"

"A mixture of trash and heavy stuff. I don't watch television because I really don't have time for it. I was taught to read when I was very young, and it was enforced. Fortunately, that didn't spoil it for me."

"Humm. Well let's talk about that later."

18.

As it often seems to happen one day turned into the next, weeks, then months past. Soon a year then another. Diva's repeated absences from my life went largely unnoticed and were increasingly appreciated. She had her life and I had mine. When in her city, life was more tolerable for me; I was getting used to and liking my office arrangements with its spartan loft quarters. I could have used her houses, of course, but preferred my own. I remained on call attending functions when she required an escort and we appeared to others as plausibly normal.

I had sold the real estate interests where she found me a few years before and oddly didn't seem to miss them. My work continued to be of no interest to her and while this initially took some getting used to, we found other ways to pass our infrequent times together. My insistence of a moratorium on political discussions was usually impossible to enforce, so when her brain bomb went off, I simply left the room without comment. This, of course, was like pouring gasoline on the fire because, the actor wanted and insisted on an audience. Politics for Diva provided the perfect target for vicious paranoid attacks on others. Her party was not in the White House and, therefore, virtually all misdeeds of government stemmed from that place and its people, let us say, those not of her kind. On her racist nighttime website, she read about "White Chocolate and burned pork," came to love these euphemisms and used them often.

An outsider might have assumed Diva was active in politics, but she was not. She wrote checks to friends asking for support, but these were bribes for friendship, rather like money in case of hard times. Friends, in turn, would be obligated to support her showboat events. I learned quickly the people she associated with allowed no political diversity or debate and for the faithful this included religion. A few were not extreme, just loyal bumbling party soldiers in search of the spoils of war. Like many of their kind, *and their opposites,* they detested those on the other side and made no effort to listen or consider alternatives other than ones dictated by party functionaries.

I found especially interesting the myopia of their views and how little understanding there was of larger more complex implications. This seemed a conflict, uncharacteristic since some were quite successful in the business world; but alas, religion and politics causes many, if not most, to suspend reality and reason. The brass ring was the Lincoln bedroom at the White House but that would, at best, wait until after the next election. As I had some experience in these matters, in reality, at their level it would never happen for any of them. Anyone questioning Diva about current events and party lines would quickly discover she didn't have a clue. The brain hernia prevented her from thinking about anything other than spending money, parties, and sex.

Diva had only one close friend, that friendship wasn't a typical friendship and not at all visible to others. Those who she thought her everyday friends repeatedly told me they did not trust her; knew she was deceitful and lied often. This confessional talk usually followed some hurtful episode involving deceits the diva was quite naturally not aware of. Unaware, since the time had long passed when she recognized the feelings of others. When I asked a confiding friend why she continued to see Diva, the answer was always the same, Diva was fun and gave her presents after the friend paid for dinner. A $75 orchid plant for a $200+ dinner wasn't a bad deal, good ROI. I often wondered why they were telling me these things, unless it was to forgive or justify their own sins of commission or omission. I was tempted to ask something about the quality of their standards for acceptance but did not, since it might easily have called in questions of my own behavior.

One evening, in whispered conversation, one of these "close friends" explained Diva was being encouraged to return to therapy and could I help. In "their" world this subject with Diva was taboo. I was unable to confirm this suggestion in any other way, but I did once suggest I would accompany her if that made it easier. Hearing this she flew into a wine tossing frenzy and the inescapable wine stain on white carpet required replacement. Occasional carpet replacement was not unusual since the dog's urine stains would reach a point where even Diva could no longer ignore them and thank God, she didn't have a cat. The smell lingered, but one gets sorta used to it like the odor of your own home others might gag on when entering. With rug man, Diva was a frequent flyer. This said, looking at the Hispanic rug man I correctly assumed they never shagged together.

On another occasion, standing near the same place on the now new carpet, and after 2 glasses of wine, she managed to teeter, then lean against a shelf. The purported collectible fine porcelain avalanche slid to the floor. Glass and china went down along with her sprawling self and carpet man was again called. As I was told later, a friend of Diva's said it was I who had been responsible for several thousand dollars-worth of expensive broken china. I, of course knew better, but did not say this. I had seen some of this same, rather common Blue Willow Asian china pattern in a Pier One store years before. Ersatz often worked for Diva and most of her friends couldn't tell the difference. It was all about presentation. When some had the balls to turn a plate over, they kept their discovery quiet, at least for a while. The broken china storyteller person knowingly smiled while telling me the salacious story of my reported drunken-caused damage.

In the winters Diva liked to travel on her own. She could avoid the nipple numbing cold she always complained about. This was fine with me as I had no preferences and certainly nothing in common with friends or some of the climates she visited. On several of these occasions she visited her ne'er-do-well son with whom I definitely had nothing in common and virtually no interest. However, at her insistence I did visit him once, where from his southern "home office" he pretended to busy himself with ill-fated business ventures. Repeatedly imploring his mother to invest in them, this unspoken but known ploy was to buy him a job in the, at best, shaky ventures where, on a resume, he could claim entrepreneurship. He eventually would leave these ill-fated businesses and put Mommy's losses behind him citing irreconcilable differences. It was family tradition to explain the reasons were always the fault of everybody else.

Back on the entrepreneurial trail, Ne'er-do-well would search for another start-up. He had a formula that included walking in representing possible capital investment. Inevitably the "mark's" desperate search for cheap, no cost labor and equally desperate need for money created a perfect opportunity for both walking-talking frauds. Along with Mommy's money, they'd take him on and in the course of a little over one year, sure enough, as office manager then head of national sales, he'd be selling ersatz watches etc. online. Other ventures followed with software for Hispanics searching for credit compromised bargain autos (Mommy hated Hispanics), a device to keep tabs on your teenager driving the family car (Mommy was not fond of kids), dreadful off label watered down imitative alcoholic spirits (basically she didn't drink), guns, and an Internet chatting service. An event application put together one night at a bar with a couple of newly met Serbian gay guys (she really liked this idea, parties are good) and the list went on. Formulas are for repeating, each time he sweetened his pie with more promises of Mommy capital and eventually hit up the old man, who sometimes paid to keep his creepy kid away from him. Word leaked out even though Diva was usually secretive about her involvement in these mis-ventures. Over time, between us they became taboo topics. With no success I once tried to explain the word grifter to her, that's when I got the cut in the side of my head requiring seven stitches. Airborne cocktail glass.

By his mid-forties, between drugged stupors and unsuccessful golf lessons, Sonny Boy, who still couldn't putt, was still trying to find himself. According to Diva he managed to pick some hole-in-one herpes along the way.

19.

Listening to her version of the story she did the heavy lifting to promote her former husband's career. She loved to talk about who really should have received the credit, and she, with no shame, took it. Always making it clear most successes were her visions, her encouragement, and only happened because of Diva's hard-won efforts. Accordingly, she was husband's inspiration and always finished the story adding, "then the ungrateful bastard turned on me." All while, she, along with a nanny, cleaning-lady and so called "executive assistant" bore major burdens of housekeeping and child rearing. Poor thing, just pitiful she didn't cook or change diapers, and especially not for a seven-year-old.

Except for toilet training, Mommy schooled sonny well. His potty training appears to continue to this day. Herein we shall continue referring to him as Ne'er-do-well rather than using his pretentious, mommy given, pompous, silly ass name.

Ne'er-do-well was an only child, a preceding infant sister died in an accident that sounded awfully like being thrown out a window by you know who. With tears in her eyes, after Ne'er-do-well Diva claims to have wanted more children. The thespian tells how "that bastard husband" offered her a choice between a cat, goldfish, or abortion. Threatening her, if such eventualities arose and she didn't opt for the cat or fish over abortion, he, her meal ticket would take the fastest road out of town. Diva was a realist, so plumped for the fish and a few abortions attributed to unregistered *daddies to be. A*ll in the name of money for life and in spite of staged tears, kids were not all that important anyway.

Ed note: Much later, bored and with less to amuse her, she changed her mind in favor of a grandchild… but made it clear just one, unless they were matching twins.

Her lone kid was more of a toy than a real person. She could dress him up, "play with him" and show him just what to do. His later STD was a no-no, but as she explained, "it was nothing more than a little accident." Like the one at the Clubby Easter Egg Roll when, according to his mother, he was "only six and boo-booed" in his little pant-pants. Quite a memorable event it turned out, causing some old dowager who felt the surge, got a whiff and literally sent him air-born off her lap. He landed with a broken arm.

Little boy diva would grow up a pasteboard perfect Ralph Loren masterpiece. Sweet little saddle shoes, white knee socks with blue shorts, white jackets or little white pants and blue blazers with, of course, cute little brass buttons. You could not escape this photographically recorded evidence from every viewpoint. Impossible to miss on virtually every flat surface in the country house and city apartment. Well... except for the many other photos of Diva herself that usually, in their silver frames, crowded out the kid. Something else here; I have never seen someone put out framed photographs of themselves signed "with luv." She loves to tell about her baby's early business successes beginning with the lemonade stand she had a carpenter built for him. "All the children," she said, "would *flock to his house,*" where Mommy prepared peanut butter and jelly sandwiches and baked cookies. If you can visualize this picture, you just popped out of the hole you dug from and to China. In his forties now, Ne'er-do-well continues to refer to *mommy dearest* as "Mommy." Behind her back and without his wish list in hand, she's referred to simply as "The Bitch."

"Later," according to *Mommy*, sweet baby was considered a star by his, according to her, "many friends." More stories of advancing successes and how others came to associate with him in hopes of enhancing their own early earthly largess. The same Ne'er-do-well that down in Sunny Land Georgia, on occasion, sought new *friends* who did not know Mommy bought the Mercedes, the house, paid for first class travel and gave him the heart shaped backyard the in-ground pool as a birthday present. The required payback from Ne'er-do-well was a dedicated, decorated to suit suite, bedroom with bath for her, in his (their) house. The place where and when she chose, especially in winter, she resided at will. Watching over her baby while at the pool, spreading nude, self-baking like a yummy Hispanic brown.

Humming "Back Home in Indiana" at the river house, Ne'er-do-well's room reflected her means and their shared values. Perfectly and artificially accessorized just like his Mommy gifted Sun Land peachy Georgia home, where luxury included a TV room + very large screen, abundantly accessorized, using for show trophies that were actually sale purchased, out of date salesman samples.

Ne'er-do-well's northern country river house featured "yachting" memorabilia from some far from the ocean marine artifacts store. A special room with displays conveying presumed active yachting skills including extensive experience and unspoken association with "the greats." After all, back then the lad, for part of one summer, had received sailing class instruction in dinghies on a very small nearby flat land lake. Poor fella couldn't tell a shackle from a cackle. Yachting no, day sailing in tiny little boats maybe. No and shoes with Velcro buckles. Same ones seen at old people's homes around the country. However, the sycophant always has the pearly white Loren smile that others *urine* for. It passes for, or in lieu of genuine, sincerity and fictionalized intelligence.

On the second floor of the out in the country house his choice of several bedrooms, all decorated (oh yeah and pigs fly) by "Mommy." Again, magazine perfect, old "real skin" Yalee footballs, walking sticks, a few *old,* and a dozen new tennis rackets from which to choose. Artifacts bought at some old junk store with added dust covered books to read from years gone by. Quite Gatsby, all from a time long before the date of Ne'er-do-well's divine birth.

The message to others was clear, the lad's arrival had been anticipated by *alleged* Carnegie related grandparents, whose quaint old tennis racquets they, of course, were. Defined and exhibited historical family pedigree, the pre-accredited child sprang forth from and with vaginal perfection. Genetic breeding shored up with evidential artifacts to prove it.

Ne'er-do-well eventually brought his Herpes home. One cannot imagine at what price or which Trollope gifted his or her STD to him, but there were many to choose from. I was told that sometime after my expulsion, Diva started presenting her own cold sores. Phew again... just missed that.

Mommy wanted a grandchild at any cost. While she was the one who told me about Ne'er-do-well's herpes, she seemed unconcerned about possible effects on an unborn child. When I pointed this out the soon to be grannie made it clear she would take a grandchild at any cost and was sure she could have whatever the baby suffered from fixed. It only took money.

20.

Like his mother, the spawned progeny was greedy, self-possessed and when gene traced, undoubtably sociopathic. It is understood such maladies can be hereditary. Going back a bit if Diva were to be believed, dysfunctional gene purveyors and their offspring should be spayed.

Diva's kid was sulky, of unpleasant disposition and perpetual smirk. Older, he looked like a snarly dark bearded Serbian terrorist. Ne'er-do-well detests his mother, he often speaks to Mommy in snide and demeaning ways, publicly criticizing her hording, endless purchases of things he does not approve of and always "The Bitch." All the while in his forties, to her face, calling her Mommy(dearest apparently not). Still he doesn't hesitate to ask Mommy. When his divorced father remarried in a distant city Ne'er-do-well called to ask Mommy if she would buy and upgrade his airfare to first class so he and HSV-1 (herpes) girlfriend de jour could attend the wedding. Father apparently didn't feel his son's presence important enough to buy sonny even a bus ticket. This air upgrade request of Mommy was common practice, but on this occasion, I took note with exceptional disgust. There really were no limits to big brat's depravation, expecting Mommy would do anything for him.

Late one night, at the country house Diva got up very quietly, opened the bedroom door and crept into the hallway. By this time, us oldsters recognized the sound, the rhythmic beat and audio, coming through the wall separating our bedroom from "theirs." After a short-time I too got up and went out into the hallway thinking Diva went downstairs, wanting to get away from the wake-up wall banging beat of the TomTom's next door. As long as the boom-boom drama continued no one could possibly sleep in the house that night.

But there was Diva, in the hallway ear pressed to the bedroom door. Earlier when they left the dinner table, she had literally given her son thumbs up. I saw it and thought it the "good to go" signal for later, and later they went. Her signal to proceed and make *her* grandchild. Pressed against the door she turned and saw me, quickly putting her finger to her lips she warned me not to make a sound, not even a growl.

Disgusted, I went back to bed and buried my head under the pillow. Having escaped the evidentiary percussive sounds of rutting, I could not believe what I had seen in the hallway and shortly after, sliding into bed Diva poked me to say she was sure she got her new grandchild. "Houston, we have a go." For those who find this unimaginable, under normal circumstances I would have agreed, you had to have made this up, once again you just had to know her.

21.

Diva went to boot camp. You may know them as fat farms. She went with a friend in hopes of leaving some of her fleshed-out bakery goods behind in a grease trap.

Before this adventure, this same friend sent pictures from her last summer's annual Tripus Grandus. Included, but not from the travelogue collection, was one of the Diva taken from behind; one might call it a trailer shot from a friend. The subject pictured was stuffed into late model Chico pants, and I recalled recently reading a description of similar women's black pants described as "lesbian pants." With her big data copious display, I thought this photograph might deter Diva from wearing the "Chicos" again but(t) she was not to be deterred or discouraged until this photo arrived in her email with a blind copy sent to me. Previously

I had been discreetly informed that perhaps Diva was, "unaware of her increasingly appending condition." Obviously, the purported friend, type of which if we have one similar who needs enemies, thought I was expendable even back then; hence there was nothing to lose by making me party and fall guy for documented copiousness.

Until that very same night at dinner, Diva hadn't known I received the same photograph. In the interest of self-preservation, I did not raise the subject but knew something was bothering her. When under duress she is not hard to read, finally she said, "I got photos from Julia today. They were wonderful, my Pucci blouse looked so good on me, I'm so glad I wore it that day."

I said, "Yes the pictures were *great*," and foolishly decided to add, "but I think the Chico's could have stayed home." Diva went dead silent, level TBD but hurricane warning certain.

The point was made, plans made, and no further comment issued other than her announcement on Saturday that Monday she was leaving for two weeks. Destination undisclosed and, again fearing for my personal safety, I didn't ask. Instead of hoping things were going well and having emailed her a few times I heard virtually nothing for three weeks. This was not necessarily unusual, since I typically believed she didn't read most of my emails anyway and I preferred not to phone.

Upon her return, I, supposedly not knowing she had taken such fast action or where she had been, asked where she had been and whom she'd seen. I was summarily told to mind my own business. I then offered that, at least, I hoped she'd had a good time. She said no and that seemed to be the end of it. A few weeks later her frustration broke, and I was told the story according to Diva.

It had been a scam of course. They had robbed her. $7,500 didn't amount to anything other than skimpy meals with unattractive well overweight women, getting up early in the morning to sweat while doing jumping jacks, or some facsimile, and later bouncing around on big rubber blue balls. Kinda like bumper cars. I envisioned mountains of chaotic mega-jumping all over the place and what is/was happening in their intestinal tracks.

There was no television, lots of diarrhea with light classics and Wi-Fi limited to two hours each evening. The losers needed prescribed sleep. In short, she left early and went to see her sister in Arizona where she ate and made up for lost time and pounds. I assumed another trip to Chico's inevitable and surely, if the store was savvy, this time she'd become a welcomed, graciously referenced frequent flyer now on the plus size floor. Out of the beautiful people's line of sight, four floors to the top (aka attic) this is actually called "The" Designer Floor if you can imagine that.

After spilling the story at dinner, she swore me to secrecy. I was to never tell anyone again about the aborted attempt to dump pounds, sums of dough. The solution was, of course, to finally buy larger clothes. I was going to suggest Mumu's but did not. Soon to super-size muffin tops were graduating to jelly rolls and no doubt at some point loaves. More skirts moved to racks in the garage, where for years a car had been, but no longer. Already one could barely walk through the stunning accumulation of clothing. To this day, under rotting canvas replaced every few years, the car she never drives but will not sell, for appearances sits draped outside, revealed only for special impression occasions. Garaged inside goods continue to increase in volume + soon, to be the added, an annex.

A new chapter in adventures of shopping began. The trip away to lose became a return to gain. Vanloads of clothes appeared once again; big buy was on to buy big. Diva shopped and on rare occasions had no problems returning things after she'd worn them once and decided she didn't need or want them anymore. A common complaint when new "duds" failed to illicit gushing favorable comments. I assume retailers caught on to this a long time ago but were helpless in the face of retailing junkies whom they hoped to see over and over again. I also figured it's factored into the price, but one wonders why they just don't rent the stuff or maybe that's the way they do see it. Apparently, it's just the cost of doing business with moneyed scammers. These orphans of retail consumed as much time after-use-returning as beginning-arrive-buying so in some ways it all balances out, but still, "More is More." A cycle of fashionable domestic life, formally diagnosed as CBD or Compulsive Buying Disorder, has been professionally described and I can attest it is an addiction with serious negative consequences. Not unlike alcoholism or drug addiction.

Ed note: A touch of reality. As we age some grow less and others more literally and or figuratively. Such is life, but there are exceptions to the natural order. As with the habits of smoking and drugs, we acknowledge the lamentable consequences of addiction. Often, we have little patience or tolerance for addictions that can, with greater discipline and will power, be controlled. When successful or even tried we celebrate those who make efforts to improve themselves and others around them. They deserve our support, thanks and smiles.

In these recorded incidents of Diva's life this book follows the flagrancy of habitual, willful abuse. This is not to be confused with the pathology or unfortunate consequences of avoidable, treatable efforts by and for those who seek peaceful solutions.
When Diva says more is more, and laughs about it, we lose patience and sympathy.
And yes, Así es la vida

22.

I am reconsidering my time with the Doctor. She asks me again what I want out of this, and I answer but later think I didn't fully respond. I did not because I don't completely know myself. I have since met others who have encountered, survived, or lived with a sociopath. There are support groups for survivors, a large percentage of them seeking therapy to recover from damage suffered at the hands of these vulturine creatures. Some described it as a kind of death experience.

Yesterday I was driving, and the words "vicious criminal" popped into my head. I started wondering if this term applied to Diva. Was she vicious, the answer was yes. Was she a criminal the answer was again yes. She repeatedly broke the law by illegally taking things that did not belong to her or returning them under false pretenses and again yes, she was and is a thief, ergo she was and is a criminal and worse yet, she could care less.

But there were still others unaccounted for. Adding to these offenses she performed other acts of malicious destruction and wonton odium. She used the law and her lawyers to subvert intentions of the law where, in our country, lamentably most have come to know fairness and truth is no longer an issue. She used her money to destroy other people who, in the courtroom and, without comparative resources of wealth for legal fees, could not legitimately defend themselves or respond in kind. This woman has bought and paid for law on her behalf. And, of course, plenty of lawyers stood ready to take her money. It's all the blood sport of law and order. It is simple, wealthy people know this and so do some lawyers and judges, who need a place to sit, eat, drink and be merry. Justice is, in too many circumstances for sale to those of influence who can afford it. Take it from me, since it keeps them employed, judges and lawyers who know this could care less about integrity and therefore are much the same as Diva. The outrage is listening to their protestations and justifications for the profit center they create and support.

Criminal acts affect many innocent people. When a criminal walks free everyone is damaged, unless one is directly affected and then others just might pay attention. They simply can't be bothered, especially if they are so-called close friends. Diva survives because people of her kind do not care and as repeatedly shown are no better than she is. No matter what evidence is presented, most of Diva's friends have little moral fiber and no incentive to confront wrongful acts with indignation or rejection. Once revealed, covens of corruption become unavoidable so one might think twice before associating, but still, they do nothing. Later corruptors plead for forgiveness, understanding, and sympathy. Santa's making a list about whether they've been naughty or nice and Hell eagerly awaits those who pray to prey. Services, with religious fervor regularly held close to where you too live.

Temerity is masking her sickness. Finished malevolent acts, with pusillanimous pleading, she has the audacity to write, "Please respect me and leave me in peace." A suitable gift of forgiveness might be offered up with a block of C4. This woman is truly crazy, she really believes that after treating people so brutally they will forgive and forget while she stuffs bon bons. Want further evidence, this is the classic sociopath at work? She simply cannot understand, much less care about, the seriousness of having made enemies for life. Sun Tzu far above her pay grade.

Avoid Strength, Attack Weakness: Striking Where the Enemy is Most Vulnerable | Sun Tzu

There are plenty of wannabe divas. Diva has a friend who, for fear of others seeing them, won't let her obese parents use the front street or side door of their house. I know it sounds preposterous but it's for real. Mixed in there are other self-absorbed, philosophically stateless people and, like a rattlesnake, Diva and company lie camouflaged among them.

So, what do I want with the Doctor? Why do I talk to her? Venting thoughts of revenge seems a place to start. Perhaps redemption for my revenge, should options ever come to pass and others might see it, they may be warned and cautious. Will I commit an act of revenge and then later after the fact, like Diva, ask for sympathy, forgiveness with understanding? Ask the victim to let the victimizer be left alone in peace. Unless you have been there you simply would not understand. The deities say leave revenge to them alone, but I say they can't take all that satisfaction for themselves, I want some too. Even so, it is not I who will destroy the diva, it wouldn't work that way, there are far better ways. I've learned plenty from her. It is the system and people I will have never known who will finally destroy this woman. I will simply make a few introductions and then watch from a distance. She will die alone in shame.

I do not hate her; it has taken time, but by this time I have come to pity this train wreck of a woman. I say, at the very least, let others make her irrelevant. Perhaps by then in their unrequited life they too will be irrelevant. Her co-conspirators will not reject her, it is unrealistic to think they will, they are too much like her. They steal unused packets of sugar from the table, stuff their pockets full of things they have little use for, willfully denying those more worthy or in need.

This is self-talk; I concede and conclude I need to return to the doctor to find my answers or at least bright light the way forward since I am not finished. To help those who have suffered at the hands of a sociopath, I first need to heal wounds of loathing and disgust that everyday have grown in my own heart and surely in those of others. My day and night resentment of the dangerous, murderous people with their ill-gotten wealth and social concealment of psychotic treatment of others. Diseased psychopaths destroying souls of good and worthwhile people who make a better world.

23.

"We have talked for twelve weeks now. I think, you need to assess your own progress. What do you think, what is your opinion?"

The man stood to respond to her then walked to and fro speaking slowly. Choosing each word carefully. Becoming more comfortable with the doctor he increasingly did this, a sign he felt safe with her. To some it might seem as if he were lecturing, but that was not the case or his intention. He was thinking, listening to his own words, choosing them carefully so as not to over-reach or erringly minimize the issues.

Today he stepped close to the window and stopped. Looking out across the street, into the park where, under the watchful eyes of parents or minders, children were playing. With no obvious predators in sight, they believed they were safe. After a full minute he resumed walking again and speaking. It had begun as words of lament.

"Doctor, I have now come to know others who lived with sick people like this. Their stories are grim. They were and are so damaged that inevitably, and if they could afford it, they seek out people like you. They were broken. It took them time, it was painful but finally they came to realize that, and yes Doctor, we both know many of them did not make it."

He hesitated and continued, "I am broken, Doctor, which is why I came here to see you, even if I had to pay someone just to listen. This all sounds different when I speak and hear it aloud. Listen, when others did not or would not even when they could. I have concluded their lack of empathy is an expression of inadequacy, impotency of the mind and heart. Little generosity of spirit, miserliness. Nevertheless, from the beginning I knew it would end, I believed there would be an end of this torment; I will survive and recover. I tell you my story, it will take me time to be repaired, heal, for this to become a lasting artifact of my life. It will never go away, and I will forever reflect and continue to learn from it. These scars will remain, but I will be okay."

He stopped and again looked out into the park, then turned back to face her and resume his pacing. The Doctor listened and what the man did not know was she too was learning. His pain, his experience, what he'd born witness to had touched her, she was growing because of him. Evil did not seem the right word. She could not yet catch the right one to describe his experience but the feelings about his victimization, as well as her own emotions, were overwhelming. In a complex world they had become a daily reminder of what dangers lay out there and still, she wanted to believe in a world of hope. Tomorrow would, in fact, arrive on schedule and she intended to be there to meet it.

"I have many questions, Doctor. Ones I did not have before and realize, most likely there will be no answers. That is or was unnerving for me. The diva stole the answers, leaving me with questions which can tell me only one thing. Answers are perishable, they change with the weather, circumstance, and our gestalt. I feel like a man standing in winter with no shoes. I think perhaps answers would never have been of value anyway. Odd that maybe her theft was a gift, don't you find that ironic?"

He paused and this time she spoke. "What answers did she take from you, and tell me then, what are the questions she has left you with?"

Pulling up the sharp crease of his trouser leg he perched on the edge of her desk as if it were his own. In these moments it seemed they were partners. He was contemplating, factoring, preparing a summary to date, like this he knew is what the two of them must do together. He bowed his head and as if to erase, reaching up, he pulled his hands down across his face to present a new one. Lifting his head slightly and looking where she sat in her usual chair, staring directly down into her eyes with a wistful smile he spoke. "I do not know what love is anymore, Doctor. I know that once I had it, knew it and was cherished in its embrace. Not with her but another woman. After it was lost I thought I could bring that back, transfer or share it with another person but I have discovered I cannot. For me this will never happen again in my lifetime. She stole that from me, Doctor, what has been stolen can never be recovered or restored in any way."

"I no longer feel capable. I no longer feel I have the capacity to share love with another. I fear this terrible thing may happen again, that there has only been one person in my life who would not betray me, and she died long ago. I want to be wrong about this, I want to be wrong about never loving and being loved again. Diva took what was most personal to me. It is the worst sort of theft I think could ever be possible. I want to be whole again." He stopped, pressing his lips tightly together as if to seal them forever. His pleading palpable, it hung in clear still air of the room. Something had changed, as if another's spirit had entered to join them, comforting them, giving them hope.

He stood away from the desk and paced again. This time she thought he was going to leave; he was headed for the door but suddenly turned and came back. Close. Now he stood inside her personal space. She was still seated and he, she thought, looking down dominated her, but reconsidered. He was compassionate, wanting her to understand, wanting her to care. She not fearful or apprehensive in his presents nor he in hers. For the brief moment she felt this closeness, thinking he was going to reach out and touch her, being protective.

But he did not reach out, he smiled and stepped back saying, "She will not win, Doctor. What she has is deviant in a way, only a spiritual pervert could never understand. While she has nothing, I now have a question to take into my death. Already spiritually dead, with every breath she takes she is being emptied. Do you understand that? She will leave here empty; her time of opportunity has passed, been wasted and because she is a sociopath this means nothing to her."

He felt a tear and turning away quickly wiped it away, hoping she had not noticed. Backing further away this time glancing outside, seeing children playing in the bright sunny day. Safe, they owned this day, it belonged to them.

"She cannot win or succeed because she knows nothing of meaningful triumph. It's like air, no weight or mass, not money or material with weight. Diva is a vicious criminal offender, but we have ways of dealing with them. Some of us know to put the hard ones away, we isolate them with others of her kind. And she is with those of her kind, just not yet locked up."

"May I call you something else?"

As if he'd accidently revealed himself to her or made a mistake he moved on, too fast for her to respond to his question. Quickly saying, "I know too many of them. I have walked with them, heard them. Seen them and listened to things that should not matter nor be spoken aloud. For now, I do not know what love really means. What is the difference between love and deep affection? I am making progress, Doctor, and I will live while Diva and those like her die in the squalor of their dismissability. Their own obsequious obsoleteness, empty clothes, empty hearts, spirits of wind-blown dust, empty souls."

"I have made good progress with you. I have learned what to do with this, the possibilities of it. I see a path forward. I know to walk around them, through them… it is slow in coming but I am learning, beyond anger, not to glance in their direction. They are increasingly irrelevant to my life and my purpose."

He sat down finally sinking back deep into the soft cushions peaceful and content. He had crossed over, was tired, safe and for now had found a home.

The doctor could have made comments, many of them for sure but for the moment she did not. Instead, she listened in silence rich in comforting resignation. And she watched. As she did, she drifted along gently with just her own soul, getting reacquainted with the softness of considering her own life and its purpose. This man with no real name or at least one she knew, had become a mirror. Looking around her office, with him sitting there, sharing this man's arduous journey she renewed her own, one lost for too long but not forgotten. He had become a prophet to her, a teacher presenting new opportunity. They shared what each had to offer and then, with mutual compassion, to receive. It was more than fair; at its best it was what life has to give.

They sat for some time. Deep in their own thoughts, together just sharing with no spoken words.

24.

After the man left, she sat quietly at her desk. His appointments were always the last of the day so she could sit now and reflect further on their meeting this day and the others. Fiddling with her pens she carefully lined them up and stood away from her desk. The doctor, there to heal, went over and sat down in the chair patients usually occupied. It was still warm. His chair. A different perspective, a different comfort.

Whole. She did not feel empty, instead greater now than the sum of her parts. She was doing her job well, her client, or patient, as he would not like to be called, was himself becoming whole again. The first signs of completeness, his wondering, his questions, his attention to the children outside in the sun playing. He had said at the outset the diva could not wonder and now she better understood and felt the impact of that statement, the insightfulness of his observation. "What," he had asked, "would it be like if you could not wonder or imagine?" Now she too wondered about what it would be like to not wonder about the smallest or greatest of things.

The anecdotes of Diva were appalling, at times humorous and at others pathetic. Yes, on occasions she had laughed but mostly the stories were sordid. She saw that and shivered slightly. This had become far more than a challenge to fix a man's broken heart and wounded spirit. Despite what he said or thought, this man was not broken. He was more whole than most of those she knew or had tried to fix. This man leveraged experience; introspection brought it to a higher level. This was rare in her treatment of patients but then he was like no others and was, she thought, why she'd been drawn to this profession, looking, hoping for the exceptions. He asked for no medications, and none had been offered. Using what he had he was treating his own soul. The question was what really was her role, why was she there or here for him? When would she not be?

Unlike some in her field, this doctor believed Diva could not have asked for her illness, she was born with it just as others with debilitating mental illnesses were. But the question remained where did tolerance and compassion fit into this picture? Where was the line between forgiveness and blame, feeding or starving the beast and most of all the abilities or opportunities for self- control? Were there any lines at all? Now more deeply than ever before, this woman, who was a doctor, wondered about such things. The diva was easy to despise for her actions, but the doctor wondered if she really understood the whole picture. In their recitatives all patients were biased.

What would she do if Diva presented herself for repair? What would the doctor's reaction be? What would Diva say and how would the fixer, the healer, the professional react? Was there anything she could do, was there anything anybody could do for someone who had done these reprehensible things? Was there hope for the fixor and the fixee?

And the picture reappeared, he had been standing at the window, his back to her. Looking out he stared at children playing in the park across the street. There had been a prolonged moment of silence while he stared and, then almost abruptly, turned to stare at her. His arm raised gesturing with a finger pointing toward her, ready to say something of importance to her. Just as quickly his arm dropped, mouth closed, and he said nothing. For years to come she would wonder and imagine what he had been about to say.

BOOK 3

1.

The soft knock on the door was easily recognized, Lover had arrived. This time at the "other house," their covert house of pleasure. The one Diva had, some time ago, bought just for the two of them. No one else knew of its existence, the secret safe place. On entering, before reaching the inside play areas, one passed through other well secured doors. Lover had personally seen to those just as she had managed the installation of their security system. Originally there were two bedrooms at the end of a short hallway to the left, and together Lover and Diva made plans for expanding their pleasure palace. The wall between the bedrooms was demolished making the space larger, room for a luxurious mirrored bathroom added, along with elaborate dressing rooms for each of them. At the beginning it had been a small house, but the additions more than doubled its size. Outsiders really wouldn't have noticed, hidden far back from the road in the trees.

In the living room, behind a locked door that always stood open when they were there, another door, the soft black glove leather-covered door to their playroom. Inside, Xanadu with reflecting side walls that mirrored those in the ceiling. Like the rest of the house, heated hardwood floors contributed to a naked body's comfort. Wood floors provocatively echoed recognizable sounds of high heels resonately clicking until stepping into deep plush area rugs muffled the cadence, softening the touch. Every consideration given to promoting and the enhancement of one's tactile senses. Xanadu indeed!

When slid back the panels of mirrored walls revealed an assortment of medieval looking devices, all tastefully arranged to please and excite expectations of the flesh. Hanging on hooks and resting on glass shelves the display was better than any sex-shop most people had or would ever see. Lover had even crafted some of the device offerings herself. Choices, options all for sexual pleasures of the flesh.

Diva has no, or certainly limited, imagination but Lover does, making up for Diva's shortcomings and in their secret spaces expressed it with abandon. The vision and handiwork were impressive, it was all quite elegant, no expense spared. Diva's ample funds made any wish of Lover's a reality. Lover was handy; at various places in the floor, ceiling and walls, provisions for the attachment of assorted "appliances and devices," some inquisition worthy.

The workers had typically come from far away and had no idea who their paymistress was or obviously the final intended purposes of their applied craft and skills. They were only told these areas were to be an *exercise room*. In a rare moment of truth; yes, in fact, places to secure writhing real live dolls for playtime exercising.

At long last, with the workers gone, the house was ready for unimaginable pleasures. At one end of the main rectangular playroom they liked to call a chamber, a free-standing latex sheet-covered bed; at the other, two opposing black leather flat-topped benches with brass rings at each corner and places in between. In the center of the room, on castors, a smooth red leather covered hydraulically operated chair with fold out legs and arms, much like those used in a gynecologist's office. Bright brass hardware, all hardware in the room was polished brass to look like gold. Diva loved leather and the color of gold.

Through one of the far end doors the black marble bathroom with jetted black bathtub for two, maybe three and even four should opportunities arise. A door off to one side led into large but separate mirrored dressing rooms complete with ample drawers and plenty of hanging space. Diva, the great collector, has numerous costumes and bought more for herself and Lover. Exotic wardrobes any theatrical enterprise would have been murderously envious of.

Tonight, as most times, there will be pain followed by its sublime sister. Twisted sisters of exquisite pleasure, the two sensations orchestrated with delicious slowness, scored, and conducted to an explosive finish. There will be aftershocks of trembling continued pleasure, shouts for mercy quickly swallowed by sound-proofed walls. Begging, laughter and sighs. Pain-panting pleasure can be such sweet sorrow.

"I'm not wearing panties." Lover had written on Diva's bathroom mirror. "No Panties Today."

This is a bit risky for Diva because if she doesn't wear a girdle she can't, or shouldn't wear most of her *street* clothes, but these days, in the *cuntry,* she usually doesn't care or bother. Like other parts of her anatomy, she doesn't see, or even comprehend her gradually changing image. Lover has chosen to overlook Diva's potbelly going to full boiler; just as selectively, Diva ignored her own muffins overflowing the muffin pan. She is, after all, a woman with a plus size appetite, she's also like a Murphy bed.

The burlesque queen she always wanted to be is getting wet. They kiss, long and passionately rubbing tongues moving on to tribbing rhythms. Tribalism at its practiced best, but first, after a long day in the dirt Lover needs a break. Time for a warm bath, perfuming, powdering and just a *touch* of lubrication. With a go-hither-smile she excuses herself. Diva knows she will not be long, she never is, and settles into the plush sofa cushions rubbing her legs together. She's all ready to go, waiting with moistened hands and moving fingers placed just where they should be.

On the coffee table two Waterford crystal wine goblets. Diva has set them out with an opened bottle of expensive wine that with rising expectations will not be finished, exquisite, imported cheese and dark colored grapes. No champagne, it gives Diva gas soon after; experience has proven she burps and later farts at inopportune times. This prequel cocktail and hors d'oeuvr ritual repeats often, foreplay for KY Queens real life exotica.

The diva dressed carefully for this evening. Stretching out her legs, she admires the red seamed black Wolford hose and black patent leather 4-inch heels she can't walk in; some time ago abandoned the 5-inch versions. It is well-known among those in the know, many women's shoes are not meant for walking. Posing for short periods of time is okay. When wearing some of her shoes, she is far better off seated, then soon laid.

For now, with legs crossed she continues to admire herself. Diva still has nice legs, no dark blue highway and byway lines yet. Lover's are chunky, scratched and bruised with large veins beginning to show. Unattractive from outdoor work hence, opaque stockings and sometimes dark crotchless tights.

Powdered and perfumed Lover is back and looking at black garters beneath the transparent material of Diva's dark green chiffon skirt. Her demi cup brassier, Diva calls a brazier, with enhanced breasts pushed up until they runneth over. Perky an ignored distant memory.

There is no music, so they sit and talk quietly. Sipping, sharing, and purring. Two women luxuriating, never pushed by the urgency of slam-bam-thank-you-mam men. Instead long silent pauses, each with thoughts of what will *cum* tonight and who's first.

Standing then walking across the room, Lover turns to Diva conspicuously licking her lips then a suggestive tease pursing them to a letter "O" blows out gently. Her face eases to a naughty smile and she rotates her shoulders. Walking toward Diva she's making little cooing sounds. It is her own practiced seductive stripper's routine done to perfection. Quite unlike like the one who, a short time ago arrived with irregular dirty fingernails and tangled hair. Lover's a born to be pole grinding stripper and there's a sturdy floor to ceiling brass model right there in the living room for her to work on. She likes to say she keeps it "pussy polished."

Sliding down, with Lover bum bumping the bottom, talk turns to explicit sex. These girls are not particularly poetic. Diva wants to know what Lover will do tonight, what's planned and how it will be done. With a demure smile L tells her to wait and see. For impatient Diva, it's maddingly provocative and as usual Lover seems in no hurry. Diva's getting wetter by the second. Hot moisture seeping between her legs, she squirms and shifts her hips. Diva's idea of foreplay is about ten minutes and then it's off to the races of sensuality and endless orgasms. First the purring then the pain, followed by more purring and then, like falling stars the shattering of her body breaking into a thousand pieces of glittery pleasure.

Lover sits back down and reaches over to stroke Diva's silky nylon covered legs. Beginning at her ankle, she slowly moves circling fingertips to Diva's knees then further still until finally to the inside of welcoming thighs, Diva's own lobbied reception area. Her breathing now audible… she's panting while Lover is softly purring.

"Please," begs Diva, "Please." The partner slows down, knowing if she does Diva will plead more desperately. No matter how often it repeats, both love this sweet torture, knowing just what to do and… Lover's very good as a tormentor.

2.

If you've ever made or eaten dumplings, you know they are slimy on the outside and puffed up in the inside… pure carbs.

These days Diva barely makes it to the across the pond UK Hajj once a year. She is chummy with the founder of the Annual British Hajj. Snarky Grand Ma-ma dowager queen of the Anglophied events is that same one who'd sell you out for the cheap drinks. No rapprochement unless you have money to spend. The old grannie is all about money and power. After spilling her guts about her husband's affairs, the cycles of going broke and she along with her husband's climbing back up the social ladder, Grannie, with feigned sincerity, tells me how sincere I am and she is being with me. I'm her new best friend ever she says, so smart, and trustworthy. Telling me she's the dumpling in my chicken soup.

"Darling, I don't know why I am telling you these things, you just do something to me, and please, I feel so safe with you." No wonder she and Diva are chums, her affected speech is overdramatized, no recognizable origin but sounding more like a bad corny New Jersey movie script. A chain smoker, if you heard her from behind a wall, curtain, or headboard you might think she was Al Pacino. She should have had a better drama coach, but undeterred presses on with affectations she hopes some, and particularly I, will think are truly international, qualifying her as a royal personage or parsonage. But I don't buy it, the drama is not even B class entertainment. Puffing on her long thin "lady's cigarette" she concludes with the predictable, "I've never told anyone this before, so please, please, please darling, don't think me wicked. Promise me you'll never tell." After hearing this same line a few times, you'll believe you're listening to her answering machine or a pay by the minute sex line.

With equally feigned sincerity I respond, "Oh never, you know I'd never say a word to anyone, not even Diva." It is a game after all, or until she finally gets around to having to be more specific. It's been fun, so we smoke again while she tries to rearrange clothing in a way she hoped would clinch the deal. Regrettably, efforts in the wrinkled décolletage improvement zone looked more like Death Valley or the Badlands of Dakota.

As Grand Grannie Ma-ma confides secrets in the world of the Merry-Maids of Bedroom Lotteries, I'm finding out past and present infidelities that are not uncommon in these parts. Tales of titular talismans and catalogued willingness to sell vaginas for profitable revenge are remembered with religious fervor. There is wear and tear on the old bod of course. After heavy repeated use, she confesses hers has had more than one overhaul. On the women's side, it's an incestuous group acting like a nest of female Western Hognose snakes eating their own tails. What I am being told and didn't ask for is more about Diva's inner circle and this from her "alleged" best friend the "Bare-an-Ass grandmahh of Hajj, who swore to kiss and never tell anyone except, of course, me.

One evening, in a hushed tone of voice and her creeping hand on my thigh, the Brit-Hajj Bare-an-Ass again imparts secret information with attempted affected speech. Very confidentially, of course, and "for my eyes and ears only" she tells me what she thought I did not know. Most in the room know each other biblically. "This," she says, "naturally includes but is not limited to the conventional mano-mano and girlo-girlo." Standing she turns away to take a drag on her cigarette and with pursed lips blow out the smoke. Dietrick style she slowly raises her head to exhaust the smoke away over her shoulder and turns back down to look me in the eye. A dramatic, wordless conspiratorial stare. This is the come-hither moment to dither and *yawn*. My polite dodge is another beginning of the end to a "confidential" relationship. The culmination, delivered much later, will be her final stab in my back.

Anglo-file groupies annually pay Brit-Hajj Grand Ma-ma considerable sums to greet, meet, and eat with more rich and famous title clutchers than they are, or ever will be. Grand Ma-ma's philandering husband is a bully who, according to "wife," dragged friends and those who aspire to their association into unproductive, if not disastrous financial schemes. Somehow, with his imperious manner he still manages to survive and get the suckers to repeat at the trough with boy girl knickers around their ankles. Grannie-ass and Bad Gas's marriage, in their well-played roles, have for nefarious reasons obviously survived. Not unlike those in Kevin "Spacey's" duplicitous fun House of Cards.

The Hajji Gassers have equally dysfunctional offspring, no better than that of Mommy Dearest Diva herself. The annual trek to jolly old England is a rip off for unknowing newbie slaughterable lambies. They are bamboozled into paying thousands so organizers can ride, eat, drink, and while fraternizing at their own sucker's expense, be merry. As aspirant lambies are led to each event, it's amusing to watch them bob and weave among those they think will, in this promised land of pseudo nobility, be their new and "trusted" friends for life. No doubt, soon they expect an invitation to a castle summer soiree in Scotland. Those recently unwashed now scrubbed have no idea they're merely newly minted fiat pawns in a game of tithe and seek.

The yearly events in Britain are grand and impressive to new, across the pond arrivals in London. Long before, and certainly not with divas, when a mere teenager, I was there the first time, and it was impressive. With Diva (capital "D"), et al, it is quite different now. At the end of each activity, several times each day, Old Brit Mama bear of the club repeats her maudlin mantra to our "receiving" hosts.

> *"Thank you for your kind and gracious hospitality today." (Nod here) "We are so honored to be received and allowed in (on, up, down, around) here today (or night)." (Nod here with hands clasped in front at her crotch) "You are so kind, and we are so privileged." Nodding with a theatrical wipe-away stage tear she gestures then continues with false humility, embarrassingly obvious, head bowed then raised to the ceiling and heavens beyond. (Insert smile and gently tilt head at this point.)*

As we trek from site to site, table to table, house to house and castle to castle it's been said she lip syncs while brooding husband, Mr. Gasser stands behind jiggling her strings and works the recorded playback nobs.

As usual, the brief repeated talk, intended for the host and hostess finally gets around to money. Since the host and hostess are the real thing, what the old babe really wants is permission to use their name next year to hit up other wannabes, but a topper donation from them would be nice too. She occasionally throws in her personal story of how she is either persecuted for her good looks and works, or how others, how and why, are in debt to her for life. As thanks, she makes it clear the host and hostess are, for life, already inside the tent of her fleecing forever road show.

Reports circulate about her drinking, snorting, and clothes that appear expensive but, for style, seem to have originated at a resale shop in Omaha. The one "out there" devoted to forties couture of long dead wartime Rosie Riveters. Even talk of her sexual preferences pops up on occasion. She flutters mascaraed one hundred and fifty dollar loaded and applied eyelashes faster than a key tapping Morris Coder telling the world about a train robbery out west. It's a cover to, of course, disguise roving eye surveillance and her endless hunt for new prey. One side of a tear-soaked eyelash slips then momentarily hangs up before being brushed away and symbolically falls to the floor. All pretending not to have seen it, nobody stoops to pick it up, just a stage boo-boo I guessed, like a fart at a funeral.

One of the best-held secrets of charities are tax write-offs and ability to live well under the flag of business generosity, just causes and promotions of religiously intense kindness. Let us pray to prey. There is nothing new about this and certainly not Diva's intentions. What she hasn't told her tax accountant may someday land them both in the slammer. C'est la vie, even though they are only B level, friends know the tricks well. When entertaining it is important to create the right mix of expenses for compassion, recruitment, and lavishness. Nobody attends a pretend state dinner in Levis. All objectives are easily rolled into one and there are even how-to instructions roundly shared on the subject. What appears as garter secured or bow tied generosity to some, is more often social advancement and security bought with tax-exempt dollars from taxed citizens who never can or will receive such benefits.

"Lovely to see you. How have you been darlings? Come I want you to meet…"

At the annual Christmas party, in their big city apartment, nobody cares the food is Americano blaséo. Pork dipped phosphorescent magenta edged, suspect glowing party pink Thai farmed mini shrimp, they go further, disemboweled shredded turkey bit string pieces for faster stomach filling consumption along with brown tinged "used by" crudités. It's the tell tail darkened edges of celery and dry curled up carrot sticks that gives them away, along with commoner's cheese string and block cheddar.

Brito-Grand ol' Ma-ma, who's originally from some no name desolate place in New Mexico, knows where to put her butt and bucks, hence and therefore cheap catering, instead of tell tail watered-down whisky. Guests this evening will quickly be too shit-faced to check the food quality.

Bearing gifts of the season, and you damn well better have brought one, arriving guests anxiously wait for "her" to finally sit in front of the out of scale ornate R-ah-ha-co-co mantled fireplace that has never, nor ever will, know fire. For female guests anxiety has been running high all evening. "She" will open the elaborately store wrapped bundles in the presence of these adoring women. Each jockeying to catch a glimpse gathered in the semi-circle before her, three and four deep, the female aspirants hold their breath anxiously awaiting even the slightest mention of their gift and desiring personage status. This is a big deal where points and credits accumulate, with credit cards overdrawn. Access to the high-fallutin is at stake, in this holiday drama where armpits grow moist and neathers dry up.

The men are elsewhere, drinking while wives and undisclosed but suspected lovers hope theirs will be just the perfect touch for reminding Grand Ma-ma all through the coming year. Glassy Steuben evidence of devotion, adoration, and fealty are potential winners. The crafty old girl's dispensing of favors disproportionally small for gifts received and monies paid out. Smooth-talking granny's causes will not matter, that all comes later and anyway, by that time who cares. Ascendance into this team of heavenly socialites is all that matters, "D" team people have not been invited to this ritual seasonal soirée of B's and C teams. D's and their money will, however, be invited to the summer harvesting soirée Brit-Hajj. This holiday party is annual celebration for serious sycophants who bought the full package of events, big five to six figure tickets.

Pomposity, greed, and delusion carried to a ridiculous extreme, all that's missing is legitimacy with bonified up-to-date titles, but nobody sees this, it's a charade. The party brings to mind B movies, and worse, ambitious schemers in the throne rooms of yesteryear. Whispered conspiracies, illicit intimacies, back-stabbing, mother f..king ascensions to greater positions and portions of prominence, all silly really but quite real, nonetheless. So go kill your parent, siblings or relatives, intrigue is drama and entertainment in these Lives of the Rich and… well… even not so famous.

Now we're in for it. The evening's sticking Turkish Delight. As pageantry unfolds, creepy and crooked Grand Old Grannie speaks, "And Dear God, Heavenly Father, yes, we are all Christians in this season of the year." Jews need not apply, "Devoted churchgoers committed to the faith of our blessed lord, Jesus Christ, and" … her well known wistful look, repeatedly inserted fluttering falsie lashes, and she goes on. "Sharing one fish with many. Amen. Ah, men." The ridiculous Bible story goes unchallenged and back in the dining room, the skimpy to begin with salmon is down to bare skin looking like snake and will surely be shared no more.

All the while white men remained clustered in the dining room where booze and food remnants are dwindling unrefreshed, minutes away from garbage canned scraps. Looking around, methinks half the catering crew's time ran out and they are off the clock headed home. Time for me too. From the scattered remains of now dry, nearly crispy salmon bits, on the party table you can see just how far the one fish to feed many really goes or went, to whom and why.

Charitable is on display this holiday night. Ma-ma Grande has chosen the "blessed" carefully, bestowing on them just enough to keep them in paying place most of the time, well outside the gates and far away from l'chateau. There is a PR side to it all. Eligibility for this crowd requires hospital and museum board memberships, mandatory as competition rings, and manicured claw-clutched purses. The most faithful lambies this night, not to be slaughtered for sacrifice, rather simply prepared for the harvest of again having their pockets picked. It is never a good idea to cut off hands that feed you.

Through it all Diva plays her role with hushed consistency. The increasingly abundant coquette darling stands well behind gathered gift givers, a humble reminder of her position and unchallenged role as closest friend behind the throne. Alas, nearby for verification, her temporarily interesting but secretly known to some as disposable, man is at hand. Those in the know understand that other than her presence and money, at this blessed event she has no legitimate bona fides of her own; therefore, I was admitted for food and drink. The celebration time and place where "We are all Christians here darlings." Woops, a few exceptions so quickly she tossed in reference to, "Christ, King of the Jews." Phew, oh yeah, now, even though he is no king of theirs they feel welcomed also.

Cheek to cheek, air kissing in thick Shalimar/CoCo air (breath deep). Well played Diva and I with creds for the evening. The real paramour *lies* elsewhere, alone with "equipment" on satin sheets. Therefore, on this blessed eve this is, of course, seasonal Christmas camouflage.

3.

The diva is not alone with her reprehensible actions. She calculates and circulates in the company of others who defy and disrespect reasonable explanation. Another couple also is reported have "large" parents. They do not allow the "*hugie hoagie huggies*" in their home during daylight hours. When Humpty Dumpy and wife visit, they are kept in the outback of their nearby daughter's suburban home, guesthouse, hidden from sight during daylight hours. We are told, by the married daughter, when her grandparents visited, they are lured to the guesthouse by her mother and kept inside with television and abundant supplies of soft drinks and Cheetos. I'm told the issue is the oldsters are too fat to be seen out and about in the upscale gate guarded paradise. They're only allowed to waddle around outside after dark. This all reported according to overheard divatonian conversations.

God only knows what Dumpty daughter in the big house tells her thinner friends at Club La Margee. Similar stories get refreshed with periodic *embroiderments* tailored to suit male and female entertainments. It is cultural anthropology; in this way, legends of swells are created and remembered as warnings to interlopers and especially those of unapproved religions, size, weight and ethnic origin.

Going for the throat, sordid tales of social warfare are common. Membership in clubs sabotaged and mercurial overheard whispers are society's grist sources for gossip mills. One recalls childhood pranks, pulling a chair away when someone unsuspecting sits down. Rumors enhanced with elaborations of alcoholism, drugs, sex and other perversions of mind, body, and soul, all thrown into play like raw meat to piranhas. It's blood sport of the "swells." If you don't believe it just ask the jailed Leona Helmsley, Queen of Mean.

You might wonder if these people have too much time on their hands, what their priorities are in life, and/or purpose if any. One-upmanship I suppose. Grand Hajj Ma-ma tells me of a plot to blackball her from another new country club membership. She, begging for sympathy says, "That bitch is telling people I'm on drugs and I'm an alcoholic. And she *was* my best friend, I've known her for years." Time for a stage tear, the pseudo sometimes-Brit's accent slips away, replaced having descended to original backcountry drawl with a southern twang. Time to change partners again.

No different than games the husbands play. Fair to say, other than with increasing amounts of "gear," for climbing the social ladder there are no other socially constructive priorities for divas. Many, if not most charitable works long ago cast aside, they were training grounds for competitive gamesmanship and initial recognition; kinda like going from frosh to sophomore, those tickets got punched.

Diva, who's educational level and IQ are most likely in the high double digits, or low threes, coasted into the game using her appearance, husband's skill and reputation. It's advanced sorority rush without training wheels but money is the kicker. T and A come second, and for the smarter ones, short courses at charm school. Always walk toe to heel, toe heel, toe heel, back straight, chest out, smile always with tilted head. Charm school, back in the day you could even attend one at a local Sears store.

On this day, the Carrion Sisters are seated around a table at the Women's snorting and sporting club, the topic: decorators, for parties, not houses. Specifically, the annual "Hajj project" parties start first in NYC and the final banger party finally at a rented whatever castle outside Manchester, that would be England. To accomplish all this, they annually throw several tax write-off team-planning parties, those that make the society pages all love to love and hate if they don't make it with a photograph in a party dress. It is always time to again remind others just who they know and what they have. Somebody please make sure Town and *Cuntry* has been notified. Society pages are published, scorecards with photos. Too many mulligans and your membership is cancelled, and locker sold to someone else on the waiting list. Not making it with your pix at a recent A team party, or at least once a year is an immediate bogie with your knickers yanked. Cause: déclassé.

Lepers rarely return from oblivion. One recent slippage resulted in too many pills stuffed and wine dropped into the fouled mouth of a former "sister." However, the funeral was an *event* to be remembered and well attended. Occasions such as these are always referred to as "events." Everyone agreed it was lovely and, of course, "she looked as good as she could." At the request of the Carrion Sisters the society priest blessed her white rose covered casket with a generous sprinkling of *diluted* Shalimar and a dash of white wine. After a last peek the lid was closed and all said again, she hadn't looked that good since her facelift finally healed eight years before. Some added. "Being there, flat on her back in white satin was sheer poetry." Facelifts are like tires, with heavy road use they wear out and the last one was ah…short lived.

> *Spoon to wine glass, tinkle, tinkle, tinkle. "Ladies, may I have your attention. We really do have to get a little work done here this afternoon so let's start with you my dear, how much can you get from the Chinese? I remind you here, you told me that if we invited them this year, they would pay top price. I think you said…" (insert here she smiles sweetly), a million."*

This was a first-time offer made to the Chinese. Even though the Carrion Sisters are only low 'B" class, the invite would not be lost on the country's leaders. Their government would most likely pony up all the needed funds. What the hell, it's a high-profile photographable Anglo/English do-dah "In USD's I'm told," Grand Ol' Ma-ma rocks on. Hitting big time in the west, or east of the west, is a Chinese banker's wet dream. For their wives and lovers this event will be a chrysanthemum memory of heroic proportions.

The stylishly dressed woman from New York confirms the dollar amount to the fearless leader and those gathered. The Chinese, invited for bucks, this new committee woman in charge has superior bona fides. Her husband is from an historical patrician family, but she is not; hence, at least so far on this day of "recruitment" her membership remains in a class 'B' group not A (only her husband is Class A). She went to charm school and well trained, prefers to stand looking down on those seated. "I think a million." That's all she says... The room hushed, the old birds awed with envy and excitement.

Later, in their lair, Grand Ma-ma + Diva and a few "selects" tore the patrician's wife to shreds. Much much later the entire con fell apart. It had been Grand Ma-ma's plan to bring her into their group and milk the patrician's wife using both hands, but alas, when it was over and the promised million didn't show up, there were harsh words and pandemonium among the carnivores. With the Chinese shortages, to cover the loses of soiree expenses, the ladies had to pony up themselves. That talk spilled over onto dinner tables with men present. Blame, mockery, and laughter reached new heights. The men smiled smugly, emboldened by talk that inherited money and position wasn't everything after all.

Time passed and just as with Diva's violations and episodes of false contrition, memories prone to convenience faded in favor of better times to come. Back at this particular year's meeting Grannie motions the now reinstated credible NY diva to sit. Matriarch resumes. "Thank you Dear," returning to the worshipers "and now how are we coming with the faithful?" This refers to *tickets* they prefer to call subscriptions.

Sales to the same people who every year, still not getting it, attend the feeding frenzy. They come to see newbies and the same party people over and over, every year repeating the same stories. Same food, same wine, same desserts, same people, ah, but some exceptions. Aside from the new lambies the best *newest* attractions are different houses, art, chateaux, castles, London and UK beyond nooks and crannies, Muse apartments, divorces, and a few demises of those who choose not to or no longer can attended … samo every year. A Gathering of Crones with some "nest" jumping and fresh meat. After so many repeats, for some it all looks, smells, and tastes the same.

Each year it starts like this:

THE FRIENDS OF ANGLO-AMERICA REQUEST THE PLEASURE OF YOUR COMPANY FOR A BENEFIT SUBLIME

Le Grand Gala de…

(It continues section by section.)
Extraordinary Donor's Recognition

For a gift of $X00,000 and above, per individual or couple, your name or company's name will be listed on the
Principal Benefactors Plaque

placed within the ……. and you will be *afforded* two tickets to the ………… events.
A UNIQUE OPPORTUNITY
…….AND WE WILL BE RECEIVED BY ……blah blah blah

As one man unhappily later whispered, "I feel like King Shit of Turd Mountain."

"Subscription" price, $X0,000 to $X00,000 a head, unless you get the discount and all the planners gathered here today, for the planning session, will get at least some discount. Secretly awarded graduated portions, and very secretly for a very special few, all champagne and dinners included. What the gathered don't and can't know is the sliding scale. Only the matriarch and her hairdresser really know who gets what. This, after all, is not an "A" team billionaires club, it's just mid to low "B" so they have come to economize watching their "P's" and "Q's."

In the past few years, suffering from habitual over-spending, Diva has been having financial difficulties, or as her chief financial advisor described it, "her tit's in a wringer." She, the ever survivor, will get the best party deal in the house because she sucks up to Grannie Brit-Mama with gifts and girl talk. In the Euro traditions of secret alliances, her son, Ne'er-do-well will soon be offered up as matrimonial tender to seal the deal forever or until in death's doo-doo, they parted. Diva has been sneaking around back by the dumpster. A few of "the girls" suspect this but say nothing, even though loose lips shrink slips. Soon there is to be a crisis of confidence over fair play, or whatever you choose to call make-believe.

Alien discounts can be worth more than common fiat currency and even increased charitable donations. A reflection of positioning for all except the "receiving" matriarch. She is, after all, top bitch dog and final receiver and acceptor of the collection plates. Diva will, this year, also be in for airfare and hotel. Food, wine, tours, and entertainment on the house paid by others who foolishly thought everybody paid full price. And after all, for a fee or perks, somebody has to watch over everything in the shop.

Under the guise of philanthropy, the group's goal is to create a legitimate event with lobbied influential purpose. A parading of gowns, jewelry, and dwellings that only continentals, who are not Continentals, can afford. Wandering about in their bow tied tuxedos, pompous penguins act as props for women, that with years passing continue to swell with some still appearing in now seam-busting gowns from yesteryear. Not dresses but "gowns" and yup, under those long dresses some are commando but that's really for the youngsters or those who forgot.

Remember the advertised first stop at the risqué lingerie shop in Paris? It's come to this, since that is now only a memory. Wal-Mart below the knee length hose and cotton grannie panties for the oldsters, no peek, no show'ems. If you can't see it why pay for it? Age has many in the Social Security grouping now, so while you might have plenty some start watching more carefully . Diva stocked up before she left since as of this writing, you can't find a Wal-Mart in downtown London and those in the know, know wearing Wal-Mart's you toss your undies in the never tell garbage. In fairness, at these affairs there are some real trophy lovelies. They trot around like prize awarded show ponies to be ridden later, again this time in the dark judged for fitness and style. Awareness of this, the appeal of youth and performance causes plenty of hard feelings so circling their wagons for protection, the "originals" bunch up.

"And now Dears that's enough planning for today… where shall we meet next? Any suggestions?" Somebody at the back says Nevis, another suggests Capri. What the hell, its tax-deductible party planning for tax deductible parties, why not just tax-deductible Iceland.

"Any more business," asks ol' top doggie.

Notice the suggestions were not discussed en masse. Three women will decide this later over wine and their private dinner but before that some ingrate asks, "When will we be getting information by email, and can we get an email roster?" "No Dears not yet, that I think, is for the next generation." Something like real ladies don't do email, unless of course you have a secretary of your very own, but that's generally for those in the "A" league, far above this one. Oh, and one other thing…that master roster is always kept under the mattress on Grannie's side of the bed.

The gossiped descriptions continue. Current subjects among them are hot, hand-held boutique dogs, purses, food, means of travel, jewelry and, of course, shoes. Thanks to Brazilians no more crabs, at least we are beyond that scourge of yore. Preventing or in special circumstances encouraging camel toes are just one of a few lesser topics to occupy idling conversations. There are a few who are authentic people of grace and culture, whose interests do not reflect the pettiness and destructive intentions of gathered diva crones. But why are they, those worthy ones, here at all, among the weeds? They do not stand out; it is not their style and usually they appreciate genuine treasures. Their personal qualities do not need close inspection or yearn for conspicuous display. One only wonders how they tolerate this nonsense. Therein lies a mystery of conflicting values and their own personal sense of quality which includes or may question integrity.

Diva's vilification of others positions her well in the hoard. She is an expert player among those whose pension is real dirt. They do not know her sources are often nonexistent, she usually doesn't have to make it up, she's not that creative, instead she is an actor, so like the plagiarizer, alters dialogue adapted from television or reads summaries in Cosmo. Her friends are too old for Cosmo so there's little fear of discovery or accusations of plagiarism. She is good at distortion, having practiced early with boys in high school. These are not whispered conversations; this is lunch, dinner, and evening conversation with the of *odeur* of diaper drama. A place where one sharpens skills by looking and listening for morsels of spoor. Narcissism runs wild, "Yes, it really is all about me, yes, see how pretty I am, attractive and superior we are, but really, yes, I am more than you." And so, as La Rochefoucauld said, "Hypocrisy was the tribute vice pays to virtue."

Added to odd characteristics are references to dwelling places. Early on, sitting in the company of swells their discussion is habitually about where people lived, or now live. Reference by address number instead of street name. Location number rather than streets presumed known to all seemed peculiar to me, like club exclusivity, but then I was new, and the numbers didn't mean a thing to me, nor did anyone care. Colloquialisms I decided. These people do not gather for my benefit they are longtime friends with shared histories, so I just told myself, get over it. It really was my own poor attitude and that didn't help.

"Divors" (men) were sometimes kind but often dismissive. I, after all, was not a banker, lawyer, or candlestick maker, they were experienced warriors serving lubri queens who, for kings, were trinkets. These men too had dirt under their fingernails but plenty of it in their hearts and on their books. The men, like their skirted counterparts, seemed to never forget past transgressions of others. Told and retold from one gathering to the next, these stories reached back generations.

After one party, the following evening I would be with the diva and a different group related to the previous evening but only by type and tawdriness. This second group night conversation continued in virtually the same vein as the one last night, only exceptions were the newly inserted grinding attendees' names from the previous night. If he/she or it cares, God only knows, if we weren't invited, what was said and to whom about us on night three.

With Diva and under these sheltered circumstances often a most eager participant, it would have been amusing if all these tear downs were not so utterly crude and transparent. I was reminded that in college there was a joke about the mythical "circle-de-jerk," referring theoretically to a bunch of guys sitting in a circle masturbating at porn accompaniment. That is what these groups were often like, "circles-de-jerks." Great pleasure taken in finally reaching the climax of a teardown story about someone they all knew.

As long as the body splat isn't on your new Audi R8 roof, falls from grace were especially entertaining. It's a contest, who can spin the same story all know well, heard often but now listen for an update with a creative twist. At the end, the guy who does it best gets to lift his leg and piss on the nearest fire hydrant, and until the next contest, claim it as his own. Lust and sex is good!

How often? Not every time but often enough an outsider remembers. Thinking it a waste of time, energy, and thought, no one talks of help, sympathy, or empathy, and if they needed it, none would be offered. Most of us are not angels but then most of us do not spend so much time on deconstruction.

Diva floats easily between groups and with malicious cleverness contributes bits of vituperation to both sides. For someone of limited intellect, she is an effective anarchist, but these groups are getting smaller. The swells are moving south to the warms, cold blooded reptilian creatures crave warm sun.

One wonders if duplicity was ever understood by anybody and whether they spread it to their new places of residence. If such deceitfulness was and is easily transported, others are clearly in for a diminished quality of life. When all goes according to plan the new innocents, so easily impressed and compromised, won't even see it coming.

Why is it some campaign against Wal-Mart's coming to town but do nothing when divas stage a raid? Soon, the older citizens too will be fuel for scorching fires of alienating bitter exclusivity. There are few phoenixes among these pre-combustibles, you catch your pants on fire at the ankles and it quickly spreads upward to your crotch. When correctness and facts are not an issue, talking out of both sides of one's mouth becomes easier as you go. Has anybody noticed the tendency that as many age, the corners of their mouths turn down. Kind of a comment on losing the steam of their youth perhaps.

"Did you hear about xxx and the IRS? Credit card charges. Oh boy, they caught him with a hooker in New York." Smiles all around and a few beads of sweat. No one has proof of this of course but they all believe it. Another one of them just returned from Vegas and a torrid weekend with his favorite tranny who takes American Express. They apparently got him too, same way. No one has proof of this either.

"Great job of getting "..." out of the kiddy porn deal. Must have been rough on his family. You lawyers sure know how to do it and now I know who to call if they catch my kid again." Nuff said and still no proof.

4.

Most swells are trim. Some fanatical about exercise, but Diva is not, it takes far too much discipline. She collects health club memberships like grocery coupons but doesn't cash in. In the world of appearances, one does not let oneself go too far off the grid. In all fairness Diva isn't yet obese she's just working on it and close.

There are many strategies the aging diva employs to fend off effects of blubarian blubber. When larger no-belt waistlines appear, clothing gets looser; heels lowered, no more sleeveless only sleeved ... can Mumu's be far behind?

In a counter move intended to redirect the eyes, lipstick gets redder but progressively creeps out over the property lines onto the tiny wrinkles. Like a clown it is the lipstick that's comical, followed by Botox grins and scary sunken eyes. Spreading connected liver spots are not mini suntans. It's Halloween time.

"Let me give you some advice, dear. Light fabric must never be allowed to press up against the inside form. It reveals dark crypt relics. If there is a fan or window with a breeze either stay away or really get to it fast so clothing can flow and flutter. We like flow and flutter." When cloth flies around things are blurry. Men carry their pot bellies right out there above the belt but if they're clever, women can carry theirs 'in' there, inside a tent. "While we're at it, get a better bra. That wrinkled cleavage is looking like turned over field furrows in winter."

These ironic time warriors continue to collect jewel encrusted necklaces. The crones drape themselves with as many neck focusing, jewel-weighted visuals as their waddlings can support. Each new birthday offers up and memorializes multi-folded turkey necks. What they need is what I have not yet seen, a turtleneck evening gown. Once sparkles were symbols of wealth and beauty; now, with sequined blinking lights, they only denote money and caved in wrinkle flappy or balloon stuffed flesh.

Facelifts start early. Diva had her first before she was thirty-five. Botox was a later miracle but looking over the crowd a trained spotter can these days easily recognize frozen expressions of the newly poked and filled stone faces. Teeth, eyes, butts, tits, necks, arm flaps, belly flops, thigh flaps now even feet and vaginas, all there for the eager surgeon's profit. Doctor Fixit From Flappin.

Sometimes it goes badly. When plastic surgery is botched, and it sometimes is, there's endless talk. This is still not a perfect science and while it's clear some practitioners are artists others are mere journeymen plumbers. Men seem to go for eye jobs and sometimes even belly renovation. With historical restoration in mind, and results not always successful, what was to have been a showroom trophy can wind up on the used car lot. There are many used car lots for women and certainly men. For women, they call themselves spas usually in warm places where desiccant effects tend to defeat erstwhile improvements. For men there's the card table in the 19th hole locker room at the country club.

Attributed to some kind of "fix," unexplained lengthy absences are gleefully rehashed. The laughter is uneasy since all know that there but for the grace of their own surgeon go themselves. There are spas specializing in no address, no phone ,hidey-holes tiding one over until obvious signs disappear and the overhauled can return to face the race. I am told some lady hidey-holes offer late night *"le serveeece d'carnal"* with menu choices. Sort of like "Nuit Suits de Jour, méprise, ignoble, bas, abject, misérable." The eye that no longer droops but did last month, telltale white lines into the hairline, unnaturally puckered lips, and straight-line whiter front teeth, oh my, how high we fly. Recent hot topics: vaginal rebuilds and G spot attenuation with alignments costing extra. Do they really relocate these things to a more serviceable locations? If she could choose and get it, Diva's clitoris would be on the end of her nose.

"Oh, darling who needs him, I can do so much better myself."

It's all a choice, but then, let's not complain when "he" takes up with that jail-bait bimbo. There is a point when marriage isn't fun anymore but still worth plenty.

This last time and prior to taking on a new fulltime escort, Diva suffered in a sand box desert of social despair. Pure agony, having to get by with one man for show and other men for pleasure. At her age, it was no longer one in the same, instead, more like "no man's land." To keep her sanity during these times of drought and spiritual famine, she augmented using personal pleasure equipment, vibrators with flapping ears called rabbits and other look-alikes, but not as noisy and large as jack hammers. Diva's collection included multiples of every new sex toy she could lay her hands on.

Extra points for girdled Miss Marple detectives who, when seeking ways to pass splendidly strident afternoons, one often just makes stories up for added credit. All claimed as gospel truth, of course, but nevertheless nosy investigations into how much girl-girl kissing in public is allowed? Even now there are conflicting standards and reactions to such questions and finally, these days we consider ourselves wiser and more sophisticated. There are still unwritten rules when selected thresholds are crossed. Much talk of "more than just friends" kicks and licks, in and out like a lizard's tongue, amour is a five-star subject and six if you can confirm a sighting with a credentialed girlfriend witness. The confirmation of an irregular girlfriend relationship continues to be primo conversation. It breeds and promotes extra-long lunch conversations at clubs or even a chatty aside while casually walking between the aisles at Niemen Marcus.

Any reasonably progressive person today accepts a broader array of societal choices that include ethnicity, religion and, of course, selected sex-n-gender practices. We see in the circles that included the Carrion Sisters, deeply hypocritical strains of conservative judgement, superficial rejection of actions and beliefs wider that society had already assimilated, presently considered healthier and acceptable. Diva's associations were not only contradictory and insular, but irreparably out of touch with reality. She and her friends simply did not seem to realize that what they were sneaking around with, most in society had moved on from some time ago, accepted and adjusted to. It added to the deeply dysfunctional and maladjusted nature of their "B and C" class structured insular activities. This cultural isolation would eventually criminalize and seriously harm others around them. They were all dinosaurs deserving of another great comet attack.

Here's a whopper in times of public sex clubs. Officially unconfirmed and usually only whispered, a special girl's club meets monthly by appointment in a secret location for girl-only pleasure. A Victorian club idea that's out of the ordinary. Exclusive application is made informally only by invitation and in public. Upon acceptance, initiations held at the home of a rugged old harlot the unblessed have not heard from or seen in years. Its owner known only by reputation is wealthy, living north of the city at the hacienda Grande-Carne-Grande with extensive grounds and tall surrounding hedges for privacy. No one really knows where the alleged owner is at any given moment, she's reputed to spend considerable time in Europe with other reclusive dowagers of shared similar persuasions. More than one person has suggested, in her preferred pre-femcoital lifestyle, she murdered her husband for his money and real estate. Still others ventured she's been dead for years.

During her absences, la hacienda is available to selected women who have secretly subscribed to, as they call it, "Life Behind the Hedges," where many who enjoy the rides got their first training-wheels attached and later rode bicycles built for two. If you're savvy enough, when it's mentioned in conversation, you can sometimes pick up shrewd references to *The Life*. Still odd when secrets such as these have become quite unnecessary.

Many aspire but few are chosen.

BOOK 4

1.

"Let me ask you Doctor, when you try to help others beyond their problems, how successful are you?"

"Well, of course, it depends on the severity of the situation, the diagnosis, and resources but mostly on the person themself. Really, we can only offer a pathway. I wish I, or we, could do more but so far there is a limit to what drugs and counseling can accomplish. I live with it every day and some days it is very hard and discouraging, always something of degree. I am sure you understand that."

"What is your success rate?"

"Quite honestly I feel not great, but others I know, as well as myself, try hard." Somewhat defensively she asks, "Where is this going?"

Pensively the man seemed to consider the question before speaking next. Looking down to his lap and then up again, then over and quite directly, "Can you cure a sociopath?"

"Cure is a difficult word sir. It requires and implies first a complex definition. Generally, the best that happens is the person comes to recognize this is a part of them, and, as with many bits and pieces of their personality, if successful, they learn to manage it in a reasonably constructive way. This said, first they must see and understand it. Once this is ah…" she was searching for the right word but seemed to change her mind and settled for, "Once they genuinely want to minimize its destructive consequences, a new journey begins for them. They have to care first, and that bar is high. Too high actually, or at least it is for most of them."

"And what if they don't jump that high?"

"Do you mean change or care? Either way, if they don't the prognosis is clear, it worsens with repetition and age. Increasingly they do not see or feel the repercussions. They are often marked by damaging incidents where the sociopath is rejected by, or for something they passionately want. Their friends leave them, they are progressively isolated and become bitter. People who are afflicted can become vicious, some nearly rabid, it is a sad prognosis. Sociopaths are very lonely people." She paused then said, "They die alone." Another pause and she, with some hesitation continued, "Some become criminals, others just forgotten insular waste. An additional tragedy, some pass the trait on, as apparently is the case for Diva's son. Those who are conspicuously out of control we can only isolate, often with imprisonment like rapists who can, in some ways, be one and the same."

The man held up his hand, calling for a pause in her thoughts. Thoughtfully he asked, "What can others do? If one cared, is there any way to help?"

Now the doctor looked up at the ceiling, tapping her pen on the clipboard in her lap, and then down again, returning to look almost sternly at the man sitting opposite her. She smiled reflectively, "Talk to them, show them they are damaging others and in the process themselves, but the examples must be specific. They, or you must not talk vaguely, otherwise the sociopath rationalizes it really isn't their fault. You must be very specific, quite direct. The malady keeps working to inspire and confirm to them feelings of conspiracy and hatred. When this happens they turn and direct their negative feelings and actions against those trying to help. It is, in every way, like a cancer, spreading inside, destroying as it goes. The sociopath often believes their closest friends and family are involved in treachery; a nefarious collusion directed against only them. You see this in extremists, those who are nearly always paranoid, they have come to the edge of reality.

"Why now the question, do you want to help the diva?"

"No, I am finished."

"That is what many would say for they, like you, have been pushed to the edge of the end. In most cases I can't say I blame them."

2.

I could never share my dreams with her. She wouldn't understand. Diva sets the rules and there are no other alternatives. What repeatedly amazed me was her inability to accept the views of others or, if you could call it that, be oddly creative in ways that went beyond only herself. It saddened me that she rarely ever finished what she started. She'd begin, get tired of the task then pay someone else to finish or just drop the whole thing and let the elderly housekeeper clean up the mess. Haul the debris of partially completed projects up to the third floor packed in with all the rest of long-forgotten collections hidden at the country house.

She was seriously obsessed by thoughts the floors would give way and crash in on her while she slept. If you can imagine a copious woman in an industrial strength girdle threatening to burst, you get an idea of what the loaded third floor was like.

The two-car garage was a clothes storage annex no one was supposed to ever see but all knew was there. Diva was nuts about having no one enter the sanctum to see piles of used and unused, many still tagged clothing items, first hung then piled to overflowing. The crazy thing, nearly all those close to her had seen it at one time or another and if they hadn't actually seen it, they'd certainly heard the stories.

Not looking on purpose but when they went through the kitchen out to the garage refrigerators, plural, to get a bottle of wine, a soda or ice cubes the sight was shocking to most first timers. The kitchen was large but mostly food for one, sometimes two people who were there, was kept in one of three refrigerators or two large chest freezers in the garage, so it was inevitable people would go there. In the kitchen, drawers and cabinets were so full many couldn't be opened, jammed, or overflowing with unused or more likely never used devices. China, flatware, pots and pans in there, more inventory than many kitchenware shops. Somehow, Diva chose to believe the garage was just her secret, known only to myself, the housekeeper and Paddycake, who kept her lunch and a few gardening tools just inside the back door.

While I watched one Christmas, Diva set out to assemble gift baskets for her friends. This culminated a yearlong spree of accumulation. Each year she bought more baskets and from the mixed dozens that remained on shelves upstairs one couldn't begin to guess how many had been attempted, completed, or gifted. In different colors there were twenty rolled yoga mats I assumed didn't make it to previously designated giftees. After each Christmas and on into late summer Diva's typical approach was to buy more baskets and miscellaneous contents on sale. With the annual collection she could easily stock a store.

Christmas, Valentines, Easter and Mother's Day, sales were all particularly good times to go fishing. After each holiday for weeks on end, the living room would increasingly fill with sacks, bags, and boxes. Hardly room to walk from front door to the kitchen. Within days of Christmas, and with no time to complete the gift baskets intended for others, she would do a special one, a very large version for Brito Grand'ol Ma-ma. This was payment of course, for personal promotional reasons and critical for the summer discount trip event. Utterly senseless gifts for a woman who had more than plenty of useless trinkets. Running late, the remaining baskets were forgotten while she rushed off to select clothes for Christmas parties and another pair of camel toe pants.

After the holidays her aging housekeeper, but not Paddycake, would repeatedly struggle up the steep narrow flights of the back stairs, hauling bags and baskets to the third-floor hoarder piles of dead forgotten things.

Our second Christmas was different because she asked for my help. This time I saw the process up close. In the dining room baskets were stacked around the room and proposed contents laid out in the center on the dining table. All leaves inserted and, where possible, card tables set up for the overflow. There were perhaps fifteen to twenty items for each basket. Clearly more than any basket could hold, so I assumed, there would be other tables for additional sub-baskets. More is More! On the day we were to work together assembling, Paddycake arrived and within minutes the two of them disappeared upstairs to do I knew not what nor wished to speculate about. I waited for over an hour for her to return and resume *our* task, but she did not. I thought of going to find them but decided, quite wisely, not to. There was something about this that was not right. I finally left to do other things outside the house.

Depending upon the recipient, if they were on the first tee of the B Team, I was told there was to be a small, wrapped gift piece of sorta expensive costume jewelry, a current bestselling book Diva thought would reflect well on her, and the usual idiotic useless kitchen items she had seen advertised on late night, early morning television or more likely the Dollar Store. She was a patron saint of the Dollar Store frequent flyer club. Useless items because, if they ever did, Diva's friends no longer cooked. Bath salts, soaps in colored cellophane wrappers, real perfume for some, watered-down versions for the "lesser," a deck of cards, silly toys that only a small child could love and not much, a silver framed picture of Diva herself gratuitously signed "with love." The inevitable stuffed little white dog, ersatz version of her own live, boutique hand carried, hand fed, rug peeing pooch.

Finally, there would be gourmet, cheesy smoked and tinned items in the Christmas baskets, topped off by requisite "Go-Diva" chocolates.

Piled on the table and in more than sufficient quantities, all these things were available for each gift basket. The sample "built" that day of Diva and Dirt-girl's disappearance was the only full one that ever made it to that year's Christmas celebration or, as far as I knew, any other. Not even one yoga mat included.

By this time, I understood in the soon to be next year she would start all over from scratch. It would be a new routine retailing opportunity. Only the chocolates would be eaten, and the dining room remain a mess until just before Valentine's Day when more candy would be eaten and holiday decorations came down, replaced by a giant blow up Easter Bunny by the front door…go figure! Dirt-girl, aka Paddycake, blew the bunny up each day since as a subtle reminder of the times, place and deteriorated condition, each morning it lay flaccid outside the front door. The day I finally left to do other things, the upstairs bedroom door was closed. Behind it Diva was busy grunting with Paddycake.

3.

In the country at the river house, gardener Paddycake was a thoroughly unpleasant person. Looking like a kinky Halloween wig storm, the usual tightly bound hair, when unleashed, exploded to nearly four maybe six times the size of her head, a witchy character from the bar scene in Star Wars One. Usually dressed like a shabby little man in the garden, I must agree she was quite good at what she did there. Only Diva knew of her other more important assets, ones that were nearby, well hidden from others.

Out there in the flat farmlands, Paddycake was pathologically protective of mistress of the house. She was secretive, dishonest with others, and freakish about her job. She hated the housekeeper; they never spoke unless absolutely necessary. The housekeeper, an aging kind and gentle soul, kept thoughts about Paddycake to herself, not wanting to jeopardize her job and the perks Diva bestowed upon her every year at Christmas time.

Unlike her husband, Paddycake had a formidable reputation around the town. She was known as a conniving bitch not to be messed with. On one occasion one of the more *roundly* respected men referred to her as a cunt and I nearly fell over, amazed he would use such language, much less in a dinner setting at the River Bend Country Club. But then Moochie knew about her, having regularly reported him and his wife's guest doings while they stayed in Diva's houses the year before.

Some thought her scary and many concluded Diva herself was intimidated and afraid of her. Paddycake was known to sabotage various things and cause damage to other people's property. This was difficult to actually prove of course, but widely suspected and often discussed out of earshot from Diva. Like Diva, the dirt-girl was malicious; but unlike her, stealthy, quiet and cunning. The few others who did engage her services took advantage of the nasty traits and used them to ward off two and four legged vermin. Another neighbor resident referred to her as Doberwoman, "an out-of-control nasty bitch dog" the man said. Seemed along the river even nasty dogs were of value to some.

When Diva was in residence, Paddycake was a frequent presence. The two of them spent hours talking together inside the house and in nice weather outside in the garden. Always in private, always away from the sight or hearing of others. If I or someone else appeared nearby, they would conspicuously move to another place so as not to be overheard. Diva was generous with her groundskeeper, wretch of dirt and malice. She frequently gave her gifts of expensive jewelry and clothing. It was hard to imagine Paddycake wearing gold earrings and bracelets since she was rarely dressed as a woman, stone-ass butch would be more accurate. Always quite plain, anything but attractive, slim boyish figure with a little girl's voice, the mannerisms and hands of a male laborer.

Peevish and petty, she carefully hid items from others who might be looking for something as simple as an extension cord or rake. The idea was to create and maintain total dependence. Diva relied upon her like she did no other and Paddycake aka Dirt Girl usually stirred the pot of her mistress's raging tirades with false stories and equally outrageous accusations of others. She was an endless source of guile, flotsam and jetsam.

The diva was a sociopath, but her dirty Paddycake was patently demonic. Something out of a gothic novel, one very sick puppy who others thought twice about encountering or crossing. There were many names, but most country club dowagers called her *The Scourge*.

4.

Here we are again.

"Let me ask you something? We have been talking for nearly six months. I think we should give this a performance review. Are you getting anything out of this? Am I helping you at all?"

"Yes."

"And can you tell me what that is?"

"Not exactly, but sometimes I think I can."

"And why is that?"

"Because I don't look at it in those terms, Doctor. For me this is an experience I am passing through. You see, I told you in the beginning I'm on a journey, but you didn't listen carefully enough. You are trying to fix something with the tools you have been taught to use. I don't need those tools; I just need you to listen."

"Well, if I did or didn't that isn't what I am asking, sir. I am asking if you are getting what you want or is this helping you?"

"Let's agree on this, Doctor, I will tell you when I know, but for now I'm going to leave you. I do not know just when I'll return, but most likely I will at some point. Or at least I think I will."

"May I ask where you are going? This seems quite sudden. Has something happened to you or between us?"

"Yes and no."

"Is that all you can say?"

"Yes, but I will probably see you again I just don't know when, so perhaps you might stand by. Please forgive me if I have offended you, this is not my intention. It's just time for me to become less reliant on you, Doctor, and more reliant on myself. I am ready for this and must go now, it's a test of sorts and there is much to do."

She started to speak but decided not to. He had always been the one who knew his mind and what his course would be. She must accept his decision, but he would be missed. The full effect was yet to be realized by her. There had never been someone quite like him before and, she thought, probably never would be again.

The man rose from his chair. On this occasion they had only spoken for a few minutes that was usually an hour. He put on his coat and ceremoniously wrapped the muffler carefully, around his neck and coat collar. Opening the door that led into the outer foyer he stepped through into the entry then softly closed the office door behind him. He had not said good-bye.

From inside her office, she heard the outer lobby front door open and close. It was snowing. Going to the window she watched him adjust his coat, pulling the collar of his long coat further up and adjust the long purple muffler he usually wore this time of year. He wore no hat or gloves, and snow quickly flecked his medium length grey hair. He disappeared into grey-white of the late winter afternoon.

She continued to wonder about this strange man whose real name she still did not know. He always paid in cash and for this short meeting again had left the usual five crisp new one-hundred-dollar bills on the corner of her desk. Once she thought they were counterfeit because they were always very new and crisp. She'd long since stopped counting them so scooping them up, opened the bottom side drawer of her desk and dropped them into his file folder with all his other payments to her. Nearly $11,000 maybe $15,000 she guessed, but it was of no matter to her, this particular man was far more important to her than money.

She returned to the window hoping to get one last glimpse, but he was gone. She wondered and mused that she did not know how much of all this was really true, how could it possibly be true. Swallowed up by the world, was it he or was it she who had disappeared from view.

BOOK 5

1.

"Please come in."

Stepping aside, she gestured turning her head, stretching out her hand toward the chairs. "Sit over here if you'd like, that chair is far more comfortable for conversation than the couch." With a smile to set her new patient at ease she continued, "Actually I keep it just for appearances sake and really, my own occasional nap."

"Thank you." The woman said with some hesitation, walking over to sit down. She appeared nervous then got up again.

Walking to the far end of the professionally furnished office, she briefly looked out the window as if looking for something or someone, then back to the chair where she again sat down quite formally. She perched close to the front edge of the tuxedo arm lounge chair, back stiff, straight, hands folded formally in her lap, knees together, one foot quite properly slightly ahead of the other. The woman looked very uncomfortable. The doctor took her seat opposite, separated from her patient by a rectangular beveled glass topped coffee table with inane but current magazines, an ashtray, and an unopened bottle of water at either end.

To a doctor in her type of practice, first impressions were very important. Well dressed, the new "client" did not look around at anything in particular, just the doctor. She appeared to be in her mid-sixties, perhaps older with a defined, forced artificial style. Most physicians are good at sizing up their patients quickly. This woman's suit was a bit too tight; she wore low out of fashion pointed heels, no hose, a uniform-completing diamond watch with a thin diamond tennis bracelet on the opposite wrist. The doctor recognized jewelry that was obviously expensive and, she thought, given the rest of her appearance, a bit overdone for this occasion. Large topaz ring surrounded by diamonds and a smaller, similar aquamarine on the ring finger of her left hand that did not look like a wedding band.

Something amiss. She studied her patient carefully but quickly, so as not to break the informal rhythm of their first meeting. There was something wrong here, the doctor felt this woman was exceptionally uneasy. Preparatory office notes she'd read earlier that morning showed the woman had made an appointment several weeks before and a secretarial aside notation; the new patient preferred not to give any specific reason for her appointment.

Because first impressions were necessarily important, the doctor continued her assessment noting little or no makeup with severely pulled back brown hair obviously dyed. Presumably hastily and, probably, thoughtlessly arranged for this meeting. On this occasion, the overall presentation was one of a person who cared more about her jewelry than general appearance. One interpretation might be she was not here by choice but instead, instruction or compliance. "Please," the doctor gestured again for the woman to get comfortable and indicated she was welcomed to the bottled water.

Efforts to calm did not work. As if panicked, she was sudden. Bursting, she spoke quickly to establish her own ground rules for the meeting and subsequent ones if they got that far. The imperious manner was evidently born of nervousness combined with fear. Control issues, the doctor thought and, without looking down, made another practiced brief note on the file. The patient's tone was condescending, commanding, like she was speaking to a low-level employee.

Short-clipped-sentences, "I have given a false name doctor. I will pay you in cash and understand the rates for each hour of your time. There will be no record of this for insurance purposes and again said I will pay you in cash. Do we understand each other?"

"Ms.... ahh," the doctor looked back down at her notes, "Smith, right?"

"Yes, it's Smith," she snapped with pursed lips.

"Alright Ms. Smith, may I presume you understand the doctor patient confidentiality relationship, rules, and law? So yes, your terms are quite acceptable. Now tell me, if you can, why you are here and what I may do for you, and if you don't know exactly that is just fine, we will work together." She tapped the clipboard and said, "First I have very little information here, can you help me by answering a few preliminary questions?"

Today the doctor wore a black jumper, black turtleneck sweater, opaque black hose, and low black heels. Her dark hair was relatively short, and as usual, she wore no jewelry other than, for appearances only, a modest wedding ring. The wall behind her displayed requisite diplomas from prestigious schools. MD, PhD, accompanied by certifications from various hospitals and institutions.

But collectively they all made no difference, her patient took a momentary look around the room unseeing, registering nothing of interest, appeared completely indifferent. Just gazing for affect, killing time. Wordlessly revealing herself a taker seeking only to confirm this doctor would be suitable for her needs. No more than a fulfillment issue, much like her online purchasing.

"Ms. Smith," the doctor repeated, "what brings you here to see me?" Her voice was level but this time firmer, somewhat uncompromising.

"I... want to talk to someone. I have questions and require some answers, isn't that what you do. I have been told this might be helpful." As if bored she looked away, avoided looking directly toward the woman at the other end of the low table, evasive, ambivalent, dismissive. The psychiatrist was used to the avoidance of eye contact, particularly in the beginning, but this accompaniment of announced indifference made even this professional uncomfortable, but still curious. This woman was going to be a challenge and perhaps unpleasant.

"Well, don't you have family or friends to do that with? One's who will listen I mean. I am of course here to listen, but interested in the role others play in your life as well. Are they supportive or can they be for what bothers you? Why don't you tell me about them, let's start there shall we?" She leaned back further in her chair hoping her patient would relax and do the same.

"None who I would dare tell," Ms. Smith hesitated, and the doctor thought she saw the reflection of a tear forming. Her patient was collapsing quickly, losing her bravado and with this, it was palpable, she wanted or certainly needed help.

"But there are plenty who would love to know the whole story and know that I am here talking to you. Actually, they'd eat this story for lunch. They say they love me, Doctor, but that isn't so. They know things that will destroy me, I know it, I just know it. That's exactly what they want to do." She was gushing now, talking faster and the doctor understood she needed to calm her patient, slow this down.

"I see here you've not written your first name on the form. Is there a reason for that and is this really your last name? If I may say so, Smith seems a bit common?" She looked up and smiled.

"You don't need this information Miss…err Doctor, at least not yet." She removed a tissue from her purse, wiped her eyes and blew her nose. "I can pay you at the beginning or end of this session. I have done this before; I know how it works." She reached into her reptile skin purse and withdrew several hundred-dollar bills. Seeming to take some offense, the doctor ignored the gesture.

"Oh, and is there a reason for that? You're not giving me your name."

"Yes, no one can ever know I was here, and I mean no one, ever. Will this be a problem for you, I thought doctors couldn't tell anybody about their patients?" She reached forward laying cash on the table between them.

"Well," referring to the money, "let's just let that be for the moment. For the time being I don't need your first name but at some point, it would make this a bit less formal, and yes, no one will ever know you and I have talked. Now let's start again what are we to talk about?"

Regaining her composure slightly and consciously crossing her legs somewhat provocatively, less uncomfortable than before, the woman leaned back then protectively crossed her arms. For a moment seeming to forget where she was and to whom she was speaking, or perhaps in the presence of another woman a show of superiority, renewed effort at further control. The patient was pulling herself together. Was this all an act, her rapid spooling up, down then up again?

Again, the condescending tone, "Doctor, how often have you thought about pleasure and those who want to take it away and destroy you for it?"

"Ah, well yes, I think we all have experienced this, or at least to some degree the pleasure part. And you? Do you think about pleasure? Do you do that often, think about it I mean? Why don't we start with the pleasure part, later we can come back to your friends, who you say are trying to steal it away from you."

"Yes, of course."

"Ms. Smith, have you been damaged by others or someone who has no regard for your needs or pleasure? Can I assume this is why you want to talk about it more privately, with someone like me?"

"Yes, but I want to know things about this. You might say getting from H to M but not to Z. Actually, from S to M." The woman smiled demurely just for a moment and looked down at the back of her liver spotted hands. Momentarily enjoying, for her, a very uncommon inside joke.

"I have the balance of the hour, Miss Smith. At the end of the hour, we can discuss whether you would like to make another appointment. Will that suit you?"

"Yes, I'll tell you at the end of the hour. Now can we get on with this?" More control.

"Have you ever sought help in the past, from a professional such as myself?

"Yes, often, but not by choice."

"Oh, and why that? Let's try again how would you like to begin?" Shifting yet again, fishing for some entry point. "Would you like to tell me about your previous experiences?"

"It starts I suppose, a long time ago, just as most things do."

"Then why don't you just begin wherever you wish."

As tedious as this was the psychiatrist had been down this road often, fishing for an opening, a place to start. Doctor and patient were finding their way into a conversation.

2.

When I was a little girl the people where I went to school... the other kids hated me. They hated me and made fun of me because I was not like them. My mother didn't like me and said I wasn't pretty like my sister, especially when I was in high school or maybe even before. I think I interrupted her pleasure, but that came later. I don't remember much until I was in third grade. I went to a city school where most students were Jews. I was not and they teased and taunted me about this. I really didn't understand the difference until I got older. They said I was stupid, and no one liked me. They kept telling me I was unclean, ate pig meat and that made me a pig. I didn't know what they meant by the pig meat either. They said only Jews were smart. I usually went home in tears. Sometimes, after school they'd follow me for blocks, yell, and throw things at me. In the winter it was snowballs, but other times they were rocks or chunks of dirt. Nobody stopped them, sometimes at night I still hear them laughing, shouting, and calling me a pig eating slut.

My parents were common people, very common. Because my mother never told me I was pretty I grew up believing I was not. My father was a bartender. He thought I was pretty and secretly told me so. He never did anything inappropriate to me, I mean feel me up, or things like that. He was a nice man, but my mother ran everything while he stayed quiet.

At school, I was always sad and angry and thought about how I would get back at the nasty Jewish bitch princesses who shoved me, kicked me, and stole my books. They took my homework and once slammed the locker door on my hand breaking two of my fingers. In the locker room they laughed at me, they took my underwear and called me a filthy goy cunt. At first, I didn't know what that meant either. I was not a good student... in fact I was a poor student in more ways than one. I never got good grades even when I tried, but there was no reason to try so I stopped.

Jew girls were beautiful. They had nice clothes, much better than mine. They were first to get their bras, the first to wear panties not underpants. I was the last. They had boyfriends and talked about sex all the time. No boy would look at me, sometimes they joined the girls in calling me names, but mostly then it was a girl who did it, not the boys.

The boys groped me. They didn't really care but still called me the filthy pig eater and worse. I started to get breasts and then soon, well you know. I didn't know much about sex and had no one else to talk to. I was alone. My mother took the money from our family vacation savings jar to go to beautician's school. She never practiced on me, only my sister. My hair was straight, my father cut it. He was not a beautician, so it was uneven, sort of chopped looking. I had a few pictures from that time, but I have thrown them all away. I looked ugly in them.

I wanted a boyfriend, but they were all Jewish, and in the beginning, they called me other disgusting names. Soon I was called "easy" and a whore, but they didn't know, they just called me that. I heard them because they never even tried to whisper. They wanted me to hear them. When I was twelve, I gave a boy his first BJ. The Jew boy and his friends asked me on a dare. I stood up to them and called his bluff. Three of his friends watched but I didn't care, I wanted a boyfriend. Word spread I had spread for all of them if you know what I mean. The crazy thing is, it was them who first spread for me.

That got me ahead of those bitch girls and this made more trouble. I was good, they knew it and were really mad at me. The boys were after me, I showed them how and fucked better than any of them and I liked it too. I got back at the girls and was, for a while, way ahead of them. I got my bra, bought it with my own money and soon had very large breasts. I had more to work with. I shared them with boys and didn't care as long as they paid attention to me. About that time, I learned to masturbate. That's when the real fun started.

3.

Interestingly Ms. Smith, when beginning her story started talking like a young girl. Her recollections were a form of transference. It was as if the woman was acting a part. However, the tone changed, her voice quickly got older, more woman than child.

"I left my new husband a week after we were married. That was over 40 years ago. I thought I'd made a mistake, but I went back. About ten years ago my husband dumped me. He said he'd had enough. He subjected me to years of stupid psychoanalysis with some shrink he played tennis with. Truth was he is the one that needed it, my husband I mean. I just went hoping he'd get fixed. He paid me off with lots of money, but to continue with my friends there were issues. The problem was, I was single. I had not really given this much thought before, but soon I wasn't getting invited to the parties I wanted to go to. My friends don't like single people at their parties, and I like parties. Especially single women, oh, and you know what else, that shrink, my husband's tennis buddy loved to fuck me. It's the only time I ever got crabs and from a doctor!

In those days I wasn't a real predator, but more than a few husbands came on to me. It was nice and I remembered some of the stories well, those I'd heard from other women; so, after a few affairs with my friend's husbands I decided to go looking and hunting further away. I continued near home with a few stolen moment blowjobs and that was fun. I love BJ's. One even recently at a charity ball for an old friend who that night, with his wife not far away, said he wanted a charity ball of his own. I thought that was pretty funny, so we did it in the basement and later he fucked me again on the floor and ruined my dress.

I got on the Internet, lied a little bit but soon had plenty of online men, all hot and chasing me. You could say it became my hobby; I'd tell them all kinds of things to get them turned on. They called it getting tuned up. It was naughty and I practiced. They couldn't find me, so I talked like they do on those sex phone calls, I called those numbers often and knew how they went. It was fun, they couldn't find out who I really was so I sort of opened my own little sex talk-line, but I didn't take any money, I couldn't figure out how to do that and not get caught. These men are so stupid, I loved to think about what was going on at the other end. Sometimes I could hear them working on themselves. I even made up a man's name and used that on dating sites, it was fun to talk to other women that way and some gay guys as well.

For the men I took photographs of myself dressed up in different costumes but always covered my face. I love to use masks. That was fun too and some of the men went wild. A few times I set up dates and got there early. I sat in a place so I could see them when they came in; I watched them, and if they were hot, I'd rub my legs together under the table but never go to actually meet them, you know, be with them. I was good at rubbing myself under the table. For years I practiced sitting on the washer at home, waiting for the spin cycle.

But things didn't go as I planned. When I was in high school, I had a special lover. Boy did we have fun. It didn't last long but she was some of the best sex I'd ever had. Believe me these Internet men were not nearly as good. Lots of talk but not the action I wanted; they just don't know where the hot button is even after you draw them a map.

Since I was divorced, I fucked some of the men I met at parties and even pegged a few, especially when they asked. Let me tell you that's a trip but it can get messy. One night, at a party, a new real lover came on to me. We agreed to meet and for two years we were together off and on. That lover was well known to my friends, we had to be careful, and we were. That lover was a tiger in bed, I'll tell you it was wild and one night, while on my back, with my spiked heel I punctured a hole in the backseat leather. I'd never had sex like that. She knew right where my special, you know, button was. I didn't have to do a thing except lay there while she worked on me.

But I got concerned. That lover got reckless, and I thought we might be found out. Sometimes we attended parties together, but she was getting too obvious. You know it when its two guys, but it's tricky with women. We were always invited separately so others wouldn't suspect. We'd take our time, meeting up to talk innocently. She was married. We never talked long but she started getting too close and touchy in public. If it had been a man, I probably would have not cared so much, sensitive you know.

At first, I loved the innocent touches, you know to a certain extent, women can do that. It was dangerous and I have to say thrilling, but I thought if anyone really knew, well, I knew what happened in situations like that. My girl lover didn't care so I made a plan. After six months I told her I had a man who I'd been seeing, she never objected to this before, and it started getting "complicated." Our times making it in ladies room stalls were becoming fewer and fewer. Frankly, I was relieved.

Another time when I again told her about the guy, she was furious and hit me. I had bruises on my face. I had to go away for about a month until I could finally cover them with makeup. Of course, my friends don't miss a thing, right away they spotted them underneath the makeup. I made excuses, you know, the falling down the stairs kind of thing, with a wink and a nod. Most of the time we laughed but I remembered the kids at high school, and I knew those women talked later, just like those Jew bastards did.

For a while, I took up with the husband of one of my close friends. I knew he would never tell but it was even more risky than the other one. His wife and I were good friends, but once she found one of my earrings was where it shouldn't have been and that ended it. At least it wasn't my panties, but you know, secretly I wish she had figured it out and anyway I don't wear panties anymore.

I needed a quick other lover. I found one and once found, did all the cooing and athletics to keep him in line and coming back for more. He impressed my friends and at first, they liked him. Eventually I got tired of him, but I learned a few new things. All he wanted to do was talk about things I didn't understand, much less cared about, you know cars, golf, money, and stuff. We stopped having sex. For a while I kept asking for more and we would talk, but the bastard said he wasn't in the service business, but I always thought all guys wanted service. I told him I wanted service and I had paid God damned well for it. Thank God for girl toys and in fact, by that time I had another house in the country, a place to stay and play. The final payoff was I wanted him to have me and another lover at the same time. I knew who I'd bring to the table, but he didn't like that and wouldn't cooperate. Another time I just wanted him to watch but he didn't like that either, so I just decided he was a nowhere man. I tried a few more times but he still wasn't game, so I got rid of him. I had to do it in a way he couldn't talk to anyone, so I broke that bastard good. Took his money, clothes. even his car that I hid. He really hated the car thing. I talked up the great disappointment about his STD's and tax evasion. Tax evasion was a hot-button issue, and all my friends treated it like contagious poison.

Then another man, pretty similar actually. I told this guy all the things he wanted to hear… these men are so easy. I mean they are really dumb. I had lots of money by then and said I would take care of him if he didn't, give him a place to work and play, you know all the promises he needed to hear. I mean really, who is the stupid one, he actually believed it. He got to be a bore, so I got my son to throw him out. We evicted him and made him sweat because I again kept all the clothes and his other belongings for a long time. I had plenty of money from my husband but took all his just to be sure there would be no comebacks. I knew he was helpless and had no power. Money is power and he was homeless by the time I got through with him.

Men are so gullible; all you have to do is show them a little tit and they fall between your legs and melt like sherbet.

4.

No one wants a single woman at their dinner table; when you're single, you aren't invited to the parties. We cougars are crafty, and everybody knows it. Believe me, I have bedded a few husbands whose wives knew it and practically right in front of them. Frankly, I think they were glad to catch a break. It's fun to play with their men, they think they're very clever just because they made a lot of money and didn't get caught recreational fucking. Listen, I can tell you, the power we have is between our legs and further up hanging out in front of us, most of us know very well how and where to use it. Holding on to that chrome winged lady for dear life, I even got humped on the hood of a Rolls. Listen Sweetie, you always use perfume and wear earrings to bed, believe me when its time, being well trimmed you attract plenty more with perfume than honey.

This last time, before my current mano was actually interesting to some people, and when I found a better alternative, it was a little sticky getting rid of him. He'd once been a player in the government. I think there's more to this than I know right now but I'll tell you this much, everything has its price and someday I'll pay others to finish him off. He doesn't know it yet but he's expendable and really a scary bad fuck. Viva Vagina!

He was getting suspicious, so I set my son to take him down. Didn't work so well so we just let it be, hoping for no comebacks.

My boy, when I raised him, he was like a little doll. I played with him, and he loved me for it back then, I even saw his first hard on. He needed more training, so I helped him a little bit. I'm not sure he feels the same way today. To keep him close I still have strings to pull when I need him. I want a grandchild, the first one didn't work out very well, it died just like my own first one. He'll give me another one very soon, then I'll have another doll to play with, dress up and buy things for. If it's a little boy maybe I can help him with his first hard on too, I'll use his dad as a reference.

5.

The next time the doctor saw her patient, it was different. Ms. Smith was agitated and angry, very disheveled. She started talking the moment she came through the door.

"They're after me. He's after me. I thought I put him down like a dog. They've all turned against me, all of them." Patient Smith was nearly breathless, hands waving and her hair a tangled mess. Weaving, she wasn't even walking straight.

"Here Ms. Smith, please, please come sit down, there in your chair. Take a bit of water and tell me about it." The doctor had to move fast, and she did. She got the woman seated then quickly took her own seat at the opposite end of the coffee table. Fast, leaning forward, "Now tell me what has happened since we last spoke. Something terrible has happened; I can certainly see you're upset."

The woman's hands were trembling, she'd dressed hurriedly, no makeup or lipstick, looked drawn, haggard and fearful. She appeared not to have slept in days, dark sunken blood shot eyes and kept running her hands up and down, scratching her arms. The water bottle shook when she grasped it to take a drink. Was this a hangover, no, she said she didn't drink, but the lies, was this another one of them, or what about drugs? Surely this woman used coke, really who didn't these days.

"I hear the rumors, I still have sources Doctor, I know they know. They're laughing at me I can feel it right now, my best friend who always invites me to the London affair every year, she never sent my invitation this year. It should be here by this time. I know others have theirs; I've been thrown out like dirty laundry. I don't know how they could have known. We were so careful; we are always careful." She hesitated then drew in a deep breath, gulped some water, and went on, "We have a secret place that nobody knows about. It's in a stupid, ordinary neighborhood, the perfect place. Those dumb low-class people could never have imagined what we were doing, and we weren't breaking any laws. We're just having fun."

She started to cry, then sobbing, snot running from her nose with spittle flying from the corners of her mouth. The doctor always had tissues at hand, she reached over and offered her patient several.

She waited for Ms. Smith to stop or slow down. While she did, she tried to imagine what this was about, obvious it wasn't a minor social slight. There had to be more to this. The doctor knew plenty about people like this, the woman, and groups she associated with. She knew they were sharks waiting to frenzy feed en masse. There surely was more to what the woman had done, she wasn't telling it all and if the doctor was to help, she'd have to find out what it was...the details.

Beginning slowly and with increasing suspicions, the doctor thought perhaps Ms. Smith had fucked the wrong husband this time. With these consequences she was probably on the cusp of a psychotic break. Doctors knew how to act fast in such situations lest their patient rage out of control and next stop a mental ward at the hospital. So, she queried, asking with calm sincerity.

"Ms. Smith, help me to understand, what exactly are we talking about, what did they find out? Is this about something we discussed before? Tell me so we can both put the pieces together." Offering more tissues, "I understand you've been excluded for the time being. Other than not receiving your invitation, how do you know you are no longer part of your friend's circle? Did someone speak to you or hint at something?"

"No Doctor, I just know. This is how it works." More uncontrolled sobbing, speaking haltingly, "They never tell you directly, ...that is not how...how... *we* do it...they... just let you drift. No more invitations, no more lunches...they all... Oh God." She shouted this time... "They went to New York last week and I wasn't told about the meeting. They went without me; my son told me there were things on the Internet. Pictures."

The crying was turning to rage, she was, barking now, the snakes came out. "My friends, my other friends out in the country didn't invite me to plan for their July party either. I didn't get my part in their shitty little play this year. They're worthless bastards all of 'em. Stupid hick farmer fuckers, and after all I have done for them, the little shits. Wait until I tell a few of them I fucked their husbands, and listen Doctor, my son's the one who supplies their coke. Little fucking cowards can't even make a buy themselves. Won't matter whether I really do it for them or not... it'll completely fuck'em up. Just wait 'til they start hitting the withdraw wall. Yeah, that's what I've always had over them. Those stupid, ugly, dried-up bitchy wives that couldn't satisfy a greased-up dog much less their limp dick husbands. The dried-up pussies wouldn't know a live tomcat from a country roadkill."

The doctor stood, reached over and again offered more tissues then went to her desk, got the woman's file, and returned to sit. She sat at the edge of her seat, with file in her lap and elbows on her knees hoping to convey sincerity, her focus and concern was palpable.

"So, you have not been invited, but no one has actually told you why or given you any reason other than just not inviting you to things, is that what this is about?"

"No Doctor, you don't get it. I think they found out."

"What have they found out and is this your city friends or the other ones out in there in the country, what's the name of the town? What haven't you told me, what is it you think they know Ms. Smith? You have said all this before. What could be so bad or worse this time?"

"They know about my personal life, Doctor."

"What personal life do they know about? The one about you having sex with their men, or other women. Unless I know more, I can't help you."

"Listen Doctor, you don't know anything. You don't have a clue. You're a prissy little woman sitting in a dull office everyday listening to stupid people who do stupid things. Don't you ever get that?" She blew her nose and wiped her eyes.

"You're just like them. You're naïve, you just don't get it. My son and I have had more experience than you and your husband will ever have. You have one, don't you, is he still number one?" Pointing to the doctor's hand, "Isn't that a wedding ring on your finger?"

She took the slap from her patient knowing in extreme psychotic states this is often how patients defend or justify themselves. She had heard it often although perhaps not quite this way, each one different but similar. She knew those who criticized others often did so to hide their own shortcomings. This woman was in trouble and her guess was, most of it of her own making. Well trained, she responded softly, hoping to reassure the woman she was still okay, and her doctor would stay with her. Together they would sort it out and make some sense of it, but she had to be careful. Ms. Smith was fragile, teetering today on a precipice of rejection and perhaps a great fall. Ms. Smith was not telling her something important and before she could do anything effective, she had to know what that was.

"This isn't about me my dear, it is about you. I am here to help you, make you feel safe and reassure you that you will be all right, but you must trust me. Let's get back to your problems of today, do you want to tell me about what you think I don't know, or would you prefer to keep it to yourself? I understand if you do but we really should try to talk about it."

6.

Diva spiraled down then down and further down. She felt the harsh rejection of her friends and it was devastating, she experienced it all from the other side now. What she had done to many others over the years was now bent back on her. What went around had come around, they had her pinned against the wall. A now *former* friend crudely and candidly told her she was finished, and that she would go down doggie style. By herself, that night "Smith" got roaring drunk. She threw things at the walls, broke a few windows and in the morning the devastation was messy, replacements and repairs would be expensive. Of course, her city cleaning lady did the cleanup after Diva got into her car and fled the city to her country house where she believed she was safer, hoping compassion awaited and news of the nasties had not yet arrived out there.

This kind of directed attack of disgrace had never happened to her before. She knew or was certain, perhaps for the first time, that what she had been involved in was well beyond the comprehension of those who she now believed were her newest enemies. But then again, maybe not, maybe this new worry was about something else she had done…let me count the ways. *Former friends* would this time be drawn in with details of their own, or others simply fabricated for juicy embellishments.… this was perfectly normal, the diva's way. Some would not survive and that would serve them right, she'd make sure of that, and this too was normal. Diva was a master at using disinformation of her own and, if it had to be, this would be war. She'd destroy them all before fire spread out of her control, but she needed to get to work fast, there simply was no precedent, so she was in uncharted territory here.

In the meantime, while she drove out to the country, she cried.

Like a snake, Grand ol'-Ma-ma sniffed the air and quickly knew there was the all too recognizable odor of dead rats behind the walls. Poisonous malfeasance had broken out, reportedly over missing funds from the NYC office of the annual Brito-Celebration. Only the nuclear option was open to her; she had known it would come eventually but why now after she finally set the Diva Plan in motion. Diva was becoming a serious behind-the-curtain threat. This situation was a killer. Without warning or ceremony, 'ol-Ma-ma mysteriously disappeared into her own cesspool. Having quickly recognized the signs, she acted much better than Diva but then that was why 'ol-Ma-ma was the head "mucky."

The story first leaked in the Sunday paper. A short, somewhat speculative story but, like bad Depends, in the Sunday society section, it didn't take much. Rumor had it some person or persons absconded with "a reported" considerable sum of money and coincidentally, the president's husband had also disappeared. A charity scandal in the making and all efforts to contact the aging president of Hail Britannia had gone unanswered. With calls not returned, some loyalists suggested the woman was recovering in an unnamed treatment center at an undisclosed location. One didn't have to be a rocket scientist to know what that meant but still some said it out loud… "drunk tank." Others desperately tried to smear it over with stories about sad cancer and their grieving concerns.

Back at the farm, walking closer to danger, Diva paced. Rampant speculation, some of it lurid and closer than half true. The biggest questions were about sources, where was all this coming from? Always before, the diva knew how to play her cards of money, bribery, or threats. Now what to do, which to choose? This time the options seemed empty, who were her targets and how to get at them right away. Option #1, put them down ASAP. With her phones incoming silent, she sent out a few libelous test emails and quickly received back angry serious threats. This isolated creature was remarkably familiar with schadenfreude. Always before, as salacious false stories slipped under the doors of enemies, victims and the press, Diva usually felt the scrumptious "harm-joy" when relishing the misfortunes of others. But this was different; now it was mad-crazy, Diva moving faster, beginning to suspect she might know the source of her problems, her first act had to be retaliation.

At the "girl's" party office in London, a spurious DHL package with a detailed letter including evidentiary accounting ledger copies was received, then another just like it in NYC. Anonymously, each reported detailed questionable bank transactions in the American office. From a distance, real Brits put Diva's "alleged" problems together with Grannies, and they concluded Diva was being framed by none other than… The allegations of Diva sins were just too unbelievable to be relevant, so for the present, the diva line seemed to be holding. Out in the country house, with the Sunday newspaper article on Ol' Mama's disappearance at home, things just might work out after all. Even so, more responses were being planned. Diva knew from experience most successful solutions resulted from good old blitzkriegs.

The English support for her was not surprising; she expected their backing, since over the years, behind her friend's back she'd paid plenty for it. Nevertheless, knowing nearby there was one who would never abandon her she remained relatively safe in her country house. Feeling the pained seclusion away from former friends in the city, in this time of substantial risk, especially with her playmate, the two women mutually agreed to not take risks of any public association until the shit storm was over. What was working in the UK was not working quite as well in the U.S. where a few friends, "the little shits," openly betrayed her. The U.S. versus UK loyalists was a long-complicated story with a history that presently showed itself to be exceptionally worthwhile abroad, but less so at home.

The little shits in the U.S. pressed their moments of opportunistic superiority down hard. Nearby there was a hugely different picture with ingrates showing up everywhere. The new inner war of attrition would include a run at the throne by others, which was inevitable. She had to find her way back and a little maiming or even death along the way might not be out of the question. In the States, where some didn't buy it, her total innocence was suspect because she was 'ol-Ma-ma's best buddy and therefore part of the old régime. The President's increasingly accepted sole responsibility for embezzlement was losing traction and with it, Diva's claims of innocence. Pumping it up, she needed to be seen as victim not conspirator. That had been the genius plan of diversion to take the sting out, but now it was not enough. The Diva's salacious fictitious stories still lacked enough specifics. At the same time, Diva was also fantasizing about another outcome... if she played her cards right, with old backstabbing Grand Ma-ma out, she just might just become the new leader of them all after all.

Sides were choosing up, devotion to Grand Ma-ma had run deep, increased, but now nearly everyday feelings of betrayal made the rounds. To avoid their being personally associated with the disgraces of opulence and association, some crones began weaving new cloth of incitement, indictments, and innocence.

Backfire, blow back toward all.

Unexpectedly, covered in the mud of association and sensing duplicity, a few inner circle girls suspected it was fitting together a wee bit too easily. However, there was more trouble; ladies of the carrion club hired a lawyer who soon discovered Diva's own "low cash" situation and need for annual free rides to Britannia provided by Grand Ma-ma. In retrospect, a mistake in the 'ol-Ma-ma's strategy of give, take and secure the fort. Chess is best played by those who think several moves ahead. Flame and flood spread together; fire burning on top of water. Oil always fueled fire on top.

Even with the hunt for crooks continuing into the now former socialite, Grand Mam-ma and the Gasser husband, Diva's plan for the disgraced old girl collapsed into deeper exile of shame for them both or all three. No bucks meant no power and no power meant Diva was in shit city without a limo. Like a bad child confined to quarters, unable to leave the house or her yard, she was no longer seen in the city or even much in the distant farm community. Sending her help for food, she stopped pillaging local retail establishments and of course, even with those outside the twisted circles of sisters, the country club was out. Only mysterious late-night excursions away from her house remained and increasingly, she was whispered to having become the recluse who, like a ghost, only wandered streets in the dead of night.

Deep in the night Diva sent oceans of email, and with newfound skills of hired Russian hackers she planted more disinformation. Wherever possible she threatened to disclose, with mostly fraudulent information, the illicit activities of unsupporting others and their self-serving agendas. All without proof but nevertheless... once accused...

Creating dark web aliases for her, her son and hackers helped, so enemy sources couldn't backtrack the digital missiles. For onerous fees they helped write exposés that cunningly revealed how treacherous acts of enemies explained her banishment, and why none of the accusations were true or remotely her fault. She herself wrote the talk of others was a smoke screen to cover their own reprehensible activities and they would never put their foot on English soil again, not even Barbados. With fictional supposed firsthand accounts, she exposed ol' Ma-ma as an alcoholic druggie with legs spread for all manner of men and beasts willing to keep their eyes closed, and yes, even women too who didn't care. After all, the Ol' Brito Grannie was in the pleasure business for all cumers who could pay. Diva claimed, for a fair and balanced price, to have pictures and videos altered for proof. Years before, when they discussed hackers, Diva made notes of contacts while Grand Ma-ma did the heavy lifting. These days those notes proved invaluable.

There was a great deal of scandalous talk around, but nothing reliable enough to confirm the truth for any legitimate journalist to bother with. Good ones had known for years how the games were played with this bunch; but still, since there were bits of truth to the disclosures, a few of those who threatened Diva went down and with a smirk she could claim modest successes. So far, she had two overdoses, three separations, two divorce filings and one serious disabling odd car crash to her credit. The leftover others were paranoid rants leaving 'the girls' wondering if there really would be more pictures and where would she strike next. And OMG what about recordings? Some believed Diva was not original enough to make all this up, so in fact, there either must be some truth to it, or worse she was getting damn good help. The crones were keenly aware what they themselves had been doing, and it seemed Diva did too. Rumors beget rumors and soon, paid on account snitches were everywhere.

With fires raging out of control, in various clubs there were empty luncheon tables, uneaten and spoiled food, layoffs and cash problems. Like a rolling snowball the damage was getting bigger. Attendance down even at the country club fish night dinners. Increasingly, help was talking and there was a betting pool in the pro shop over who would be the next to fall; literally or figuratively it really didn't matter which one or who. It was well over one hundred degrees in the desert, but up-country snowbirds were fleeing south in the Summer.

Diva asked herself repeatedly, "How could others know?" Since Diva had competition for her evil deeds, leaks could still not be isolated reliable attribution. The solution she and her special friend decided was an indiscriminate shotgun approach, the response could only be to kill them all. Things were moving faster and slipping backward with no real progress, she was losing sleep. Eating erratically and pulling at her hair that was already plenty thin it was wig time. Hair coming out in clumps and soon unsightly patches of bald ground appeared all too obvious.

Ms. Smith had discontinued "treatment" and was on her own. Shrinks could never fight wars like this one. In "the circles" of only slightly more imagination than Diva, gossip fell far short of the mark. In their circle, myopic world of unholy alliances, experience, complacent comfort, and wildest dreams, "swells of the city and far out farmland" memories had yet failed to capture the real truth and depth of depravity. To find her guilty with offered solid proof, nobody could accurately describe what Diva was or specifically had been a part of. For long years of convoluted destruction, the "ladies" downtown club world had been teetering and now about to suffer further media exposure. The likes of all this had not been seen since, with an audience, the symphony conductor humped the first violinist on stage after hours. A disgraced outing no one could have conceived of, but adding it up, Diva today would easily outdo the one with the conductor and video camera carelessly left on.

More than one tabloid reporter had been nosing around Diva's story and now the FOX was waiting outside front doors ready to pounce. "Friends of Britannia" were afraid to step outside by themselves. Before it was over, with specifics, most, if not all would fall into the hell of Diva and still there was the matter of missing money, the Gassers, mister and missus.

Rumors persisted about compromising photographs of Diva and others of the elusive Gasser clan. Sweating, Diva promised the man with a camera, who every day sat in a filthy McDonald's wrapper-filled old car at the end of her driveway, she would pay if he left her alone. He agreed for the time being, so she provided four, but in two the faces turned away and the others were somewhat blurred. She called them publicity shots and for the time being, photo man left happy. In his business with FOX, nobody cared about details or authenticity and certainly had no scruples about Photoshop.

If viewed from afar one had to give credit where it was due. Diva, with help from her furtive companion, had until now hidden their biggest secret in plain view. Because of this, dullards of the fields and city would, they believed, never, ever put the real story together. Far too obvious and scandalous for them to come to grips with; hence, it was certainly impossible to fully imagine. This at least put some of the fears that had sent her rushing to the psychiatrist temporarily at rest. These days she was focusing on other possibilities, the power struggle for presidency of the six and seven figure Hail Britannia boondoggle.

The Diva's companion, cunning and malicious person that she was, had long ago been first to suggest their adventurous sex descent into hell; but of course, she didn't call it that and Diva had gone along with their glorious run of licentious pleasure. Back then why wouldn't she agree, it was all about pleasure and especially since, in that regard, a sociopath had no ethics or morals to worry about. Add to that, other than laws of the jungle; far beyond the age of consent, they really weren't breaking any laws, any peekers at least had to admit that.

"Ms. Smith" and her partner assumed that if these insipid ordinary people did know the real facts, they wouldn't have believed them anyway. Thus, there had been layers of protection, and that too was operational cover for their version of reality and playtimes together. Dullness breeds dullness and assuredly, comforts of wealth provided protection while at the same time inducing myopia along with prejudice. After all, this was not California and nearby friends were as intellectually plain as their routine pedestrian lifestyles.

The city circles were not all that different than those she called knuckle dragging mongrels out near her country home; the single exception being, city people were more experienced, more worldly. Their sins of commission and omission deeper and perhaps, with spice, colorfully more corrupt. Opulent lives had style where those "rural people" had none, unless you counted corn, cops on the take and county fairs. It depended on your point of view actually, who had more legitimate and tasty style than "wannabe Amero-British swells" whose appetites ran more to cheese, crackers, caviar and champagne.

Hush money was a universal reality, usually all it took to keep things quiet with the town and country cops, who themselves had plenty of other sins to hush up. Some so obvious they forgot to brush the white powder off their dark uniform jackets when speed ticketing a city slicker. With the driver window rolled down, one speeder even had the temerity to ask the ticketing cop if he would share.

Diva was becoming the stuff of legend, but exile and whispered revelations only scratched the surface. Just before Christmas, the season of parties at country and city clubs, details about the diva's expulsion reached new heights…not replays but all new second season multiple episodes material. Like volcanic magma, trails and tails of depravity wagged beyond their wildest dreams. Confirming Diva was shortly to become the stuff of legend, indeed permanently at home and abroad.

> *Coming up and soon to be released, a cult web site devoted to the famous Mistress of Disgust. Ladies and Gentlemen, we present the Diva of Depravity. Mistress of downtown dung and farm town harvested offal.*

Acting for real would finally get its theatrical due. The author anonymous but well informed, with keen reporting from *inside* sources. Friends, soon to become infamous as supporting players with real names, they will all be co-stars.

Out in the sticks, community theater would enjoy renewed and standing room only attendance. Scandal, like war and poison for the soul was good for the economy. With sex thrown in, it all just got juicier! Fields of the Swells, with City of the Damned soon joined in bitter irony. Diva would benefit middleclass shopkeepers, carpenters, even those simple minded who mowed lawns, pumped septic tanks and local young flat-chested blue-eyed corn-fed waitresses. Gawkers would come to see where it had all happened, birthplace of contemporary disgust with mother and daddy fuckers. In the all-new Peyton Place of the 21st century, a complete cast included the very same people Diva especially loathed.

And finally, just after New Year's, the attempted suicide of one recently surfaced, particularly active former city actor who some time ago mysteriously disappeared. She was older and in public had been a bit imperious. In private she always seemed the nervous type, insecure but few ever saw that. They said it was pills but who cared when the adios note was gratuitously passed around. The maid who found the unconscious woman couldn't read English so asked the neighbor to read it and that was like buying advertising space in the Sunday Times. Apparently afraid of green card issues she, the discovery maid didn't know her mistress, the well-known former president of some Anglo Charity had named names, dates and posted "activities." Real panic set in and it was noted, several from the former circles suddenly departed for permanent unnamed "vacation" destinations. Money was still missing from the foreign and domestic offices. That would remain a mystery, but one thing was for sure, Grand Ma-ma Gasser was down, out, and confirmed dry toast in a box. She'd fried her brain with meds. Mr. Gasser was still missing in combat. AWOL.

BOOK 6

1.

    We are having dinner. This night Diva has surprised me. We use conventional tableware. In this million-dollar country house, when we are alone, we usually use plastic-ware and paper plates, and I don't like that. In front of me, for us to look over and not to be missed in conversation, the center piece is a silver couverture de plat or cloche, one of those humped up food covers. Engraved on each side is the crest and name of some unknown long forgotten owner. This one just perfect when serving a roasted stag quarter in one's very own English manor house, an apple mouthed stuffed Christmas pig would work too. The splendid sterling silver serving piece is not empty. It is so large that, like Russian Matryoshka dolls, there is another slightly smaller one inside and a still smaller one inside that one. All perfect for roast breast of horse, pig, turkey, chicken, or quail.

    Diva collects silver pieces. Usually, they are old, she prefers ones with inscriptions and coats of arms. She also has trophies from long ago families who presumably could or would no longer afford them. Here the intention is to compliment the staged environments of her homes. For the actor, props suggest pedigree, breeding, and centuries of presumed successful family conquest. Fictitious of course, or at least as they apply to this nouveau riche owner. Visitors of quality would never be so impolite as to closely inspect the engraved names for authentication or worse, turn them over to reveal more confirmation of provenance.

Most legends had been partially obscured by years of the repeated polishing by staff downstairs from the upstairs. Friends assume that the many trophies and engraved winner bowls are evidence of Diva's family treasures. Inheritance from the bartender and two-timing mom, come beautician, who in the old row house on Molder Street was reported to have stolen money from the family kitty.

Diva has no idea others have similar misleading artifacts; she is not that discerning. To the legitimate educated observer, the not so slight-of-hand is all in the game of implications and resultant expectations. This, after all, is what traditionally nouveau riche is about, and why history has despised those interlopers who claim authenticity. It is the illegitimacy of Americans that appalls European aristocracy. Yankees didn't pay for their booty with centuries of spilled generational blood and Machiavellian treachery; they just bought it with printed, not minted, fiat Yankee dollars. In Europe, gratitude is held to a different standard where and when that mystifies, and with justification, angers Americans standing to view Flanders Fields.

Diva is very insecure, seen up close she has a self-esteem problem. This is not a complicated analysis and conclusion but complex with some deep digging required. Up until now she has hidden her insecurities well. With the exception of money, her most valued possession has no real weight or mass. Ironically, it is instead paradoxically abstract social standing. Strange for a woman who usually values only things of weight and mass. Diva does not *do* abstract, her "you hold'ems," even when illegitimate are real and can be sold or traded for newer versions of wampum.

She lives in constant fear of background check discovery. To erase her unwanted past, on the Internet she has bought and erased evidentiary kernels of revealing pedigree, available to all at a price. You should know anyone can do this, erase the bar her father worked in, a beauty shop her mother took a shot at, the grim dark dreary house on Molder Street; but not the Jewish*ness* of her husband which stayed but nobody cared about except Diva. Home, bittersweet home isn't named or referred to by number like the ones her extant friends refer to. Para dejar una buena primera impresión en tu entrevista, viste con ropa elegante.

She never lived at sixteen hundred, seventeen hundred, or eighteen. Diva fears someone from the past will reveal what in recollection lies beneath. She fears someday, in a drunken or impaired feeble state, some Jewish man will recount stories of puberty days and first BJs with a pig eater in the janitor's closet at school.

2.

Sociopaths can be withdrawn for varying periods of time; they go off the grid to recharge their maliciousness. With others, and when they are in high gear, the gregariousness can be quite misleading, making it appear as though they are genuinely enjoying social interaction. This strange teeter-totter of engagement and withdrawal complicates the story. In their isolation they, she, can be depressed and morose. On down days Diva stays in bed all day, eating comfort food while wearing flannel jammies with little yellow kitties printed all over them. Without makeup and her accessories this can be disconcerting or even frightening to an outsider. Popcorn, popsicles, milk, and cookies supply nourishment, Bravo, and re-runs of Orange County Housewives. A constant stream of spiteful televised entertainment she calls important educational information. Kinda like guys who like shoot 'em ups because they are instructional. In this remote solitude, her laptop is the window to a narrowly defined world of peculiar off brand circumstances. Importantly, via eBay and similar others, they provide endless remote anonymous shopping opportunities.

These are times when the sociopath elicits and usually receives sympathy, it's like bringing child aspirin to a drunk. Sympathy is something dysfunctional people, like Diva, see as a one-way street with all roads leading to themselves. Her friends easily confuse her pretended expressions of sympathy to them as authentic and can't understand this: sociopaths do not understand empathy. There is always an ulterior motive used in one way or another to help themselves.

"No dear, send her the $95.00 one. It will be bigger than any of the others the girls will send, and BTW that should hold her for a while."

Big orchid plants are currency, they buy at least three, sometimes four months of reliable fealty. Big orchids are a Diva trademark, and nobody dares to compete in kind. You see big orchid; you see a Diva payoff. Even politicians and bookies are subtler. Recognized trademark donations are tip offs that raise suspicions of graft.

There's no suspicion, sociopaths are known predators and Diva is a predator among other predators, but not necessarily of all the same kind. The more specialized big-balled versions are the jackals among Venus flytraps. You can step on and crush a Venus flytrap, but a jackal will bite and is often rabid.

As if a flash had gone off, when drawn in close and blinded by the light, there were some diva charms to appreciate. So long as the wrapper stays on, veritable feasts for the senses. Once peeled away and contents revealed a contagion spreads. Like a striptease gone wrong, May West at 90, or a naked leper missing pieces, Diva moves slowly at first, lest her charms tarnish in the sulfuric atmosphere that surrounds her. We are in Greece.

It's Athens time. Propped up on the bed in an array of elaborate lace-trimmed pillows, Diva is lap-topped. She's just finished ironing her dress for the evening, it is carefully hung against the closet door. I step out from the bathroom where, since she took so long, there is little time left to shower before we must leave for dinner and the dancing.

"Oh, I see you ironed your dress, I didn't know we had an iron. Could you do me a favor and just quickly repress my trousers? I think you're sitting on them." She looks up as if I'm a stranger, thinking about what I have just asked. "No, I don't think so, I'm busy, I'm not your stupid maid." She returns to eBay in Europe.

A gentle knock on the door. Wrapped in a huge towel I open it. Holding the towel around my waist with one hand and gesturing with the other, "Kaló apógevma," I greet her, or however you it say it in Greek. She nods and before I can say more the floor maid comes in to remove the ironing board and the iron. I think I muttered, "Fuck it."

Later, at the champagne reception before dinner I apologize for my appearance to a very nice woman. I explain Diva sat on my dinner clothes that had been laid out on the bed. I was thinking the lady would perhaps suggest I just take them off, but Cosi sia, it didn't work out that way.

Sia fatta sempre la tua Volontà. Tutto ciò che Tu disponi è la cosa migliore per me ed io fin d ora l'accetto e Ti ringrazio. Cosi sia.

As previously mentioned, Diva's dog has a place at the table. Yes, a real seat at the table. At dinner, the small dog has been lifted into place and sits up on two large silk damask pillows piled on the seat of "its" chair. A place is set for the dog, there is a plate, a napkin, salad fork, a dinner fork, knife, spoon(s) and yup, a dessert fork and spoon at the top. Doggie doesn't care for wine and fish will not be served this evening so no fish knife. The dog is small, purse size, the silverware is baby size, and the porcelain china has hand painted images of little doggies at play. A linen napkin is neatly tied bandana style around poochie's neck. Doggie is named after some famous forgotten diva and scented with namesake perfume. The vet repeatedly says this creates persistent skin problems, but Diva refuses to believe the vet. With dogs and like scented women in the room, following one's nose in the dark one could easily mistake one dog for another.

As usual using paper plates and throwaway plasticware, we will serve ourselves in the kitchen this night and each carry our food to the table in the dining room. As requested I sit waiting, the dog is, of course, first to be served and food is spooned onto its plate from a small tureen. Doggie's plate arranged much as ours except her meat has been cut up into little bitty pieces just as you would for a small child, old or disabled person. The dinner conversation will consist primarily of Diva talking to doggie and encouraging "it" to eat its vegetables. We, that would be Diva and myself, obviously have nothing as interesting to discuss as she and la pooch. When asked for comment on the food the dog remains silent, which seems comment enough. I am hungry, clearly have less to offer, so just eat chewing with my mouth closed and some gratitude for not being a part of the absurd conversation.

A fashion update here: The dog's wardrobe includes a complete compliment of costumes de jour. Coats, sweaters, collars, bejeweled leashes, baskets (plural) to sleep in, raised car seats (plural) so *it* can look out the window. Little boots, one pair for rain another for snow so it will not slip or freeze. I've never heard of a dog slipping on ice and breaking a hip and even a little toboggan with an attached basket to sit in. Dog is dabbed and wiped each time after it goes poopee and tinkle-tinkle. This concierge service is performed first, even after the damn thing has just crapped on the bed comforter. And a set of gossamer fairy wings for "let's pretend" drama night or it had them until it chewed them up. The same fate befell its butterfly wings and dog sized bunny costume.

I suspected the canine peeing are protests rooted in anger or resentment from the indignity of it all. They do, of course, have doggie shrinks for these problems but as with Diva, that will not be optioned. Alas, it was just a bitch being a bitch. In the city many was the time I was tempted to set the wing attached animal on the eighth story window ledge to see if the thing wanted to use its wings and really fly. Give it an Icarus shot at freedom.

Dogs like "doggie" are born and bred to be carried, not walked. Giant Betsy Johnson sparkle-bags or designer dog carry-alls reek of status, old urine, and crumbly dried fecal matter in dark corners of the inside bottom; putting my hand in there once was enough! Pet-i-cures, regular baths with white brightening conditioner, air fluff, scents applied, routine inspection of orifices and this dog, every three or four days is good to go, weekends and holidays included. Cashmere wrapped dogs may seem extreme to some but in this crowd, nothing is too good for old rover and the swimming attire with water wings is a scream.

And finally, the dog days of travel. Diva is just fucking furious that she cannot take her doggie lapped and strapped in her seat on the airplane. First, they tell her only downstairs with luggage and other beasts where

Diva has found out temperatures are unacceptably low and there is no company. Rejected. The next possibility is, purchase the creature a seat beside her in first class where the thing can only be caged and other than water no free drinks. That option too is rejected. The third option is only available for "service dogs." This is a pathway forward but there are problems. A service dog is a legal FAA designation and requires proof not just owner's desire. Solution... Diva finds and pays a vet $850.00 dollars for a fraudulent slip of paper. A prescription showing the dog will prevent its owner from melting down aboard an airplane and jumping out the emergency door, going otherwise nuts or endangering the lives of all aboard including the pilots. It is not clear just what the dog can or will do to prevent these episodes, but the problem is solved. Dog flies first class but can't look out the window because it's on the floor jammed under the seat ahead.

Older women do indeed treat their dogs better than their men.

3.

There were few or no projects or interests we shared in our life together. When she was not traveling far away Diva resides only in the country house or city apartment. She says she's busy when in the city, but this seems absurd and typical overstatement since she really does little to nothing except veg out, dine out or shop.

Other than the occasional city lunch, she has actually only two friends there, the next-door Orphan Annie neighbor who she secretly loathes but needs and a meek but pleasant woman down the street with a slightly bigger version dog to match her own. The dogs do not get along. The women giggle hysterically as the old and bigger down street dog tries to hump Diva's up street toy dog in Diva's downtown city apartment. While working in the other room, on more than one occasion I overheard the two friends sitting in the living room watching the doggie show which, knowing the little dog's resistance, can only be called canine rape. Blitzed on afternoon white wine and squealing with delight, they grade sex show of canine copulation using a point system just like ice-skating competitions.

"Ooooo," one howls, for the furry offered ass, "That's a five for approach but I have to say only three for presentation." These babes, working as self-appointed judges really know how to enjoy their sporting time entertainments. They have fun sharing play by play assessments of dogs-do-it fuck games. Think about it, what else is there to do on any afternoon in the big city and… its weatherproof?

As near as I ever figured out, when in the city, all the diva does is watch TV, the doggie show, eat junk food, cruise the streets making rounds to discount stores where she, each day, buys more stuff and, frequently but defiantly not always, having worn it once, returns the goods a few days later.

She bought me seven identical black zip up the front black cashmere sweaters. Just perfect "swell accoutrements" along with, at last count, fourteen identical black Polo tennis shirts which I particularly dislike and repeatedly say so… However, all these were bought at discount places so at least she isn't paying full price. It does not register that I do not want any clothes from her EVER. She insists I wear clothes with conspicuously embroidered logos over the left nipple. Fashionista passé is not something she gets, even I know that much.

Diva is very good at not paying full price. She is incredibly extravagant in some things and in others very cheap. That is why she buys gems, photographs the authentic jewelry then sends photos and eBay gems off to Asia to get back the same recently photographed for a song, yen or whatever. Diva is a blend of contradiction, fraud, and destruction. She will not take the safer tollway drive to the country house because she's angry they charge instead of tax her to use the road. Her route trip sans tollway takes much longer at proven greater risk and more fuel.

This is Diva's workweek in the city. Once back in the country, where I spend most of my diva time, other than me working and she in her garden with Dirt-Girl playing Paddycake down by the river, we do nothing together. That is why, each morning I leave and travel the relatively short distance to where I usually work 8-10 hours a day, almost every day. City events excluded, I like my work, it's not an escape and I don't do this because Diva is a bore. She does nothing or at least nothing I can see other than buy, bitch and feed.

Not that I haven't tried to suggest things we could enjoy together, but she only wants to amuse herself chatting with mud-bound Paddycake or, nose in her laptop, cruising eBay. She's a true eBay junkie, each delivery day there are packages left by front doors in the city and country.

4.

The look on her face was clear. "Well, this is a surprise."

"How are you doctor; it's been a while." His smile was genuine and relaxed, he stood there like a long-lost friend. She felt in that way he was more friend than patient.

"Yes, I think almost two years, isn't that about right?" She had thought of him often, wondering where he was, how and what he might be doing. As soon as he left the last time, she hoped he would come back. She hoped that often over the past two years.

He pretended to think a moment and said, "You know, I think you're right. I didn't think it had been that long. I guess time flies when you're having fun." His smile was warm and genuine. "Yes, I guess it has been two years. My-my."

He looked good, well dressed, appeared successful, happy and the doctor knew this was not by chance, not at all serendipitous. This was a man who did not welcome random events any more than he liked divas. Smiling she was amused, knowing they both knew perfectly well it had been two years.

"Please, please come in and tell me how you are, what has happened, what's going on in your life. Come, come sit, tell me everything."

"Well, I've been quite well actually, and you look well too, Doctor, you look very well, in fact you look great." The smile with sincere warmth not lost on her.

"I have traveled some, visited old friends I'd forgotten and even a few cemeteries where there were others I also remembered well. Happier than I've been in a very long time, that's the short version, and you Doctor, what about you. I know doctors don't discuss their personal lives, but I think we went a little beyond that, don't you?" His big smile and, "I hope I'm not being too forward."

The question and statement directed outward. A clear sign of good health and well-being, the man seemed transformed. Unpretentious and natural he was indeed now a friend rather than patient with additional time, she thought probably more than that. Easily recalling there was far more to him back then, when two years before he disappeared into that snowy, blowing white-out afternoon.

She deflected his question away from herself. "Well first I am so happy to hear what you are saying, your report from the front so to speak, and yes," somewhat sheepishly, "we became more than doctor and patient. That rarely happens, you know there are rules. I don't suppose in the interest of perhaps 'our friendship' you might finally tell me your real name. It would, after all this time, make conversation easier." She was teasing him. Again, her smile was warm, charming, and inviting.

"Well," he thought about it a minute, raised a finger and tipping his head to the side said, "Why don't you just call me Rumpelstiltskin. It will be better that way. Yes, I think Rumpelstiltskin would work just fine." It was his turn to again smile and tease.

"Okay, Rumpelstiltskin it will be but Rumple for short. Not like the Rumpole of Old Bailey, you certainly don't look rumpled. They laughed and she knew he was not finished.

Nodding his agreement, he went on, "I have come to terms with several things because of you and have you to thank for some of this. I've come to tell you that. You should know about your successes, even with evidence unfolding far away I imagine sometimes this takes a while. I easily imagine you sometimes can't see it firsthand. And too, I realize things now I didn't before. Perhaps the one I still find most disturbing is the utter waste of her. That woman we talked about still contributes nothing; she only takes. She's done nothing to advance the human race. I remember asking you how successful you were at curing people of their problems. I recall and know your answer still."

She did not respond but sat smiling with affection. Titling her head slightly she sat back, crossed her legs, arms high on the chair arms and listened intently as he talked.

"I've given it a great deal of thought and when successful, others deserve to hear about that. Most people just report the failures. In my case you were and are instrumental in my having returned to the living."

With a deep sigh and shaking head. "And yes, I've learned a great deal more over the past few years about what Diva does, with and to whom. She's been watched very carefully. What's been seen, some of it recorded and witnesses confirm, it continues to be disgusting. I'm pretty sure eventually she and others will pay a heavy price. But to be clear she will not be asked to pay me, Doctor. I am not a violent man, sometimes harsh or too direct with my words perhaps, but not my actions. You might say I'm now more of a clinical observer taking notes. What happens will be her doing; after they are finished with everyone else, people like that have a way of destroying themselves. You know that too. I'm rather well read on the subject... almost an expert you might say."

She looked concerned, "Have you threatened her in any way. What you are doing could be against the law, I assume you're aware of that and you're keeping safe."

"Oh, I know well, Doctor, I know all this very well, but you see I don't have to be involved directly, I only watch and certainly have no intention of breaking the law. I am and have been only an interested watcher that continues to do just that. She's become my important project to observe, analyze and learn from. I make lots of notes. It's a compelling drama. Someday, using my notes someone could write a good book about it. For now I just read periodic reports and pay others to do the real up-close observing for me. We don't touch, we never touch. Long ago I decided that would upset the natural order of things and possibly invalidate the natural outcome."

"I don't yet know the specifics of a final outcome but can assure you it will reach a peak and I'm convinced rapidly descend. Things like this almost always do. I'm what you might say, ...ummm... philosophical about it. You could say, for verifiable authenticity my contribution was made several years ago. Since then, those I have engaged for some time now only watch from a lawful distance; but if I were to choose today, Doctor, I could tell you what her bank balance was yesterday."

"This is a curious social experiment, and I am sure you would be interested professionally. Unfortunately, for now the information is secure for my eyes only. However, if I'm right, someday, not too far off in the future you'll know what happens. It will capture the attention of blood sucking sensationalists in the media, and perhaps even more thoughtful inquiring people who wish to help others with their understanding of this terrible human flaw. Of course," he smiles, "this assumes I am correct with my prognostications."

The doctor watched him closely and after a few thoughtful moments asked, "How soon do you think?"

"I believe this time the ball is finally in play but again, I didn't put it there nor did I even give it a nudge. It's been rolling faster with each passing month. Unexpected forces building and another player whom I suspect has probably unleashed the last act; I think as sure as you and I are sitting here, the time is near. I'm beginning to think the diva will not survive it, nor will some others and there's nothing you or anyone, including me, can do to stop it. No laws have been broken by us, so we just watch and wait. And anyway, there's really no recourse one way or another. But there is one realization, something I have learned; just breathing is not necessarily a reliable sign of life."

"Oh my," the doctor said. "Did you come here to tell me all this?"

"No. I came to say thanks for what you do professionally, and have, at least in my case done well. I did not pick your name at random, and I have a hunch you have known that for some time. I knew things about you before we met. After you and I finished talking it was I who, quite anonymously from a distance, arranged that Diva become your patient.

I know I said I didn't want to help but that was not entirely correct. I still had hope then, despite what you told me about any possible success. I arranged it all just as I now watch what, with considerable sadness I think is her last chapter. I had hoped, with you she would have a chance for redemption and perhaps some forgiveness, but sadly that has not been for either of us to decide. You and I are just observers now, not even monitors."

The doctor shifted uncomfortably in her seat; she was concerned but had no idea what to do other than agree. It seemed any or all intervention was beyond them both. Yes, maybe he was just what he said he was, simply the observer of a tragic human drama. Some things just had to run their course. Thinking about it she recalled over two years ago he had told her he was a trained observer. Now, oh my, how had she missed the importance of that?

"You see doctor, once the characters were well understood and in place, let's say I just left the stage to sit in the audience. Again, it is Diva, the actor herself who created and made this theatrical drama possible. Were it not for her, this spectacle would be just so ordinary none of us would have paid the least bit of attention. But now you and I both know the diva will dance, while unknown, unidentified puppet masters work strings from a safer distance. I can and will assure you I am not among them. The puppeteers are simply coincidence and consequence; it was she who created the stage and the theater, the lights the action. I feel no guilt nor should you."

The doctor decided to challenge him just to test and see if, despite what he was saying, he was a vindictive voyeur. "So," she said, "You just played us all, is that right? Has this all been a charade to justify your personal verdict, your justice, or maybe is this a personal form of revenge?" It sounded a bit harsh, but she needed to know… know if there was authentic closure here, if his words were as authentic and reasonable as they sounded.

"Ah, but of course you would ask, and these cards would be played, but I believe none of them madam. I had told you, when doing my work,

I watch. I have always been a watcher. It was and continues to be about players performing on a stage of their own making. That is where Diva always wanted to be and, in the beginning, I missed it, because while I watch I do not, cannot see everything. I bought and paid for my ticket to be in the audience, never thinking I would have a part to first appear on stage myself. My mistake, for a time regret was becoming part of the troupe. The allure was too great, I vacillated, should have known better and consequently literally played the fool's fool. You recall, she said she was a good actor. I just gave her, and a few of her friends, the opportunity to remember the mission with intentions of Punch and Judy. Getting help, her former friends became contributing writers of her program notes, still others, her artless erstwhile audience. But none could ever do the star roll performance of Diva, that is only for a real diva to enact."

"I have read your case summary, written for the journal you contributed to. Quite good doctor, I must say, and if I'm any judge, quite correct. Good job. But there will be more so stay tuned, ready to write your conclusions about all the players including judgements of myself."

"Thank you," she said, "That seems damning with faint praise, Rumpole, and of course, I will wait and see." She was smiling once again, more friend than doctor. "In this area you appear to have become quite accomplished yourself. Maybe you should consider my line of work or to at least write the book so others might better understand, and who knows, maybe even comprehend. As I recall you have plenty of recorded material." They smiled at each other recalling his disclosure of having recorded their sessions together.

"Thank you, that's high praise indeed." Not knowing whether she was being sarcastic or complimentary, he rose from where he'd been sitting, the old chair he'd eventually found safe, comfortable, and reassuring. "I must be on my way. I don't think we will ever meet again, Doctor, but you may wish to watch media reports over the next few months. Diva's show is not over yet and what is perhaps the last act may not have yet fully begun but it will. I may have overstated matters but when it happens, I suspect the reviews will be interesting. I can assure you every player has qualifications, what exactly they do with them at this point, I have no idea."

His stay had been short, he had not taken off his coat and just as before left quickly. There was no hug, no handshake not even a farewell kiss on the cheek. Again, just as before, from the building's lobby she heard the front entry door open then softly close. Looking out her office window she could only wonder while watching him walk out into the street, across and into the park, remembering what he had said at their first meeting …Diva could not…wonder.

Once again, snow was blowing hard, this time almost horizontally. The predicted storm had arrived more ferocious than before; the long purple scarf around his neck fluttered freely with what seemed a show of enthusiasm, a colorful symbolic gesture of freedom. Footsteps in the snow quickly covered as he disappeared into the darkening grey winter afternoon. Soon the night, darkness then light, darkness again and again more light. The doctor wondered if these past few minutes had been an apparition. She wondered if this all had been a dream.

Turning back, there on the corner of her desk were five, crisp $100 bills. They appeared as if by magic. Out of a nearly forgotten habit she swept them up, opened her bottom drawer and dropped them into a folder with the others. Still there, the contents unused, her guess was there probably at least one hundred of them by now. He had sent more after their last parting, never a return address. They were a precious symbol now, personal treasure and yes, magic. Perhaps someday that would change but for now she had no interest in using them for anything other than as a keepsake.

The doctor had never known his real name nor exactly what he did for work. This time there were tears, hers came from the heart and bled to the floor.

BOOK 7

1.

He was not sure, two maybe three years ago his suspicions had begun. There had been inklings, but in those days, he'd pushed them away as far as he could manage. Subtleties were well beyond his imaginings, not a particularly smart man, but not entirely dumb either. A simple creature with a life and expectancy of elementary understandings, prejudices he kept mostly to himself along with routines including Sundays at the local Lutheran church. Apart from his wife, he had always been a loner, never a dreamer, a simple man in mind, heart, and manner.

He was a different kind of doctor, not an MD; instead, one who practiced and performed alternative versions of naturopathic therapies who called themselves doctors. While he and his like-minded friends called themselves doctors still, even his parents remained unconvinced. He only had a few patients in this small rural town where there were few who believed in his approach. If they did, mostly they were people seeking cheap medicine or a quick fix. To fill the hours of his empty life and office time he worked as an itinerant handyman. This is how and why most knew him as Handi, he and his wife were "the Handi's." As far as anybody could recall she was a semi-skilled gardener and, since neither of them were of any special importance, most couldn't even remember their real names.

No one in these parts called him Doctor; only he believed he was and said he was one. This didn't matter to him much, but he wished at least his wife would call him Doctor. Nevertheless, he got along, condescension and snubs usually lost on him, but every small town needs a handyman, so wannabe doctor was it. Even after all these years when he passed them on the street no one said hello. With no drama or peril and minimal existence, he led an invisible life.

Today Handi, that's the way he spelled it, was walking back from the park, where every day he sat on the same bench to eat his baloney sandwich and drink bottled water he filled from the tap at the kitchen sink with a rust stain around the drain. Weather permitting, he did this the same way, same time, same place, on the same bench each and every day even in winter. Two pieces of bread with baloney, butter, yellow mustard, and off brand mayonnaise. There were exceptions if it rained or snowed hard and he couldn't work, he just sat at home in his threadbare Lazyboy chair, listening to whatever through the earbuds that seem permanently attached to his ears. There was to be nothing exceptional about this day, not even his thoughts, or at least that was the way it was supposed to be. Every day the same except for today. However, something had come loose rolling around inside his usually passive resting brain.

He married his wife the same year he graduated from the state school for Naturopaths, miles away near the state capitol. Finishing just okay and graduating with seven others, mostly farm boys, all seven were proclaimed, by others of their persuasion, affirmed *real* doctors recognized by the International Naturopathic Congress of North America.

Still, even though they all got a certificate to prove it, not even his wife believed he was a real doctor. But that was no matter since he did and that's what mattered most. The course had taken two years and his wife, who graduated from their high school that same year of his "doctor" graduation, was two years younger. It all fit quite nicely; she soon joined him as a handyperson when he wasn't "practicing." Had anyone noticed or cared, they were a blurred predictable fulfillment of an equally bland predictable world. That's just the way things worked in this rural farm community, down near the river's edge that eventually included a contradictory oasis of wealth and privilege.

Many years before, when Handi was just starting school, a big city developer had been taken with the scene of bucolic peacefulness, especially down at the bend where two rivers came together. He first built his own house and that brought others out from the city to enjoy the family's easy going country life. Eventually the man, who was a residential housing developer, started building large houses along the usually gently flowing rivers that met and flowed together west to the Mississippi. Bigger houses than anybody in that small town had ever seen.

Pursuant to their nuptials, Handi's talked about it but decided on no children. This was a good thing because Handiman, that's the way they both spelled it, now was impotent. Not a clinical diagnosis but they guessed this themselves and it made little difference in their relationship. Handiwoman especially did not seem to mind so life played out in an orderly, albeit uninspired way. If virtually every day you eat baloney sandwiches on Wonder Bread self-dosed with ample amounts of butter, yellow mustard, and white mayo there seems little else to think about and certainly no stress over decisions about what to eat.

Without fail, each working day he ate lunch sitting on a bench he came to believe, by rights, was his own. His wife would be off somewhere, at someone's big house on or near the river, working outside or in doing domestic chores for those who could afford to pay others to turn the soil, scrub their toilets or after Thanksgiving, if they were spending the holidays away from the big city, decorate their Christmas trees in the country.

The beginning years passed quickly, and suddenly one day, Handi's were celebrating their 15th wedding anniversary. Both were bashfully observant of this event, and one would have thought this was nothing more than a low-grade occasion in their low-grade lives. They were both nearing 40 years of age, childless, had rarely ever crossed the county line and never further than the state line in any direction. Along with most other humans on the planet, simple Handi homebodies treading water.

A flashing stoplight had been installed eight years ago but other than that not much changed. They went to church every Sunday, were unquestioning believers like the rest in their Godfearing rural congregation. When asked if he thought theology was a good thing, Handi just asked what the word "theology" was. Once a month Handiman drank the wine and bit the biscuit while the Mrs. declined.

While Handiman maintained a predictable schedule, his wife often did not. Sometimes, when her employers entertained, she worked late, arriving home after midnight. Out here in the rural counties she had become a reliable party service person who also did clean up. Years into it, some man friend of a woman she did most of her work for called her the Paddycake Dirt-Girl and it stuck. There were other names as well but generally saved for other times. She hated the shortened name Paddycake but had started the fight because she was jealous and didn't like the man from the beginning. Both Mr. and Mrs. Handi were comfortable with her working arrangement and the name issue was never discussed. Between husband and wife there was very little Handi conversation.

2.

The woman from the big city found Mrs. Handi through friends. In those earlier days Mrs. Handi, the woman working outside her home, was developing quite a reputation for herself. Handi women were not common, especially ones as versatile as Mrs. Handi. A hard worker, when pressed she could clean house, paint, garden, even decorate for holidays, even serve food and later, if requested clean up after guests departed.

She could do several things but was a terrible cook. If food required anything more than a poor replication of her mother's meatloaf and mashed potatoes, she was just awful. Usually scorched, even her gravy was terrible. Mrs. Handi, it seemed, had left her taste buds buried in the garden.

On a warm summer day at one of the grand summer residences, a city woman was visiting another of her kind. Handiwoman happened to be weeding in the nearby flowerbeds. Dressed in gay summer dresses and drinking full on southern iced tea with a wee touch of bourbon the two women chatted amicably on the veranda. Handiiwoman walked by pushing her wheelbarrow filled with tools and brush clippings but stopped when mistress asked to introduce the employee to her friend. The visitor had moved and now lived part time in an equally large nearby house on the river. The three spoke courteously but briefly and that seemed the end of it. Several days later, the woman to whom she had been introduced, called Handiwoman and asked if she could stop by her own home for a look at the troublesome roses that failed to reach their potential that season. Thus, began a long and unusual relationship.

Handiwoman would work and later play with and for Diva over the next 25 years.

3.

Until more recently, from Mr. Handi's point of view, minor changes in their married lives really didn't warrant serious thought. There seemed little need and this was too deep an exercise for him. Marriage was an institution created by God and, as far as men were concerned, intended to be worry free.

But now, like tiny particles of dust, odd bits and pieces of information had been falling onto the table of his life. At first, they went unnoticed until finally one day, through the dusty glaze in his brain there were enough of them for him write his own name with his finger. Something was going on he did not understand, he couldn't quite put his finger right on it, but situations were not aligning easily.

For the first time in years, or maybe forever, it occurred to him little things were bothering him. some things out of order giving him a wee bit of a headache. Whatever it was, ever so slightly things had shifted, changed and like any simple animal, whatever the cause it brought on creepy low-level stress, like a hinge that only seasonally starts to squeak.

In recent times Handiwoman was making a habit of arriving home late and when he thought about it, particularly over the past year or so. On some occasions one woman she worked for asked Handi's wife if she'd come to her home in the city and be paid do work there. He'd paid no attention at first but now it seemed more frequent. Driving into the city took over an hour and that seemed to him a long way away so sometimes she stayed overnight. In the past six months her stays were getting longer, sometimes more than just over night and a return late the following day.

Squinting his eyes, he was recalling for the third time, in the past two months his wife had been gone for over three days at a time. This wasn't right or certainly not usual, and she'd said little to nothing about what she'd been doing. Not a curious man by nature, at the beginning "Doctor" Handi didn't ask Mrs. Handi what was going on. That was then but now, staying in the city three days in a row changed things. Maybe it was time to find out why.

Undefined disturbing feelings were gnawing at Handiman. With no volunteered explanations all this activity prompted greater concern. He only had a hunch, just a little one, but still a tiny bit troublesome or probably just curious.

For over ten years each had their own bedroom and since the door to hers was always closed, Handiman could not recall when he had seen the inside of hers. For some undefined reason he thought perhaps he might find an answer in there. He convinced himself he was not spying it was just curiosity so tomorrow after work he was going to go back to their home early and look in her room for a quick peek.

4.

The air was still, not a breath of wind and it had been that way when he got up this morning. He stopped for a moment to look out at what had once been a garden, but that was a long time ago. These days only an accidental flower or two struggled up through tall weeds and the grape arbor, now just a mass of black sticks from vines that died long ago. Why was it, he wondered, everybody else's garden his wife worked in was so pristine and theirs such a messy tangle of weeds? It had mostly always been this way, it never looked as if anybody cared and that went for outside in the front, and really, inside their ramshackle disorderly little house as well. Out there in the far back corner, their backyard was filled with rusted old riding lawn mowers, broken, discarded, and retrieved by his wife. She always said she would fix them one day and they could sell them, but she never did, and he didn't either. Inside, on the floor by their washing machine there were three broken fancy coffee machines from her client's homes. Mr. Handi thought they had so many button controls and small lights no sensible person, who just wanted a cup of coffee, would ever use them.

He fished in the side pocket of his droopy khaki shorts and pulled out a ring of keys. Letting himself in he walked the short distance from the back entry, past the old washer and dryer with rust-colored spots on the front and around the base, through the kitchen and into the living room.

The floor by Handiwoman's threadbare chair was strewn with backdated gardening magazines she brought home from her "client's" homes or sometimes just taken out of their garbage. Since cable arrived and they'd had to pay, neither of them watched television, and in fact they didn't have one that even worked. There were two stacked in the corner back by the washing machine, it was pretty cluttered there too. Instead, when she was home and while he sat expressionless listening to something in his ever-present ear buds, she just thumbed through magazines and tore out pages that lay on the floor scattered on the other side of her chair. Patches of threadbare carpeting were getting progressively smaller, and vacuuming had long been out of the question.

Handiman went to the right, into the hallway and stopped in front of his wife's bedroom door. Hers was the first and he paused, having second thoughts about entering her room. He knew she was not in there because her rusty little red truck was not outside in the drive, but he hesitated, nonetheless. Finally, tentatively reaching out he slowly turned the knob, almost expecting her to be waiting for him on the other side. It would not open. Thinking it stuck, he tried again but the knob turned only partially around and stopped. There was a small hole for an old-fashioned skeleton key below the doorknob, so he bent down to look more carefully. He could easily pick it; he'd done this before on other door locks like this. In the short dark hallway he still could not see the lock inside well enough.

Handiman straightened up wondering why this door would be so hard to open or maybe locked. What would be the point of locking it? They had no secrets from each other and if there was something of value why lock this door and not some other? He reached out turning the knob again this time jerked it hard. Still the door would not budge.

Why lock the door to her bedroom and not the house entry doors? He was the only one who locked the backdoor and no one had come through the front door for years, he thought they'd nailed it shut years ago. How long had she been locking her bedroom door, when was the last time he tried to open it?

Handiman returned to the kitchen and got a glass of water. Standing by the sink he was thinking and wondering, mulling over the idea, there was no reason for the locked bedroom. This was a problem and probably not all that serious, after all she went in and out of that room every day with no issues he was aware of. He would ask his wife about it tonight but then remembered she was in "the city" again with the diva. This is how they referred to Handiwoman's "client." Others called her that too but never to her face.

Handiman would have to wait until tomorrow. He was sure there was some easy explanation. There just had to be.

5.

Tomorrow came and went. Handiwoman called to say something had come up in the city and she would stay another night and return the following day. Through the previous night and all day, the locked or jammed door had eaten away at Handiman; he was not used to this and what had started as a smoldering ember was becoming a full-fledged fire.

He was replacing old windows on a widow's house along the river. It was hot again, the work monotonous and mindless. He had done this many times over the years, fixing windows in homes and this one was a regular. As each hour passed and with little else to think about, he became increasingly obsessed about the door. Finally, unable to wait any longer he picked up his tools and called it a day. By this time, it was only 30 minutes from his usual quitting time.

He drove home slowly, always very carefully because the local coppers enforced the town's tricky speeding laws. Tickets were an important source of cash; they didn't take credit cards. Cash came mostly from over the state line "Out of Towners." Easy prey and good revenue. It kept the property taxes low.

At home he turned onto the short, cracked cement two track drive that ended in front of his ancient garage doors. Dead grass between the concrete two track was black with oil spots and the old vertical double garage doors that hung crooked on rusted hinges no longer opened. For years, the garage had only been accessible through a side door that was never locked, Handi had long forgotten what might be in there.

As usual, he went in the back door that if the Mrs. had been the last to leave usually needed no key. Today it was locked, so pulling at the chain attached to his belt loop, many keys attached at the other end fell into his hand. Sorting through them and finding the one he wanted, he unlocked the back door and took slow purposeful steps inside. His intention was to give the bedroom door just one more try and he hoped this was all his mistake. But when he tried no such thing. Same result, the door into her bedroom would not open.

He went back to the kitchen and from a drawer beside the stove fished around to retrieve a small flashlight. Returning to the hallway, he got down on his knees and shined light into the dark keyhole. Deeper inside he saw what he had not seen before. Cleverly hidden, the reflection of a newer brass lockset showed the unmistakable line pattern of a modern Yale or Baldwin keyway. It had been disguised, set further in the keyhole so as not, he assumed, to raise suspicion. This quite cleverly prevented any cursory outside examination. Any other time Handiman would have admired the work, but not today.

He stayed crouching down in front of the door, looking with blank and confused amazement; he wasn't thinking, his brain had come to full stop. He just stared and finally, deciding he could not believe what he'd just seen, he shined the light again and looked more carefully this time. There it was the unmistakable brass zigzag line for modern key entry access.

With aching knees Handi stood up and looked down again at the doorknob and key plate. He had no idea what to make of this. There must be more, he knew that now. What might he expect to see behind this closed locked door now? Obviously, he was not supposed to look or see, but he was going to find out very soon. She was hiding something and that might explain why he had such odd feelings lately, but for the moment what was this hidden keyset all about? It would have taken some doing to disguise the lock, and cleverness too.

It was late afternoon and Handi had never been an excitable type, but this time was a real exception, so he went into the kitchen and opened a beer. It was the first of five he drank that night and three more than his usual self-imposed limit.

Later Handiman slept sleep of the dead, which was probably good, since it would be the last good night's sleep, he would have for a long time to come and maybe ever.

6.

She told him it was traffic. That's why she'd arrived after he had eaten. He was not hungry, but since he had not eaten anything that day, he forced himself to have something. With his wrapped sandwich still in the frig the frozen meatloaf TV dinner would be just fine.

Hearing her drive in and the truck door slam shut, he'd remained seated in his chair. He didn't know what he was going to do, how the subject would come up much less what kind, if any, explanation could possibly be made. The only thing he did know, or believed, she was protecting something. As he thought about it, he knew it was important to both of them, so he persuaded himself this would not be a difficult conversation.

The biggest question was, what did they own that was so valuable, and he could think of nothing. Certainly, nothing even a B&E druggie would find worth stealing for money. They were simple people with simple things. They lived in a simple town with other simple people, and he could only remember once in the past year or so when a house had been broken into down the street. The only thing taken had been an ancient HiFi most likely worth nothing.

She came in and dropped an overnight bag on the floor next to her chair. He glanced at it and noticed it was new. He asked and she told him it was a gift for a job well done over the past few days. She went to the kitchen and from the refrigerator took a bottle of flavored iced tea. It was still quite warm out and very humid inside. The old fan in the corner groaned occasionally making an effort to rotate and grind through its changing directional routine. Occasionally it stopped completely and then inexplicably resumed.

He asked how the job and gone, and she told him about planters that were planted and miscellaneous chores she was involved in, like beginning to repaint one of the three bathrooms which she would complete next week. Another trip to the city. Because he had never been there, he didn't know there were no such things as planters at or in the city apartment and only one guest room.

Her husband appeared to be listening but really thinking how to bring up the subject of the bedroom door. While he did, he noticed her fingernails were clean and seemed to have a gloss to them. At last, he said, "I was going to oil the hinges on the bathroom door this morning. While I was at it, I decided that it had been a long time since that had been done, so I'd do them all."

Handiwoman was calm but interrupted and said, "I thought we agreed I would do everything inside and you would handle the outside. Wasn't that our agreement a long time ago?" She was pleasant but there was a slight edge to the sound of it.

"I guess so," he said, "but I forgot. Anyway, when I got to your bedroom door, I couldn't open it. How do you get it open, is there something wrong with that door? I tried jiggling it but couldn't seem to get it to budge." There, he had said it, and it sounded to him like it was quite natural. He waited.

"No, you just have to lift the door handle while you turn the knob. I'll take care of it. Don't worry I'll take care of it tomorrow." She passed it off so easily, as if it were nothing, but there was firmness in her voice.

"Oh, guess I didn't think of that," he said as pleasantly as he himself could manage.

Handiwoman picked up her new overnight bag and quickly disappeared down the dark hall. There was a pause and after a moment went into her room for the night. He heard the door close, and her husband sat in his chair for another hour staring at nothing in particular. In total confusion, he was thinking hard.

7.

Handiman had not forgotten, and try as he may, he could not decide how to raise the issue again. Handiwoman could get really angry when she wanted to so if he could avoid it this was something Handi did not want to get involved in. She'd never given him the yank, but he had seen her do it to others and it was blistering when she did.

Any form of excitement, anything out of the ordinary assumed larger proportions than it might have for others. As such things always do, the unexplained locked door mystery grew and started to undermine confidences. Each of them grew increasingly wary of the other and it seemed they were watching for some sign that might suggest something not just amiss but seriously wrong. The mystery continued with escalating animosity.

Although he knew nothing of it, the following day, after he had asked about the door, she watched him leave for his window renovation project. She waited a full half hour and then hurriedly began carrying packed bags and boxes to her little truck. When it was full, she carefully relocked the door to her bedroom and left. In the evening, when she returned the truck bed was empty, and that afternoon the newer hidden locking mechanism had been replaced with the old one. She made quite a show of displaying the new bookshelf inside her room. It had been bought that afternoon and she, of course, assembled it herself.

There had been little comment from Mr. Handi.

8.

On the evening of "show the shelves" Handi's enjoyed perhaps the most pleasant dinner they had ever shared together. If not ever then maybe as far back as they could remember. They had grilled pork chops cooked on their small charcoal grill set on parched ground outside the back door. After replacing the lock, Handiwoman grocery shopped late that afternoon and bought the grill at Walgreen's. It was on sale. Baked potatoes, broccoli, and even small dinner rolls. Both ate with surprising animation and toasted twice with a sparkling fruit wine that would have been far too sweet for most wine drinker's tastes.

It was quite exceptional, they talked about what they were doing, and once Mr. Handi thought the Mrs. had slipped, contradicting herself when describing the project in the city. No matter, they both had more wine than they were accustomed to, and he thought they were getting a little silly. She knew they were, just as planned.

After dinner Mrs. Handi suggested they forget the dishes and take a look in his room where she said there was a surprise waiting. As they passed down the hall Mr. noticed her door ajar which was unusual if not unprecedented. He quickly peeked in to see her bed neatly made up and bedside table lamp casting a homey glow. It could have been romantic.

They entered his room and lying on the bed was a pair of pajamas. Not regular pajamas but dark blue satin top and matching bottoms. If he had seen them in pictures, he did not remember but knew he'd never seen ones like this in real life. His first reaction was they must have been hers but that was quickly dispelled when she said she would be back "when he was *ready*."

Mr. Handi had limited imagination for most things, a genetic and environmental shared condition in the area that some attributed to bad water. If he thought about it, which he didn't, to get the job done in the quickest and most efficient way possible, he would have concluded the missionary position was best, ordained, he was told, and prescribed by God "himself." In his brief analysis, to achieve the greatest likelihood of success, "missionary" seemed practical and poetically reasonable. However, in this instance his "costume" it seemed, was intended for something other than what Our Lord intended, and it mattered not since long ago, with evidence he had concluded he'd only shoot dribbling blanks. Now overcome by what any other time he might consider "unclean thoughts", he would not be analyzing options this night.

Mrs. reappeared in a cotton robe and matching furry pink slippers. The robe hung open, and he saw a short slinky putty colored nightgown beneath. Mr. felt a bit awkward so just rubbed his hands together and with a big smile on his face said, "oh boy." He had seen these moves in a movie once. Maybe it was too much wine, but he could not recall anything like this in years or maybe ever, so… not for us to reason why but for us to…ah… do… ah… and lie.

It did not last long. Mrs. Handi immediately took charge and Mr. thought this was because she was drunk, so it amused him and "inflamed" his rare desire for her. Mrs. was on top taking the lead and would ride this pony all the way to the finish line. When they finished the initial stages, which was pretty quick, she planned for him to go on to the winners' circle by himself. She, job done, would be tired and off to bed.

But that's not quite the way it went. Despite her plans and to the contrary she rode that pony that surprisingly had become a wild horse, as long as she could, until they were both completely exhausted. Finally, a bit bowlegged she wordlessly dismounted and hobbled out the door before Handi could say good night.

9.

If the idea was to distract him from his suspicions, it worked. A few days later, when he remembered to again inspect the door lock, he found the hidden keyway empty inside, it was just a dark old empty place for a regular ancient key that had been lost long ago. Now it seemed the matter had come to a close and all was again right with the world. He could forget all about it and just wait, saving his blue satin PJs for next time with grilled pork chops and broccoli.

A week went by and then a month. Handiman, despite his efforts had not forgotten but decided to not ever raise the door issue again. Handiwoman could get very aggressive when she wanted to, not yell or scream, but Mamba snake deadly. Handi just wanted to remember PJ night at the ranch.

Their marriage was more like an arrangement. If sex was any measure of such relationships, then theirs was a low two or maybe one on a ten-point scale. PJ night had saved it from going into negative numbers. She was good, he was bad, but when they were trying, she was better than him. Neither complained nor even brought the subject up in all the years he could remember. Two very lowball people living out a sexless lowball life.

As was typical in their part of the country, months proceeded with monotonous unoriginal sameness. The norm, summer came and started to go, autumn was coming, harsh winter would follow. Diva had been to her country home more often than usual that year. Her house by the river was at the end of a long drive, so unless a fisherman saw activity from the water, other than Paddycake and sometimes the housekeeper, no one really knew when she was in residence. Not that they really cared, her now infrequent appearances at parties, especially in the city, and other events came and went, forgotten with increasingly passive disinterest. Occasional gossip was the final social *coup de grace;* like snakes hunting rats in the dark, deadly old lures of scintillating gossip came and went. There were always other subjects to prey upon.

The gardener, Mrs. Handi, continued with her seasonal attentions. If one were looking outside the small town, it would seem Diva's gardens got more attention than most others nearby.

Diva had never been a home entertainer, at least socially. Throughout the year in earlier times, she attended other people's dinners and events with rare reciprocations. Once a year she paid off her social obligations with a season of invitations sent to chosen members from selected groups, each designed to even the score. For simplicity's sake the same dinner each one, and its time every year at her private dining club in the city. Table settings grew smaller, but pretending everything was just as it had always been Diva said nothing and soldiered on. Rather like pretending not to smell a fart somewhere nearby. She seemed not to have noticed her invited guests' declined invitations and increased unavailability. Most had even stopped RSVP-ing which was a cultural taboo. Further confirmation of Diva's irrelevancy.

Of course a few, who still needed the occasional overnight use of her city home accepted invitations with feigned grace and afterward out of earshot, venomous stories. On one occasion, visitors to the city apartment helped themselves to a few of Diva's toys. Apparently, she had forgotten to lock a door, so the oldsters took a night-time ride on the fantasy train. Too old for such things they never did reach their intended destination but still, just traveling was more excitement than they had seen and done in years. The only reason this came to light was the older fellow suffered a mild heart attack that brought EMT's to come rushing. Terrified wife, having forgotten to re-hide 'em, the heart-busting evidence had lain all over the bedroom. Yes, ambulance people talk, and the Sunday paper ran a vaguely disguised story with reference to the thinly undisclosed address. It included a health warning of caution to oldsters about things that giggle, jiggle, and go squirm in the night.

There were repercussions from the newspaper story. Connections made, even with the address deleted pieces were put together into what easily morphed into a juicy diva sex-bending story. A few got the cautionary message to elders, as well as its source, and some others just howled.

By Christmas and with Diva seen less in the city, rumors were circulating she suffered from some incurable disease. Some said it was an STD and gossip "spreaders," by some so old they assumed it could only be syphilis or crabs. For more contemporary minded opinionators AIDS was the outside limit of older folks' understanding.

After the holidays that year, a previously close friend of Diva's said she had recently been institutionalized by her son. A few had long known of her "never kiss the cold sore king son" who carried un-named STD blistering baggage of his own. To confirm, there was the story of an irate father allegedly throwing Ne'er-do-well bodily out of his home, over the protestations of his naive weeping daughter. It made for another, this time Valentine's Day, splash. Rumor and friends verified daughter got STD anyway, and there was some reported financial settlement offered to keep the matter quiet or *from spreading*. Just who gave and who received was to remain a secret.

Didn't work.

In all those previous years, people seemed not to notice, or mind, that Diva had long been a social mooch. Her leafy gifts of orchids, for a long time covered this reality quite nicely and she continued to be recognized by the more simple minded for her generosity. Bribes can, without a doubt, keep one active on the party circuit, but the Diva joke making the rounds was, "How does a mooch, mooch from a mooch"? The answer, with laughs was, "Pretty diva mooch." These days, and after all the talk absences, there was little to mooch on so options, with examples, were shriveling up faster than her friend's aging genitals.

She still bought and paid for tickets to benefits staged by various organizations for the Hot to Trots. This act of giving money to attend organizational functions was, in effect, the most basic form of payment for other unlisted dues, sometimes referred to as assessments; however, eventually even this no longer carried the intended weight. In more recent times if she dared to show at all, she was usually late and ,when overhearing too many whispers, departed early. If it was dinner and with no man to accompany her, she was seated in the last empty seat at the widows and divorcees table over in the corner. Picking at their food the women would sit, wordlessly waiting for everyone finish their food so the singles could get up again and "mix." Diva was becoming the Done For Donna. The increasingly haggard, soon to disappear Grand Ma-ma of Britannia coined the term for her friend at one of the Hajj planning sessions, aka gabfest in New York. Diva, where Diva, of course, had not attended nor was she asked, hence the appointment and appearance with a shrink.

Long fearing she would commit some unforgivable sin of social disgrace, Diva left personal city party planning to professional felicitation and the ambiance of her clubs. But at last and in some desperation, to make up for lost time and fealty, she'd gather city friends out in the country for a sunny summer riverside soiree. There was however an exception to entertainment rules; she would organize a birthday party for herself. It was a biggy, a decade birthday she felt worthy of attention and perhaps, if she were lucky, redemption. Add to this a few more accumulated gifted collectables and she would be back to the good old days. Believe it, she would lick her fingers and be a come-back-kid and maybe something even better.

Regrettably, but perhaps predictably, few of the "official" 108 invitees responded or attended. Those who did were of the class C and D farm club variety, but hey! they filled seats, ate the food, and sucked up expensive liquor and first-class wine. In the trade these guests were known as "filler fellers."

All was well until, headed to the Porta Potty with monogramed paper towelettes, a geriatric guest tripped, fell, split her head on the front step and Diva panicked. Blood, moans, tears and initially a presumed heart attack, oh Christ! a death.

Party went to bloody hell. 911 called, ambulances plural from near and next county arrived. So far, the only thing missing was the not-yet-coroner. Cops rushed in a few minutes too late and one of them smelled *Eau De Cologne d'Cannabis,* with hinted undertones of (strike that) heavy overtones of much Joy and Shalimar.

Bumbling local coppers called the State Fuzz for a Diva level society bust. In spite of the speed ticket revenue 'dah pole-eees' hated big city swells and, despite the lady's injury while EMTs did what they do, the lady was not dead and the pistol packin' local native cops were all shits and giggles. Gottcha smiles accompanied rolling eyes and resentful legal beagles, ready to even the score, quasi-professionals smelled more than blood on the pavement. Really, an old folks bust was just too much to hope for on a slow Saturday night down by the river. Best to get out the fresher jail cell linens, then call TV and the papers.

The cops had been to Diva's many times and knew the history. While taking her payola, they particularly disliked Diva for all the nuisance calls and dry runs they had to make to the annoying tax-paying citizen. Her complaints were treated with a wink and a nod and generally regarded as a first-class pain in the ass from the bitch down the highway, across the bridge and back up the other side on the north side of the river de-looooxah. Hence response times tended to be slow.

Diva had a rap sheet down at the cop shop. They were particularly irritated about the near fatal accident Diva caused some months ago, when she threatened them about reporting it as her fault. They did report it that way and one of the victims was permanently disabled. Diva claimed it was all their fault (driver and cops) and she was being persecuted. Screw the lady who was badly injured, it was Diva who was gravely injured, it hurt her feelings and not that she much cared, it increased her insurance. The woman she hit, aka victim, definitely didn't get a "get well soon" diva brand orchid plant.

Back at party central, hemp smoke that birthday night actually came from the closest neighbors who also despised Diva and her pals. With no parents in sight at the vacation house that weekend, the older kids with a whoop 'em up of their own next door decided to haunt the birthday party. When police arrived, they took up the opportunity with a vengeance. Thinking quickly and recognizing the confusion, some pretended to be weed-smoking guests or older invited children of aged legitimate guests. In the bushes where fast-thinking younger people huddled over a smudge pot, they erected a smoker that, with a squeeze please bellows breeze, blew pot smoke into the crowd. It was all just rich.

This party bummer was too good to pass up for the, proving quite capable, "let's get even" neighbors. Since there were no ashtrays, smoldering joint butts were surreptitiously left on dinner plates, in saucers and soggy at the bottom of not quite finished wine glasses . A short distance away upwind, another hard at work kid was pumping out clouds of telltale MaryJane fog using a bee smoker.

With sirens and flashing colored lights reflected all around, drama of two ambulances and more arriving coppers the real guests panicked like pigs at the slaughterhouse with a welcome sign over the door and smell of barbeque. The narrow driveway down to the house at river edge was blocked with police and medical emergency vehicles so oldsters couldn't leave. With a firetruck last to arrive, now skidded crosswise completely blocking the narrow one lane drive, nobody could leave, not even the cops and the ambulance with the injured lady drove around through the trees and got stuck. I kid you not!

Like shooting fish in a barrel and the cops, who were sometime robbers, knew it. Names were taken; real and false ID's presented, accepted and collected without question. A few drivers' licenses deftly pulled from table orphaned purses and other swapped identities in the moment and later created greater confusion. Pandemonium continued and young uninvited neighbors could hardly contain themselves.

Movie worthy, at the direction of Diva's completely stoned son, and throughout, as if they were playing the last dance on the Titanic, the small combo band periodically struck up some oldy music for those who felt like dancing.

Much later with firetruck gone, up the road, waiting to leave, a few 'officers' with beers in hand were seen talking to the clamorous young people. Everybody having a great time with laughter heard all the way back down to the riverbank.

But it wasn't over. Getting that far out of town, TV was too late, but the speeding press got hold of it. The party assumed enormous proportions on a slow rural weekend news night. Diva again in the news, all the way to the big city. As if she needed more, this time stop the presses, Diva's stock took a deeper nosedive. With first person elaborations lasting for days, it was the newest juicy scandal in the city, and why not, this one a real Academy Awarder. Sister of the grossly unpopular governor, himself a 'D' Class player and later jailed, the uninvited guest was present. She used what turned out to be a false ID belonging to some old man who was still AWOL. He, presumed dead, next morning high tailed it early out to Arizona and later found by police quite mimosa disoriented in some stranger's hot tub. C'est la vie.

The party became legendary. If nothing else, Diva had been entertaining that evening. It became a badge of honor for a few "low level swells" who had not attended, to falsely claim having been present at the bawdy birthday party. And, of course, they added more fuel to the fire, inflating stories even further. Like "does a bear shit in the woods. No, only a few oldies with bad bowels."

More pay-backlash to Diva. Somebody later said there was food poisoning, requiring old guests to stay home seated on their potties for days. Ya know, given their age it was probably just nerves. Better and better when later the caterer went broke and sued for libel.

And a postscript: Ne'er-do-well, who all thought loathsome, took perhaps the biggest fall. Some said it was all caused and started by the kid pimp and his arrogance for having given the injured old lady more than a few sample tokes. She got a seven-stitch splitting headache for her party favor gift. According to sources, he'd been party favor gifting little cellophane wrapped white-powder samples that evening. Only Mommy's money kept him out of the slammer, but it was big money and shortly afterward two brand new, extravagantly over equipped local police cruisers appeared on the road. All just too funny for words, and the media, God bless 'em, performed admirably.

And a follow up: That following Friday at the ritual Friday night country club fried and refried again fish dinner, they discussed supposedly authentic scorecards that showed 175 guests invited and, at last best guess fewer than fifty accepted or showed up. Before the actual Diva event start time, one of her *friends* had given a pre-game party for selected elder invitees over at their place, directly opposite on the south side of the river. With a few drinks under their copious belts, "the wrinkles" noting the hour advancing toward bedtime, 7:30 PM and skipping the birthday action, just went home from there. Diva really was not all that interesting anyway and God knows, with that caterer, they all knew the hors d' oeuvres by heart, just samo samo.

It was roundly reported there were twenty-eight empty seats at the dinner tables set for eighty-five, and even with a small dance band, nobody apparently felt jovial or limber enough to dance for the Diva. Sometimes, at these affairs the odor of Extra Strength Balm BenGay overpowered colloquiums of competing perfumes. Another witness confirmed Diva legend had been created but ones that followed were not so funny.

In short, Diva's birthday party was a disaster. Her expensive dress and new jewelry for naught. The "B" teams never made it and never would. She went into hiding again, this time deeper than before and it was again rumored, after 25 years, she, in shame and disgrace, was going to leave her house, the state and maybe the country if another one would take her. The days of wine and roses were gone forever. Diva was a goner. The Done For Diva.

But not quite yet.

Still more unforgettables. Other Diva party stories were also just too good to forget. "River lore" added and regularly told at many a Friday night "Club" fish dinner, comedy central, frequently at Diva's expense.

A few old timers could still get a laugh when recounting an oldie great one, usually with embellishments. The time she and her former husband threw a party for the alumni of a well-known private eastern school. They desperately wanted their son to attend, so she convinced her husband letters of recommendation could be bought with chits from regional social notables. Diva's assured success scheme would fix the game by offering these letters of recommendation in support of sonny boy's acceptance. All they needed to do was *buy* an impressive party. Shoot the moon with distinguished alumni guests then follow up afterward with requests for "just a little letter favor."

For a mere bracelet, a close friend had given her an alumni roster and with it, Diva went to work on a guest list.

The big day arrived; many well knowns were invited to the impressive, alleged, historical farm town and elegant river house. All invitees were bunker busters from the city but by not adding RSVP to the invitation the implication was, of course, many would attend the regional special event of the summer. In their world, attending summer lawn parties were for frocks with fops. That day in late-June the weather was perfect, well-known out from the city uptown caterer sublime and expensive, as was the champagne and, of course, the table floral arrangements. Intending others recognize it, waiters were instructed by the diva, how to serve the carefully white linen-wrapped champagne with front facing label casually but recognizably exposed.

Diva, son, and father anxiously awaited their guests. The start time arrived then passed, in anticipation and with increasing anxiety Diva, father and son paced the veranda. Husband started to criticize Diva, sure she had screwed up the dates. This was not an altogether unfounded accusation and it turned ugly. In his preppy seersucker jacket and spreading dark wet under arm stains, Ne'er-do-well, whose candidacy was at stake, started to look like a cowpoke on roundup day. Mommy sent him inside to change his sports jacket, this time preferably something darker.

An hour after the grand lawn party was to begin, and no guests yet present, a dark much older model sedan slowly and silently coasted down the hill, into the circular drive and partway around off onto the grass. As the car slowly drifted past the hosts, the driver was seen frantically gripping the steering wheel while jerking to apparently pump and stomp the floor brake pedals. The engine had died taking the ancient power brakes and steering with it, so the car slowly rolled off the pavers out onto the sloping, perfectly manicured lawn twice-mowed that morning. The car, thank God, stopped several feet further down the incline, four feet short of the still spring flooded river. Wearing their white gloves, not seen in these parts for over a century, uniformed local high school valet parking attendants swarmed over the car and all four doors sprung open like Jack in the Boxes. Extending their hands, the young local schoolboys assisted antique passengers out and then attempted to start and remove the automobile off the grass. No such immediate luck. A tow truck was called and while they waited one young man was overheard to say there was a foul, quite offensive odor coming from inside the vehicle.

Four guests there that day, that was all. Two old ladies, who according to the roster were, if you could believe it, "class of 0'nine." Graduated from the target school when it was a women's college, gentlemen not allowed. Neither woman could remember the other woman, or frankly, the name of the school back in those days. One man, the one who at everyone's peril had driven the car, thought he did recall his own graduation from a nearby school but not its name either. With his head bobbing up and down like one of those dashboard neck spring hula dolls, he was fussed and obsessed by not being able to figure out how Diva got his name for "the lawn party." With, as yet no offer from the host he asked for scotch, saying they did not allow it at the Presbyterian home where he lived by himself. He explained to all he was still hunting for the right "girl."

The other smaller man it seemed was not a graduate of anything where or what. It was unclear who, what or where he was about. The car backseat passenger, who until then had not spoken, reported the stowaway had repeatedly passed gas in the tightly enclosed car, all the way from wherever it was they came from, she could not recall. As far as anybody knew, he just got in the car somewhere when the driver stopped somewhere and got out to tend to his persistent bladder issues. Twice, with no rest room or area in sight, he just barely made it out behind the car to piss himself. From several feet away, behind a tree this matter evidently was again continuing, even with a light breeze the recognizable pungent odor was noticeable. To some credit, he had apparently learned long ago that old men should not wear khaki pants.

Documentation of this event came reliably from a home across the river. Reports from neighbors who gleefully watched out of their windows, and catering people who, after no tips, later ratted out yet another Tale Of The Diva.

The caterer's contract employees for whom Diva was, so to speak, their bread and butter are a talkative group who, to off-set low wages, derive some job satisfaction telling stories of the swells. For those who write gossipy trash for a living, caterers are a great source. Moral here is: Never trust your caterer… never. As for your neighbors, either buy them out or burn 'em out.

Suffice it to say the effort to buy letters of recommendation was easily sniffed and snuffed. However, a substantial donation to the college building fund did the trick and to his mother's repeatedly spoken satisfaction, sonny boy attended. Perhaps his only credit in life, Ne'er-do-well actually did finish. As of this writing it appears to be the only thing he ever finished with verifiable success.

P.S. Diva was so thrilled by his graduation that, in later years, she reminded anyone who would listen that she too had graduated from this school but back when it was "just for girls." Another sweet thing mother/son shared. Everyone swallowed that one until a friend in her group did a little fact checking and discovered the fraudulent claim, confirmed and reported by the institution itself.

10.

The slip fell out as "Handi" reached down and picked up the empty package, so he reached again to pick up the small-folded piece of paper. He opened it and quickly read what had presumably been inside. The contents obviously gone but not a packing slip from Amazon. He dropped the box and re-read the paper. His jaw dropped again when he saw the addressee was his wife and the address a post office box he'd never seen before. It was in a small town close by, a short 15-minute drive.

The receipt listed toys used for sex. On the first line of listed items: "For Your Pleasure and Your Playmate's." The names of more items were lurid and ridiculous but not descriptive enough for him to understand what they essentially did or how they did it. He read on, "Make her scream for more," and "All Night Double Dildo for You and Your Girl Friend." Actually, not quite, he was confused by "double." What he thought he did not get was what a "double-ender for pegging" was, how it would or could be used, and by whom unless it had a hole though it and you could use it to siphon gas for a lawn mower. Unfortunately, Mr. Handi could not appreciate the humor of his own joke, nor did he have a lawn mower. "The Jiggler," seemed self-explanatory but "Premium Seven Speed Silver Bullet with Flavored Sensitizing Jell" again was not. Nor the as promised added "gift" of a Jeweled Tapered Back Door Stopper aka "Plug."

Handi was used to more specific technical descriptions at The Home Depot. Plug, something like what might be used to presumably keep the screened back door open. *With your fingers slide the silver washer along the shaft until it hits the bump at the end. Rock back and forth to ensure it is well seated then gently push it further to ensure the entry door stays open.*

With all this and a confused mind he went into the house, left the box open on the kitchen table with the receipt conspicuously displayed. He walked down the hall and finding it locked with his new but unused skeleton key entered his wife's room. He searched it thoroughly this time. Finding nothing to confirm or deny his renewed suspicions he went into the living room sat down and waited for Mrs. Handi to arrive. The box on the table a reminder he had been in a somewhat similar situation months ago... waiting for his wife to come home and make explanations. Back then, he'd asked a friend on the local police force for help on how to pick locks or get a skeleton key to fit places where he was working, if the owner was far away and unreachable.

She was not late this evening. From the back door he heard the screen door with broken hydraulic closer slam behind her. She paused in the kitchen and then after a few moments appeared in the living room holding the box from the kitchen table in one hand and paper in the other. Efficacious and with acting lessons from her friend she was a model of composure.

"What is this?" She asked in her innocent little girl voice. He simply said, "That is what I was going to ask you. It was on the ground right where you parked your truck last night."

She was quick and she was smart. Ignoring the shipping slip she rushed on, "I don't have any idea, I've never seen this before. You know these

Internet companies often send the wrong things to the wrong people. Diva gets them all the time and has to send them back. It's really a pain."

"Oh," was his only reply, drawn out and slow in coming. He could think of nothing else to say. Handi was not dim witted, he was just dim.

Then he added, "What do you think happened to what was inside?"

She shrugged, pretended not to read the paper, and wadded it up. "I have no idea and really, who cares." Without another word she quickly disappeared into her bedroom and closed the door hoping there would be no further discussion about the Post Office box address.

The next morning, he asked her if she was going to work at Diva's all day. She told him yes and when they finished their coffee in silence, she left for work. Long ago they had abandoned the idea of a good-bye kiss or best wishes for each other's day.

The Mrs. backed out and went gone, followed by Mr. who did the same but after a block he turned right to drive along the south side of the river and his current handyman job. The 25 MPH drive would take him 15 minutes. As he drove, he decided on a plan. Mrs. Handi's explanation for the box the previous evening had not satisfied him.

11.

At noontime Mr. Handi put his tools in the toolbox, got into his truck and drove off. No baloney sandwich on the bench today, he headed to the diva's home where his wife said she was working. He wasn't 100 percent positive, but he strongly suspected that at least some answers were there. One was that Diva had asked Mrs. Handi to receive mail for her or even more likely, perhaps on behalf of her son.

Approaching Diva's house, he turned into the driveway just ahead of hers. He knew the owner of this home and knew this time of year they were only here on weekends. It was Wednesday so he would be alone. Should anybody ask, he would just say he was there to look at a repair job.

Driving slowly, he turned left and parked out of sight behind the neighbor's three-car garage. He got out and walked over to the edge of the hill that looked down onto Diva's house and out to the river. He saw his wife's little truck parked in the place where he had seen it before. Suddenly he heard doors slamming and a car starting. Diva's car backed further away from the space in front of her clothing-packed garage. He could see Diva behind the wheel and in the bright midday sun, squinting his eyes to look more carefully, he saw his wife in the passenger seat.

Diva backed around then putting the car into drive slowly drove up the hill then a hard right around the curve toward the main road. From where he stood, he knew they could not have seen him.

Mr. ran back to his truck and quickly got underway. He would follow them and continue his surveillance from a distance. One might have thought he believed this a thrilling adventure, but he did not, he was angry, anxious, and apprehensive. Probably this was just a run to the nursery to buy more plants, but he was committed to this plan of observation for as long as it took. He would track her every move until satisfied he had answers to questions that continued to build and keep him up nights. The dim light of Handi mental abilities was growing brighter.

He slowed well before the end of the road behind him leading down to other homes along the river. Looking left through the trees he saw Diva's car ahead and waited for her to drive onto the main river road. If she passed in front of him, he would follow and go right, if not he knew they could only go left. After pausing for a few moments, he did not see her car so drove forward and turned left going even slower so as not to be recognized. If he were discovered he had his clipboard and, "What a coincidence seeing you, I'm visiting what I hope is a potential job out here."

Ahead he watched them come to a stop at the main river road then drive straight across to the other side and up the hill. This was odd since off in that direction there was nothing he could think of that might interest them. The nursery was to the left toward town.

He crossed and fell further back as they sped up and then ahead turned right. He knew this road and for a few miles there were no cross streets that could lead back to the river. He continued to be cautious. Cresting the hill, he saw them about a half mile ahead, they turned onto a street he knew led only to houses on a cul-d-sac. There would be no other way out that he knew of, but it had been a long time since he'd been out here. Handi knew practically every street in the area, and this made no sense at all. Maybe they were visiting one of Diva's friends.

Driving on a bit further, past where they turned right, he pulled left into a county park. The gates were open, and he drove to the back where, relatively unseen, he could look out onto the road and down a bit to see Diva's turn. Shutting off the ignition he watched and waited. He waited for nearly an hour thinking, increasingly persuaded they must be seeing one of Diva's friends. His patience wearing thin, another hour went by. Finally he decided to go have a look. Back up the road a short way, left turn, then quickly into the cul-d-sac. If they saw him, he had no idea what he would say to explain his presence other than use the clipboard, but by this time he was more curious than worried about discovery. Driving into the cul-de-sac turnaround area, Diva's car was nowhere to be seen. There were only six houses around the circle with a wooded circle in the center, Diva's car was not parked in any driveway he could see or on the street in front of any of them.

He drove around the circle again, and this time saw an unobtrusive low hanging chain. It was pulled across a dirt drive running alongside one of the adjoining well-spaced homes, with trees and underbrush on the other. Prohibiting entry, on the right side a heavy chain was fastened and locked to a plain steel post. He looked up the road, past the chain but this time of year there were too many leaves on the trees and in the brush to see what might lay beyond where the drive seemed to curve off to the right. He could only conclude this must be where they might have gone since there were well used tire tracks on the other side of the locked chain. It was the only explanation. But why, and why would it be now locked after them if that is where they went? He got out of his truck to have a better look.

He was about to step over the chain when a UPS truck drove into the cul-de-sac circle and parked in front of one of the houses. The driver got out carrying a large package and went up to the door of the home. He rang the doorbell and after a few moments it was opened. Mr. Handi could not hear what was said but more importantly, when a woman opened the door, realized he may have been seen standing near the chained drive entry.

He was nervous but walking normally got in his truck and was out on the road before the UPS truck. He turned right on to the main road and drove past the park entrance. Perhaps thirty yards further he noticed a driveway on the right, headed back, more or less, in the direction of the cul-de-sac. What lay further back was completely obscured by trees, but he knew this driveway, it led to the house of an old school friend. But that was a long time ago, he wondered if anybody he knew still lived there.

Odd he thought, such a coincidence with the road back in the cul-de-sac and this driveway in the front. Away from the road this drive also had a chain across it with a sign forbidding access. Someday soon, he should come back and have another look. But not today, something was very curious about this, and he needed time to think.

12.

"Someday soon" came more quickly than Mr. aka Dr. Handi expected. After following Diva's car Handi had tossed all that night, struggling, wondering about the driveway off the cul-de-sac, speculating about whether it had anything to do with his old friend's house across the road just beyond the park. This annoyed him so much the next morning, just after five, in the dark he got up, dressed quietly and slipped out the back door. He was certain his wife had not heard him leave. She often slept late, and it was not unusual for him to have left for work well before she did. That is why he sometimes parked out in the street.

After following his wife and the diva he had gone back and worked late then arrived home after his wife. Last night he had done the same, so fortunately, now his truck was in the front position on the two-track driveway. She was already in bed, and he had not even seen her, which was probably a good thing for them both.

At this early hour there were virtually no cars on the road. He drove first to the driveway that led into the friend's house. The chain across the driveway was several yards back from the road and relatively unseen so he backed in and parked his truck. Debris covered the drive; it was clear nobody had driven in here for quite some time. No one would pay any attention to his parked old truck, and if they did would probably assume it had malfunctioned the night before. The road was rather narrow, so the owner most likely would have rolled or pushed it into this safer location.

He got out and after locking the truck doors, stepped over the chain to walk further up the curved driveway. Given the hour and no one around he didn't worry about being seen. He rounded the last bend and looked toward the front door. The driveway was empty, suggesting to him the house was vacant. Further confirmation were dried leaves piled up around and against the front door. Walking closer to the house he was surprised at how well the small yard had been kept up and even more about the size; he had not remembered the house being this large. He walked around the side of the house and lower down, off from the walk-out basement door, he saw a driveway curving into the woods. It headed away from the house, opposite direction and he thought from where he had just come, it could only go to the cul-d-sac. He had not recalled this means of entry but since it had been several years, perhaps there had been additions, or he had forgotten. To look at the back area from a different vantage point he continued walking and rounded the corner of the house again. He remembered some of it now, the house overlooked a sloping, heavily wooded area with thick ground brush and tree cover that, for practical purposes was nearly impenetrable. At this early hour, the woods were still very dark and gave the impression this house was isolated. Close to town, but even after all these years no other houses or lights would be visible.

From where he stood, he saw it and was stunned. There below him in the dark sat Diva's car, in a cleared area large enough for at least two maybe three cars, maybe even four. The drive into it, he was now pretty certain, came and went to the cul-de-sac where a chain would prohibit any unannounced newcomers from entering. But why? The drive he had walked in on came from the north, this property now had ways in and out from opposite directions. Now he was positive it wasn't that way years before. With the car here, Diva must be inside the house, but why? From where he stood all the lights were out. What could she be doing here at this hour? The building was well cared for, grounds maintained, but he could still not imagine why here? So many "whys", something was very wrong with this picture. If one entered the usual way, near the park, cars might be seen. This way, from the cul-de-sac they were hidden and that would make it appear as if no one was here at all. This didn't make sense.

In the stillness of early morning a light came on briefly, he faintly heard a toilet flush then the light went off. Handi turned and was suddenly struck with the idea he might be spotted, police called. Dawn was a sullen grey turning to bilious yellow but despite the early morning light, under the trees it was still quite dark.

Running for the deeper woods, knowing if he were to get back to his truck and not spotted he'd have to go first in the opposite direction and make a wide circle around to the highway and hurry home. For the moment, he could not risk anything other than staying invisible to Diva or whoever was inside the house. If asked by authorities, there was no reasonable explanation for his voyeurism at that time in the morning.

He was well hidden in the brush for now so stopped, turned around and crouched down for several minutes in the darkened tree and brush cover. Moments later another light went on, then another. Now a blurred indistinct figure walked past on the other side of a semi-shear curtain. He decided there was time, so remained hidden until finally all the lights went out.

Moments later a door beside the large garage door below opened; he panicked, seeing his wife step out followed by Diva. He had believed his wife was at home, in her bed asleep. Mrs. Handi got in the driver's side and Diva took the passengers' seat. The car started, backed up, turned around and slowly drove off heading for the cul-d-sac.

As soon as they were gone Handi ran for all he was worth. Taking the short cut, running up, around the house, along the drive and jumped in his truck. Headed back to his house hoping to beat Diva's car if that was where they were going, he drove like a fool. Handi took another route thinking it might be shorter and praying he would not be stopped by a cop.

He swerved around the last corner and pulled up behind his wife's truck. Jumping out he raced to the kitchen where he busied himself with an illusion of making early morning coffee.

A car stopped outside and within a minute or two Mrs. Handi walked in. With considerable ease, she casually said good morning. When he asked, she said she had been out with Diva on an early morning errand. Diva, she said, had picked her up some time ago. Walking down the hall to her room and without looking over her shoulder she said, "I knew you'd be asleep, and I didn't want to wake you."

The coffee was ready. His hand shaking he managed to pour himself a cup and sat down at the kitchen table. First the key, then the box with packing slip and now this. He knew she was lying and had not known his truck had been gone for some time. He prayed she hadn't heard the hot engine still ticking as it cooled. She said Diva was coming back to get her soon so his old truck in front was okay for today and overnight. They were headed off to the city.

Handi finished his coffee and went to his room and lay down on his bed, staring at the ceiling. Soon he was back asleep. When machines are overloaded, they just shut down.

13.

Over the next six months, Handi watched his wife and Diva at every opportunity. He learned everything he felt he needed to know. It had been tricky not leaving footprints when it snowed and without the foliage, he was fully exposed when approaching the house.

Easy at first, but as time went on Handi made it more complicated. He taught himself the art or skills of surveillance, surprised to find he was quite good at it. He kept careful notes, many of which were captions for photographs he initially took with his phone. Later he got more sophisticated, using small hidden wireless video cameras, and them some with microphones discreetly attached to glass panes of the windows.

Sounds had been the most disturbing, the words, the descriptions and dialogues were nothing short of shocking. Mind numbing when he heard his wife's demanding voice ordering Diva, it was as if they'd come from some unknown, otherworldly demonic presence. Her normally youthful voice actually dropped a few octaves. She was harsh at times and at others soft and flirtatious. Diva's, on the other hand, were nearly always little girl-like, speaking in a plaintive little girl voice. Although at first, he thought it disgusting, her desire to obey was understood and gradually accepted by him as something she liked, wanted, and at times begged for. It was clear she enjoyed this role of obedience but in the beginning, it seemed like a rehearsed drama. He could not believe it was for real, it had to be play-acting, they were rehearsing something; after all, even he knew Diva said she was an actor. In the beginning he wanted, or chose, to believe they were reading from a script.

Even though it happened over weeks and then months, he felt everything was happening too fast. He started to think he was going mad; he'd stepped or fallen into another world of total debauchery and utter mayhem. If it were not for the cameras, he wouldn't have believed any of it. Until he saw the pictures, he really hadn't believed it was real. Handi had once seen part of a pornographic movie, but this was way beyond that, he knew the actors.

Handi had become a voyeur, it was frightening at first, then repulsive, then seductive and finally depraved. The repulsion came after he witnessed acts to his mind so reprehensible, he never wanted to talk to or see his wife or Diva ever again. He watched his wife becoming someone warped and debased. Seeing a person so perverted this was, he believed, far different than personal choice. There was nothing about this ongoing drama that was even minimally acceptable or tolerable. He was at a genuine loss about to what to do. Perhaps the oddest thing was that he watched, listened, and waited for so long. And yes, he thought about the police but when thinking as clearly as he could, he was unsure whether this was against the written laws of man. That said, he was very sure they were sins against God.

He had the video, he had the sound, he now had hundreds of photographs showing Diva laid back on the anomalous red leather chair-like device, legs spread, wrists cuffed and when secured, all manner of things done to her by Handi's wife. Diva would scream, laugh, she would laugh some more then scream some more, she would cry and giggle. He saw it all too well, her words and facial expressions begging, pleading for his wife to stop and then for more begin again. None of this part he could hear in those early days, he could only watch. The room had been heavily sound-proofed, and his earliest microphones could not intelligibly pick up those sounds. Much of this changed when once, on one particularly dangerous sortie, using a ladder he brought from home he placed tiny cameras and sensitive glass pane microphones high up on thin slit windows of the playroom.

Many times Mrs. Handi said she was in the city working. Handi believed and came to know, without exception, she was with Diva, not always in the city, but at what Mr. Handi heard them call "The Office."

In Handi's mind the debasement of both women was so complete, he knew the two women had gone far beyond the limits of any definition for sanity. He truly believed them insane. Their devices were ingenious and on rare occasions Diva was asked to tie Paddycake to the wall and whip her, slap her then repeatedly insert both exotic and common objects inside his wife. There was no limit and Mr. Doctor Handi no longer knew or recognized the woman who, as his wife, often dressed like a little man.

Handi only knew his Mrs. had forsaken God. He knew she was possessed by the devil himself or perhaps herself. Together these two women, possessed with demonic evil, eventually had to be held to account. God would guide him and show him what to do. He prayed and took to reading his bible more regularly, confirming to himself he had been chosen to end this debauchery. Handi was a chosen man. Chosen by God himself.

14.

Handi finally stopped being a regular voyeur. Reaching the limits of his ability to look and listen. He knew every day God was at his side, guiding him. By this time, most of what he saw was repetitive, so really there was no reason to involve himself in this part of the drama anymore. It was time to just consider what was to be done.

It took another five long months for Mr. Handi to decide and mentally prepare himself for what he would do. During that time what he had seen and heard changed from unimaginable to moribund insanity then beyond to sinfulness without end. He was depressed, losing sleep, thinking about his depraved wife and Diva. His disgust metastasized into unrelenting hostility. He hated his wife for having deceived him and not having been a wife at all. He hated her depravity and her having gone against God. It had come to this, from inside out he was being eaten alive.

The life he lived and now examined was a lie-filled atrocity, all a façade constructed by his conniving sin ridden wife. He'd been used so she could create and have a world that most people could never imagine, comprehend, or even want for any conceivable reason. With his own ears he heard his wife telling Diva they had been selected for their roles and pleasures. He often thought about this, particularly when each Sunday the two of them sat together, side-by-side in church. While the minister spoke, in his mind Handi rolled the tape. She and Diva were deviants, the problem was that God had yet to reveal himself, give him specifics. Handi was God's way to punish them; he could only conclude that was why he, just as Job, was being biblically tested. Handi waited for God and his wrath, but it did not come so Handi could only conclude he'd been selected to act on his own, in God's stead.

Initially, other than wait for divine intervention, he had no idea what to do. For months he felt he was in a fog, waiting for instruction and revelation with literal instructions. There was nothing or no person he could relate this dark secret to. He'd never had close friends so there was no one to confide in and Handi was not by nature, an introspective person.

Had he been he might have some time ago, seen signs of his descending into the Hell of madness. Handi was going crazy and crazy was going to come to a very bad end. Despite his rapacious and repetitious reading, God had still not spoken or at least in any way Handi could understand.

One warm sunny day he walked to the park where he used to sit on the bench by the river and eat his sandwich. It had been a long time since he'd done this. Before, it was always a simple pleasure for him, but now he could not recall ever having been happy. He opened the plastic bag he'd put the sandwich in that morning and was about to bite into it, but that bite did not happen. Without warning, the sandwich dropped to the ground and Handi emotionally collapsed. Leaning forward with hands covering his face, he wept uncontrollably. The weeping turned to sobs with his body shaking uncontrollably, eventually so violently he fell off the bench, into a curled fetal heap on the ground.

From the somewhere of uncertainty, life pictures in his mind turned black and white, morphing into morose grotesque sepia tones. Images, sharp sounds then screeching deafening noise inside his head. Definition transmogrified to surreal, objects moving that should not move, others stationary, as if in death.

Mr. Handi, having a mental breakdown, right there on the ground at that bench beside the river where pieces of yellow mustard smeared baloney sandwich scattered. He was disintegrating, sitting on that bench; in his mind, he'd descended into his own hell, falling, knowing he could never rise again. With no longer an anchor to reality, Handi finally reached up and grabbed the bench seat.

More minutes passed then an hour. Because he believed himself a doctor, he slowly took hold and stopped crying. He rose, breathing deeply, and sat motionless for a long time. Finally, occasionally shivering, he looked out at the river; his breathing slowed until he no longer felt his heart pounding, but the river has turned into an endless sea. At last he was able to summon enough strength to stand then walk the few blocks to his small office. With so few patients it was closed most of the time. Inside he pulled down all the shades, checked again to be sure the door sign was turned to Closed and walked out without locking the door. He would never return to this place again, Mr. Handi was re-organizing his life, preparing his future, he knew now what he must do, and believed God had finally sent him a message, "permission granted." How he did it, what he was going to do was now up to him. God would have to understand and accept that. It was all in Handi's hands now.

BOOK 8

1.

Totally unaware of her husband's suffering, Mrs. Handi was completely focused on her own life. For some time, she and Diva shared pleasures with greater freedom and increased regularity. It had been easier since her husband seemed to no longer express interest in her or her absences nor she in his. Like Diva's former man prop, for legitimacy's sake, she'd had and used her own "handy show-man." Handi's were more roommates than husband and wife now, and Mrs. Handi liked this just fine. In the diva's case she missed the idea that cancer, left untreated, is a progressive disease and, finally, never goes away even with treatment, like sociopathy.

The timeworn increasingly former socialite was having an increasingly difficult time. Yes, there were all the rumors and horror stories but for a while, with her for-show-man she had still managed to hold on by a fragile thread, but after she threw her latest man-prop overboard, there had been repercussions. It was slow at first although as time went on, friends and acquaintances outside the circles and in treated her differently. They'd had a look under her skirt and the old times of shared biting gossip with her were gone.

After prop guy's unexplained disappearance, only rarely a few girls, and boys, were willing to take a risk for extracurricular rolls in the hay. They were no longer interested or afraid to see if there were possibilities for some kind of relationship, or maybe even money. In the city, her Ne're-do-well son ran interference and as more issues arrived, took inept control of some of Mommy's problems but this too had failed. Ne're-do-well was essentially incoherent now... drugs and more drugs. Outward signs of ill health appeared; Diva now had confirmed Herpes, "The Curse". Only she and her son knew real answers to questions of where her STD came from, and they were not good.

She and for a short time *a new presumed mysterious other man* thought they had hidden their tryst quite well, but something leaked. The documented covert relationship with *"another new man"* happened while she was cohabiting with her more recent, but now gone, historical man prop. Shortly before casting the latest show-man-prop out like so much trash, he accidently discovered her infidelity. It was true they were never married but it got very public notice and for friends was oddly considered untoward. Diva's infidelity in her circles of diversion and deception, hypocritically discussed and judged, especially by a few friends who had sort of liked her previous consort. At least he had class, breeding, sophistication.

Nearly everyone knew *the so-called other man* with whom Diva had recently become illicitly involved. They knew the philanderer's wife and family quite well, children, parents, brothers, sisters etc. In her interest of self-preservation, the man's wife punished him publicly and quite harshly. With substantially reduced funds the society lawyer was exiled. Another launched inevitable suicide on its way to the line of finished, this time male not female. To be exact, in late August the end, just after the country fair and lots of tasty last rights of roasted butter-dipped corn on the cob.

But Diva never quite went away completely, like the saying: old golfers never die they just lose their balls, she just faded away with none. Stories still unraveling, friends departing almost daily, Diva's irrelevance was accepted some time ago, unnoticed with no one to explain because no one cared to understand. Now she was 75 with not even a single invitation to warm winter havens. Not even a suggested tiny birthday party. The last one at 70, was still a revival joke and even Diva with all her tricks could stop or top that. The river bend story retold by old timers who increasingly, even when they tried their best, only had a few memories left. With Old Brit Mama in a dirt filled box and Mr. Gasser probably the same somewhere in some unknown location, what did it matter anymore. The only thing that did was Lover; she would matter all the way to the end.

This 75th birthday evening it was just her son Ne'er-do-well who joined her. For some time, he had been regularly referred to as "The Curse." Certainly, Paddycake could not be in attendance this evening, at least for dinner. If any took note, and they didn't, any appearance of mother and son together was rare. Alone, at a far corner of the club dining room, table set for two, this birthday night at The Club they sat as lepers. No one would join them tonight. In years past everyone knew everybody else's birthday date all week. Information posted on an easel board at the entry to the dining room. This was usually cause for a Friday fish fry party including cake and cards, but for The Curse and cursed not tonight. Diva had not made the dining room display board for nearly two years.

They saw little of each other these days, mother and son. She invited him out from the city for this evening together and gazing off at nothing, they sat avoiding each other's eyes. Neither were big drinkers, and her buzzy sniffed pre-dinner coke high was wearing off. For his part, some time ago The Curse moved on to the big H. This night the food was excellent, as it occasionally was, but they had no taste for it; emptiness by definition leaves nothing to share. Diva certainly could say nothing about Lover, and Ne're-do-well spent most city days alone now, drugged, watching videos from the past or staring at his blank unrung cell phone. He too had become a pariah.

Since he no longer had respectable women friends, he, by phone or email would occasionally engage an unsuspecting prostitute to pass his venereal disease onto. He rarely came to the country anymore; old friends shunned his unpleasant demeanor and certainly any association with Mommy and her reputation. Together they were poison. In past times he bragged, and it was well known, he had years before manipulated his mother to "grow" his trust fund by releasing more money to him. The story was she was going insane and wasn't dying fast enough to suit him. These days The Curse was so stoned he wasn't even selling any more. The whole thing was quite gothic.

Each year Diva paid dues at the Country Club, more from habit than substance or benefit. It had been two years since she'd been in the dining room for any birthday. Gone forever, only memories now of New Year's Eve parties, birthdays with friends, dinner parties for no special reason. On this dismal night, with her accursed partnered son, it was bitter. His sour countenance and her depression made them quite the pair, tableau of wilted beauty and squandered youth. The dining room staff neglected them, hoping they would leave before the evening of fresh morsels began for others of pompous self-importance. Finally, without comment they silently got up and disappeared like ghosts.

It seemed so long-ago Diva had worshiped her son, Ne'er-do-well. Golden boy years before could do no wrong. Back then he'd been handsome and ingratiating, but about 15 years ago, maybe 20, it started to visibly degrade and if memory serves, rather quickly. Somewhere there was a "best if used by" sticker on him. He took on the disagreeable habits of his mother. His father reportedly, with a new wife and "normal" family, continued to flourish, was reported to be quite happy without his long forgotten former wife and child of rumored questionable authorship. Generally agreed assessments were, he too was a very sick person.

Ne'er-do-well offered up his STD to the daughter of one of Diva's closest friends and, biting gossip said, also her mother, but that had not been positively confirmed from even the usual quasi-reliable sources. With STD gabfest treatments, the mother, Brito-Grand Ma-ma learned that no good deed goes unpunished. She eventually found out her husband too was an STD graduate, more questions and speculation. Socially transmitted disease via Ne'er-do-well to Diva, on to daughter, to wife, to husband was not a difficult tracing exercise even for an idiot.

And lo, mouth sores, scratching, itching, and festering swollen members would follow them for the rest of their lives.

Ne'er-do-well became untouchable. Forced by reputation, he traveled further away seeking companionship of increasingly questionable origin and quality. After a few years, rumors of his activities quieted until out of the blue, a paternity suit was filed in the city by a Hispanic woman from San Diego. Diva was grannie to a child of now mixed pedigree and get this, of all things Hispanic.

People were simply no longer interested so the lawsuit never really gained traction in the media but was, of course, settled quietly with stipulations.

2.

Diva at 75 was slipping badly but at age 55, Handi Lover was still going strong. Both kept their thirst for the other, although Diva's staying power was wilting. Not to worry, Lover had a suggestion to fix it all.

For years, Diva supplied money for their relationship. It was formidable, but she hid the details, costs, and continued purchases for their lives together. In truth, for a long time the financial advisors suspected something but, for obvious reasons of continued employment and annual fees, did not discuss suspicions with their client. As long as she paid their onerous charges there was no need. Like many other things in life, wealth had taught these financial predators well: it was always about money, how much you had or could accumulate at someone else's expense. The *so-called* advisors were in just as much of a hurry to grab OPM as their clients.

For a time, Handi Lover and Diva took trips to distant places together. The difference in their ages made it appear to some as though it was a mother daughter trip. One evening, aboard a Caribbean bound ship, Lover and Diva were dining, Lover was speaking.

"I want to make a suggestion my darling. I have a friend who is a few years younger than I am. I don't know for sure, but there could be a few occasions when she might like to join you and I at "The Office." What do you think my sweetheart? I know we've never discussed this before."

OMG, Diva did not have to think about this as if it were a new idea. For some time, she'd felt apprehensive about her role of diminishing returns. She was not keeping up with Lover who usually set the pace. With increased lubrication, for years Diva had done as requested because she craved L's orders and imaginative scenes. They were both actors on the stage they'd created, but while the sets they'd created remained in good shape, one of the players had not.

At the restored house, soon after they had begun the Office, Diva promised Lover she would always have The Office. No matter what might happen to them together, Lover would have it for life. Once before she had made that same promise to a man for the very same place, but later, after she became bored, the sworn promise was retracted, her betrayal never forgotten. The promise this time was important since Lover had, euphemistically, put all her remaining eggs in one basket.

They were getting older, and Diva was aware of maybe not playing her part to Lover's satisfaction. Unlike the old days she knew Lover was now often going into her own pleasure alone, time and again leaving Diva behind high, dry, and frustrated. The persistent torturous thought was Lover would find someone else and leave her for good. At 75 she thought she still knew what a good orgasm was but needed more time and "attention" than before. Vibrating rabbit's ears and spin cycles of the washing machine weren't enough, so in the meantime she was faking it a lot and L knew it.

The suggestion of another younger woman to join them was perfect. The Office would continue and Diva would be still a part of it all. It would be more comfortable for everyone and ensure continued pleasures with Lover. Just perfect, she was game for it all and who was to say that, like some other world-class secret pleasure palaces, The Office might just make the Michelin five-star 'must for lust' visit list. This set her to recalling the pleasure palace behind tall shrubs north of the city. It was still famous among the nearby chosen. Perhaps someday, the diva would become "infamous" and remembered for similar reasons.

And so, it came to pass, "Girlfriend," as they called her, joined them a month later. With renewed excitement, as if that could ever have seemed possible, their ménage à trois brought even greater pleasures to Lover and Diva. They were set, good to go and go and go.

The new girl, Catherine, Girlfriend, was quite adept with the whip and lurid manners with an ever-twitching twat that drove Handi wild.

3.

It was the ménage a trois that brought Mr. Handi to his own quite different climax. Precipitating the last act, watching the three women, he could no longer cope with what he saw. Something was different, a change in the video feed that continued to arrive at recording devices and servers he used, to then be carefully secreted away for a future debut. At first, he didn't notice because it was automatic, he rarely looked at them anymore, he just collected data and stored it. Instructions for later use would follow. But the change was insidious, like something crawling up and out of a malevolent subterranean darkness. If perversion was a growing malignancy, Mr. Handi himself had become terminally infected; he now had his own unique self-induced STD and treatment for this would be especially harsh.

It was a Saturday night. For no particular reason, he signed in and connected directly to the server he used to observe Diva, Mrs. Handi and more recently Girlfriend. This time he saw the three women in an episode that was beyond what even he, in his relatively recent experience could have imagined. The "can you top this" girlfriend had offered new toys and devices she got in Germany, where fetish had a strange exotic erotic history. After seeing girlfriend in full body red latex, with appended "toys" Mr. Handi found so bizarre, he turned the video feed off and that night drank more than he ever had in his entire mediocre life. He was so drunk he got violently ill; the entire house smelled of vomit.

He awoke the next morning with a terrible headache, but managed to fix breakfast and drink as much coffee and water as he could stand. He was still running from both ends and afterwards, exhausted, went into the disorderly living room, collapsing into his worn third-hand LazyBoy. Reclined back and closing his eyes he started making plans. The time had come to stop it all.

He would begin by finding Diva's son. That was her weakest point and Ne'er-do-well would serve quite well as her greatest punishment. He had not known much about Girlfriend so next he'd find out where she could be found when she wasn't at "The Office." Once he knew where all four players were, he would set up the order of events, some kind of schedule and then execute it. The more he thought about this, the more he realized it was going to be complicated. He understood that at every stage, each "event" would need to unfold in exacting sequence, details with perfection. There would be five actors in this final scene, Diva, his wife, the one they called Girlfriend, Diva's worthless son, and of course, himself. All would have their roles and place in this drama of the end. God's will. Theater he would direct with skill and precision, Handi was turning out to be quite the meticulous planner. Messenger. Producer. Director.

For a man who had never been known for his creativity, a new side of Handi was emerging. This consummately dull man was becoming a very interesting person and eventually his own imagination would far out-perform those who thought him an incipient fool. In fact, with this said, his twists of mind were not without precedent, there had been Stephen King, H. P. Lovecraft, and Edgar Allen Poe with his "Quoth the Raven *Nevermore*." These new ideas were unique to him, perhaps remembered for a very long time. Handiman was destined to become history with his own *Nevermore*.

He needed a place for stage properties, as they were referred to in the acting business, a place to store things. A place to test equipment so there would be no mistakes. Once it all began there could be no miscalculations. The first solution was nearby, the home where he had recently been working, it was perfect. With the owners in Hawaii, it would remain unoccupied for the time he needed. They were retired and he was nearly certain they would not return for some time. As a precaution, he'd construct a false wall in their basement where they never went, and everything could be kept secure, out of sight; it also had its own access with a shrub shielded private drive along one side of the house, so from the front he would not be seen coming and going.

Sitting there, recovering in his LazyBoy chair he mentally went over his plan several times, adding little details here and there. He knew he needed to write it all down. At last, with his hangover wearing off he fell asleep. When he woke again it was late afternoon and getting dark. His stomach was still queasy from the night before. He felt he should not stray too far from the loo, so drank more water and went to bed early. Tomorrow he would begin writing down his plan and make the first of several purchases. Not too many and not too expensive, since they wouldn't be needed for long, and the KISS principle, keep it simple stupid was essential here. One performance only, supplies lasting just long enough for the actors, and last act, when their time came for the final call to center stage. He was plenty handy after all.

4.

He did not hear the soft footsteps behind him. Diva's son walked to his car and had just put the key into the lock when a needle pierced his neck. It only took a few seconds and he fell to the ground; the attacker threw the syringe away. Opening the door of the older model pickup truck, the man with the needle picked up the body he'd wrapped in a blanket; then dragged, pushed, and pulled Ne'er-do-well onto the floor behind the front seats. Adding the plastic ties cinched around hands and feet then duct tape over his mouth, he pulled a black hood over the head and lastly threw a filthy oil-stained tarp over the unconscious body. Just in case, a spare tire was tossed on top of the tarp. Keys to the empty car had been retrieved, used to lock it and thrown over somewhere near the discarded needle. The driver of the nondescript truck where Ne'er-do-well now lay unconscious, pulled out from the parking place and cautiously headed off into the night, the trip would take about an hour. It was late and traffic light, he didn't speed.

In a totally dark, cold, damp concrete soundproofed underground space, Ne'er-do-well spent the next several days painfully collared with a neck-chain leashed to a ring recently mounted in the ceiling above him. Standing was torturous. The weather outside turned quite warm for that time of year but in the basement with no windows the chill had subsided only slightly.

In darkness Ne'er-do-well had no sense of time or where he was. Regaining consciousness the first time, he was nauseous and didn't understand it was a side effect of the second drug he'd been injected with. Stripped naked he panicked, shivered and as soon as he was able started to yell. He had no idea what this was about; Ne'er-do-well was not at all well and, as he should have been, he was very afraid. Cowards, who are usually bullies react quickly to threats, but in spite of the chill he was sweating. The symptoms of heroin withdrawal were already upon him and would only get worse.

All he could remember was unlocking his car door. His internal time clock suggested he'd been out for at least 12 hours but with no source of outside light his circadian rhythms were confused and unreliable. Even with the hood now removed he could not be sure of anything. He was, however, intended to see or at least feel where and how he was secured. After a while, exhausted and with no response, he yelled only intermittently. Finally, he gave up, completely spent, his throat dry, raspy and hoarse, the sweats continued. He was used to quitting so giving up was not difficult for him.

Sometime later, when a door finally opened, a dim hanging light was switched on and revealed a hooded figure dragging a naked body across the floor further into the room. Ne'er-do-well had no idea who it was but as the figure got closer, he started talking again, asking questions.

With no answers he switched to yelling threats and finally, just as in the movies, he offered money. This display of desperation was met with total silence. Ne'er-do-well's eyes nearly popped out of his head when he got a better look and concluded the body was that of a dead woman.

But she was not dead, only unmoving. The stripped figure's only accompaniment was a rigid leather neck collar with a small lock attached to a short chain, secured at the other end to a solidly embedded floor ring. Ne'er-do-well squinted to see ornamental piercings halfway down the nude body and confirmed the figure appeared to be a middle-aged woman. Eventually there were slight movements suggesting the body was perhaps breathing, but only barely. In other circumstances Ne'er-do-well would have found this quite exciting, but now his excitement was only one of increased fear and more serious dread. His sweating continued, fear and withdrawal symptoms solidly setting in.

The son's locked collar and leash attached higher up than he could reach when standing, permitted him a walking radius of at most, two to three feet. The new figure's leash attached to a steel ring in the floor offered no such latitude. Her head was secured tight, inches from the cold cement floor. At best, when or if the woman woke, she could only lift her head a few inches from the damp concrete and securing ring. Unable to rotate her head in the collar she faced away from Ne'er-do-well. If she tried to get up, she would simply flop around on the floor like an out of the water fish dying in the bottom of a boat. Her hands and feet were unsecured so any struggles would soon be quite animated and horrible to watch.

Having not yet said a word and work completed, the dark figure left and as the door closed the light went off. Ne'er-do-well continued to yell, again offering money, but the sound of the door lock was audible. He was beginning to understand no one was going to leave this place any time soon. With the tiny light bulb off and pitch black returning the two prisoners looked into empty cold nothing.

The figure on the floor stirred then moaned. She and her cell mate had no idea how long it had been since she'd arrived. Her sounds grew from a moan to muffled high-pitched screeches, like that of a child in pain. Through the screams Ne'er-do-well tried to ask questions. With no coherent reply her mutterings were unintelligible and finally she again was silent.

The next time she regained consciousness, their mutual sense of despair deepened, the shivering woman was mumbling again like a crazy person. From where Ne'er-do-well stood chained, he could not see her mouth had been securely taped shut. Her efforts to kneel only resulted in hands slapping at the floor and feet repeatedly slipping across the floor. Ne'er-do-well imagined what it looked like in full light and that made everything worse.

It can be terrifying to be in a strange dark place, particularly when one is so firmly pinned down, and in Ne'er-do-well's case, strung up. With hands tied he could not even use his sense of touch to understand any limits, specific means or true place of his confinement. With no sense of time or place and forced to stand he couldn't sleep for any length of time, as soon as he did his knees gave way and he, secured by the chain, would hang by the neck.

Truly in limbo, once they both stopped yelling or mumbling, only their breathing confirmed to these two people, they were alive. This was precisely what their jailer intended and why, for interminable hours there would be no further contact by him. To this point everything was in order, everything going according to plan. Eventually with no explanation or encouragement, sips of water were offered through a tube but no food.

On Handi's schedule, two days later the door opened a third time. This time another unconscious figure was dragged past the other floor bound woman. The dim light was on and the new figure, also naked, short-chained to a floor ring had both ankle and wrist restraints that were connected. In this fashion the figure was curled into a forced fetal position. Through murky light the previous occupants peered at the new woman also with her mouth taped shut. If she tried to stand, in her confining fetal crouch she would most likely fall and roll over or at best be forced to kneel.

Laying prone on the floor, straining to look, the first woman was sure she recognized this newest addition. The man, obviously in charge, and who was always himself hooded, reached over and with a snap jerked tape from the new woman's mouth. She screamed; it was painful but not life threatening. He wanted her to express herself over the muffled cries coming from faceplanted woman still taped and chained close to the floor. Throughout this newest episode Ne'er-do-well remained strangely silent; however, in dim light he thought he recognized the new prisoner. With her naked and covered with dirt that seemed like paint, he still was not quite positive.

Finally, Ne'er-do-well interrupted the howling woman, now shouting questions and threats at their jailer. He promised more money this time if his tormentor released him and added he would never tell anyone about the other two women. The jailer, whoever he or it was, could keep them, Ne'er-do-well said, but with continued silence the dark figure made no response. He left and again the room went dark with one woman mumbling frantically while the other still screaming her invectives.

5.

On May 5th, 1981, 66 days into his starvation protest the IRA protester Bobby Sands died quite painfully. However, generally humans can go only three to five, sometimes six days without water, and depending on circumstances nearly three weeks without food. After two days without either one, the effects are not pleasant and if one is a heroin addict it is far worse. What had been learned from imprisoned IRA Irish protesters years before was each day becomes increasingly painful, up to the point where hydration is of no further interest to the body.

Using the night vision cameras, the basement prisoners, even in darkness, were monitored by the naturopath doctor... so called. The watcher aware of medical issues at stake and knew more about what he was doing than an average person might.

Before final action was taken, his plan was to take the three to the edge of nearly unbearable physical and mental pain, but in their final moments they needed to be fully conscious. It was decided on the morning of their third day they would be offered a mixture of rice, mashed beans and water, to be followed by a brief burst of energy. After that part of the show, he would give them each an injection of adrenalin. In this state of mind, with sharply, medically induced increased senses, they would put at least a few pieces together and have a vague idea of what was going on.

Day three. With the prisoners fully awake, efforts to talk became increasingly frantic. They, of course, did not know outside it was early morning but in the basement a blinding light turned on and after his eyes adjusted, Ne'er-do-well suddenly knew exactly who the third woman was. Using her name, he called to her but there was no response. Her head had been crudely shaved. Without her voluminous hair rarely seen, in its unleashed entirety it looked fake, but now she looked even more horrible.

The hooded figure reappeared and dropped pie pans of food near each person. Ne'er-do-well's chains were loosened so he could finally squat and lean over to reach the food.

The second woman's neck chain was also adjusted so she could lift her head slightly above the floor. Only their fingers to eat. With no trips to a toilet, the physical mess on the floor was overpowering.

A large screen flashed on the far wall. The blinding illumination hurt their eyes and was followed by continuous audio and video images of depravity from "The Office." Painfully loud, accompanied by edited video, the loop repeated for hours. Their persecutor had learned that particularly loud sound greatly contributed to a prisoner's misery and viewing the monitors the effect was obvious.

With her leash lengthened the first woman was exhausted and to the other two prisoners soon it appeared she was unconscious or perhaps dead.

No matter, in the relentless screened chaos of blaring demands from Mrs. Handi and compliances from Diva, all efforts to communicate between the three were useless. The video soon enough included a third, younger woman parading in pink, black or red latex with prominently featured dildos. Initially only one of the two current basement prisoners knew who she was. Using her appendages and tools with pleasure, particularly the short horse whip she seemed to prefer, the effects were quite visceral. Inside sound-proofed walls of the dungeon, where the three were restrained, the amplified pitiful words of obedience and shouts of orgasmic intensity repeated again and again. No popcorn and a Coke here, combined thirst and hunger were taking their toll. As predicted they were by now completely disoriented, close to the sharp edge of complete and utter madness. Impossibly aware of a bigger picture to come and its purpose, they were being driven certifiably insane.

In reflected light from the screen and, even with eyesight blurred from the effects of dehydration and starvation, the prisoners could recognize each other. All in unspeakable squalor, him hanging and them chained to the floor, scenes of Diva with her drugged out son in congress; the prisoners knew they were in serious trouble. Dread is a progressive disease.

The screen went black with speakers silent. After a time, the now recognized and identified Girlfriend, with her face to the floor, and the other, newest of the screen dramatists having gone silent, Mrs. Handi worked her retaped mouth covering loose. She, in a screeching high-pitched voice launched her attack, yelling out what a worthless son he was. On the glare of the video, she had clearly recognized Ne'er-do-well in congress with his mother and then close by, hanging from the ceiling. Recognizing her voice, he too worked tape loose and screamed back accusations followed by threats of his own. Mrs. Handi yelled again and in the now fully lit room, quickly reverberated with repartee of barking screaming threats. All recorded to later be posted on the Dark Web. Among other things Mr. Dr. Handi had become quite the publicist; perhaps to be one of the greatest horror directors and producers of all time.

It took hours plus twenty-four more, off and on, for them to completely exhaust themselves on day four, then five. By the end they grew quiet, each privately only guessing what was ahead. Interestingly, and maybe a mercy they didn't deserve, their pitiful imaginations could not begin to match that of the tormentor. Even he agreed, he had exceeded expectations, had become demonic and meticulous, strangely disconnected from it all. But Handi would not fully admit to that just yet. In real time most anybody else would have agreed the Handi doctor had created a Pieter Bruegel quality masterpiece. Perhaps such things are only possible when a human being becomes completely disconnected from their human...being.

6.

Even in the black of night it was actually quite easy. To ensure compliance each of the prisoners was injected with a carefully timed sedative the wannabe doctor had semi-professional access to. Bound, then wrapped like mummies, they were in turn taken and placed in the back of the rusted little red pickup truck that belonged to his wife. Laid in the back like fire logs, covered with a tarp and two old tires added to weight it down. The ground and every surface, now wet with heavy seasonal dew, was cold. Everything in order, no reason to hurry. Premeasured memorized plans with a meticulous schedule scrupulously being adhered to.

Handi drove to Diva's home at the river. He called her just before arriving saying the security company just called him about a water leak in the basement, he knew it was early, but she should, under no circumstances, go down the stairs into the basement. There was a danger of electrocution if a hot wire contacted the water. She was to wait for him by the front door after making sure all security had been completely turned off. He confidently told her he would handle everything.

When he arrived, she opened the door, then gesturing turned away looking toward the basement door. Falling to the floor she didn't feel the needle prick the back of her neck. Props previously hidden well back in the garage now needed to be recovered and taken outside. Working confidently and quickly in the twilight of early morning he knew precisely what he must do, where everything would be placed and how.

First a tall ladder brought from the garage along with ropes and pulleys. Part way down the hill from the veranda, against a sturdy old tree near the water, the ladder was placed against a tree limb. With the aid of the ladder, he climbed up to the thick branch where the first pulley and rope was secured, close, about three feet out from the tree's trunk. Moving the ladder further out along the limb a second pulley rope was attached six feet from first pulley and finally, a third pulley beyond that. The ends of each rope was passed through its own pulley, fell and lay directly on the ground beneath the strong limb.

Less visible a thin piano wire of shorter length passed through the pully and firmly secured separately to the branch. It too fell down to the ground. Removing six-inch nails from his pocket he worked a nail halfway through the braids of each rope and carefully wound the ends of the wires back and forth over the nails. The nail and wire were securely fixed at the precise locations Handi intended. On the ground lay three body harnesses; Handi attached the rope to rings with a breakaway carabiner at the center of each harness.

Mr. Handi moved efficiently, checking his watch periodically to confirm his timing so far was perfect. He removed the ladder from the tree and carried it up to the top of the hill where he thoughtfully, in plain sight, laid it down beside the house. He knew others would need it hours later.

Returning to his wife's little red truck, he unloaded each of the mummy wrapped unconscious bodies, dragging them one at a time, to place each in predetermined order. Beneath each pully he unwrapped each of them and cut the hand restraints; then with effort worked each unconscious body into its now rope-connected harness, attached and checked the carabiner at the back. Finally, he slipped a wire loop around each of their necks and pulled it tight. On the ground, now in harness, the previously wrapped bodies began to stir. With mouths taped, they started making muffled sounds.

Handi returned up the hill to the house and fireman's style, over his shoulder carried Diva, still unconscious, and placed her in a large white lawn chair facing the tree and river then moved another smaller chair a short distance setting it perpendicular to the first. Seated and still groggy he taped her body upright with arms firmly secured to the chair. Finally he covered her mouth with a short length of duct tape.

Glancing at his watch he smiled to himself and noted again, right on time, just as expected. With everyone in their place all was readied for Dr. Handi's drama to begin. The final act.

Diva barely felt the adrenalin needle. With her heart pounding, she came fully awake. Looking around, blinking rapidly her eyes went wide. She felt tape over her mouth and realized she was in her nightgown, outside in fading darkness of the chilled early morning light. She quite clearly saw Mr. Handi sitting calmly beside her in a smaller white chair with low matching table to the side. There was a small black object on the table and certainly what she could not know, a computer terabyte hard drive with all Handi's recordings.

He was fiddling with some other objects on the table, things she recognized but could not understand. A bottle and an eye dropper. Reaching in his pocket he withdrew a pistol. Spreading a towel on the ground at Diva's feet so she could see it, he lifted the gun and dramatically inserted a single bullet in the pistol's chamber, clicked the safety off and set it back down on the towel. In a calm voice he slowly began to speak.

He explained to her that as the morning grew lighter, just below her, soon to be hanging in the air she would see and feel retribution for her depravity and God's punishment. She would be allowed no explanation or offered any easy way out. That, he said, would only be for those who lay on the slope down below her.

Raising his voice, he explained why she would feel their pain. It would be visceral he concluded and said nothing more. The two sat quietly for several minutes. Diva, with no strength to release herself, was still unable to fully understand the scene before her. With confusion and increasing panic her face told it all. She held her breath and waited for prescribed revelations of the dawn.

7.

A cloudy day with storms forecast for later, the early light was slow in coming. Diva remained fixated. Down the hill, three hooded naked figures lay side by side, each with their head down and feet pointed up hill toward Diva. Ropes attached to harnesses were plainly visible but from this distance not the wire.

Minutes past, Handi allowed Diva more time to absorb the sight. At last, the doctor stood from the chair beside her and carefully made his way down the hill. Handi stopped and pulled their hoods off, and it was then… Yes!... she knew exactly who they were. Diva knew with staggering disbelief, confirmed realization roaring in on her like a speeding train.

Face down in the middle, laying on the hillside his slightly turned head distorted and barely visible, she recognized her son, then Lover and finally Girlfriend. All three on their stomachs, each in harness with rope attached to a pully. Now she got the picture. In probably the fastest moment of awareness she had ever experienced she understood it completely. The gun with a single bullet lay on the ground before her, she believed she knew what was going to happen.

Moving to each one, he rolled them over their backs and in turn gave the condemned their adrenalin shot then waited for it to take full effect. He allotted time for the scene to worm its way deep into their consciousness. He knew they would still not fully understand but returned up the hill and again softly spoke to Diva. Pointing to the gun he told her he was going to remove the tape over her mouth, but if she made any loud noise, right now, for those below to clearly watch and see he, would shoot her in the face.

Seeing it all from where she sat the diva understood. She looked down at the gun on the towel, knowing for certain, she had seen him do it, there was only one bullet in the chamber.

A racing picture of her life passed before her and merged with others more recent. Images dissolving, back to the scene before her. Details of her son who counted for nothing to others, but everything to her. Lover, the passion they shared, girlfriend, toy for their amusement and pleasure.

She saw it all and had precious few moments to think about it. Dr. Handi knew this, had seen to that, waited, and then rhetorically asked, "Do you know what this is about Diva? Do you know what you have done and been a part of?" She made no sound, did not shed a tear or try to scream, she just looked, staring mesmerized, first at the Doctor and then down the hill.

"Do you now want to say anything?" He tore the tape away from her mouth.

Showing no emotion she shook her head. This was it, not a normal person, there was no obvious remorse, no pleading, no asking forgiveness. She was a sociopath, a diva after all. Looking at the gun, she believed it was to be her end with no regrets.

Not surprised the mister doctor stepped away. He again made his way down the hill to confirm each figure was awake and looking around, each beginning to realize their connection to the limb above feeling the rope but not the wire that connected them. As Handi watched, Diva took a moment and looked down again at the gun, even more sure it was intended for he; believing this was all a drama those three would at least survive.

He walked over and cut the plastic zip ties around their hands and ankles. Stepping back to the tree trunk calling them by name he instructed the women to stand; laying on the ground Ne'er-do-well was told not to move.

The women struggled but stood and since they had heard talk from above faced up that way. Their eyes focused on Diva, and they felt weak in the breaking morning light. Soon there would be thunder followed by torrential rain. They saw the house behind Diva, her sitting there in a plain white nightgown. Bound, silent, with piercing eyes staring down at them saying nothing. For the first-time, the two women clearly recognized Mister Dr. Handi. He seemed at peace, moving slowly, silently, wordlessly contributing to their dread. They looked to each other and saw on their neck what they could only feel on their own. Confused, the rope, the harness, the wire loop now finally visible around their necks.

He decided then they would not be allowed any last words, the tape covering their mouths would remain. He had no interest in cries of supplication, pleadings, confessions, anger, their sobbing. In these moments of private madness, he was far beyond that. He knew they would each die alone.

The evening before, Handi silently prayed the cosmos would forget them all as he too entered through their gates of Hell from a different direction. It was just as God intended, he was a sacrifice, they were retribution. Really all quite biblical he thought. Yes, Mr. aka Doctor Handi would finally find peace with his maker but never see him.

Picking up the first rope he pulled and hoisted Girlfriend away from the Earth, into the air and tied it securely to the tree's trunk. Next, his wife until the two women were hanging in their harnesses, swinging slowly in the air. Handi looked up at Diva to confirm she was seeing it all and then down at Ne'er-do-well staring up. Bodies high-up squirming frantically, their freed legs flung out causing them to twist, turning helplessly, jerking in harness.

Exhausted, Girlfriend was the first to slow down until she finally stopped and stared down at Handi who untied her rope and held it tight for a moment... then let go.

She fell.

The freed rope raced toward the pully until at the embedded heavy nail it abruptly stopped. With slack still in the wire, she continued for another fraction of a second until her body jerked to a stop below, severing her neck just below the chin. Cutting in deeply the thin wire partially severed her head until her face fell forward onto naked breasts. Girlfriend hung swinging in a silent gushing red mist.

He untied the rope connected to his wife. Having witnessed this unfathomable horror Mrs. Handi aka Lover squirmed more violently, making a desperate effort to scream and free herself. Behind the tape covering her mouth it was futile.

Mrs. Handi fell.

Her wire too cut deep but not enough to completely sever her head. The sprayed fountaining blood was copious, gut wrenching, unimaginably shocking.

Handi remained calm and silent.

Now the son, instructed to now stand alone. Moments ago, he had lain on the cold ground in the center with fresh cadavers showering blood from above. Above him swinging wildly on either side he was being drenched, deep red. This was not finality, only a prequel for his mother's watching from above. The sole intended audience.

Handi slowly pulled the last third rope to the top where it stopped. He hesitated, in his hands holding it tight, looking up at Diva. Ne'er-do-well hung, moving only slightly, making no effort to protest behind the tape covering his mouth. He did not look at his mother, instead looked away. Having already entered Hell, the twisting bodies on either side slowed or stopped.

Handi let go.

Ne'er-do-well fell.

This time a longer drop, with greater force the wire caught. Cutting deeper than the others the severed head fell further. With little sound it hit the ground and rolled down to the water's edge, into the river and was swept away.

On this cloud covered day, rains would soon come to cleanse the earth.

Only a madman could envision such a thing.

From below Handi looked again up to motionless Diva. She had not moved or changed expression, just continued to stare. Climbing the hill, Doctor Handi approached and administered a final drug to prevent her from going into shock.

8.

Earth and heavens wept. With profound sadness there was more to this drama of contrition. Handi stood aside looking away from the hanging bodies, staring at the woman in the chair who had yet to shed a tear. Not at all like the one he'd seen too often in video recordings of the past few years.

With purpose he pulled his chair closed in front of hers but did not sit down. He leaned down and retrieved the pistol. Unfamiliar with firearms, he carefully placed it on the table then picked up the filled hypodermic needle. Moving over to stand behind Diva he grabbed her hair pulling it back, away from her sight of the carnage. She looked up into his face. Using his thumb and forefinger, one at a time, he pulled each eyelid further open. With his other hand he held and pressed the needle's plunger down until drops of acid fell into each wide opened eye.

As the blinding acid burned and dissolved delicate eye tissue, over her screams he spoke in a calm measured voice.

"This is so you will remember what you have done and now witnessed today as retribution. It is God's will that for all the time you have left on earth you will see only this scene and replay it in your mind's eye. One day you will take this image into the hell of your eternity."

He walked around and turning to shift the empty chair even closer he sat, his head not four feet from her face. Faced away from her, he put the gun to the side of his head.

Diva's face was instantly covered in viscera.

THE DENOUEMENT

Years passed. On a bright sunny summer's day a dark car slowly made its way down a weedy road toward the river. It pulled around and stopped in front of an old house that badly needed painting. Hopelessly overgrown, the gardens had long ago faded, no flowers, but one could still hear faint upstream sounds from the river rapids. Fruit trees remained but most had died, only dark limbed skeletons with few survivors that grew wild and free. To those who saw it from the new road across the river, this property looked overgrown and abandoned.

Haversham

The car's driver got out and went around to open the rear door for his passenger. A well-dressed man slid out and leaning on a cane stood for a moment. He looked at the house then glanced at the river he knew from long ago and back to the house again. Reminiscing, thinking this a house truly cursed.

He slowly walked toward the front door. A long time ago he passed through it many times. If the walls, the trees, and the gardens could talk, they would recall stories in the time of their lives, some humorous, others with irony and many of regret. He had read some, heard others, they were never far from his memory. Today a pilgrimage to this ruin tragedy, not a monument instead a marker in a field of Earthly remorse.

The recordings from years ago were never made fully public, most only seen and heard by the authorities. With Internet reveals there was, of course, leaked information some real but mostly speculation. Lurid rumors persisted even now, still embellished by people who relished such matters. Stories of the house in disrepair, holding on, slowly failing just like its mistress.

Through his sources the man had been told executors received specific instructions. Upon her death the house was to be burned to the ground and land gifted to the county for a riverside park. No plaque or acknowledgement of any kind. She was to be forgotten.

As if she had been waiting, the door was opened by a young woman who appeared to be Hispanic. Curiously, she seemed to have some of Diva's features. Not so much pretty as Diva had once been but handsome, ironic he thought. She stood in the doorway self-assured and petite in her formal starched service uniform. He had written some time ago to ask permission and most probably she was the one who read the note to Mistress. Before he could speak the stooped old woman appeared behind her. The man took note of how reliant and compliant the older woman was. Wordlessly the younger woman took the lady's shaking outstretched hand and slowly led the two of them onto the veranda. Once seated the pleasant service woman left them.

Quietly facing forward and with some intensity staring at nothing in particular, the old lady, with some apparent anticipation, sat rigid. When the weather was warm and she could hear the river, he imagined she often sat here waiting. Even with her stiff posture it told him she was still resolute. No doubt confirming to herself, each and every day there had been a vast conspiracy for which she was the primary intended victim. He knew too well how it went and, in many ways, she still appeared to be the same.

The old oak stood as a sentinel. There was no talk at first, the man looked at her and he was sad. She was very thin, gaunt, sunken cheeks with dark eyes deeply set with paper-thin transparent skin that impressed him as empty and lifeless. The veins in her cheeks too were dark, more prominent than before, a few thick but most thin as he remembered, just more of them. She did not wear glasses, her sightless open grey clouded eyes plainly visible. Hair pulled back, tight as always but more or less the same style, these days only held with a rubber band, no more jeweled clips.

Hands trembled, the lipstick appeared as if she'd attempted it herself, far too much and outside the lines of acceptability. This added to a macabre visage. Another time, in another place it would have looked theatrical. Someday the mortician would make things better. Cotton stuffed cheeks for a final facelift, but really, who would be there to see her flat on her back? Who would care? Finally, he spoke to her in a near hushed tone.

"You look well."

She responded slowly, "And you, for your age, do you?"

"I suppose, for my age I am adequate," he responded softly.

She spoke. "It is warm today."

"Yes," he said.

She spoke. "Would you like something to drink?"

"No thank you," he said.

She asked. "And why have you come?"

"I suppose to see what has become of you. More than just curiosity you know. I once thought I had a vested interest here. I am sorry," he said.

"Yes," she said dragging out the word, and she followed with, "You are sorry."

He asked, "Why have you stayed here all these years?"

She breathed in deeply, paused and after several moments said, "You should know... I have no other place to go, just like you, once upon a time and long ago. This is all I know now, especially in the dark. You know, of course, this all started with..." her voice trailed off, but he knew. She wanted to blame it all on him or others... any others really. Divas never change, sociopaths never blame themselves.

Another long pause, "Do you have people who come to see you?"

"No. Nobody since then." No suggestion of wistfulness in her manner or her tone. She was more matter of fact, as if this was the way it was always supposed be.

"Ahh yes," he said. It was his turn to pause again. "I suppose."

Just as the maid reappeared and had set the tray with lemonade down and departed, the old woman, looking off said to him, "You must go now," she was dismissive and moved forward in her seat to reach for the small silver bell she knew would be there.

He stood, helped her to her feet, and gently took her arm to lead her back into the house. The door was opened, the woman in the starched uniform took Diva's arm from him and led her inside. Diva said nothing and did not turn her head to look back. Without another word the door closed softly behind them. Nothing else said. Nothing more to say.

Returning to the car, the driver opened the door and he slid into the comfortable backseat. With doors closed and windows down letting in fresh air, the car moved forward and up the rarely used drive, this time a little faster. The visitor did not look back, he only looked forward. No remorse, only feelings with no regrets.

On this warm summer day, in his mind Rumpelstiltskin was disappearing into the grayness of a cold snowy day. He knew he was watched and from his pocket withdrew an addressed envelope. He leaned forward and dropped it on the front passenger seat requesting his driver to post it at his earliest convenience.

L'extrémité

THE AUTHOR

 Joseph Kinnebrew is an acknowledged autodidact polymath. A man with many talents and uncommon proven abilities. Among other things he is an internationally recognized artist, writer, mentor, and consultant.

In his role as visual artist, he is a keen observer of life and especially the individual traits and characteristics of people. Writers of books are often advised to write about what they know, and the story of DIVA is no exception.

Kinnebrew has written several books of fiction and nonfiction, inevitably they offer imbedded messages with questions provoking serious consideration and debate. Preferring to focus on his work today he lives reclusively with his partner and manager Siri Struble in the Pacific Northwest.

He may be contacted by email: siristruble@gmail.com

Printed in the USA
CPSIA information can be obtained
at www.ICGtesting.com
JSHW081416270823
47119JS00001B/15